The Cormac and Amelia

Case Files

A Collection

The Cormac and Amelia

Case Files

A Collection

Carrie Vaughn

Carrie Vaughn, LLC

P.O. Box 20982

Boulder, CO 80308

www.carrievaughn.com

Print ISBN: 979-8-9864682-0-4

Credits:

Cover Design: Joe Campanella

Book Design/Conversion: E.M. Tippetts

Also by Carrie Vaughn

1.

Cormac was pretty sure he was being watched.

On the one hand, he was usually being watched. He'd made some enemies over the years. He was an ex-con who'd done time for manslaughter, which meant any cop running his plates had an extra reason to stop and hassle him. He rarely drove over the speed limit these days—not that that kept him from getting pulled over. That was background noise to his usual life, though. This was something different, a shiver at the back of his neck, a shadow at the corner of his vision.

A couple of clues drew his attention, such as a dark sedan he'd never seen before in the parking lot of his apartment building. That only happened once, but after that he couldn't drive without feeling like he was being followed. If he was, whoever doing it was good—Cormac never spotted them. He took different routes to his usual destinations.

Then for the first time in all the years he'd lived there, the management company set up security cameras in the walkways outside the apartments. This place was a run-down rattrap in a shitty part of town, but *now* they were worried about security?

"Somebody put you up to this?" he jokingly asked the handyman, who was up on a ladder installing a dome camera that would look right at Cormac's front door. The guy shot him a startled glare, full of guilt.

He really had to get out of this apartment. Get out east on a chunk of land with good line of sight.

1

And space for a garden, said Amelia, who dreamed of growing herbs. She went through a lot of herbs in the spells she prepared.

"I'd be doing all that gardening, you know."

Oh, I think you'd like it once you got started.

Amelia was...he wasn't quite sure what she was anymore. A disembodied spirit. Far more than a ghost, a word that didn't explain their situation. They'd become partners. Friends. More.

"Mostly interested in security right now," he muttered.

I'm not sensing anything. The magical shields are holding. She didn't seem worried. She was, as usual, supremely confident in her ability to get out of trouble. Cormac worried enough for both of them.

"Maybe we should get out of town for a few days."

She doubled up the usual protection spells on the apartment, the Jeep, and himself, shoving charms in the pockets of his jacket and jeans. She cast triggers, spells that would alert her if magic was being cast nearby, or if anyone of ill intent approached within a certain perimeter.

He was careful. He'd been raised to be careful, he'd lived his whole life being careful. He prided himself on protecting what needed protecting, even after he put away his more conventional weapons.

But he really wanted to figure out if someone was watching him, and if so, who and why.

The list of people and beings who had grudges against him was long. He'd been a bounty hunter—he'd killed vampires, werewolves, and a couple of things in between. He'd already had one vampire minion come after him for killing her master. *That* had been a mess. He'd gotten on the wrong side of vampire cabals. He didn't quite believe that the Long Game—which might or might not have involved actual angels and demons and Lucifer himself, he still wasn't too sure—was really over, and if it wasn't he might have some really nasty people coming after him. And then there was the *really* old stuff: his uncle had just gotten out of prison after a long stint for weapons and conspiracy charges, and Cormac had, half his lifetime ago, gotten mixed up in some of that militia and sovereignty mess. A lot of those old tangled connections definitely held grudges. Didn't matter that Cormac had left that world. He'd call his cousin Ben, see if he'd heard anything about what his father was doing now and if Cormac needed to worry.

So yeah. The list of what might be out to get him was too long to give him any clear sense of what might actually be gunning for him. If it wasn't just paranoia and his own frayed nerves catching up with him.

Maybe he needed a vacation.

Do you even know how to have a holiday?

No, he did not. "I hear beaches are nice." Except his last time on a beach he'd been arrested.

This state of mind made even taking out the trash an adventure. He paused at the second-story railing outside his apartment, checked over the parking lot. Right before dusk, the shadows were long and the street lights hadn't come on yet. Traffic on the nearby freeway was heavy but moving fast. The parking lot was half full, with no unusual activity.

He carried the bag of trash down the stairs, checked over the parking lot again, and kept close to the wall as he walked out to the Dumpster, located between the concrete wall and a chain-link fence separating this property from the next. Came at the Dumpster sideways so he didn't have to turn his back to the wide-open lot. Dumped the bag, dropped the lid, and was turning to head back along the building to the stairs when something punched his shoulder.

He stumbled a step, spun to look—and a pinching sensation stabbed through his muscle, followed by a warm wash of tingling along his nerves, then numbness. Craning his head, he reached, batting at himself, trying to get some sense of what had happened. His hand hit something small, hard, and cylindrical sticking out of his shoulder. He yanked it out. His flesh twinged, but he felt no pain. He wasn't feeling much of anything, suddenly. His legs had turned to cotton, and he dropped to his knees, hitting the asphalt hard.

His vision swimming, he looked at the thing in his hand that he'd pulled out of his shoulder. Small, silver, the width of a pencil, with a needle on one end and plastic fletching on the other. A tranquilizer dart. Of all the stupid, idiotic, bad '80s movie bullshit...this had *not* been on his list of things to be worried about.

A black SUV pulled up in front of him. Someone got out. Two people? He squinted, unable to focus.

Cormac, what's happening, what's—

"Goddammit," he muttered and passed out.

He woke up groggy, his mouth tasting like old socks. He squeezed shut his eyes, blinked them open again but couldn't see much better. This was because the room was dimly lit by a single lamp on a nearby table. The walls and ceiling of the room were lost in darkness; he might have been sitting in a void. Calmly, keeping his breathing steady, he assessed. He was on a metal chair with a high back. His hands were cuffed behind him. He rattled his arms a little—definitely metal cuffs. His phone had been removed from his back pocket.

Around the chair, white powder marked out a circle about ten feet in diameter. Salt. He was sitting in the middle of a circle of salt. Okay, then.

"Amelia?" he murmured, because he needed her, he expected her to be right there calling for him, but the back of his mind was silent.

"Who's Amelia?" asked a voice from the darkness outside the salt circle. Male sounding, curious.

"Shit," he muttered, then cursed himself again for not paying attention. A pounding headache between his eyes was growing more painful. He wasn't sure he'd be able to stand even if he wasn't tied up.

I have no idea what to make of this, Amelia finally whispered. She seemed distant, like she was speaking from another room, and he wasn't sure if that meant something was wrong with her, or with him.

Salt won't do any good against us, we aren't demons.

Yeah, but these guys might not know that. And who were these guys, anyway?

"So," he spoke as clearly as he could, but the words still slurred; his mouth felt thick and sluggish. "How are we doing this? You gonna ask questions or make threats?"

He listened—for breathing, for footsteps, for anything that would tell him how many people were in the room. He craned his neck, but except for the pool of light encompassing him and the salt circle, the room was dark, hiding anyone else here. The bad movie bullshit continued.

"We have questions," the male voice spoke again. He was standing on Cormac's right. "About you, your power. Who you're working for."

"Same here," he replied. Then under his breath, "Jackass."

The silence dragged. Cormac leaned back against the chair and wondered if he could go to sleep until the headache passed. He really needed a drink of water.

"We've been following your career," his captor said conversationally. "Your most recent career, that is, after you got out of prison. You've landed in the middle of some interesting events, some of which are difficult to explain without resorting to...magic."

How are we going to get out of this? he asked Amelia.

As I've explained many times, magic can't solve everything. Particularly handcuffs. And sedatives. I'm not sure I could occupy your body right now even if I had a solution. Her frustration was adding to his own anxiety. Was this vampires? He didn't think so. This guy didn't have the chill he associated with vampires, the feeling of age and power.

"You're a close associate of Kitty Norville, but even associating with a werewolf doesn't explain everything about you. Her accounts of many of these events don't entirely make sense. There's something she isn't saying."

Cormac jerked against the cuffs, as if that effort would be enough to get him out of the chair. If they'd caught Kitty, if they had her tied up somewhere and were questioning her— "Leave her alone. If you've hurt her—"

"We haven't touched her." He might have sounded surprised. Offended, even? "But she does talk a lot all on her own, which makes what she *doesn't* say very interesting. And she doesn't much talk about you, does she?"

Cormac settled back. Even if he could come up with a good story to feed this guy about who and what he was, that didn't mean he'd be released. If this guy wanted information, he could have just *called.* "What do you want?"

"Who's Amelia? A colleague? A girlfriend?"

He laughed a little. Yeah, something like that. The drugs were wearing off. His whole body was cramping and he couldn't stretch.

Maybe you should tell him about me, see how he reacts. We need information.

"He wouldn't believe me," he murmured, then realized he'd spoken out loud.

"Try me," the man said. "I've got some experience with the unbelievable."

"Not like this you don't."

"Mr. Bennett. You're a magician. A powerful one, and you got that way with no history of magic, no apparent training, no connection to any known disciplines of magic—"

What disciplines of magic? he asked Amelia. Do we know about this?

Amelia hesitated. *It's not a community I ever actively engaged in myself.*

Right, fine, he wasn't worried. Not at all.

"The only explanation I can come up with is some kind of bodily possession or mind control."

Well, that explained the salt circle, if they thought he was possessed. In spite of himself, he was impressed that he'd gotten this close to the truth just by deduction.

"It's not really like that," he said. "It's more like...a sublet?"

God help us, Amelia muttered.

The following silence seemed choked, as if his interrogator was at a loss for words.

"Amelia," a new voice said. This one sounded female, light and urgent. Cormac thought he caught a flash of movement ahead, someone coming right up to the edge of the light. "You're not the magician. She is."

"How?" the man asked.

"You haven't given me a reason to tell you anything," Cormac said.

He said, "I could arrange any number of charges to be filed against you that would put you in prison for the rest of your life. I know you've been working very hard to avoid that."

Captivity was probably the one thing he and Amelia were most afraid of. Might have been the only thing they were really afraid of. Amelia's very existence made the prospect of death rather ambiguous, after all.

"You could also shoot me dead right here," Cormac said.

"We're not the bad guys," he said. "We're trying to do some good, here."

By what definition of good? "Tell you what: undo the cuffs and get me a bottle of water and I'll talk."

Footsteps sounded from his right to his front. The man, moving to consult with the woman in a low voice. Cormac could just about make out what they were saying.

"But what if he—"

"What if *they*," she corrected. "I can handle them. I want to hear this."

They were scared of him. Of what he—and Amelia—could do. Maybe they could use that.

Steps on the concrete floor went away, then returned. The woman still wasn't entirely visible—she remained a shadow, her features obscured. She stepped in just far enough to sweep open a section of the salt circle with her foot. She was wearing low-heeled, black pumps and a suit, that much became visible. The man entered through this break, came into the light, and Cormac got his first good look at him.

He had an athletic frame; his ear-length hair was gray, swept back. His pale face was weathered, and he looked back at Cormac with an air of resignation. He could have been anywhere from forty-five to sixty, and Cormac wondered if this was his last big job before retirement, just to keep the bad movie tropes going. Slacks, dress shoes. No suit jacket, no tie, but picturing him in those was easy enough. His shirt sleeves were rolled up, adding to his careworn look.

He tucked a bottle of water under his arm as he moved to the back of the chair and unlocked the cuffs, which popped open. Gratefully, Cormac stretched out his arms and rubbed his wrists.

Then he turned on the man with hands outstretched and shouted, "Boo!"

The man didn't react, except to give a wry curl of his lips as he offered the bottle of water.

"So you have seen some shit, I guess," Cormac said.

"Yeah." He left through the opening in the circle. The woman remade the circle, scooping salt from a bag and spilling it while whispering indecipherable words. Cormac listened hard, but he— Amelia—didn't recognize the incantation.

Cormac took the water and drank. His whole body seemed to suck in the moisture at once, and he sighed with relief.

"Now," the man said, stepping to the edge of the light and crossing his arms. "Who is Amelia?"

LONG TIME WAITING

Manitou Springs, Colorado, 1900

Amelia's scrying brought her to a cottage perched on the hill overlooking the road. Tucked in the woods, the place was meant to be charming, but the blue paint had faded to gray and the shadows of the surrounding trees fell across it strangely.

The feeling of doom that had brought her here grew stronger. *I am too late.* For the thousandth time she rebuked herself; she should have heeded the warning on that crossroads tomb . . .

Dismounting, she tossed her horse's reins over the porch railing, and charged inside.

Lydia Harcourt, nineteen, lay in the foyer, sprawled on her side on the hardwood floor. A pool of blood had spread around her, a scarlet carpet. Her blue cotton dress was stained and spattered with it. Her throat had been cut so deeply, the head lolled back at an angle that caused it to stare inhumanly over her shoulder. The wound exposed muscle, bone, torn vessels, and windpipe. One would think the girl had been mauled by an animal, but the cut was too clean. A single swipe of a claw, not the work of teeth and limbs. The blood was still wet, shining in the light coming through the window. This hadn't happened long ago, but the perpetrator was gone, vanished into air quite literally, same as last time. Last month, she'd tracked the demon to a village in Juarez, where it had slaughtered a herd of cattle. She had known it was only a matter of time before it chose a human target, and one likely to most infuriate Amelia.

10

Nothing in the place was broken, no struggle had taken place, no one in the neighborhood had been alerted by screams. Lydia might have simply fallen where she stood.

"Damn," Amelia whispered. She cursed herself for having the ability to know what was happening, to mark it and track it, but not the speed to catch the thing. As if the demon knew this, it seemed to taunt her.

She opened the satchel she wore over her shoulder.

Chalk. A red candle. A bundle of sage. Flint and steel. A round mirror the size of her hand. The body had not yet stiffened. A trace of warmth still lingered in the blood. If Amelia hurried, she might be able to catch the trail of the demon. Keep such slaughter from happening again.

She set the candle near the girl's head and lit it. Next, she drew a circle in chalk. To contain the girl and all the blood, she had to draw it clear to the walls. She paused a moment to take direction, found north, and drew the proper symbols, the ancient signs that communed with the stars overhead and the elements on earth, that opened doors between worlds.

Lydia watched her with eyes like frosted glass.

"Rest easy, my dear," Amelia murmured. "Soon you can tell me what you know, and I'll stop the thing that did this."

She lit the sage, set it smoldering. Placed the mirror by the candle. It reflected golden light back into the room. Amelia knelt before it, and watched Lydia.

The smoke from the incense set Amelia's eyes watering. Closing them in a moment of dizziness, she drew a breath. Her mind was entering another state. Opening passages, picturing a great ironbound block of a door that separated the world of the living and the world of the dead.

"Lydia Harcourt, I need to speak with you," she said, and imagined the door cracking open.

Fog appeared in the mirror.

"Lydia. Can you hear me?" Amelia breathed slowly to keep her heart from racing. If she panicked now, she'd lose the trail and would never vanquish this creature. She focused all her attention on the room, the door, the body, the dead eyes.

"Lydia, please. I know it's difficult. I want to help. Can you hear me?"

The eyes blinked.

Amelia's heart jumped, and she steadied her breathing. The dead eyes swiveled to look up at her, and something stared out of them. Amelia found the courage to look back.

"Lydia. I know you can't speak. But I need you to remember what happened. Think of who did this to you, live through it one more time, just once. I'll see it in the mirror here. Then I can find what did this. Punish it. Do you understand? Can you do this for me?"

The eyes blinked.

"Oh my dear, thank you." Amelia brushed a strand of the girl's chestnut hair off her forehead, as if she could still feel comfort. But who could say what she felt, with the door open? Even if it was only a crack. "Follow the light. Show me in the mirror."

The mirror presented an image of fog. Figures began to emerge. A dark form had the shape of a man, tall and stout, but it was featureless. When it reached, the fingers were as long as its arm, and it had claws, extending, curling. In the mirror, Lydia showed a picture of herself, her mouth open to scream as one of the claws raked across her neck.

"Lydia, you must try to remember. Where did it go?"

The shadow in the mirror took on red eyes. Again and again, the claw tore through her throat, and she fell before she could make a sound. That was all she had, all she could give Amelia. The corpse, its gaze still locked on her, blinked again, and a tear slid from the outside corner of its eye, down its cheek.

Amelia sat back and clenched her hands in her lap. What was she doing here? Abusing the dead for no good purpose. She fancied herself a wizard, an arcane scholar, a demon hunter. She'd traveled the world to learn what she knew. It all should have been good for something.

She touched Lydia's face and closed her eyes. "Sleep, Lydia. Leave this world. May the next treat you better." In her mind, she closed the door, slid shut the bolt. The mirror was a mirror again. She snuffed the candle with her finger.

Then she heard footsteps on the porch. Perhaps Lydia had had time to scream after all.

The rumble of a carriage and horses came up from the road beyond. More steps on the porch. Her heart in her ears, Amelia was too shocked to move, so when the men opened the door, they found her kneeling by the body with blood on her hands and the occult circle drawn around her.

Cañon City, Colorado, Four Months Later

Doors, passages, worlds. A skillful magus could travel between them by his thoughts alone, or so Amelia had read. In the East she had seen orange-clad monks who could stop their own breathing by meditation and seemed to be dead, but they awoke safely.

Did she believe a person could travel between life and death? Pass through that iron door and return unharmed?

The bricks of the prison where she was housed were old enough, at least by this country's standards. Their roots stretched into the earth. They had seen forty years of life and death. They had passages and portals the wardens did not know about. Lying on her canvas cot at night, she traveled them. She bound together a bit of candle and a lock of hair and burned them until neither remained.

Would it work?

The iron door was open wide, gaping like a mouth.

They had cut her dark hair short and put her in a poor cotton dress, a bleached gray prison uniform. They had let her keep her boots, thank God. These boots had traveled the world and were well broken in, comfortable. At least her feet were not sore. The boots would walk her to the scaffold. She could travel between worlds, but not escape a steel-barred prison. A sore irony.

The day was blustery, a wind pouring from the mountains, carrying dust and the promise of rain. For now the sky was hazy, washed out by an arid sun. A crowd of spectators had gathered, all men in proper suits and hats, hairy mustaches making their frowns seem fiercer, more judgmental. They were all no doubt horrified at what she'd done. What they thought she'd done. The bastards had no idea. They would truly be horrified if they knew what lived in the world, dime-novel monsters they could not believe.

She stood on the platform. A man tied her hands in front of her. A noose hung. Part of her wanted to look away, but part of her studied it. She had seen men hanged, but had never seen a noose from this angle, so close. The knot had been tied correctly. She had never seen a woman hanged.

Her thoughts were scattered, her mind already partway gone. Not through the door, but into a little room she had built beside the door with hair, candle, and incantation. She would fool that iron slab. Doors and rooms existed between life and death.

The candle, the hair. The light, her life.

How had it come to this? part of her wailed. Her parents had been right, she should have stayed home, married the unremarkable suit they'd put in front of her. Too late, the scientific part of her mind reprimanded. She followed this path of her own free will and she must continue on. When the path seemed to end, you blazed a new trail through the wilderness.

"Amelia Parker, you have been tried and convicted for the murder of Lydia Harcourt and sentenced to death according to the laws of the state of Colorado."

She cleared her throat and tried not to sound nervous. Her voice came out halting anyway. "Lady Amelia Parker. I'd prefer my title

14

entered into the records, if you please." Her throat closed, and she swallowed. *Just a little longer. Stay focused on that room beside the iron door.*

"*Lady* Amelia Parker, do you have any last words?"

"None whatsoever. Thank you."

"Then may God have mercy on your soul."

Closing her eyes, she left the scaffold. It was a strange feeling. She merely thought, *Breathe out.* Breathe it all out. Focus on the small symbols she had built, make them real, go there. Light, life, the room beside the door. Then she was watching a slim waif of a girl standing on the scaffold. It was her, pale and despairing. She'd hardly eaten for days and it showed. The prison dress hung limply on her. Hood over her head, rope around her neck. Still she could see. Was pleased the body did not tremble. But the executioners had to guide it into place, as if the person was no longer truly conscious.

The floor dropped with a creak and a snap, and everything went dark.

Cañon City, Colorado, The Present

Cormac took another step forward in line and tried not to think too hard. This place was built on routine, rhythm. If he let himself fall into it, the days flew by. He'd be out of here in no time, if he could keep up the rhythm and not let anything—anyone—knock him out of it. He made sure not to get too close to the guy in front of him—big guy, beefy shoulders, white, tattoo-covered—and tried not to think of the guy behind him—shorter, wiry, which probably meant he was quick—breathing down his neck. Cormac didn't look at anyone, didn't meet anyone's gaze. Let himself be carried by the rhythm. He'd pick up his tray, his plastic utensils, find a place to sit where he wouldn't have to talk to anyone, and eat to keep himself going for another day. Try not to think about the way the orange jumpsuit didn't fit right across his shoulders, or the way this place smelled like fifty years of bad cooking.

He had his tray in hand when a shove hit his shoulder. Because he'd been expecting it, the tray didn't go flying.

He didn't have to look to know it was the guy behind him, the scrappy freak who'd tried to stare him down before at meals or out in the yard. It wasn't an accident, though if Cormac confronted him the guy would say it was. More than that, he wouldn't apologize; he'd turn it around, accuse Cormac of trying to start something, then he really would start something—a fight to knock him a few pegs down the pecking order. Cormac had seen this play out a dozen times. The black guys had their gangs, and they picked on the Latino gangs who picked on the white gangs who picked on everybody else, spouting some kind of superiority shtick, which was a riot because they were all locked up in the same cinder-block box wearing the same prison jumpsuits. Even their tattoos blurred together after a while. Cormac didn't try to keep score.

He turned his head just enough to look at the guy, whose eyes were round, whose lips were snarly. The collar of his jumpsuit was crooked. He was bristling, teeth bared, like he was getting ready to jump him. But Cormac didn't react. Just looked at the guy, frowning. Cold. The big mistake these jokers made was thinking Cormac cared about his rep, cared about the pecking order, wanted or even needed to join up for protection, for friendship, for some sense of belonging. Like they were all some pack of wolves, he thought with some amount of irony.

They stood like that for maybe a full minute until the next guy behind muttered, "Hey, move it." Cormac only turned back around when the scrappy freak ducked his gaze. No need to get excited, no need to say a word. You just had to keep to yourself. He wasn't here to make lifelong friends or be the boss of anyone.

No one else bothered him as he picked up his tray and went to an empty table at the far end of the cafeteria. Prison guards stood at the doorways, watching. Cormac didn't pay them any more attention than he did to his fellow prisoners. There was no point to it.

He hadn't been trying to earn a reputation over the last few months, but he seemed to have one anyway. No one else sat with him; the others gave him plenty of room. He didn't talk, didn't try to make friends. That cold stare was enough to keep trouble away. So he ate greasy chicken and mashed potatoes with watery gravy in silence.

He didn't want to think too hard about it, but keeping stock of his surroundings was too much a habit to quit: noting where the people around him were, how they carried themselves, where the exits were, what dangers lay in wait. The hunter's instincts. He should have been grateful—those instincts were keeping him safe here. But they also made him edgy. Maybe it was the feeling of being trapped, that he couldn't go anywhere in this place without being watched, without the chance that one of those uniformed, frozen-faced guards might decide to take him down for no reason at all. He hadn't seen open sky in weeks. Even the yard was ringed with concrete and barbed wire.

He set down his fork and flattened his hand on the table, just for a moment, until the tension went away. He was doing all right. He just had to keep putting one foot in front of the other.

And he had to get rid of the tightness in his spine that said someone was watching him. That something around here was just a little bit . . . off.

The inmates told ghost stories.

"There's a warden fifty years ago who hung himself," the guy in the next cell, Moe, was saying. "Can you believe that? A warden. Hung himself on the top floor. That knocking sound? That's him. Walking around."

"Shut *up*," hollered another inmate in another cell.

"You've heard it," Moe insisted.

"It's pipes. It's old fucking pipes," Cormac's cellmate Frank said.

"You know the story, you know it's true."

The pipes acted up once a week or so, and every time Moe had to talk about the ghost of the warden who hanged himself. Cormac thought it was just the pipes.

Trouble was, inmates told lots of stories, and something here wasn't right. That tingling at the back of his neck made him reach for a gun on his belt. Easy enough to brush it off, to tell Moe to shut up. But something dripped off the walls here. Of course a prison was going to be tense, all these angry guys penned up together.

The trouble was, Cormac knew what was really out there. A prison filled with ghosts wasn't the worst of it.

"I'm going to beat you if you don't shut it!"

"I'm just telling you. I'm *warning* you!"

This would go on for another minute before Moe finally shut up. Wasn't anything anyone could do about it.

Cormac pressed his pillow over his ear and tried to think himself away from this place. To a meadow up in Grand County, miles from anywhere. Tucked on the side of a valley, east facing so it got the first sun of the morning. Green grass, tall trees, blue sky, and a creek running down the middle of it. His father had taken him hunting there when he was a kid, and he never forgot it. Camping, waking up before dawn when a layer of mist clung to the grass. Drinking strong coffee heated over a campfire. He went back there, when he needed to get out of his own head.

The nameplate sitting on the desk read "Dr. Ronald Olson." Cormac sat in the not-so-comfortable chair across the desk from an unassuming man in an oxford shirt and corduroy jacket. He even had glasses. He was maybe in his fifties, and his hair was thinning. He looked soft rather than weathered. Cormac classified him as prey.

"How are you doing today?" Olson asked.

Cormac shrugged. This was just another hoop to jump through.

Play nice for the camp counselor. He doubted the guy could tell him anything about himself he didn't already know. Both his parents had died violently when he was young, his whole life had been filled with violence, he'd fallen back on violence as a solution to every problem, and that was what landed him here.

He didn't know if Olson expected him to try to manipulate him, play some kind of mental hide-and-seek, Hannibal Lector-style. Cormac didn't want to work that hard for so little payoff. But Olson was free to think Cormac was a puzzle he could pick apart and solve.

"How are you adjusting?"

"It's just a place," Cormac said, shrugging again. "One day at a time."

"Any problems? Anything you'd like to talk about? It can be a shock, going from the outside to this."

Cormac smiled and looked away. "Am I supposed to get pissed off because I can't run out to McDonald's and get a hamburger? That's a waste of energy."

"That's an admirable stoicism. Are you sure you aren't in denial? That can be dangerous as well."

Cormac had a feeling the two of them looked at dangerous in completely different ways. He resisted an urge to glance at the clock, to see how much time they had left. He hadn't asked for this—the guy had gotten hold of Cormac's file and decided he must be crazy.

"I figure I keep my head down and get out of here just as quick as I can."

"Goal oriented. That's good."

Now Cormac wondered if the guy was for real. He shifted, leaning forward just a little. "There's one thing you could maybe tell me about."

"Go on."

"You hear many ghost stories around here? Do guys come in here telling about . . . things. Noises, spooky stuff."

Olson's smile seemed condescending. "I suppose every prison has its share of ghost stories. Some inmates have active imaginations."

"There seem to be a lot of them around here. Like the guys have passed them down over the years. They say some warden hanged himself and now his ghost walks around, that a serial killer came in slitting inmates' throats, that sort of thing."

"You believe that?"

"The one about the warden? No. Not that one."

"But you believe . . .something."

"People tell stories because there may be something to some of it." He wasn't trying to rattle the guy; wasn't sure much would rattle a prison therapist. That wasn't a game Cormac wanted to start. But there had to be something to the constant chill that had settled in his spine.

Olson leaned forward to study a page in an open folder, Cormac's file, as if he hadn't already memorized it and was working from a script.

"In your deposition, you claimed your victim wasn't human," he said.

"I didn't say that. I said she wasn't *all* human."

"Then what else was she?" He didn't ask like someone who was really interested in the answer. He asked like a psychologist who expected his patient to say something damning. Hell, how much more damned could he be?

"It's hard to explain," he said.

"You think something like that is going on here? Something that's hard to explain?"

This isn't about me, Cormac wanted to yell at the guy. But he settled back, didn't look away, didn't give an inch. "Maybe it's just being in jail."

"I just have a couple of more questions for you. Your parents both passed away when you were quite young. What do you remember about them?"

Cormac stared at the guy, his expression unchanging. "I don't remember anything."

Of course Olson didn't believe him; Cormac hadn't expected him to. They stared at each other, waiting for the other to break.

Olson glanced at his watch and said, "I think that's enough for today. Until next week, then." He smiled kindly. A guard took Cormac back to his cell.

Part of the general population, he was allowed out of his cell for meals, showers, time in the yard, and his work detail washing dishes. He'd put in for a better job, but that would take time, a review. He had to prove that he wasn't going to cause trouble. He was trying to do just that. The days ticked on, hour by hour. Best not to count the time, but there it was.

His half of the cell was starting to look like it belonged to him—his small shelf displayed a growing collection of books, a small stack of letters he'd gotten, a couple of magazines. Frank had been here longer and had a radio and pictures of his two kids on display. None of those details could disguise the bars, or the fact that their bedroom was also a bathroom, with a stainless steel toilet and sink mounted in the corner. This was a cage in a zoo.

Yet another night after lights out he lay on the top bunk, staring at the shadowed ceiling, waiting for sleep to pull him under. He could almost hear the shadows shifting across the walls, moving through the building, claws scratching on concrete. The place was old, haunted. A prison had been on this spot for almost a hundred fifty years. If any ghosts had taken up residence during that time, he was stuck with them.

"Hey," said Frank from the bottom bunk. Cormac didn't answer, but Frank continued. "You got a girl waiting for you on the outside, don't you?"

It was an odd question. Cormac kept staring up. "What makes you say that?"

"The way you stare, like you're looking somewhere else. Guys only stare like that when they're thinking about a girl. Not just a hot piece of ass, but someone they really like."

Cormac's thoughts flashed on a face and a name. The girl he liked. The one who wasn't waiting for him on the outside.

He rolled over on his side and didn't say a word.

Ghosts haunted the place. She built up her walls and they left her alone. She waited.

The first one who went mad was a veteran of the Great War who'd returned home to few prospects and been caught stealing an automobile. She had thought perhaps the chaotic visions swirling in his mind would prepare him for her. She was wrong. She slipped in quietly, tentatively, like dipping fingers in the surface of a pool of water to test the temperature. She whispered words, told him what would happen, that it wouldn't hurt—she didn't think it would. She hoped it wouldn't. But it did. Her presence pushed an already disturbed mind past breaking. He woke from sleep screaming and wouldn't stop. Said he heard voices.

Madmen who speak of the voices they hear was such an awful cliché. And yet.

She tried to be more careful. Her second attempt was a family man convicted of fraud. A stable, quiet man who'd committed a nonviolent crime and had much to keep him levelheaded. When he heard the voice, the whisper, and felt her tendrils in his mind, the spirit that wasn't his own moving through his flesh, he split his skull trying to fight his way out of the cell.

And so it went. No matter how carefully she chose her targets, how gently she pressed against their thoughts, she broke minds, searching for one that would fit her. She was waiting for a certain quality of mind: intelligent, astute, observant, patient. So many of the minds that passed through here were troubled, ill, wracked by demons of their own making that had nothing to do with the supernatural. Weak, prone to

22

violence, which was what brought many of them here in the first place. She waited a long time.

She might have given up entirely, let what was left her fade to shadow, but the murders followed her. The curse of the demon should have ended with her death. But she hadn't really died, had she?

She needed a body to resume the hunt, to finally destroy the curse. So she kept trying, kept making morbid sacrifices.

If she'd had any fear in her state, any feeling beyond the instinct to seek out what she needed, she'd have been afraid. She would lose herself in this place. The spell would never work to completion. She'd never find the vessel. She would fade, become simply another voice calling purposelessly to madmen. Another shade to the miasma seeping from the stones.

Then, one of the minds recognized her.

He'd been primed, and he had the instincts. He recognized the irregular, the uncanny. Magic. He didn't even know it. He'd lived with it so long, he only noticed it as a tickling in his mind.

He was violent, here for killing. But it was a controlled, chilled violence of necessity and will. In some ways, his ability to kill was less understandable than the ones who lashed out in the heat of violence and caused mayhem. They lost control and that was reason enough.

This man approached it like a job, with no more passion than he might mend a shirt or dig a hole. She was drawn to him and horrified— her, horrified! What was he?

Human, nothing more. She could see by the glow of him.

Most of all, though, she felt he was a hard mind. Resilient. He might hear a voice, but wouldn't break from it like the dozen before him had. She was sure of it.

After breakfast the next day, an alarm sounded. Lockdown. Cormac lay on his bunk, waiting for news. The grapevine would start feeding rumors soon enough. Probably it was just someone trying to get out. It happened more often than he would have thought, inmates packing themselves into crates to be shipped out or squeezing through barbed wire. He didn't understand how that could look like a good idea to anyone, even someone who spent twenty-three hours a day in a ten-by-ten cell. People succeeded more often than he would have thought, but seldom for very long. The guy who packed himself into a crate was found when they unloaded the truck at its destination. He was hauled back with a few more years added to his sentence.

The gamble wasn't worth it. Just a few years, keep his nose clean, get out. That was the plan. He'd still have a life when he got out of here. Maybe even more of one than when he arrived. He could stare at the ceiling for a few years and not go crazy.

Moe, the flighty guy in the next cell over, said, "They found Brewster."

Frank stood by the bars in the corner to talk to him. "Found him where?"

"Dead, throat cut, blood everywhere. Right in his cell."

"So Gus did it?"

Cormac listened, almost amused. Gus must have snapped. The guy was half Brewster's size, but he could have managed it.

"No, that's the thing, Gus's pissing his pants. They don't think he did it."

That piqued Cormac's attention.

"They were locked in together, what else could have happened?" Frank said.

"All I know is he got cut up, but they didn't find a knife, and Gus is pissing himself. Says he didn't even see what happened."

Frank chuckled. "Yeah, that's a good story. That'll get him off the hook for sure."

"It's just like what happened with that serial killer, the one from the thirties, remember?"

"I thought that happened in the sixties," Frank said.

"Maybe it was a vampire," Cormac said. "Turned to mist, come in through the bars."

Frank stared at him. He was young but worn down, a stout white guy with a dozen tattoos scattered piecemeal across his back and arms. He'd spent more of his adult life in prison than out of it.

From the other cell Moe said, "What'd he say?"

"You're not serious," Frank said. "Can they do that?"

One thing was for sure, the world had gotten a whole lot more interesting over the last year, since the NIH went public with data proving that vampires and lycanthropes were real. Cormac loved throwing out bombshells like that. He loved that people acknowledged the existence of monsters without knowing anything about them. It made terrifying them so easy.

"But it probably wasn't that," Cormac said. "Vampire wouldn't have left all that blood lying around."

"Jesus Christ," Frank muttered. "Now how am I supposed to sleep?"

Cormac knew that vampires didn't turn into mist. They moved quickly, with faster-than-the-eye reflexes, and that was probably how the mist stories started. They couldn't break into a locked cell. But if Gus had nothing to do with the murder, then *something* had gotten in and killed Brewster.

It was just the rumor mill. He'd wait for more reliable information before drawing conclusions.

That night, Cormac woke up sweating, batting at a humming in his ear. The place had bugs. Rolling to his side, he settled his arm over his head, and tried to imagine he was outdoors, camping at the edge of his meadow, his father sleeping a few feet away, his rifle beside him. Any sign of trouble, Dad would take care of it.

Cormac hadn't thought much of his father in years, until he ended up here. Here, he thought about everything. What would his father think of him now? Would he be surprised his kid ended up in prison?

The breathing and snores of the dozens of other men on the block echoed and kept Cormac rooted to this place. Best not to let his mind wander too much. Had to stay here. Pay attention. He shouldn't have thought of his father.

A voice plucked deep in his mind, a buried place carefully covered over, where not even his dreaming self went. That place had lain quiet as a matter of survival.

What are you?

A shadow stirred, rustling, looking for the light. Cormac shut the door on it.

Olson would see him next week and ask, *Anything troubling you? Anything you want to talk about?* That shadow would start to rattle around the inside of his mind, but Cormac would just shake his head no. *Nothing to talk about.* Except that the inside of his skull itched. Again Olson would ask, *What's on your mind?* And Cormac would say, *Let me tell you about my father, who died when I was sixteen. Let me tell you how, and what I did to the monster that killed him.*

The buzzing wasn't a fly; the legs crawled on the interior surface of his skull. He suddenly wanted nothing more than to take the top of his head off and scratch.

It was just this place getting to him. Well, couldn't let that happen. Had to hold on, stay sane. He had too many reasons to stay sane and get out of here in one piece. He never thought he'd say that. Never thought he'd have anything to live for except the next job, the next hunt.

He drifted off and again woke up sweating. This time it was light out, sun coming in through distant skylights. Cormac still felt like the bugs had gotten to him.

He thought of all the things that could slice up a man in a locked cell. A guy could do himself in like that if he put his mind to it, and it wasn't too hard to think of how captivity could drive a man—the right kind of man—to it. That was the simplest explanation and the one the warden would probably settle on. Let the psychologists hash it out.

While Cormac had been joking about vampires turning to mist and coming in through the bars, other things could appear from nowhere, things that didn't have physical bodies, demons with knifelike claws that fed on blood, curses laid from afar. Ghosts that tickled the inside of your mind. If he'd been in charge of an investigation and the physical evidence couldn't explain it, that would be the first trail Cormac followed: Did Brewster know anyone who could work that kind of magic, who also had it in for him? Without seeing the body for himself, Cormac didn't have much to go on. They'd probably find some reasonable, nonsupernatural explanation.

Two guards didn't come to work the next day.

Yard time was cut short. Half the block didn't get time at all, which set up an afternoon of trouble. Guys yelled from their cells, hassling guards during counts, which happened half a dozen times a day. The warden even added a count, which started up a rumor that somebody was missing and probably cut up the same as Brewster.

That couldn't have been the case, because when a count turned up short the whole facility went into lockdown, and that hadn't happened since the body was found. Lockdown then had only lasted a day, but that made two days now that the routine had been trashed. Without routine, inmates floundered.

At dinner, Cormac took his tray to his usual corner in the dining hall. A couple of tables over, his neighbor, Moe, was tugging on another guy's arm. Big guy, bald, tattooed arms, glaring across the room with murder in his eyes. Cormac followed the gaze to a group of black men who seemed to be minding their own business. Moe was trying to get the guy to sit back down.

Cormac took his tray and moved another table down, farther away from them, and put his back to the wall. Sure enough, the shouting started, the big guy broke away from Moe's grasp and lunged toward one of the black guys, who lunged right back at him. The fight turned into a full-blown melee in seconds, two gangs pounding into each other, surrounded by a ring of more men screaming them on.

This was what passed for entertainment around here.

Cormac kept quiet and wolfed down as much of his dinner as he could, because sure enough, guards swarmed into the place, clubs drawn to beat the crowd into submission and drag the worst offenders to the hole. They cleared the whole room. When a guard approached Cormac, he raised his hands, lowered his gaze, and went back to his cell without argument. The prison went into lockdown yet again, which mean a lot more staring at ceilings and grumbling.

"He said it was voodoo," Moe said right after lights out, in a hissing voice that managed to carry down the row. The guy had somehow managed to extricate himself from the worst of the mess and got out of any kind of punishment. "Hal said that Carmell knew voodoo and made a voodoo doll of Brewster and ripped it to pieces. That's what got Brewster."

Somebody muttered at him to shut up.

"Voodoo doesn't work like that," Cormac said. He shouldn't be encouraging the guy.

"It don't work at all," Frank said.

"You know so much about it, how does it work?" Moe said.

Cormac sighed. Maybe a scary enough story would shut him up—or make it worse. "That voodoo doll thing is Hollywood. Saturday morning cartoons. Real voodoo, you want something done you have to make a sacrifice. Usually a blood sacrifice for something big. You'd slaughter somebody in order to do the curse, not as the curse itself."

Now there was a thought that halfway made sense. It wasn't a murder, but a blood sacrifice. That still didn't explain who or why.

The others shut up for at least half a minute.

"Christ, you're worse than him," Frank grumbled.

Moe perked up with what seemed to be a new theory. "Hey, if it wasn't Carmell, maybe it was you. You seem to know all about this shit."

"Forget I said anything," Cormac said, rolling to his side and pulling his pillow over his head.

"Maybe it was Satanists. I heard this story about a cult of Satanists here like twenty years ago—"

In winter, the creek froze solid, but in spring it ran white and frothing with snowmelt, lace waterfalls tumbling over sheer boulders. He could watch it for hours and stay calm.

Elk came down into the meadow to graze early, an hour or so after dawn when the sun began to peek over the mountaintops. Dad would stake out the herd, choose his target, and fire. Never missed. This was where he'd taught Cormac to do the same. He didn't bring his clients here. He'd run an outfitting service, worked as a private guide for hunting parties made up of folks with more money than sense. Got them their big stuffed trophy heads and stories for their fancy cocktail parties. But this place was different. This place was for family.

As Cormac watched, the elk vanished. Like someone turning off a TV.

A woman appeared before him, gray, ghostlike.

Terrifyingly out of place, she stood on the dewy grass, hands folded demurely before her, chin tipped up. Her clothing was old-fashioned: a dark skirt that draped to the ground, a high-collared neckline with tight little buttons going all the way up, lace around the wrists of her long sleeves. Her black hair was twisted at the base of her neck, and she wore a hat, a flat thing with a brim and a few feathers curling down the side.

Cormac had an urge to unwrap that hair to see how long it was.

She opened pale lips to speak. The inside of Cormac's skull itched.

Shivering, he opened his eyes to darkness. Twisting, he looked over his shoulder through the bars, fully expecting to see the woman standing outside the cell. His instincts told him someone was standing there. But deep into night, the place was still. Nothing moved. No one stood there, the pressure at the back of his neck notwithstanding.

"Goddamn," he whispered. He scratched his head, fingers scraping through his rough hair. The itching faded, but didn't go away. The skin on his back crawled.

This place was doing its best to make him crazy but he'd be damned if he let it.

Moe's cellmate's screaming woke the block at dawn.

Cormac hadn't slept well and was already awake. He jumped off the top bunk and pressed himself to the bars, trying to see next door. Frank was right beside him.

In the next cell over, Moe's cellmate, Harlan, was throwing himself against the bars, reaching through them, lunging like he could push his way through. His breaths came in full-throated screams, over and over.

Cormac smelled blood, and the only way he could smell it from ten feet over was if there was a whole lot of it. Looking down, he saw a dark puddle pushing out, oozing on the floor from the cell to the walkway outside. Harlan must have been standing in it.

A pair of guards came, annoyed looks on their faces, as if they were fully prepared to beat the shit out of the guy. When they reached the cell, their expressions changed. They radioed the control room to open the door, and as soon as the bars slid away, Harlan fell out and ran smack against the railing opposite before the guards caught him and hauled him upright. He was gibbering, unable to stand on his feet. He kept looking back into the cell, eyes wide and horrified. His socks left bloody footprints on the concrete.

It had happened again.

Cormac thought they might move him and Frank to another cell while they investigated Moe's death, but they didn't. They didn't have anywhere else to put them while the block was under lockdown. Harlan had been dragged to the infirmary.

Frank paced. The prison equivalent of cabin fever was getting to lots of them. Some of the guys were shouting about cruel and unusual punishment, that none of them should have to stay here until the warden figured out why men were dying. Someone had started an Ebola rumor—the disease had infected the prison and was now spreading. Or that the government was using the inmates in experiments. None of that was right. Cormac wondered if that ghostly woman carried a knife under her skirt.

He leaned against the bars, arms laced through, to watch as much of the investigation as he could. The lead investigator, a burly middle-aged guy in a blue Department of Corrections uniform, stepped carefully around the pool of blood. A photographer snapped his camera, recording the crime scene.

An hour or so later, the guards brought the body out on a stretcher. They didn't cover it up at first, and Cormac got a pretty good look. Moe's throat had been slit from ear to ear, torn maybe, though the edges weren't clear through the blood. He didn't seem injured or cut in any other way. Cormac was willing to bet the same thing had happened to Brewster.

The investigator noticed him watching. The guy had probably been around long enough to have seen a few wild crime scenes and was probably already cooking up some story about how Gus and Harlan had gone crazy and killed their cellmates in exactly the same way. He studied Cormac, taking in details, probably figuring he knew everything about him from those few seconds of looking. Gruff-looking thirty-something hanging on the bars of a prison cell. What else did he need to know?

"You see anything?" the investigator said. "Hear anything unusual from over here?"

Cormac made a shrugging motion with his hands. "I was laying on my bunk. I didn't hear anything until Harlan screamed."

The investigator smirked. "Does that mean you didn't hear anything, or you 'didn't hear anything.'" He put up finger quotes the second time.

Why the hell did the guy bother asking if he wasn't going to believe him? "I figure he must have woken up and seen Moe already like that."

"Then who do you think killed Moe?"

"Don't know. Bogeyman?"

Now the guy looked disgusted. "What are you in for?"

"Manslaughter."

"So you killed somebody but you didn't mean to?"

"Oh, I meant to all right. I'm here on a plea bargain."

The investigator walked away in a huff.

"Christ, man." Frank eased up against the bars next to Cormac. "It's like I watch you trying so hard to stay out of folks' way but you just can't help aggravating them."

"I just told the truth."

"Yeah, right," Frank said, laughing. The laughter sounded wrong and put Cormac even more on edge.

He wasn't much surprised when a guard came for him and went through the process of pulling him out of the cell. Frank, standing facing the wall, hands on his head, was still laughing, quietly, like he thought Cormac had brought this on himself.

He expected to be put in a closet and worked over by the smug inspector, but the guard led him to Olson's office. The doctor looked busy, gathering manila folders and setting them aside, indicating for Cormac to sit while he did. He slouched into the chair opposite the desk.

"Thank you for coming," Olson said.

Cormac chuckled. "Seriously?"

Olson granted a thin smile. "That we're sitting in a prison is no reason not to be polite."

"I didn't think I was up for another session yet," Cormac said.

"You're not, but I wanted to talk to you. What have you been hearing about recent events?" He had finished filing and now leaned forward, arms on his desk, his full attention on Cormac.

"My cell's right next to Moe's," he said. "Kind of hard to avoid it."

"Do you think his cellmate did it?"

"What—both his cellmate and Brewster's, going batshit and turning killer in the same way? Neither one of them's a killer."

"But if they didn't, what did?"

"'What did.' Not who?" Cormac said.

Olson paused, considering, gathering his words. "I'm sure you're hearing more rumors than I am. People are saying what killed him couldn't have been human. It was too brutal."

For a prison full of medium- to high-security inmates, that was saying something. "So what else could it have been?" Cormac said, straight-faced, disingenuous. "Some kind of monster?"

"You've had a long association with monsters."

Cormac wondered how much he'd have to say before he got a referral to the psychiatric ward. Deciding to play out a little line, he said, "Some of my best friends are werewolves."

"Yes, so your file says."

Nothing flustered this guy. Olson was starting to look less like prey.

Olson continued. "An autopsy on Brewster's body showed no fingerprints, no fibers, no sign of a struggle. His throat seemed to have spontaneously opened, the cut reaching all the way to his backbone. Gus is in the infirmary, under sedation. He hasn't been able to communicate since the guards found him with Brewster's body. No weapon was found, and Gus didn't have any blood on him. Because of that he's not being considered a suspect. Now Harlan is in the same state. I suspect Moe's autopsy will reveal the same set of mysteries."

"Why are you telling me this?" Cormac said.

"I'm asking for your advice. Do you have any idea what could have done this?"

Cormac's first impulse was to blow him off. Olson was part of the establishment that locked him in here. Bureaucrats like him didn't have room for the bizarre, couldn't understand that the woman he'd killed was a wizard, powerful and evil, and he'd had no choice but to destroy her. As Frank had observed, Cormac could piss people off just by sitting in one place and looking at them funny. Olson couldn't force him to help. Why should Cormac volunteer?

"There's so much shit out there that could have done this," Cormac said.

"Vampire? Werewolf?"

"Maybe. But you've got the same problem with them—how'd they get through the locked door?"

"So what *can* murder someone behind a locked door? What should we be looking for?"

"Something without a body," Cormac said. "Some kind of curse or magic. Ghost, maybe. Demon."

He could see Olson trying to process, trying to keep an open mind, his mouth pursed against arguments. Finally he said, smiling wryly, "You're getting into issues of physics, now. A physical action requires a physical presence. Doesn't it?"

Cormac couldn't tell if he was being rhetorical or asking a genuine question. "There are more things in heaven and earth," he murmured.

"Hamlet," said Olson. "You like to read, don't you? You have a friend who sends you books."

"I thought this wasn't about me. This is about your bogeyman."

"Do you have any ideas?"

A werewolf had transformed on live TV late last year. Congress had acknowledged the existence of vampires, werewolves, and psychics and brought them to testify in Washington. Cormac had known his whole life that these beings were real, and now the rest of the world was catching up. That didn't stop a lot of folks from pulling the shades down. If Olson were one of those, this whole thing could be a setup. A trap. Get him in here, get him talking crazy, giving them an excuse to pin the deaths on him and lock him up good and tight. No visitors, no parole. Then he really would go crazy.

Cormac said, "Are you serious about this? Are you serious about looking for something that a lot of people don't even believe exists?"

"I wouldn't be asking if we had a logical, mundane explanation for what's happening here."

Not that Cormac had a choice but to trust him. Like so much of his life right now, the decision was out of his hands. "This place has been around a long time. Has anything like this happened here before? Rumor, ghost story, anything."

Olson glanced away briefly, nervously. "It's hard to tell. There've been so many attacks over the prison's history—"

"But have there been any cases of somebody getting their throat cut in a locked cell?" Any sightings of a dark-haired woman in Victorian clothing?

"In fact, there have," Olson said. "A handful over the last hundred years. But they were isolated—never more than one at a time. In every case another inmate was charged with the murder. Are you saying they may be connected?"

Cormac was both shocked and thrilled at the news—he hadn't expected Olson to answer. This meant there was a thread tying these deaths together. Which meant there was a way to hunt the thing doing it.

This thing had been killing here a long time, but that didn't bother Cormac. He was even a little amused—even inside prison walls where he ought to be safe, this shit just kept following him around.

"Even if you don't know what's doing this, you can try to protect the place. Put up crosses above the doorways, at the ends of hallways. Get a priest in to throw some holy water around, do an exorcism."

"Seriously?" Olson said. "That works?"

"It's not a sure thing."

"That's the trouble with this, isn't it? It's never a sure thing."

Cormac had to grin. "That's why it never hurts to cover all your bases."

When he arrived at the visiting room, he saw that Kitty had joined Ben this time. The joy—or relief—at seeing them both was a physical pain, a squeezing of his heart, though he kept his face a mask. He wanted to melt into the floor, but he only slumped into his chair and picked up the phone.

"Hey," he said, like he always did.

"Hey," Ben said back, and Kitty smiled. They sat close together so they could hold the phone between them. Cormac had gone to live with Ben's family after his father died, and now he was the closest thing he had to a brother. Kitty was . . . something else entirely. The two of them had gotten married a month or so back. Ben had sucked her into the family. She couldn't escape now.

Kitty was cute. Really cute, and not just the way she looked with her shoulder-length blond hair, big brown eyes, and slender body. She burst with optimism, constantly chatting, always moving, and usually smiling. She and Cormac never should have met much less become friends. She represented a lot of lost chances. A lot of things he should have done, and maybe some he shouldn't have. But he wasn't sure he'd want to change any of it. Better to have her as a friend than not at all.

She was better off with Ben. He was man enough to admit that.

Small talk got real small when he didn't have anything new to say. What was he supposed to tell them, when the same thing happened every day? But this week was different, and he wondered: How much should he tell them? Wasn't like they could do anything to help.

Then Kitty mentioned her own demon, derailing the whole routine of their usual visits. It seemed she was in the middle of an adventure, and he couldn't do a thing about it. He didn't know whether to throttle her or laugh. He ended up just shaking his head. He'd come to her rescue, all she had to do was say the word, any time. Except for now. He hoped they didn't get themselves killed before he could get out of here to help them. He hoped whatever was haunting this place left him alone until then.

He'd developed an inner clock—they were running out of time, and he had a bad idea.

"Can I talk to Kitty alone for a minute?" he said to Ben. Ben wouldn't understand—he'd try to fix everything, and he couldn't, not this time. Kitty didn't know him well enough to be suspicious.

Ben left, not looking happy about it.

Alone now, Kitty seemed almost accusing. "What is it? What can you say to me that you can't say to him?"

His lip curled. "You really want me to answer that?" She looked away; so did he. "I don't want him to worry. Kitty, do you believe in ghosts?"

He liked her because nothing ever seemed to shock her. "Of course I do."

He leaned forward. "Can you do some of that research you're so good at?"

"Yeah, sure."

"I need to know the names of any women who were executed here. Let's say right around 1900, give or take a decade. And any history you can find on them."

She narrowed her gaze, and he wondered if he'd said too much. Now they were both going to worry, because she wouldn't keep this secret from Ben. "Are you being haunted or something?"

"I don't know. It's a hunch. It may be nothing." That last was a lie.

"Is everything okay?"

He hoped she didn't tell him to get some sleep, that she didn't see the stress written on his face. He tried to smile, failed. "Hanging in there. Sometimes by my fingernails. But hanging in there."

He played the visit over in his memory, like he did every time, even though he knew he shouldn't. He made himself sick, worrying that maybe this was the last time they'd visit, maybe they'd skip next week, maybe they'd decide they didn't need him— they wouldn't do that, they weren't like that. But he had a hard time not imagining it, so he dwelled, reflecting on every word they spoke, every loose strand of Kitty's hair, just in case they didn't come back.

Noises here echoed. The hollered complaints kept up even after lights out, and the warden and his guards couldn't do anything about it. They'd have had to put every damn inmate into solitary. Cormac was betting that nobody even knew why they were leaning out, as far as they could, faces pressed to bars and yelling. They were scared and had to do something. Nothing was right and as far as they could tell the folks in charge weren't doing anything about it. The idea that they didn't know what to do was worse than the usual apathy.

Cormac could take care of any problem that bled. But this— without the help of someone like Olson or the warden, he couldn't do anything. He lay on his bunk, staring at the ceiling, trying to block out the noise. Trying not to think too hard about what might be lurking in these walls.

No priests came in to perform an exorcism. Cormac wasn't surprised. He made a cross of his own, borrowing scraps of pine from the wood shop and lashing them together with a shoelace, and hung it over the door of his and Frank's cell. Things got worse.

The dream was a form of escapism, he recognized that. The

images kept him from wanting to break things, and that was good. Here, he remembered being safe, when everything was right. Almost everything. Enough of it was right that he didn't think about the rest, the vague memory of a woman who'd died when he was young. He should have loved her, but anymore she was a shadow. A face in a few old snapshots. She didn't enter into calculations of whether he was happy. But sometimes he wondered, *What if.* What if she had lived. Would having a mother have kept him from all this?

He sat on a rock overlooking the stream, squinting into a searing blue sky. Crystals embedded in the granite dug into his hands. He could even smell the sunbaked pines, meadow grasses cooled by the running water, snow-touched air coming down from the peaks. If he had to pick an opposite smell from the prison, this would be it. Clean and natural instead of antiseptic and institutional. Bright instead of sheltered.

He saw the woman again. Not at all ghostly this time, she walked obliquely up the hill toward him, watching where she stepped, lifting her heavy skirt with gloved hands. Some ten paces away, she stopped, smoothed her skirt, and folded her hands before her. She had color in her cheeks and wore a gold cross on a chain. Donning a small, bemused frown, she regarded him as if she had walked a long way to get here, but hadn't found what she expected. Her gaze was cynical.

She didn't look like a murderer or a demon. She looked far too real to be a ghost.

They could stay here, staring at each other for hours. If this had been real, he would have asked her what she was doing here. Or she would have spoken. This was a dream, his imagination, and so they simply stared. Trouble was, he'd never have imagined anyone like her. Nothing in his conscious mind could account for her. His mother had had auburn hair, not so dark as this woman's.

He finally asked, "Who are you?"

The woman's frown disappeared, but her smile was not comforting. She wanted something from him.

"I should be asking you that," she answered. She had a crisp British accent, clipping her words like she was in a hurry.

He looked to the distance. He could wait. She wouldn't stand there staring at him forever, and he was willing to bet his stubborn would outlast hers. Then again, how long had she been lurking here?

"Why won't you let me in?" she said next.

This was getting a little too obvious to be a stray bit of psychoanalysis bubbling up from his subconscious. He didn't *want* to be talking to his subconscious, his feminine side or whatever. Or maybe he was reading too much into it. A woman he didn't know was standing here, asking him a question that had an obvious answer. Why not just answer her? Why not treat it as real?

"I don't know you," he said, looking at her. "I don't know what you want."

"That's wise, I suppose, and I ought to respect that. But you see, Mr. Bennett, I've been waiting such a long time. I need you. More than anyone I've met I think you'd understand that."

For the first time, she looked uncertain, clasping her hands together, ducking her gaze. Cormac thought, *It's an act.* She was trying to soften him up.

"Wrong sales pitch," he said. "Is that what you told Moe and Brewster? Is that how you killed them?"

Clenching her hands into fists, she said, "I did not kill them. I could have saved them, if you'd only listened to me."

He felt the thunder of a sudden storm in the core of his bones, and his skull screamed in pain. She'd done something, he hadn't seen what. Like banging on a door—*Let me in.*

With the flashing light of a migraine, he jerked awake, nearly toppling out of his bunk. He sat up, clutching his sheets like they would anchor him and gasping for breath. Sweat chilled his skin.

"Jesus, fuck, what is it?" Frank, half out of his bunk, clutched the bed's frame and looked up at him.

Cormac felt the remnant of a scream in his throat. Closing his eyes

40

tight, he swallowed and forced his breathing to slow. Everything was fine. He wasn't in pain. Nothing was happening. Except for that almost constant itching in his brain. He scratched his head hard, ripping at his hair. The cell block was dark, quiet.

"I don't know," Cormac said. "Must have been a nightmare."

"You're not getting killed?"

"No. Doesn't look like it."

"There's no blood? Look around—you don't see blood?"

Although he felt silly doing it, he checked himself—and was relieved when he didn't find any blood. "I'm in one piece."

"Jesus Christ man, don't ever do that again. You have another nightmare I'll beat it out of you, understand?"

Cormac didn't argue because he couldn't blame him; he'd have told Frank the same thing if the roles were reversed. His cellmate was still muttering as he rolled back into bed.

Lying back, Cormac didn't try to sleep. He stared at the ceiling, a field of thick, institutional gray paint full of cracks and shadows. How many hundreds of eyes had stared up like this over the years? What did that do to a building? Cursing himself, he looked away. That was how far gone he was, attributing malevolence to a building.

Somehow, this woman, this demon, whatever she was, dug into his brain and found his meadow, his refuge. The chink in his armor.

She thought she could get control of him through that weakness. Fine. He just wouldn't go there anymore.

Her overriding goal, the purpose of her being—however truncated it had become—became more imperative than ever.

She found herself in a bind she had not expected. Not that she'd even known what to expect. Hacking her way through a jungle of unknown size and density was the least of it, really. But she was hacking and had faith that if she continued long enough, she would persevere. She had lasted this long, hadn't she? At some point, time had no meaning. Science had discovered that fossils could lie in the earth undiscovered for millions of years. So would she.

Once she found her proper vessel, though, she assumed it would simply let her in. The paradox presented itself: A mind pliant enough to recognize her and not go mad would also have the ability to resist her. A mind that recognized her would know better than to let her in. So it was with this man. The door between them remained closed, barred with iron, stubbornly locked.

How much simpler it would be if she could persuade him! She called through the door, picked at the lock, tried battering it down with her will, which was all she had left. And he resisted.

She found another entry, however—a wedge he himself provided: the meadow. A magnificent, beautiful scene she would not have thought his troubled mind capable of conjuring. He himself didn't seem to recognize that the memory of the place was filled with sadness and regret, the safety of a world and home he believed he had lost forever.

She hadn't been able to delve farther, to learn where this memory had come from or the circumstances that tainted the air of his refuge, that he didn't even seem to notice or refused to acknowledge.

She must win him over. The rituals of thought had become second nature over the century. The focusing of the mind, visualizing action, making action real. When nothing was real, the world became nothing but thought. She focused on the single cell, the single bed, where a man lay and put himself to sleep with thoughts of a meadow. She became tendrils, thin lines of energy melding into the patterns of his mind. Think of the meadow, put herself there, approach the man sitting on the rock. Listen to the birds in the trees, the water of the brook tumbling over smooth stones—

But the meadow wasn't there anymore. It had lain so close to the surface before, almost as if he could transform this prison into his mountain vista through force of will. Now, he'd managed to lock her out.

There she was again, back at the start, battering at the door.

Oddly, she found herself admiring him.

"You can't keep me out forever!" she shouted. "I'll drive you mad! I've done it before, to men better than you!"

A smug satisfaction barred the door. The emotion roiled off him.

Time for a different approach—send a quiet thought, so quiet he would think it was his own. A bit of intuition granted from the supernatural. Surely he believed in such things.

"I can help you." She didn't even imagine her voice, did not give the words form. Merely let the thought linger. "I know this murderer, this demon. I have hunted it. I can help you."

Create the thought, set it drifting, let him find it. That was all. She felt one impression out of the thought snag him: hunted.

The request for a visit surprised Cormac; this wasn't Ben and Kitty's day for it. He wasn't sure this was a visiting day at all, and he didn't need another anomaly making him twitch.

He sat, looked through the glass, and saw Detective Jessi Hardin of the Denver Police Department sitting across from him.

"Christ," he muttered, looking away, rubbing his cheek.

"Hello," she said. "You look terrible, if you don't mind me saying."

"What do you want?"

"I have to be blunt, Mr. Bennett," she said. "I'm here looking for advice."

Cormac had picked up some bad habits when he was young. The way he looked at cops, for example. They were the bad guys. They wanted to take your guns, they put bugs on your phones, they followed you, they worked for a government that wanted to suck you dry. They were fucking Commies—never just "Commies," it was always "fucking Commies." That's what he learned from his uncle when he was a teenager. That's what he learned from his dad, before he died.

He had to work to not think of Detective Hardin as an enemy. But she wouldn't be here unless she wanted something from him, and he remained suspicious. What his family had taught him: Cops weren't your friends, they weren't going to help you, they'd take you down the minute you did something wrong—the way they defined wrong. He learned to avoid the cops; he definitely never learned to respect them. Especially not after they sent Uncle David to prison. He didn't go to prison because he was wrong, but because he got caught. Same as Cormac.

Hardin didn't have a whole lot of respect for Cormac, either, to be fair. She'd have locked him up herself if she'd had the chance. She came from the overworked and driven mold of detective, her suit jacket worn and comfortable rather than fashionable, her dark hair pulled back in a functional ponytail. She didn't wear makeup, and the frown lines around her mouth were more prominent than the laugh lines around her eyes. The nicotine from cigarettes stained her fingers. She always seemed to be leaning forward, like she was listening hard.

"Not sure I can help you," he said.

"You mean you're not sure you *will*. Maybe you should let me know right now if I'm wasting my time. Save us both the trouble."

"Did Kitty tell you to talk to me?"

"She said you might know things."

"Kitty's got a real big mouth," Cormac said.

Hardin was still studying him, glaring through the glass in a way that was almost challenging. Maybe because she felt safe, because she knew he couldn't get to her here. Except she'd looked at him like that outside the prison, the first time he'd run into her.

"How did you two even end up friends?" Hardin said. "You wanted to kill her."

"It wasn't personal."

"Then, what? It got personal?"

He considered a moment, then said, "Kitty has a way of growing on you."

That got Hardin to smile. At least, one corner of her lips turned up. "I have a body. Well, half a body. It's pretty spectacular and it's not in any of the books." She pulled a manila folder out of an attaché case, and from there drew out a pair of eight-by-ten photo sheets. She held them up to the glass, and he leaned forward to see.

The first showed a crime scene, lots of yellow tape, numbered tent tags laid out on the ground, a ruler set out for scale. The place looked to be a small, unassuming backyard, maybe one of the older neighborhoods in Denver. The focus of the photo was a small toolshed, inside of which stood a set of human legs, standing upright. Just the legs, dressed in a pair of tailored feminine slacks and black pumps. He might have guessed that this was part of a mannequin, set up as a practical joke. But then there was the second photo.

This showed the top of the legs—which had clearly been separated from their owner. A wet vertebra emerged from a mass of red flesh, fat, and organs. The tissue all seemed scorched, blackened around the edges, bubbling toward the middle, as if someone had started cauterizing the epic wound and stopped when the job was half done. The wound, as wide as the body's pelvis, was red and boiled.

He'd seen a lot of gory, horrific stuff in his time, but this made his stomach turn over. In spite of himself, he was intrigued. "What the hell? How are they even still standing? Are they attached to something?"

"No," she said. "I have a set of free-standing legs attached to a pelvis, detached cleanly at the fifth lumbar vertebra. The wound is covered with a layer of table salt that appears to have caused the flesh to scorch. Try explaining that one to my captain."

"No thanks," he said. "That's your job. I'm just the criminal reprobate."

"So you've never seen anything like this."

"Hell, no."

"Have you ever heard of anything like this?"

"No." She'd set the photos on the desk in front of her. He found himself leaning forward to get another, closer look at the body. The half a body. "You have any leads at all?"

"No. We've ID'd the body. She was Filipina, a recent immigrant. We're still trying to find the other half of the body. There has to be another half somewhere, right?"

He sat back, shaking his head. "I wouldn't bet on it."

"You're sure you don't know anything? You're not just yanking my chain out of spite?"

"I get nothing out of yanking your chain. Not here."

Wearing a disappointed scowl, she put the photos back in her attaché. "Well, this was worth a try. Sorry for wasting your time."

"I've got nothing but time."

"If you think of anything, if you get any bright ideas, call me." She looked up at the guard who had arrived to escort Cormac back to his cell. Hardin had a parting shot. "And get some sleep. You look awful."

It was almost nice that she cared.

He could have sworn he heard banging on the bars of the cell, as if someone was hanging on the door, rattling it, trying to get his attention.

You have to let me in! You have to trust me!

Not even bothering to tell her no, he put his hands over his ears and squeezed shut his eyes, ignoring her. That didn't stop the noise.

I know what it is! Listen to me! I'll prove it to you. Those photographs— —I know what did it!

He woke up, covered in sweat, a foreign word on his lips and knowledge he didn't know he had flitting at the edge of his mind. He'd had a nightmare—another one, but this one was different. Images of a tropical country full of brown-skinned people. A village wailing in despair because so many women had suffered miscarriages over the last few months, losing babies before they were even born. The vampire has taken them, the vampire has drunk them. Which didn't make sense to Cormac. Vampires drank blood, not babies.

This one takes babies. It travels by separating from its legs and can be destroyed by salt.

He knew what it was. She'd told him. The word was on the tip of his tongue.

When he asked for an extra phone call that week in order to talk to a cop in Denver, the warden gave it to him. Apparently Hardin had left the request in advance, like she had a hunch that he'd get a sudden attack of memory. But this wasn't memory, it was—

He didn't want to think about it.

He called collect and waited for the operator to put him through. She answered, sounding surly and frustrated, then rushed to accept the charges when she heard his name.

"Hello? Bennett?"

"Manananggal," he said. "Don't ask me how to spell it."

"Okay, but what is it?"

"Filipino version of the vampire."

"Hot damn," she said, as happy as he'd ever heard her. "The victim was from the Philippines. It fits. So the suspect was Filipino, too? Do Filipino vampires eat entire torsos or what?"

"No. That body *is* the vampire, the *manananggal*. You're looking for a vampire hunter."

"Excuse me?" she said flatly.

"These creatures, these vampires—they detach the top halves of their bodies to hunt. They're killed when someone sprinkles salt on the bottom half. They can't return to reattach to their legs, and they die at sunrise. If they're anything like European vampires, the top half disintegrates. You're never going to find the rest of the body."

She stayed silent for a long time, so he prompted her. "Detective?"

"Yeah, I'm here. This fits all the pieces we have. Looks like I have some reading to do to figure out what really happened."

She was *really* not going to like the next part. "Detective, you might check to see if there've been a higher than usual number of miscarriages in the neighborhood."

"Why?"

"I used the term 'vampire' kind of loosely. This thing eats fetuses. Sucks them through the mother's navel while she sleeps."

"You're kidding." She sighed, because he clearly wasn't. "So, what—this may have been a revenge killing? Who's the victim here?"

"You'll have to figure that one out yourself." He could hear a pen scratching on paper, making notes.

"Isn't that always the way? Hey—now that we know you really were holding out on me, what made you decide to remember?"

"Look, I got my own shit going on and I'm not going to try to explain it to you."

"Fine, okay. But thanks for the tip, anyway."

"Maybe you could put in a good word for me," he said.

"I'll see what I can do."

Maybe she even would.

He was curious. Itchingly curious. But if he let her in, he'd never get her out again. She already had her foot in the door, and now she was pushing. The bars of the cage rattled, claws scraped the inside his skull, worse than ever, a coarse rasp working on him, over and over. He could beat his head against a wall to make it stop.

Kitty came through. He could tell by the smug, triumphant look on her face when she put a manila folder on the desk in front of her, before she and Ben even sat down on their next visit.

"You found something," he said.

"I did." She grinned.

He tried not to laugh; it would annoy her. "Which means, I assume, that the demon problem is all fixed and everything's okay."

"Would I be smiling if it weren't?" she said.

"Sorry," Ben said. His cousin leaned back in his chair, smirking at Kitty just as much as Cormac was. "We forgot to tell you. The genie is bottled and everything's okay."

Cormac pointed. "See, I know when the problems are solved even when you don't tell me, because you just stop talking about them. And did you say *genie*?"

"Can I tell you about your executions now?" Kitty said quickly, clearly not wanting to explain the adventures they'd been having without him. She opened the folder, and he leaned forward, trying to see. "If you take in the twenty or so years before and after 1900, there were about a half-dozen women executed. There was only one woman executed in 1900."

"What was her name?" Cormac said.

"Amelia Parker. Her story's a little different." The pages looked like photocopies, text from books, a couple of old newspaper articles. She lectured. "Lady Amelia Parker. British, born 1877, the daughter of a minor nobleman. By all accounts, she was a bit of a firebrand. Traveled the world by herself, which just wasn't done in those days. She was a self-taught archeologist, linguist, folklorist. She collected knowledge, everything from local folk cures to lost languages. She has her own page in a book about Victorian women adventurers. She came to Colorado to follow an interest in Native American culture and lore but was convicted of murdering a young woman in Manitou Springs. The newspaper report was pretty sensationalist, even for 1900. Said something about blood sacrifice. There were patterns on the floor, candles, incense, the works. Like something out of *Faust*. The newspaper's words, not mine. She was convicted of murder and hanged. Right here, in fact. Or at least, in this area, at the prison that was standing here at the time."

Bingo. He hadn't expected Kitty to hit the jackpot like this. The fuzzy, old-fashioned photo of the young woman on one of the photocopies even looked like his ghost—black hair, serious frown. Everything fit. Cormac leaned forward. "The victim. How did she die? Did it say what happened to her?"

"Her throat was cut."

They were connected. The murders and his ghost were connected. It was a revelation, she'd been a murderer in life, and kept murdering in death—but no. *Hunted.* He remembered the words, the thoughts she'd flung at him. She was *hunting.* And she'd been wrongly executed. No wonder she was still around.

"What is it?" Kitty asked, probably seeing the stark shock on his face. The wonder in his eyes. "You know something. This all makes sense to you. Why? How?"

Finally, he shook his head. "I'm not sure. May be nothing. But she's got a name. It's not all in my head."

"What isn't?"

He met her gaze. "She didn't kill that girl. She was trying to find who did. *What* did."

She blinked back at him. "What do you mean 'what'?" Ben's lips were pursed, his gaze studious. So much for not making the two of them worry about him.

"Never mind," he said, leaning back and looking away. "I'll tell you when I know more."

"Why is she important?" Kitty said. "She's been dead for over a hundred years."

His smile quirked. "And you really think that's the end of it? You've been telling ghost stories for years. Are you going to sit here now and tell me it isn't possible?"

Ben leaned forward. "She just doesn't like the idea that someone else is having adventures without her."

Kitty pouted. "I'll have you know I'm looking forward to a good long adventure-free streak from here out."

50

As long as he'd known Kitty, she'd been getting in trouble. She couldn't keep her mouth shut, or she had to swoop to the rescue like some kind of superhero. She was a lightning rod for trouble. *She'd* been the werewolf caught shape-shifting on live TV. Cormac and Ben had been there to clean up after that mess.

"A month," Cormac said finally. "I bet you don't go a month without getting into trouble."

"How are we defining 'trouble'?" she said. "Are we talking life-or-death trouble or pissing-off-the-boss trouble? Hey, stop laughing at me!"

Ben said, "I'm not taking that bet."

Kitty straightened the papers and closed the folder. "I could try to mail this to you, but I'm not sure it would get past the censors."

"Just hang on to it for me," he said. Like the rest of his life. Just hold on.

They said their farewells, and they both wore that pained and pitying look on their faces, the one he'd put there because they could walk out and he couldn't. At the door they hesitated—they usually did—glancing back one more time. He almost stopped them, standing and reaching, calling back. He'd have to shout through the glass because they'd put the phone down. He could feel the guard at his back, but he had the urge to do it anyway. Press his hands to the glass and tell Kitty everything: *I have to tell you what's going on, the murders, the ghost, my meadow and what it means and why I can't go back, I want to tell you everything—*

But he didn't say anything. Just like he always didn't say anything. Without a word, without a flicker in his expression, he stood when the guard told him to and allowed himself to be marched back to his cell.

It sounded like claws scraping on concrete, an insect mash of legs running straight up the wall without rhythm. Like a million other nightmare noises that anyone's imagination might trigger, that would freeze the gut.

But Cormac hadn't been asleep. He was on his back, staring at the gray ceiling, refusing to sleep, refusing to let her in when the noise rattled outside the cell. He remained still, wondering what would make a noise like that. The sound of a thousand souls that didn't know where to go.

Cormac rolled to his stomach, propping himself up just enough to look out, letting his eyes take in the patterns of light and shadow that made up the prison's weird internal twilight. Resting on his pillow, his hands itched for the feel of a weapon. This was like hunting; he could lie still for hours waiting for the prey to come to him. But here, when he was weaponless, behind bars, which one of them was prey? Did he think he could just stare it down?

He kept his gaze soft, not letting himself stare at any one thing, which would reduce his peripheral vision. So he saw it, when a clawed black hand reached across the ceiling, brushed his throat . . .

He half jumped, half fell from the top bunk, stumbling to the floor in a crouch. Pressing himself to the bars, he looked in the direction the thing must have gone

"Hey! Dude!" Frank hollered. "What did I tell you about your fucking nightmares?"

"Quiet!" hissed the guy in the next cell over. Not Moe's old cell but the one on the other side.

Cormac had his face up to the bars, but he couldn't see anything to the sides. He couldn't see a damn thing from here, though he could still hear claws on concrete, maybe even a voice, growling. He didn't know where it was coming from. If he could just get out of here—

A light shone, the deep orange glow of coals in a forge across the prison block, inside one of the cells. It flared, turned black—like an eclipse of the sun, a moment of dark terror—then collapsed. All of it without a sound.

He could see it, a demon's claw scraping across a man's throat, and in his mind he heard a voiceless, inhuman laugh of triumph. Another inmate dead.

"No!" he screamed at the block, the sound echoing.

Hands grabbed the back of his T-shirt, twisted, and yanked him back. Cormac led with his elbow, striking hard, hitting flesh and bone—a man's chest. Frank wheezed, falling back, and Cormac followed through, swinging his body into a punch. Frank's head whipped back, but he stayed on his feet and came right back. Deceptively powerful, his blows pounded in like rocks, hitting Cormac's cheek and chest. He was dazed, but he shook it off. He should have explained, but it was too late, and this was more his speed anyway.

Ducking another blow, Cormac delivered his own, tackling Frank in the middle, shoving him against the bunk frame.

Lights came on in the cell block, an alarm siren started, and the door to the cell rolled open. Guards came in, swinging batons. Cormac didn't have a chance against them. They dragged him away, though he kept lunging forward, into the fight. Blows landed on his shoulders, kidneys, gut. He fell, then was hauled up again by his arms.

Waking from his fog, he saw the guards surrounding him. He was totally screwed.

Frank was yelling. "I don't know, man, he's gone crazy! It's not my fault, he jumped out of bed screamin' and he just went crazy!"

Frank's protests didn't matter; the guards dragged both of them out, hauling them in different directions. Cormac tried to get his feet under him—they were keeping him off balance on purpose. Again, his instinct was to lash out. He locked it down, tried to keep still, tried to speak.

"There's another body. Another guy's been killed, I saw it, I saw what did it. I need to talk to Olson. To Detective Hardin. Somebody. Let me talk to somebody!"

It wasn't their job to listen to him; they were dumb brute enforcers. But the walls were closing in around him. All he really wanted to do was scream.

Another inmate was already screaming. The newest body had been discovered.

The cell in administrative confinement—solitary—had a solid door with a wire mesh—reinforced glass window at face height, a single bed, a toilet and sink, and no room to pace. This was what he'd been so desperate to avoid. They'd put him in smaller and smaller boxes until he couldn't move, couldn't breathe, couldn't think. Only thing left to do now was lie on the bunk and sleep. Escape to that meadow, breathe deep and imagine he smelled pines and snowmelt.

No. This had all started with her, that thing, lost spirit or demon, whatever she was. Everything had been fine until she appeared and started scraping the inside of his skull. His head ached. The walls were collapsing.

He leaned on the wall opposite the bunk, refusing to even lie down. His jaw ached in a couple of places. Bruises bloomed. In a strange way the fight had felt good, and the bruises felt real. It had felt good to finally hit something. To strike back. He hadn't had a chance to strike at anything in so long. He could take his gun to the range, unload a couple boxes of ammo. Feel a hot gun in his hand. That cleansing noise.

Put the gun against his own skull next and make it all stop.

He paced. Three steps one way, three steps the other. Stopped, sat down against the wall. He had to pull his knees up to keep from hitting them on the edge of the bunk. But he wouldn't lie down. He couldn't.

He couldn't tell the difference between exhaustion and the pain of insanity gnawing at him. But he'd beat this thing. Beat it to a bloody pulp.

He closed his eyes.

A storm rode over the mountains and into the valley.

He didn't want to be here—it meant he was weak. He'd let his guard down, and now she'd found him, battering at him with wind and thunder—that rattling of the bars again, even though there weren't bars anymore. On a slope, he ducked toward a tree at the edge of the valley with his arms over his head, trying to wait it out.

Her shouts were the wind. "Let me in, damn you! I must speak with you! You stubborn fool, let me in! I *will* speak!"

It was a cosmic wail. He, who could wait out statues, couldn't stay silent against it.

"I can't help you!" He turned to the sky, screaming a year's worth of frustration. Maybe a lifetime's. "Leave me alone!"

"Let me speak!" She was a ghost, a stuck record, a moment in time. She was drawing him into her loop, driving him mad. He would never again leave this room or crawl outside his mind.

"No." The only word he could throw at her, his voice faltering to a whisper. The blowing wind made him deaf.

"Listen, just listen to me! What must I do to make you listen!" she howled. The wind blasted through the forest; trees groaned.

"Try *asking*!" he shouted to the sky.

Then, like a whisper through pine boughs, a breath against his cheek, "Please talk to me. Please."

His legs gave out, bringing him heavily to the ground, sitting on grass that was damp with rain. This was all in his mind. He shouldn't feel the wet soaking into his jeans. He shouldn't smell the clean, earthy damp in the air.

"Okay," he said.

And she was there, standing a few paces away, clutching her hands together. Still poised, back straight and chin up, as if refusing to admit that saying "please" had cost her pride. Like she didn't want him to see the pleading in her gaze. The wind-touched strands of her dark hair, curls fallen loose from her bun and resting on her shoulder. He might touch the curl and smooth it back into place.

He looked away from her and across the valley. The stream ran full, frothing over rocks. The green seemed even greener. It was high summer here, and he relaxed. Maybe because he could see her now he knew where she was, what she was doing. He could keep an eye on her.

She'd wanted so badly to talk, but she just stood there, like she was waiting for punishment. Waiting to be hanged. If she really was a ghost, if she really had been executed, she would have been hanged. He didn't want to think about that.

"Well?" he said finally. "After all that you going to say anything?"

She glanced at the hem of her skirt and wrung her fingers. "I've not engaged in conversation in a very long time, and even then I was not a paragon of courtesy. I'm sure I'm more than a little mad."

That made two of them. "Amelia Parker," he said. "You're Amelia Parker. What the hell's going on?"

She blinked at him. "You know my name? How?"

"I looked it up. You could have just *told* me, instead of this garbage you've been pulling. You want to explain?"

"It's difficult," she said, glancing behind her.

"Try me. I have a pretty open mind," he said.

"Yes, I know. That's how I found you. I needed an open mind."

He glared at her. "For what? So you could break it into pieces?"

"No, so I could . . . so I could control it. I need a body, Mr. Bennett."

"Let me guess: It's harder than you thought it'd be."

"Yes. Minds . . . they tend to twist up into knots in spite of my intentions."

"You've tried this before?"

She didn't answer.

"Jesus," he muttered.

She swallowed, wetting her lips to speak—which made no sense, because she was a ghost. Cormac could almost smell the soap on her skin. The contradiction was making him dizzy.

"I was hanged for murdering a young woman, but I didn't do it. I'm innocent. I know what *did* do it, and it's here now. I hunted this thing a hundred years ago, Mr. Bennett, and while I'm not inclined to believe in an omnipotent God, I believe I have survived—or rather that this small part of me has survived—so that I can stop it now. But I need help."

Put like that, it did seem like fate. How much did she know about him, besides his name? Had she done enough digging in his psyche to learn that he was also a hunter? That she couldn't have picked a better body for her purpose?

He said, "Olson—the psychologist here—said this has happened before. Half a dozen bodies over the last hundred years or so, with their throats cut in locked cells. Just like the girl you were hanged for. You say you didn't do it, but you seem to know a lot about it."

"I hunted it. Tracked it to Lydia Harcourt, where they found me. Then it followed me here."

"Why? Why you? You were supposed to be dead, why'd it stick around?"

"I know I can stop it—"

"Where'd it come from in the first place? Do you know?"

"—but I need hands, a voice. I'm so close—"

"I'm not giving you my body," he said, turning away. "Why not tell me where this demon came from?"

Her brow furrowed, and she seemed to grapple with something. Guilt? Shame, even? "I suppose I ought to have taken it as a lesson not to meddle. Yet I keep on meddling, don't I?" Her smile was pained.

"What happened?"

"A scene from a boys' adventure novel. I'm sure you've had a few of your own. Something had been buried at a crossroads—imprisoned, rather. I should have heeded the warning carved into the headstone. But there was a promise of treasure."

"This is all about a pot of gold?" he said, disbelieving.

"No. A Sumerian cuneiform tablet meant to be buried alongside. I thought I could secure the demon, prevent its escape, obtain the tablet that promised tremendous knowledge. I was wrong."

"The tablet was bait, wasn't it?" Cormac said. "It didn't really exist."

Bowing her head, she hid a sad smile. "The thing bound itself to me. Cursed me. It always stayed just out of reach. I could watch it kill and never stop it. Even now."

He could almost feel sorry for her. He considered the saying about the road to hell.

She paced a few steps down the slope, across his field of vision, looking at the scene, his private valley. Hilltops emerged through misty, breaking clouds. The air was cool on his skin, a different kind of cool than a prison cell in winter. This felt like living rather than being in storage.

"You've gotten better at this," she said, gazing around, squinting against the breeze and surveying the valley as if it were real. "What is this place? It's somewhere in the Rocky Mountains, I should think."

Don't open the door, he thought. After a hesitation, he said, "My dad used to take me here when I was young."

"What was he?"

"A hunter," Cormac said, remembering, and flinching at the memory.

"And you?"

"Same," he said.

"You were sent here for murder, yes?"

He considered his words. Picked at the grass, which felt real, waxy between his fingers. "I killed a skinwalker. She was a monster and needed to die."

"Who are you to decide that?"

"She was trying to kill my friends."

"Ah." She paced a few more steps; her fingers were no longer wringing, but her expression had turned thoughtful, almost resigned. "The friends who come to visit you?"

"That's none of your business," he said.

"I'm sorry—it's hard not to pry. I can tell they're good people."

"Don't touch them."

"I won't," she said and paced a few more steps. "So you hunt monsters."

"Yes. I do."

"Then you understand. You must let me in, you must let me do battle with this thing."

"Do battle yourself," he said.

"I need physical form to work my spells."

"Then tell me what to do. I'll do it, I'll get rid of it."

"I spent a decade learning what I know, I can't just *tell* you."

"Then I guess that's it."

"Is it because I'm female? You don't think I'm capable?"

He chuckled. "I hadn't noticed."

"Then why are you being so stubborn?"

She'd keep picking away at him, like a swarm of gnats. "Look. My mind, this place—it's all I have in here. It's all that's left until I get out. You can't have it."

"You would sacrifice everyone here because of that?"

The situation wasn't that bad. Couldn't be that bad. Somebody would notice before the whole cellblock was wiped out. Somebody would do something. Except for a tiny suspicion he had that maybe she was right.

He started awake. Aching from his shoulders to his hips, he straightened from where he'd slumped against the painted cinderblock wall and stretched out the kinks. He hadn't meant to fall asleep. He hadn't meant to even talk to her.

A wave of shouting echoed down the corridor. Hundreds of angry male voices raised in frustration, turned fierce, animal.

He was blind and stupid inside this box. He could look out the window—to the opposite wall, more institutional cinderblock. He couldn't talk to anyone—he didn't even know the time of day. His stomach told him it was late. Somebody should be bringing a meal soon. But the shouting told him that the whole place had been turned upside down. This wasn't right.

Standing, he rammed his shoulder into the door, pounded it a couple of times, hit the intercom button, called for a guard. The shouting outside was like an ocean, like a war.

No one would come to his call. No one would be bringing food. Of all the things that could have happened here, of all the things that could make serving time harder than it already was, he hadn't expected this. If it wasn't a riot, it was close to it. A cold knot grew in his gut, something he thought he'd built walls against a long time ago, so he'd never have to feel it again. He hadn't felt like this since his father died.

He was afraid.

His father taught Cormac as much as he could before he died, because that was what their family did. Cormac's grandfather, his father, and his father, who'd fought in the Civil War and then come west, part of the great migration of fortune seekers. At least that far back. The family didn't have any stories telling how they'd learned about werewolves, vampires, and the rest of it. Maybe the line stretched farther back than that. Cormac had always known that monsters were real. When he was twelve, his father started taking him hunting. At first it was the normal kind, deer and elk, living off the land, all that crap. Then they'd tracked and killed a werewolf. His father trailed a wolf where there shouldn't have been any—wild wolves had been hunted to extinction south of Montana fifty years before Cormac was born. More than that, the creature was bigger than any wolf had a right being. They'd tracked it, baited it, Douglas Bennett had shot it dead, and brought his son to watch the body transform. It turned into a naked, bloodied human as they watched, a scruffy guy maybe thirty years old, rangy and dangerous looking even as a corpse. They weren't like us, Douglas had said, and it was us or them. That had been the order of the universe, laid out by the center of his universe.

When he was sixteen, they tracked another werewolf. This one turned the hunt back on them.

They'd gotten word a month before—wolf kill in Grand County, a couple of head slaughtered out of a herd of cattle. A lot of ranchers would have written off the loss and not thought about it again. Maybe set traps or poison. But too much about this didn't sit right—the care with which the prey had been chosen specifically not to draw too much attention, stragglers that weren't as likely to be missed. The fact that wolves hadn't been seen in the area in seventy years. There'd been a light snow and the prints were clear in the damp earth. Douglas Bennett had a reputation for being able to handle problems like this.

Douglas and Cormac spent the week before the full moon checking the lay of the land, where the lycanthrope had struck last time, where it might be likely to strike this time. There was always a chance that it would head out for new hunting grounds before then and they wouldn't find anything. But the creatures were territorial—it'd probably stick around. They asked the ranchers in the area to keep their cattle penned for the full moon and the nights on either side. Except for one fat cow, which they slaughtered as the sun was setting. Then they hunkered down to wait.

The blind, made up of deadwood and laid over with sap-drenched scrub oak, was twenty paces downwind from the carcass. Cormac's father sat on a piece of decayed log, his rifle resting across his lap. His hand lay across the stock, the finger on the trigger guard. He could fire a shot in half a second from that position. Cormac copied him, sitting behind him and a little to the side. Studied the way he held his rifle and tried to do the same. Admired the quiet way he sat, not fidgeting even a little. He barely seemed to breathe. Cormac struggled to stay quiet, though his heart was racing. His breath fogged in the chill air. This prey wasn't like any other, his father said over and over. It had the mind of a person under all that fur and monstrous instinct. You could see it, when you looked into its eyes. His father told him he could fire the killing shot this time. If he sat quietly.

The carcass smelled of blood and rot. The blood had poured out and soaked most of the clearing where it lay. The moon blazed down and painted it black and silver. Cormac caught himself bouncing his foot and stopped it, glancing at his father to see if he'd noticed. He hadn't seemed to. Cormac blushed, wanting so badly not to make a mistake. He hunched inside his army surplus jacket, thankful for his layers of clothing. He adjusted the sleeves, pulling them over his bare hands. He didn't wear gloves; neither did his father. Gloves interfered with the trigger.

A werewolf's natural instinct was to hunt people. A smart werewolf might avoid attention by keeping away from people; but eventually he'd drift back to civilization. He might have a pack to keep a rein on him, but if that pack ever fell apart, then it would scatter and a dozen werewolves, without leadership, would wreak destruction. Best to get them before that happened.

Nobody knew about the threats that lurked not just in the wild, but in cities, everywhere. Wild and inhuman, all the old nightmare stories grew out of truths that most people had forgotten. Didn't want to remember. Folk didn't want to consider that there was something modern technology couldn't solve. It was up to people like the Bennetts and all who'd come before them to protect, to stand guard, with silver bullets and wooden stakes, protecting humanity against evils they didn't know they needed protecting from.

Cormac had learned all of this from his father, as his father had learned from his. He felt proud, part of an unbroken tradition. They were warriors, and no one even knew.

His father pointed with the barest movement of his left hand, no more than a finger lifted from the barrel of the rifle, replaced just as subtly. Cormac wouldn't have seen the wolf as quickly. It didn't make a sound—the clearing was as quiet as ever, but a huge beast, a furred canine as big as a Great Dane, two hundred pounds easy, stepped carefully from the trees across from them. Dark gray and silver, it might have been a shadow come to life. Its fur made it indistinct, its outline hard to see. A few paces from the cow, it paused, raised its head, its eyes sparking gold in the moonlight. Cormac couldn't breathe.

His father's hand had closed around his rifle stock, but he didn't yet raise the weapon. This was going to be Cormac's shot.

Cormac worked to keep his breathing steady. He had one shot, had to make it good. Couldn't move too fast or the creature would see it. Best thing was to let it start in on the bait, distracting it. With silver bullets, they didn't have to get a good target. They only had to break skin and the silver would poison it.

His father leaned out of the way, giving Cormac a clear shot. He watched the wolf, large and unnatural, pause, nose leading, searching the carcass. Any second now, he'd aim and shoot, all in a heartbeat. He could do this.

Then the wolf was gone.

Its coloring blended with the wooded clearing, but Cormac had been watching carefully, he'd followed the thing's movements, he knew where it was. He imagined putting the bullet into it—a good clean shot that meant they wouldn't have to track it. But it had just vanished.

"Where'd it go?" Cormac whispered in a panic.

"Hush," his father breathed. He raised his rifle in a clean movement. Didn't take aim yet; just looked out, waiting.

Somehow, it had sensed them. Maybe smelled them on the cow or noticed the knife cut in the animal's throat, showing that its death wasn't natural, that this was bait and not scavenging. Maybe it had simply backed up the way it had come and slipped into the woods, avoiding the hunters. Cormac started to feel disappointed.

Then his father hissed, "Get back, get back. Cormac—" Douglas threw his arm and hit Cormac, shoving him out of the way as the creature leapt.

His father was strong, and Cormac fell hard and rolled, reaching to stop himself while keeping hold of his rifle. Turning onto his belly, he scrambled to look.

Another thing that made werewolves and wild wolves different: A wild wolf would have run away from the hunters, disappearing into the trees, finding safety in speed. This one attacked.

The thing planted front paws on Douglas Bennett's shoulders and shoved. Douglas fired, the mouth of his rifle flashing, but the shot did nothing, flying uselessly into air. The man screamed while the monster clawed and bit, shaking its head, ripping at flesh like this was an unfortunate rabbit. Douglas kicked and bucked, his hands on the wolf's head, fingers digging at its eyes and twisting its ears. The wolf kept on, lips curled back from red-stained teeth. Emanating from deep in its throat, its snarls sounded like the revving of a broken engine. And still Cormac's father screamed. Full-lunged, tortured, gasping screams.

"Dad!" It happened in a heartbeat. He couldn't breathe, he couldn't think. His scream was an echo of his father's.

He raised his rifle, took half a second to aim. Fired. Later, he'd never know how he managed to hold the weapon steady, to exhale and squeeze the trigger rather than blasting off in a panic.

He got it. That perfect shot in the wolf's head. The blast knocked the wolf away from Douglas, and it lay still.

"Dad?" He dropped the rifle and ran, sliding to the ground next to his father's prone form. His voice sounded suddenly high-pitched and weak, no better than a child's. He was five years old again. "Dad?"

His father reached, clutching at his son with bloody hands. Looking at him, Cormac's gut jumped to his mouth, but he didn't vomit.

Douglas's face was gone, gory meat instead of nose, eyes, lips. His throat was gone, turned into frayed tubes and tendons and a hint of backbone, glistening in moonlight. A wheezing breath whistled and gurgled. Somehow, Douglas pulled another through the mangled windpipe, and his hand closed on Cormac's arm, bunching his jacket in rigid fingers. He didn't breathe again, and the fingers went slack a moment later.

64

Cormac knelt there for a long time, holding his father's hand. A pool of blood was creeping under him, soaking into the ground. The air reeked. He'd never get that smell out of his nose.

A couple of feet away, a naked man sprawled on his side. He had stringy, shoulder-length hair, black going to gray. He was burly, powerful, the muscles on his arms and back well defined. He was weathered, older, maybe in his fifties. Blood and fragments covered his face.

"Dad?" He swallowed, trying to get his throat to open up. But his father didn't move.

Cormac didn't know what to do. The truck was a couple of miles away, and had a CB he could use to call for help. He was pretty sure he had to get help, though he wasn't sure what anyone would make of the situation when they saw this. He couldn't tell them it was a werewolf.

He squeezed his father's hand one more time, placed it gently on the body's chest, found his rifle, checked it to make sure it was loaded and ready for another shot—just in case—and set out for the truck.

He radioed an emergency channel, told them where to go, then went back to wait with his father. To chase coyotes and ravens away from the body. A forest service ranger, county sheriff's deputy, and EMTs arrived to find him standing guard, still holding the rifle, covered in blood.

Slumped against the front corner of the cell, he stared at his hands. *It wasn't your fault.*

Everybody said that. But they didn't know, they hadn't been there. They were just words, didn't mean anything. "Leave me alone," he muttered. But he could *feel* her, as if she'd put a hand on his shoulder. He batted the imaginary hand away.

He heard shouting, ringing—inmates banging on the bars of their cells, echoing, thunderous. He couldn't see anything out the window but the wall across from him. Pressing his ear to the crack along the door, he tried to make out what was happening. Not that it helped. Not that it gave him a clue what to do next. Not that he could pick his way out of this door. He couldn't do a damn thing about anything.

Cormac had once felt that he'd been part of an unbroken tradition, a long line of warriors, secret and proud. It had all fallen apart. The line would end with him. He'd made his father's legacy worthless. No better than dust. Nothing more than blood on his hands.

He was trapped, helpless in the face of a threat his father hadn't taught him how to handle.

You aren't helpless.

He tried to shut out the voice. "Leave me alone," he muttered.

It's a prison riot. I've seen it before. Too many guards stopped coming to work after the murders. The prison is understaffed and the inmates are frightened.

"What am I supposed to do about it?"

The demon will take advantage of it. There will be slaughter.

"I'm safest here."

Not if the rioters unlock the doors.

The locks were electronic, connected to both individual and master switches. They'd have to take over the whole prison to do that. Which it sounded like they were on the way to doing.

He put his hands over his ears, shut his eyes, tried to block out the world. "Get out of my head. You're driving me crazy."

She scratched at the inside of his skull, like fingernails on a chalkboard. With the pain came a promise—that it would stop if she would just let him in. Open wide the door to his mind. He was almost there.

I won't hurt you, she said, and he imagined the young woman in the meadow, proud and calm. *If I tried to dominate you we'd both go mad. I see that now.*

"I can't trust you."

You don't trust anyone. He could see the scowl on her refined face. He almost laughed because it was true. Mostly true.

You're strong, Cormac. I'll need that strength, to do what must be done. We both will.

He wasn't strong. He just faked it real well. He saw his father's blood on his hands and felt like a child.

Cormac—

Don't use my name he almost shouted at her. The noises outside grew louder, closer. The sound of the riot had changed, from defiance to triumph. A celebration, chaotic and fierce. It didn't sound human anymore.

Then the lock on the door clicked and slid back with a metallic *thunk.* Cormac felt the vibration of it under his hand.

He thought of weapons, whether he could break off part of the bedframe, use the sheets as some kind of garrote, or find anything he could throw. Even a shoe. He had nothing but his hands.

Best to stay out of the way, then. Maybe he could get outside. Participating in a riot wasn't going to get him anything but more years to his sentence. The door was unlocked, but he didn't have to walk out. On the other hand, he sure as hell didn't want to get stuck in this hole with no place to run if the mob came after him.

Carefully, he slid the door open, keeping his back to the wall. Waiting, he listened.

A man ran past, a young guy Cormac didn't know. His orange jumpsuit was torn, hanging off his shoulder, one leg shredded, and he bled from a wound on his temple. He was trying to hold his jumpsuit up while looking over his shoulder as he ran. Not that he had any place to go but in circles.

A second later, a mob of about a dozen followed, screaming in fury. A few of the men held makeshift weapons—a broken two-by-four as a club; a toothbrush handle, melted and sharpened, as a shiv.

Cormac waited until they'd passed, and the corridor was empty again.

The cells in solitary were in a long corridor off the main block. From there, the sounds of riot swelled. Bullies used the chaos to take advantage. A prison riot was a thousand angry men trying to show they couldn't be kept down. It was all a big lie.

To get to a corridor that would take him to the yard, where he could hunker down to wait out the riot in relative safety, he had to go through the central bay of the main block. He crept along the wall, looking ahead and behind, trying not to move too quick, careful not to get noticed. This wasn't hunting; this was stumbling across a mama bear with her cubs and hoping you didn't catch her eye. It was the most nerve-racking thing he'd done in his life. Any minute now, the goon squad would arrive and the tear gas would start flying. He had to get out.

He'd meant to take a quick look, just to get the lay of the land, then slip out. But the scene froze him.

They'd killed at least two guards, it looked like. A mob of maybe a hundred or so was crowded together in the main block, passing the bodies overhead, ripping apart the blue uniforms—and more, when hands couldn't get a grip on fabric. On the fringes of the crowd, inmates turned on each other, clawing and fighting. Others cheered them on. Another group of a dozen moved along the cells, slamming open doors and pulling out the few people who hadn't rushed to take part. The established gangs had splintered. No longer organized by race, affiliation, or anything visible. They'd become opportunistic, chaotic.

Good God, Amelia said. *This isn't right.*

"I thought you'd said you seen prison riots," Cormac whispered.

This is something else.

Rage, fear, a million emotions that made a guy crazy when he was lying in a prison cell at night and the quiet closed in on him. What did that taste like to a demon who gained its power from fear and blood?

There!

He could almost imagine the woman pointing. He liked to think he'd have seen it on his own, eventually, but he wasn't sure. Human in shape but somehow otherworldly, the figure lurked, slinking across the edge of the ceiling, no brighter than a shadow, no more real than the phantom hints of movement anyone might catch in the corners of their vision and discount as imagination. The little voice that whispered sometimes, *Take it, steal it, break it.* Or, *Kill him, you know you could kill him.*

A lot of the guys in here probably listened to that voice more often than most people.

Cormac could not have said the thing had eyes, but somehow he knew that it looked at him. That it saw him and didn't like him. The thing had clawed hands and feet that clicked on I beams as it traversed the ceiling. The claws glinted like steel, sharp as knives. There must have been dozens of them, like the thing was holding bouquets of daggers.

Cormac stood at the end of the corridor, watching the creature run toward him, a figure made of oil, and wondered what to do. Running wouldn't help. Doing so would only rile it. Like a gang of bullies. But he also couldn't fight it.

It's looking for me, she said. *I told you, I've been hunting it for a century. It knows me.*

"And you think you can kill it? Get rid of it?"

I can.

"I don't believe you." He believed in bullets. He believed in being stronger than anything else on the range.

Cormac, we must stop this.

He shook his head. He'd worked too hard to hold on to himself to let his identity—his soul—go now. He'd kept such fierce control, all so he wouldn't lose it and do damage that he couldn't recover from. Now, he nearly laughed, because it had all been for nothing. The thing drew power from blood, and it would kill them all, slicing them to pieces.

"I can't let go," he murmured.

You can. You can keep your core. I'll keep you safe, I can do that, I promise you. But I need you!

He felt how easy it would be to let go. He understood how it was that a psychotic gunman could walk into a crowded room and open fire. It was because they had let go, given themselves over to something that wasn't them.

Please trust me. He felt something, someone, take his hands and squeeze. Soft hands, but firm, as if he and a woman were about to jump off a cliff together. He suddenly wanted to kiss her. Not an abrogation, then. A merging. He wasn't giving himself over. He was loaning. Sharing.

He hoped she was right.

He couldn't feel his muscles suddenly. His nerves were fire, but he couldn't move. Closed his eyes, tipped his head back, thought of a meadow, opened a door, and felt Amelia step into the place where he was—

—and she looked out of his eyes, living eyes, for the first time in over a hundred years. Her body flared—his body. It was powerful, brilliant. Already rangy and athletic, he had kept himself fit, even locked behind bars. She wanted to shout, to sing. Tipping her head back, she felt the smile on her face, and hair on her jaw, odd and tingly, scratchy. This anatomy was most certainly not her own, feeding her a confusing flood of sensations that must have been *maleness*.

Time for that later.

With a body came life, and with life came power, and that was what she had traveled all this way for, waited for all this time, so she could face down the darkness, raise her hand, curl her fingers into a fist as if holding a ball, and shout a word of Latin in a strange, deep, male voice that wasn't hers.

A crackling purple sphere of light came to life in her hand.

He felt it, the power burning through him, and it was like dying, because he couldn't move, react, or change the outcome, and he didn't want to because he felt closer to the source. To God, maybe.

Amelia was using his body to create something astonishing.

The demon approached, arms raised for a killing blow.

She lifted her hand and the light crackled and snapped, sending out tendrils of static, like some mad scientist's machine. The demon paused as if confused, its claws extended midreach.

"Back!" she shouted, startled again that it wasn't her voice, but his, the vessel's. Cormac. She had chosen well—he burned with so much life. The man watched through her eyes, which looked through his.

Respect him. He wasn't simply a tool to be used at will. That had been her mistake. No more.

Her power struck it. It might have been their combined wills as much as anything that forced the demon to fold back on itself. It shrank, screaming—the sound of static dissipating, of a star contracting. The shadow turned red.

It lashed out with fire. The wave of heat scalded—please, let his body be strong enough!—but she stood her ground, raised her other hand and built a shield, an unseen wall painted on air with a gesture and a word of power. The demon beat itself against the shield—it buckled, and she stumbled back before she could brace herself. She was still not used to the bulk, solidity, and sheer inertia of this male body. Cormac was a man who relied on brawn more often than not. Perhaps she would do well to learn to use such brawn.

If they got through this, and did not go mad after.

His muscles strained against the force. What this must look like to an observer: A great clawed shadow pushed against nothing as if throwing itself against a door, and a man dressed in an orange jumpsuit braced and leaned forward as if trying to keep the door closed. She couldn't stand this for much longer.

But she had an ally. She needed to call up power again. To do that, she needed life, energy that a bodiless soul and a shadow creature couldn't draw on.

She turned inward and cried, "Cormac!"

And he *shoved*. Imagined every muscle in his body working at once. Wondered what it might be like to have light pour from his soul and illuminate the world.

Spheres of energy formed in both his hands. She brought Cormac's callused fists together, aimed them at the beast. She couldn't contain the power, couldn't guide it. Could only force it away from her and hope for the best.

Colored light bathed the world, at least the space of it in front of her. She closed her eyes, ducking away from it, and still it burned.

The demon took the full force of it. The light chipped away at its form, tearing off pieces until it became pockmarked, full of holes, and the holes grew larger, and it screamed. Then there was nothing but light, and the light itself disappeared.

She blinked—or he did. She was having difficulty with pronouns. They looked around together.

An amplified voice filled the cavernous room, barely audible. Prisoners milled, confused, staring perplexed at bloodstained hands. Projectiles flew in from far corridors, people scurried out of the way, and white smoke began to fill the air. Someone shouted.

Tear gas, Cormac supplied. Then he collapsed, and Amelia fainted for the first time in her life.

A soft hand lay across his brow. A woman's hand, smelling clean, like soap and lavender. He opened his eyes and saw Amelia sitting at his bedside.

Taking stock: He wasn't in a cell, but in a soft, single bed, part of a row of them lined up, heads against the wall. Several of the other beds were occupied by sleeping, bandaged figures. Prison infirmary.

He didn't feel hurt. Only tired. He also didn't want to try and move.

Amelia smiled at him. "Good morning."

He was confused. He was here, awake, and she looked solid. He could feel her, flesh against flesh.

"Are you real?" he said.

She tipped her head, acknowledging the question. "A bit. Partly. I'm not sure." The smile faltered.

"I can smell you." He reached for her hand. She gazed at his for a moment, almost startled. Then took hold of it. Then disappeared.

A man in a white lab coat walked to the bed. "Good, you're awake. How do you feel?"

His fist was clenched at his side, as if he had grabbed at something that had slipped away. That was it, then. She'd done what she came here to do. Stuck around long enough to say goodbye. And now she was gone.

He tried to tell himself that was okay.

The doctor checked his chart, then picked up Cormac's wrist and counted against the numbers on his watch.

"I'm a little tired," he answered finally. It was his body she'd used to battle the demon. Of course he was tired.

"You have second-degree burns on your face and hands," the doctor said. "There was a fire—you're probably lucky to be alive. You're sedated to help you rest and to keep the pain down, but in a week or so you should be back to normal."

He remembered the fire, the riot, and the demon—but what did the people in charge think had happened? So he asked, feigning amnesia.

"The warden's still trying to figure that out," the doctor said. "Now, get some rest."

Cormac felt like something was missing. He'd lost something.

At night, the infirmary never got completely dark. A nurse was on duty in the next room, and light from the hallway filtered in. A piece of monitoring equipment made a faint clicking noise. Red status lights peered out. Cormac stared at the ceiling, wondering. He could live a million years and never understand what had happened. Maybe she wasn't a ghost but an angel. Trying to give him purpose in the world.

So. Now what?

Lift your hand. It was a woman's voice, speaking from a distant meadow.

"Amelia," he said.

I'm still here. Lift your hand. I want to show you something.

He uncurled his right fist, the one without the IV needle in it, and raised the arm a few inches. It glowed. Faint, blue, with a nimbus of static. Without his bidding, his fingers, snapped, and the glow dissipated in a crackle of energy. A wizard's spell.

She was still with him, her power still flowed through him.

We're bound, you and I. And I thank you for it.

He settled more firmly on the pillow. He hadn't realized he'd been fighting the sedative, holding himself taut. But now, he was floating. He had stopped worrying.

He was ready to go after two days, even if it meant returning to solitary. He still didn't know what the fallout from the riot—and his part in it—was going to be. If the powers that be would blame him for something and add a decade or so to his sentence. Hardly seemed to matter because he'd won. They'd won.

But two days on his back was plenty. He didn't even hurt much. The aggravating itching was all on the outside, now—the burns were healing. At least they'd let him take a couple of books from the prison library. He was in the middle of another of Kitty's recommendations: *Middlemarch,* by a guy named George Eliot.

George Eliot was a woman. Can't you find something modern? This was stale when I read it as a girl. Cormac smiled.

When Olson entered the infirmary, Cormac scowled, preparing the arguments to get him out of here. The counselor didn't seem to notice and pulled over the chair at his bedside. "You're looking much better."

When had he been here before? Cormac wondered. Thinking of Olson looking over his unconscious form made him twitch.

Cormac frowned and looked at the ceiling. "You're going to ask me what happened, and you won't believe what I tell you."

Olson made a thin, wry smile. "Actually, I think I might. We have surveillance footage of most everything that happened. We've collected the evidence we need in a few assault and murder cases we'll be prosecuting. You're not involved in any of them, if you're worried. But you did . . . something, didn't you?"

"That didn't actually show up on film, did it?" Most of this stuff didn't record too well in any form, or it would have come out a long time ago.

Olson narrowed his gaze, a perplexed expression. "I can't exactly say what I saw. I saw you. You did something—and it all ended. I was hoping you could explain it to me."

Cormac stared. Where did he even start? There are more things in heaven and earth . . . "I don't know how to explain."

"Just tell me," Olson said. "Tell me everything."

Cormac did. Everything except Amelia. He made vague explanations about a demon haunting the place, hungry for blood, gathering power, and about how he'd picked up a spell that banished it. He tried to make it sound matter of fact, like he hadn't even been sure it would work and he'd have been just as happy to mind his own business. It all sounded crazy and Olson wasn't buying any of it, he was sure.

"What would have happened?" he said at the end of it. "If you hadn't done what you'd done to stop it?"

Cormac shrugged. "I don't know. I suppose you folk would have dropped in your tear gas and knocked everyone out anyway. The riot would have died down eventually."

"But that thing would still be on the loose."

The statement didn't require commentary. Cormac kept quiet, lying calmly, book folded across his stomach. Olson's smile was grim, tired and his eyes shadowed. He probably had a lot more patients after the last week. He straightened his jacket as he stood to leave.

Cormac said, "What happens to me now?" He had a flare of hope that they'd be so grateful they would just open the doors and let him leave. He could call Ben, *Come get me, please.* The hope burned, no matter how unrealistic the thought was. But maybe they'd shave a few months off. He was pecking away at his time, day by day.

"You'll go back to your cell when the doctor okays it. A regular cell, not the hole. Things go back to normal." He shrugged. "I'll put in a good word with the parole board. We'll see what we can do."

He walked away.

About a year later, lying on his bunk, staring at the ceiling for the last time, he was scared again.

Maybe it was more accurate to say he'd been scared his whole life. Fear had become background noise that he never noticed. He'd built up this front, these walls, trying to convince everyone he wasn't afraid. Sometimes the walls cracked. He was starting to notice now that he was scared of being normal, scared of being dependent—scared of being scared, even. He could observe it, acknowledge it. But he wasn't going to take down the walls. They kept him upright.

He noticed fear when it slipped over the wall: his lack of control during the riot, his fear of having friends because they might leave. And now.

He was getting out tomorrow.

Hardin and Olson had both spoken for him to the parole board. Ben had put up a hell of a case, showing that Cormac had family, a place to stay, potential work waiting for him—legitimate work, even. It had gone so smoothly. Despite all the help, Cormac hadn't expected it to. He'd expected to have the parole hearing go wrong, but it hadn't. He was getting out more than a year early as a result. Surprise.

When he had a job to do, he wasn't afraid. The job kept him focused, and the scary usually came so fast he didn't have time to think, only react. His reactions were fast enough to match, most of the time. If they hadn't been, he wouldn't still be around.

Right now, he had to wait, which wore him down. He should have been excited. Happy. Anticipating. But transition was hard, and the world he was about to enter was a different one than he'd left two years ago.

No, tell the truth: The world was the same. He'd changed. He wasn't sure he could handle it anymore.

Closing his eyes, he let out a sigh and thought of his meadow. His muscles unclenched, and he fell into sleep.

In a bright and magnificent summer, wildflowers covered the meadow, purples, yellows, blues, reds dotting the grasses like a painting on a postcard. The sky was too blue, it couldn't possibly be so blue in life. But he knew if he hiked out to the valley and looked, it really would be that blue, and he'd stare up at it marveling at how his memory hadn't done the scene justice. The air smelled fresh, clean, as if a thunderstorm had just passed, scrubbing the world, making it new.

Amelia was there, standing close. He could touch her with a straightened arm if he wanted. He almost did. Her face was calm. The storms were long gone, but he couldn't seem to tell what she was thinking.

He moved toward the set of boulders overlooking the stream where he was used to sitting, watching elk, or sunrises, or just the water playing.

"You want to sit down?" He gestured. She nodded, and he picked a smooth, flat stone with room enough for both of them.

He expected her to be awkward in the long skirt and formal clothing, but she wasn't. She moved like she was used to it, even in wilderness like this. Tucking her skirt just so, she perched on the boulder, back straight, and folded her hands before her.

"You'll be fine," she said. Even her smile was serious, like she couldn't quite stop thinking about tragedies of past and present.

He shook his head, only able to think, *What am I going to do with myself? What can I possibly do?* He couldn't imagine what guys who'd been in here ten, twenty, thirty years must feel like, when the world outside really had changed in their absence. What would it be like to disappear into prison before cell phones and come out to find you had to learn a new technology? A new language even? He'd only been out of the world a blink.

But still, the world looked different to him, and he wasn't sure how he'd live. Tomorrow, the gates would open and he'd walk out a free man.

"Except that you're saddled with me," she said.

"No. Both of us walk free. That's the plan."

She put her hand on his arm and squeezed. She wasn't wearing the thin leather gloves anymore, and he wondered where they'd gone.

The weight of her touch was strange—she wasn't real, she didn't exist. But here she was, with her hand on his arm, her skin warm against his, and he didn't quite know what to do next. If this had been real, if she had been real, he might have turned away. Walked away to avoid the contact entirely. But this wasn't real, so it didn't matter. He could do anything. So he put his opposite hand on hers, just resting it there. He waited for her to flinch, to pull her hand away, to argue. But she didn't.

They sat like that until morning, watching the meadow.

2.

"I've never heard of a spell that can move a soul like that," the woman whispered urgently, in a conversation that was supposed to be hushed, but voices carried in the empty room.

"Oh my dear, there is so much none of us have ever heard of," Amelia murmured, using Cormac's voice. The change in diction and tone made it clear—Cormac was not the one speaking. But he was the one to smile broadly, amused at the startled looks they gave him.

Cormac wondered what they would do if he just got up and walked out. By now, though, he was really curious about who these guys were and what they wanted. He'd only find that out if he stuck around.

What have we got in our pockets? Cormac nudged Amelia. Anything we can use? She had charms that could obfuscate a person's perception, that could lull someone into a sense of complacency. If they had the right ingredients, they could maybe turn this interrogation around—

"Please keep your hands where we can see them," the man said, as Cormac was reaching into his jeans pocket.

"Or what?"

His voice held a smile. "Try it and find out."

Cormac held up his hands, showing them empty, and rested them on his thighs. Guy might have been bluffing—or maybe not.

The woman was a magician herself—talking about spells, casting

80

the salt circle. Amelia wanted to press, to find out how much she knew, how skilled she was. Talk shop. Until Cormac knew what was motivating them, what their goal was—and if they intended to let Cormac go at any point—he didn't want to talk.

"So," the man asked, still calm, still in charge. "You inherited a ghost, got out of prison and went into business for yourself? Is that it?"

"Amelia's not really a ghost—"

"Semantics," he said, and from the back of his mind, even Amelia had to concede the point.

"If you really wanted to talk to me, why not just call? Send an email? I'm not hard to find."

"We needed to control the environment," the man said.

They thought he was dangerous—magically dangerous. He supposed he was, but that didn't excuse this. "You can see how this doesn't look friendly? Who are *you* working for?"

"Mr. Bennett," the woman interrupted. "You investigated a case in Truckee, California. The unexplained death of a park ranger there. I read the report, and the conclusion of that episode was a bit vague. I was hoping to learn more about what you did there."

"What report?" he drawled. "Who the hell wrote a report—" Annie Domingo, the ranger who'd hired him to investigate. "And what are you doing digging through park service incident reports?"

"What really happened at Donner Pass?" the woman asked.

"No."

"We know your activities," the woman—the magician—said. "We're just looking for details, so you might as well tell us."

They didn't know shit. They were looking for secrets—not just what Amelia had done, but how.

The man said, "I promise you, tell us what you know, then you can leave."

"And what're you going to do with what you learn here? Who are you trying to hurt?"

"Quite the opposite, Mr. Bennett. But until we've established what

81

your power is capable of, we can't risk revealing ourselves."

"We're done here," Cormac said and stood to walk out.

And stopped at the circle. He couldn't move past it. Amelia knew salt circles, knew how they worked and how to make them, and they were meant to contain magic, power, creatures who derived their power from magic. Cormac was flesh and blood, bog-standard human. He should be able to walk right past it like it wasn't there. It didn't feel like a wall stopping him. He couldn't make out any kind of barrier. He just couldn't take another step.

"Tell us about Donner Pass," the woman said again.

Cormac made his way back to the chair. In the back of his mind, Amelia's thoughts were racing. *Perhaps we could offer a trade, teach each other what we know—*

And if these two were bad guys? Part of a mysterious cabal trying to take over the world? It sounded ridiculous except he knew of *several* such cabals.

The man prompted, "Ranger Domingo reached out to you with a job. What happened next?"

DARK DIVIDE

One

Cormac didn't really know cats. He didn't *get* cats. The cats he'd known as a kid had been barn cats. They lived outside, took care of themselves, earned their keep killing mice and baby rabbits. Aloof creatures, they stayed out of Cormac's way, he stayed out of theirs.

Standing in the middle of this close and cluttered apartment, looking up at the giant, tangled furball crouched on the top of a bookshelf, he was at a loss. That thing was twenty-five pounds of pure hate, teeth bared, hissing and spitting. Pale fur shook from it every time it moved. Whenever anyone approached, it swiped with long, sharp claws. Nothing like daggers—more like hypodermic needles, and they'd draw just as much blood.

The animal tipped back its head and yowled to the ceiling, an otherworldly noise that made Cormac's spine clench. Hell, maybe the thing really was possessed by a demon.

There is nothing supernaturally wrong with this cat, Amelia declared. *He's simply a cat. Amplified, rather, but still. . . .* The cat hissed again, shuddering, letting loose another rain of fur.

Apparently, Amelia knew cats. Cormac caught the edges of her memories involving a whole series of kittens and cats she'd grown up with in her family's lush Victorian manor house. Beautiful, soft animals born to sit demurely on laps, to be petted, to have satin ribbons tied around their necks, to ride in a little girl's doll carriage. Those cats had followed her around the house, batting tiny paws at the edges of her petticoats while she giggled.

This was a side of herself Amelia rarely revealed. She didn't like to think of her past—she'd left her home and family as soon as she could, to travel the world and study magic. Anymore, she didn't like to think of her old life. Before she'd died.

Those cats from her childhood had looked much like this one: a luxurious Persian with brushable fur and an aristocratic face. But this one was, the owner confidently reported, possessed by a terrible demon.

"Schubert didn't used to be like this," the old man said. He was a widower, the cat his only companion in his assisted-living apartment. "He was always a little stubborn, but can you blame him? A fine old gentleman like that?" Mr. Wegman chuckled then, nervously. "But then he started hissing at everything, yowling in the middle of the night, clawing me." The fine skin of his liver-spotted hands was covered with slash marks and thin scars.

Cormac—and by extension, Amelia, though their clients mostly didn't know about her—had been referred to Wegman by friends of his daughter's, a family who really did have a haunted house. They lived off of Cheesman Park in the center of Denver, the site of dozens of hauntings over the last century because that was what happened when developers plowed over a cemetery and built residential neighborhoods on top of it without moving the bodies. Cormac and Amelia had successfully exorcised the place and set the restless spirits at peace.

Surely they could do the same with a possessed cat?

He isn't possessed, Amelia insisted. *He's ill.*

Cormac and Amelia both had met demons. They'd fought demons, alone and together. In a way, that was how they'd met: fighting the demon that had invaded the Colorado Territorial Correctional Facility. She'd been a disembodied spirit trapped in its walls, after being wrongfully hanged for murder a hundred years ago. He did time there on a manslaughter conviction—a bit more recently.

He'd deserved his sentence. Probably worse, too. He'd been lucky. When the demon started killing prisoners, he'd been lucky she was there and knew how to destroy it. Lucky she'd been able to contact him. Lucky he'd been patient enough—eventually—to listen to her. To let her in.

Yeah, standing here looking at that cat, he had to remind himself how lucky he really was.

"So what are we going to do?" Cormac murmured. Mr. Wegman waited in the kitchen for the verdict. If Cormac could suddenly make the cat well, maybe he could get paid anyway. He had a feeling this wasn't going to be that simple.

Well, Amelia said, matter-of-factly. *A veterinarian should see him, I suppose.*

Cormac returned to the kitchen and asked Mr. Wegman if he had a carrier for Schubert. He did, and Cormac and Amelia spent the next hour in the back room where the cat had been lurking and terrorizing everyone. Cormac let Amelia take over then. In the years since they'd begun their partnership, he had never entirely gotten used to the sensation. It was like stepping aside, closing his eyes and moving to the back of his own mind, and Amelia—her soul, her essence, whatever that part of her was that had survived—came forward and took charge of his body. She was the magician, really—she needed to use his body to work her spells, to scry her magic. He was merely the muscle. The front man. The bounty hunter turned. . .whatever it was that he'd turned into.

We are partners, she said firmly, as she often did. She never took control of his body without warning him, without them both agreeing to it. It was part of their understanding.

With a can of tuna and more patience than Cormac could have managed by himself, Amelia lured the demon cat into the carrier. The animal set to howling again as soon as the door closed—and he had finished eating the tuna. Hunkered down in the carrier, he was at least safe, and Mr. Wegman was safe from him.

The cat whisperer. Amelia always seemed to be revealing new and amazing talents.

Cormac was back in charge when he brought the carrier to Mr. Wegman and told him that the cat really needed to see a veterinarian, that these changes in behavior were likely medical rather than supernatural.

"Oh," Mr. Wegman said, sounding a little disappointed as he regarded the carrier on the kitchen table. Because wouldn't it have been simpler—and far more interesting—for the problem to be solved by someone waving a magic wand and chanting a few words? Wouldn't that always be simpler? As it was, he now had lots of expensive tests and an uncertain diagnosis ahead of him.

"How much do I owe you?" Mr. Wegman said, reaching for a wallet sitting on the kitchen counter.

"Nothing," Cormac said. "No charge, since it wasn't anything I could fix. Just get that cat to a vet and get him healthy."

"Well, thank you, son. Thank you very much." He shook Cormac's hand as he showed him to the door.

It was an afternoon of work with nothing to show for it. Cormac didn't remember exactly when he'd turned into a nice guy. He didn't used to be a nice guy. Prison had changed him.

Or I have, Amelia said.

Same thing, really.

When he—when they—had gotten out of prison, the studio apartment in a middling part of Denver had seemed perfect. It had four walls and a door that Cormac held the key to, and could lock and unlock whenever he wanted. What more did they need?

The place was a box, with an efficiency kitchen in one corner and a bathroom tucked into another. The kitchen table was usually covered with books, papers, bags of herbs, maps, arcane alphabets, and whatever else Amelia was working on at the moment. He usually ate standing over the sink. Shelves held more of her tools: boxes, crystals, a staff, more books, carved pieces of wood, and little planter boxes with things growing in them. Cormac slept on a futon with a makeshift bedside table made from a crate. More books were piled on it, as well as his laptop.

Not a lot of Cormac himself was visible in the room. Since prison, he'd put his guns and weapons into storage and hadn't gotten them back out. He'd promised his cousin Ben he'd keep out of trouble. That meant his bounty hunting days were over. Mostly. The duffel bag full of sharpened stakes, silver spikes, and jars of holy water couldn't technically be perceived as weapons to most anyone looking at it. *Those* belonged to him, at least.

The place—maybe a little small, a little rundown—was his, while most everything inside belonged to Amelia. That cut somewhat close to the truth of the situation for his taste. Maybe this was right where they belonged.

Memories intruded. Amelia had grown up in a mansion, with acres of land, gardens, lawns, and forests. Carpeted halls, rooms crammed with furniture, windows framed by luxurious drapes, and not just a feeling of safety, but of an abiding comfort supplied by wealth. She never criticized the little apartment Cormac had chosen. She never complained. But she wanted things.

Just a little yard, she'd begun to hint. *I could grow my own herbs. Work spells outdoors in privacy.*

With a little planning, they could have a place that didn't share walls with anyone. No midnight shouting, no smell of pot outside their door. They could aspire to anything they wanted. But Cormac had grown suspicious of hope. Wasn't what they had enough? Or was he afraid to aspire?

And if I could catch a bit of rainwater now and then. . . .

They could move out of the city, up north maybe, to a little peace and quiet. Getting expensive around here anyway, wasn't it? If he was working for himself he didn't need to live any place in particular.

Well. If he kept catching cats for old men for free, he wasn't going to be upgrading anything.

Much of his work came through the internet, which had taken some adjustment. This wasn't how he'd worked in the old days. Back then, there'd been a lot of footwork and networking, talking to people, getting the word out that he was a man who could solve a certain kind of problem. He rode a little bit on his father's reputation; Cormac had learned the trade of hunting supernatural creatures from him. After his death, Cormac continued, and enough people knew that to keep him in business.

Then he'd spent a few years in prison and most of his old networks assumed he'd died.

Starting from scratch had been just as well. This was a new kind of business he was running these days: supernatural problem solver. Paranormal detective. Now, word of mouth happened via email and forums. He hadn't gotten as far as putting up a Facebook page for himself; that seemed a step or two too far. He didn't want to be too easy to find.

His email inbox seemed to get a little more activity every week.

"Picked up a Ouija board at a garage sale. Needs cleaning. Can u help?"

"I need to curse my boss right now."

"Haunted restaurant, need help please!"

"How do I keep vampires out of the laundromat?"

They didn't do curses. Amelia could, but as she pointed out to Cormac, they were trying to get out of the assassination business and the one seemed awfully close to the other. The Ouija board issue seemed straightforward—whether or not the thing was actually haunted, Amelia could work a purifying spell or two, the owner would be happy, and they could charge fifty bucks for half an hour of work.

The haunted restaurant might or might not be, and Cormac wasn't sure what was going on with vampires and laundromats. He could respond, ask for a basic consulting fee and not feel too bad about taking money from people who didn't know what they were talking about.

The next email read: "I've been told you're someone who's good with mysteries. Weird mysteries. I might have one for you. Really, I'm absolutely certain something terrible is going on here, but I can't get anyone to listen to me. Here's what happened: one of my colleagues starved himself to death. He was in a fully stocked cabin, his car was full of gas, he didn't need to starve. But he did. The medical examiner says it's a fluke—some weird undetected medical condition. If it had taken place anywhere else in the world, I might say yes, it's a fluke, he got sick and it's just one of those things. But Mr. Bennett—we work at Donner Pass. This man starved to death in a cabin at Donner Pass."

That caught Cormac's attention. The presence that was Amelia also seemed to lean forward with interest. "You know about Donner Pass?" he asked.

Of course I do, it was one of the most lurid tales ever to come out of the American West. A group of pioneers was caught in the Sierra Nevada mountains over the winter and resorted to cannibalism—or so it's said. Even in my time, fifty years later, survivors were publishing memoirs, and dime novels covered the event incessantly.

The message continued. "We're a tourist area, a lot of people come through here. If this is some kind of curse, if something's really wrong here, it could get bad. I can't let that happen. Can you help?"

The message was signed by Annie Domingo, U.S. Forest Service Ranger, Tahoe National Forest. Her tone throughout was even, straightforward. Not someone prone to panic, but she was definitely disturbed. And desperate, to be reaching out on the basis of a scrap of reputation.

"Do you think there's something to this?"

Amelia considered. *I'm not sure. I knew of magicians who were interested in the location. Some feared that such a terrible event would turn the spot into some kind of psychic sink—a pit of despair if you will. Many were sure the place must be haunted.*

"Still are, I'd guess. But is it possible something's there?"

Oh my goodness, do you even need to ask such a question?

Two

An internet search brought up a local news story about the man, a Forest Service ranger who'd been working a month-long shift at a research station near Donner Memorial State Park when he stopped checking in. State troopers found his body lying on his cot, apparently peaceful. The coroner determined that he'd died of malnutrition—he had starved. That had been just a week ago. Tests were still being done to determine if he'd had some disease or condition that would cause such a death. The coroner and other authorities interviewed for the short article all agreed that while the incident was strange, and the death tragic, it didn't require any more attention.

Cormac called the number in Annie Domingo's message.

"Hello?"

"Annie Domingo? My name's Cormac Bennett, I got your email and wanted to follow up."

The woman had a young-sounding voice, full of energy. "Oh, wow. Thank you so much for calling. Did all that sound crazy? It must have sounded crazy."

"I don't follow up on the crazy ones," Cormac said.

"So you think there may really be something weird going on?"

"Well, that's why I wanted to talk. Why do you think something weird's going on?" He also wanted to get a better idea of her definition of weird. Did she think this was a cult, a serial killer, that kind of weird? Or *weird* weird. His kind of weird.

"I think there's some kind of magic working up here."

Yeah, that kind of weird. "Yeah?"

"Just a feeling. It's hard to explain. It's sort of like. . . ."

She was hesitating. Self-editing, trying to figure out what to say. What wouldn't make her sound crazy. "Just say it," Cormac said firmly.

Her next deep breath sounded over the phone line. "It's a sense. Almost a boundary. I was with them when the cops found Arty's body, and walking into the place almost made me sick. Not physically, not nausea or anything, even though it was a pretty ugly scene. But heartsick. Soulsick. Something." The feelings she described were vague, as if she couldn't put the sensation into words. But she'd certainly experienced *something*. Not only that, she recognized the wrongness of the experience.

She's magical herself, Amelia observed. *She must have some kind of connection to the supernatural, to be able to sense that. She might not know it.*

"Whatever happened—you think it's connected to Donner Pass? To the Donner Party?"

"It almost has to be, doesn't it?"

It might have been the power of suggestion. Or it might have been some kind of dark magic evoking the power of suggestion. Fine lines, here. "Not sure, without knowing more," Cormac said.

"Can you come look at the place? Would that tell you more?"

"I need to do some research. I can let you know tomorrow. You should probably hear my rates, see if you really want me there." He told her a modest daily rate that was a fraction of what he charged in his hunting days, but still decent money. Plus the mileage to get himself out there, plus expenses.

"That's fine," she said, without hesitation. "Just please tell me you can come help."

He thought she would have balked at the money. That she didn't showed how serious she was. "I'll call you tomorrow. Early."

She thanked him and hung up.

Well, this sounded like a job. A strange, fascinating job, and maybe nothing would come of it—the death was natural, and Domingo was prone to paranoia. But Cormac felt like he used to feel before a hunt, when he had to size up his prey and consider his strategy, arrange his weapons and choose his ground. When he had a mission and purpose, a job no one else could do, that he was uniquely suited for by upbringing and disposition. He felt, in a word, *happy*.

Kind of weird.

So we're taking the job? Amelia displayed an eagerness to match his own. They were both desperate to get back to work.

Cormac slept, and dreamed.

He was in a valley very much like one high in the Colorado Rockies where his father had taken him hunting when he was a teenager. A stone-laden creek ran through the middle, and grassy meadow climbed up the sides of the bowl, giving way to thick pine forests. A hazy summer heat lay over it all, and the sky above was searing blue. Cormac sat, or imagined himself sitting, on an outcrop of gray boulders near the trees, partway up the slope, looking down on the water as it frothed and foamed on its way.

A woman in a high-necked gray dress, the skirt of which brushed the grass at her feet, stood looking at the same view. She clasped her hands in front of her and seemed serene.

He wasn't really sure if it was a dream anymore, if this was something that happened in his sleeping mind, his waking self, or someplace in between. This was a cloth woven from memory, imagination, and whatever threads tied him and Amelia together. This mindscape was where they'd first met when he was in prison, and a forceful, ghostly presence demanded that he listen to her.

When they first met her hands were gloved. They weren't, anymore.

Hadn't been for some time, and he couldn't remember exactly when the gloves had vanished. He wondered if he'd stopped imagining them, or if she had somehow removed them from their shared vision. Likewise, her hair had changed. She used to wear her dark hair tied in a prim bun under a simple hat, the picture of a proper late-Victorian woman. Now, she clipped it back from her face and left the rest to hang down her back in curls. She had grown comfortable with him. When she turned to smile at him over her shoulder, his breath caught.

Had he been born a hundred years too late, or just in time?

"You believe something unnatural killed that man," she said. Here, she wasn't just a voice. They could talk face to face. It almost felt normal.

"I've seen a lot of crazy in my time. This is new. But Domingo didn't give us a lot to go on," Cormac said.

Pacing a few feet, the fabric of her skirt shifting the grass as she moved, she said, "Even if there's nothing to this, even if we get there, speak to this woman, and find nothing—if she's willing to pay our fee, it's only a few days of time, and we might have a story to tell at the end of it. We'll definitely have the payment."

Cormac agreed with this point. It would be good to be *doing* something. And paying the rent. "And if there is something to it?"

"Our last adventure was saving the world," she said. "We can do anything."

"Then let's call Domingo and pack up."

Three

In her former life, her actual life, Amelia had always intended to come to this part of California. She'd been distracted, made a detour, arrived in Colorado, and then— Well, and then it had all come to an end.

But she'd made it here eventually, hadn't she?

A hundred years before, she'd arrived in this country in the port of Seattle. As she almost always did when arriving in a new place, she started a search for magic. For magicians. For whatever she could learn. There was so much to learn.

As she often did, she started with local Theosophical Society, spiritualist lectures and gatherings. She rarely met with anything, or anyone, useful at these events—popular movements sanitized for general consumption, with much belief and hope but little practical application. Easy to judge and dismiss, but not so many years ago she'd been among the general public who attended these gatherings. The difference between them and her was all the work she had put into her passion over the years. She had never been satisfied with vague hopes.

In a newspaper she found a listing for a lecture by a member of the British Society for Psychical Research. She had encountered the man before; he made a living traveling around Europe and America lecturing on a variety of topics. He attempted to bring a rigorous scientific methodology to his work and had the endorsement of Sir Arthur Conan Doyle himself.

She arrived at the meeting hall just as the event was starting. She paid her coins and found a spot at the back of the room, standing against the wall because all the seats were taken. A gentleman tried to offer her his seat; she declined. The place was full, an excited audience attracted by the lecturer's reputation and by Conan Doyle's endorsement, blazoned on all the flyers and the program. The bulk of the audience were upper-class ladies who had the leisure for such esoteric pursuits and the money to spend on foreign lecturers and the pamphlets they invariably sold at a table in the foyer. The evening's topic: The Possibility of Detecting and Measuring Electronic Fields Surrounding Ectoplasmic Emanations.

In all her travels and studies, Amelia had never encountered an ectoplasmic emanation. She had found auras, spheres, and lines of power, but they were insubstantial, and while she was interested in what steps could be taken to measure such fields, it became clear in moments that the lecturer was speaking of the solid masses that were meant to emerge from mediums in the course of séances. She knew of at least one so-called spiritualist who used cheesecloth to produce the effect. One didn't need wires and magnets to detect cheesecloth.

To his credit, the lecturer acknowledged the existence of frauds, but he believed some real phenomenon existed behind the stories—and he would prove it as soon as he perfected a way to measure it.

Amelia felt as if he rather missed the point of the mystical—scientific method was all well and good, but science had not advanced far enough to be able to truly examine these phenomena. This lecturer approached his work from an assumption that science had advanced as far as it possibly could and therefore could entirely explain everything—with a little philosophical effort.

If he missed the mark he at least did no harm, which was more than could be said for the charlatans who charged outrageous sums of money to conduct theatrical séances rigged by cables and hidden trapdoors and electrical effects. A reprehensible practice.

Amelia wasn't really here for the lecture. What she looked for were the other people standing in the back of the room, the ones in practical suits and walking dresses, with their amulets and charms discreetly hidden under ties and scarves, or inside the cuffs of sleeves. The ones who frowned and unconsciously shook their heads at what the lecturer said, rather than staring raptly with unquestioning acceptance. The ones like her, in other words.

As the lecturer went on about wire gauge and strength of current as it related to strength of ectoplasmic presence, one of these others caught her studying the audience rather than the lecturer and held her gaze when it passed to him.

He was a Caucasian gentleman in his thirties, clean shaven, with a beige suit and a high-collared shirt, a plain tie around his neck. His dark hair was ruffled, and the lines around his eyes indicated he smiled often. His walking stick had a smooth silver head engraved with a pattern she couldn't quite make out. It was the walking stick that intrigued her—both elegant and unobtrusive, it jostled her instincts. There was more to this man. She wondered what detail about herself had attracted his attention. He nodded at her, and she returned the gesture. A secret recognition of their secret avocation.

When the lecture ended and the audience began to disperse, she waited, and as she thought he would, the man approached, bowler hat tucked under his arm, walking stick loose in his hand.

"Good afternoon, ma'am. Did you enjoy the talk?" He had a delightful American accent, with just that little bit of a drawl that stage actors made so much of.

"Yes, it amused me," she said. "But I'm not sure I agree that science is yet able to measure all that is measurable."

He smiled politely. "I hear you share a country of origin with this evening's scholar. May I welcome you to the fair shores of America?"

"You may," she said.

"Welcome," he said, bowing politely. "I'll go one step further and say that there is an aspect of the universe that is unmeasurable."

"Such as. . . ."

"The soul, ma'am."

"Ah. Yes, that. I would also say art, perhaps."

"Oh? How so? That painting over there seems to be about forty inches by thirty inches, I'd reckon."

He was joking, of course; she smiled in appreciation, and studied the painting he had indicated: a small copy of Leutze's "Washington Crossing the Delaware."

"I don't mean the physical object, but rather the feeling it evokes," she said. "This particular scene, for example, evokes little emotion in me. It is a fair representation of an incident that is part of another nation's history, nothing more. However, for you and for most of the Americans in the room, for the people who chose to hang it here at all, I expect this piece evokes a great upwelling of patriotic feeling, pride in the scene and admiration for the man portrayed. *That* is the mystery, and those feelings cannot always be predicted or measured. That, sir, is the mystery that represents the gap between science and magic that our esteemed lecturer this evening has failed to address."

He regarded her with an interest that bordered on insulting, as if she were some foreign curiosity and not a respected colleague. She suppressed the incipient blush spreading across her cheeks and also the urge to apologize for her forwardness. This was what her older brother James meant when he said she would never attract a husband. She merely had to speak and instantly became an oddity to men.

But then the charming American said, "Did you know it's said that President Washington had wooden teeth? I admit, I can't look at a picture of him without thinking about that."

She laughed as she was meant to, and thought no more about what James would say.

The American gentleman, Mr. Roland Langley, invited her to tea at a nearby café. She accepted, and they discussed the quantifiable power of art and many other ideas besides. She no longer remembered which of them claimed the status of magician first. They seemed to slip into conversation about amulets, wardings, arcane circles, summoning, banishments, and all the rest of it without conscious acknowledgement. They simply recognized that part of themselves in the other. It had been like this at other times during her travels; she recognized a magic symbol carved above a door or the particular scent of incense drifting from an otherwise unremarkable bookshop, and known that something more lurked behind the façade. She always looked for such places, such moments. This was how she learned.

Mr. Langley was also a pleasure to talk to, and this delighted her. He asked her where she had traveled from—he would have expected her to travel across the Atlantic to America, not the Pacific, and she explained that she had set off from Britain to the east rather than the west, across Europe, the Slavic countries, Turkey, and then the British colonies of the Middle East and South Asia before reaching Singapore, Hong Kong, and then the ship bound for Seattle. She had almost completed the circle back home, but she planned on spending a good deal of time in the Americas first.

"And do you travel, Mr. Langley?"

"I do, but maybe not as widely as you."

"Tell me where you were before you came to Seattle, then."

"Well, this may interest you, now that I think of it. I've just come from California, a spot in the Sierra Nevada mountains called Donner Pass. I don't suppose you've heard of the tragedy of the Donner Party?" he asked.

"I certainly have. This is where I will be forced to reveal my secret vice of reading penny dreadfuls."

"Well, I'll try not to judge you too harshly for that. Fifty years gone and fascination with the Donner Party seems to only grow in the public imagination." He was no longer smiling, and his voice had taken on a serious cast. She had thought of him as affable, without care. Perhaps his public demeanor was a mask for more studious depths.

"That seems to worry you."

"It's like you said about art. Maybe we can't measure it, but there's power, when people react to something. Something beautiful, or something awful.'"

"More people, stronger reactions—" As in the horror evoked by a particularly lurid description of the events that transpired in those mountains: starvation, cannibalism, despair.

"More power," he finished. "I traveled with some of our colleagues to the pass to try to. . .how should I put it. . .disperse some of that power. Ground it out like a lightning rod."

"You believe such a concentration of. . .ill history. . .could be dangerous?" She thought of all the terrible happenings throughout history—wars, massacres, plagues—and all the power that might possibly surround such events. The world would be a blazing crater of hell by now.

Had magicians always worked to temper such events, such locations?

Langley offered an expansive shrug, in the demonstrative way of Americans. "Sure can't hurt to settle things down a little. Folk like us have been going up there since the start, making sure it's not haunted, or that nothing worse than ghosts show up."

"Fascinating," she murmured. "Although I'm not certain I agree with you. It seems as though the whole world must be covered with ghosts and ill power, if such tragedies anchor harmful power to the material world."

"Who's to say it isn't?" he answered with his ready, charming grin. "At any rate, time will tell. If nothing bad ever comes of the events of Donner Pass, we may never know if it was our work that helped—or if there was never any danger to begin with."

"It's likely neither of us will be alive to witness it, in either case," she said, and poured herself more tea from the pot.

And now here she was.

Four

It's beautiful, Amelia murmured.

The interstate climbed into the mountains, and Cormac had exited and pulled into an overlook. The view spreading before them was a postcard picture of tree-covered hills rising up to ragged granite peaks. The air smelled clean in the way only mountain air could. Ancient stone and young pines, the sharp edge of lingering snow.

The valley was busy. The town of Truckee nestled at the base. The interstate arced around it on one side, the railroad on the other, and in between was a tourist mecca of shops, ski resorts, parks, and people.

After the reading about the Donner Party Amelia'd made him do, he'd gotten a picture in his mind that this would be some desolate, remote place. Instead, it was where everybody crossed through the mountains on their way to and from northern California. And a big chunk of those folks stopped for vacation. Lake Tahoe was a dozen or so miles south. The traffic was bad, and the roar of semi trucks on the freeway was constant, inescapable.

Perhaps it's more peaceful in winter? Amelia suggested.

"Not with all those ski areas," he muttered. He was from Colorado. He knew how mountain tourist towns worked. If anything, the place might be worse in winter. Hard to imagine the twenty-foot blanket of snow that had socked in the Donner Party.

If the members of the Donner Party could see this, the land that killed so many of them so brutally, what would they think?

102

"That maybe they should have stayed in St. Louis?" Cormac said.

Haven't you ever wanted something so badly you'd have gone through any amount of hardship to achieve it? Believed in the chance of a new life so much the risk would have been worth it?

He thought about it a minute, and decided that no, he never had. He'd had to take risks to get out of situations, not in them. But Amelia—Lady Amelia Parker—had taken that kind of chance when she left her family, along with its wealth and status, to become a magician. She had traveled the world, taking risks until it killed her. Sort of.

"I think they didn't know what they were getting into. They didn't believe in the risk," he said. They'd been fed a line by guides and outfitters trying to get rich on the wave of settlers moving west in the 1840s. Apart from the gruesome details about that terrible long winter when they'd been trapped on the mountain, the whole story was ultimately sad. A tragedy.

He took another deep breath of pine-filled mountain air, surveyed the valley one more time, and climbed back in the Jeep.

"Let's go track down Annie Domingo."

He called Domingo, who asked him to meet her at the visitor center at the state park, a few miles down the freeway.

Literally right on the freeway. The site where forty people starved to death, where the survivors engaged in cannibalism and participated in one of the most famous tragedies in American frontier history, was no more than a hundred yards from a major interstate. A massive statue put up to commemorate the place by an overly enthusiastic heritage group back in the nineteen teens was visible from the interstate. The cognitive dissonance of it might actually give Cormac a headache.

In the parking lot, a set of tired-looking parents leaned on the hood of their minivan and watched three squirrelly school-age kids run around screaming, full of pent-up energy from riding in a car for hours. The dad had a camera in one hand but appeared to have given up trying to get everyone to stand still for a picture. Mom had a hand against her temple like she was nursing a headache. Years from now, this would be a treasured family memory. Or something.

Cormac gave them a wide berth, walking through the lot to the new-looking visitor center. Like the visitor centers at a hundred other parks all over the west, the place was rustic—painted brown, suggesting a cabin with its sloped roof and backdrop of trees—and yet had plenty of wide concrete sidewalks that met Federal accessibility standards. Signs pointed to nearby nature trails and reminded visitors not to litter or feed animals. The parking lot was full, but most of the visitors seemed to wander out to the giant statue of an overwrought pioneer family, take pictures, and wander back to their cars. They were families with hyper kids, or older couples belonging to tricked-out RVs. Cormac—alone, frowning, studying the area through his sunglasses—felt out of place. Anywhere he went around here, he was going to stand out: that surly-looking guy all by himself, glaring at everything.

He went inside to find Domingo.

The old woman behind the desk just inside the main doors wore an olive-green uniform with a "volunteer" tag on it. She smiled broadly at him. She seemed tiny and earnest to Cormac, and did not look like she could be Annie Domingo.

"Welcome to the park! Do you have any questions I can answer?"

Such a broad offer, Amelia murmured. *So many questions. . . .*

"Is Annie Domingo here?" Cormac said.

The volunteer opened her mouth to tell him when a door behind the desk opened, and a woman in her thirties in a Forest Service uniform emerged, as if she'd heard her name spoken. She was average height, with an athletic build and skin like weathered sandstone. Her thick black hair was braided down her back. Her dark eyes were piercing.

"Oh, here she is! Annie, someone's here to see you."

"Thanks, Mary."

Mary smiled happily at him. "Have a lovely visit!" she said before moving off to help another visitor. That left Cormac and Domingo regarding each other across the laminate counter, between the bins of brochures and park maps.

Native American, isn't she? Amelia answered. *There were several tribes located in this area, weren't there?*

"Hi, can I help you?" she asked.

"I'm Cormac Bennett, we spoke on the phone a couple of days ago."

She blew out what looked for all the world like a relieved breath. "Oh my God, thank you for coming." She came around the front desk, all business. "We should go somewhere to talk."

Bemused, he followed her out the building and across the parking lot to some kind of nature trail, marked with gravel and plastic educational signs.

"I just want to get out someplace no one will overhear. I'm already on the outs with a couple of people over this."

"What, for calling in a supernatural consultant?"

Her answering smirk suggested she had some sense of humor. "The medical examiner is doing another round of blood tests, trying to figure out if Arty ate something poisonous that affected his digestion, so that he either couldn't eat, or even when he ate he couldn't absorb nutrients. Like that McCandless kid from *Into the Wild*? You hear about that?"

Cormac had. A suburban kid abandoned everything and fled to Alaska to live in the wild. Starved to death in a matter of weeks. The initial assumption was he'd been too stupid to hack it. Turned out, he might have eaten seeds containing some kind of toxin.

"I suppose that makes sense."

"Arty—his name was Art Weber—was a backwoods ranger here for fifteen years. He knew what not to eat. Something else killed him."

"You sure he didn't just. . .pass away? He have any emotional issues?"

She gave him another look, her brow furrowed. "Starving yourself to death is a real inefficient way to commit suicide."

"Stranger things have happened."

"Yeah," she said thoughtfully.

They stopped at a rustic, rough-hewn wooden bench along the trail. A nice place to rest, for anyone who needed to rest on a half-mile circular trail. For all that the area around the visitor center and monument was crowded and noisy, they had this trail to themselves. Even noise from the freeway was muffled. The running water of a creek trickled nearby, and the underbrush was thick with birds calling.

Before sitting, Domingo took another look around. "I think something happened to Arty. Something the medical examiner's never going to find."

"What do you want me to do?"

"I don't know—what do you normally do in a case like this?"

"Not sure there's ever been a case like this."

Amelia said, *We look for stories, scour the old texts for symptoms, for similarities. We examine the site and look for symbols carved or painted on the walls. We look for bits and pieces of spells that have been used up. We hope for a lead, to make scrying easier. If we don't find a lead we scry anyway.*

Amelia had a spell that woke dead bodies, so she could question them about their final moments. He was pretty sure this Arty had been dead too long to try that. He hoped.

I do have other methods. I think we should see this place, where the man died.

"Can you show me where your friend died? I'll know more if I can have a look around."

This must have reassured her—first that he was going to investigate, and second that he might actually be able to learn something. The tension in her shoulder slipped, and she let out another relieved breath, like she hadn't believed he was serious. "I can take you there right now."

She drove him in a Forest Service truck, twenty minutes up a couple of increasingly unkempt dirt roads. She had to stop and unlock a steel gate on one of them, and soon the road faded to just a couple of ruts worn into the forest.

A little further on, she finally parked, and up ahead sat the cabin. The thing was small, maybe twenty feet on a side, with a tool shed and narrow porch attached. It looked like it might have been built in the thirties, of simple plank board and a shingled roof. A stone chimney rose on one side. Cormac's father had worked as a hunting guide and outfitter in the northern Rockies of Colorado. He'd have brought his clients to stay in places a lot like this: functional cabins with few amenities, a woodburning stove but no electricity, no plumbing to speak of. But the walls were solid and the roof stayed dry. A place like this could stay toasty warm all winter. You could live here just fine, assuming the pantry and woodpile were stocked.

Yellow caution tape wound around the outside.

Domingo carefully peeled back a length of tape and invited him onto the porch while she unlocked the front door. When the door opened in, she paused as if steeling herself, and Cormac felt it, that sense that she'd talked about on the phone, a stomach-churning wrongness. He looked around, thinking he'd be able to see something, a shimmering in the air or a shadow covering just this area of forest, the cabin, and a little space around it. But nothing looked out of the ordinary or wrong. It was all in his head, in the shiver traveling down his spine.

"You felt that, yeah?" Domingo asked.

"Yeah."

"Everybody does. I've always had kind of a sixth sense—spend enough time in the woods you get a feel, you know? But I mean everyone—the cops, the coroner, everyone who came in here. They write it off as the power of suggestion. They know what happened here, they just think it's creepy. Even though they're all tough, experienced guys who've seen a lot worse than this. What is it? What's making us feel like this?"

Magic, Amelia offered. *But it's. . .off.*

Since meeting Amelia he'd encountered a lot of magic. That was where his own sensitivity came from—not any natural ability, but an instinct developed over years, like an allergy that grew worse over time. A demon might crawl out of some rift in reality and exude dread; even a benevolent magician might cast some kind of protection that produced a vague sense of ill feeling in someone who wasn't welcome. Most of the time, it felt like little more than a tingle on the skin that faded as soon as he was aware of it.

This—the magic had already happened. Any lingering sense of it should be indistinct. A prickling of hairs and nothing more. This—

It's like some kind of hole in the world.

Domingo seemed hesitant to enter the cabin, so Cormac pushed past her and took a look around.

The place had a sour, musty smell that indicated the man had been dead for a few days before he'd been found. That only contributed to the unconscious creeping fear tugging at his perception. A spot of movement at the edges of his vision. He looked, but nothing living was here. There should be mice in an uninhabited cabin like this. Bugs. Birds. Anything.

As Domingo said, the pantry was stocked. A set of shelves on the back wall was filled with canned food: vegetables, tuna, pasta. A couple of cupboards likely held more. Out of curiosity, Cormac opened a drawer and found a can opener, so that wasn't the problem. He was willing to bet the propane tank outside was full enough to run the gas stove by the wall. In another corner stood a desk covered with USGS contour maps, pens, pencils, a stack of worn notebooks, binoculars, compass.

"What was he doing here?"

"Arty was a field biologist. He spent a month or so up here every summer doing wildlife surveys, maintaining trails, that sort of thing. He called it his vacation." Her face was screwed up, her eyes shining, tears ready to fall. She scowled and looked outside. "Nothing was different. Nothing had changed. So why did this happen?"

"Where was the body?" he asked.

"On the bed. Like he just lay down and gave up."

"He wasn't on drugs or anything?"

"No! The blood tests came back negative. They're running a second round of tests for plant toxins. There weren't any signs of violence or illness."

The bed where he died was a basically a cot, with a thin mattress, made up with white sheets and a government-issue-looking wool blanket, a single pillow. The pillow still held a depression, a crease where a head might have lain. The blanket had been smoothed out.

He knelt, looked under the cot, and found two things: a jackknife, blade open and ready to use, but then dropped, discarded. And a piece of bone, smooth and flattened, probably part of a rib. It was just a couple of inches long, so no telling what it came from.

I've no idea what those mean.

Might not have meant anything. Guy dropped his knife. He was a biologist, so the bone might have been a sample he brought in and lost track of. It was smooth, bleached. If it had been magical, part of a spell maybe, it would have had something written or carved into it. He set them on the table, and wondered if the cops had missed the items, or figured they weren't important.

He held the knife up. "Ms. Domingo, that look like Weber's knife?"

"Yeah, that's his." She stood with her arms tightly crossed, unhappy. "He always had it with him. Where'd you find it?"

"Under the bed."

Her brow furrowed, maybe thinking what he was: it didn't make sense, but it also didn't *not* make sense. Both the knife and the bone might have just fallen out of his pocket.

Look around, Amelia said. *There must be something more here.*

He let his vision go soft. He might miss something, so Amelia had to be present, slipping into his eyes, occupying not just his mind, but his body. She had knowledge and skills, but needed physicality to use them. She would see the magic where he might not.

Domingo wouldn't know the difference. She'd see Cormac standing in the middle of the cabin, turning slowly, studying the walls, the roof beams, the furniture, the floor. She wouldn't see Amelia looking through his eyes.

Anything? he murmured inwardly.

Let's try something else.

They'd been doing this long enough that he knew what came next. Before she could instruct him, he drew thread and iron nail from the pocket of his jacket. He unrolled the thread, held the end of it so the nail hung in perfect balance, a compass needle pointing at random. He whispered the words she told him.

Hard to notice at first, if the thing moved or not. The gentle swaying it displayed, shifting left, then right, then back, came from its own natural movements, a draft in the air, or maybe the tiny vibrations of blood pumping through the capillaries of his fingertips. Dowsing alone was inconsistent, unreliable. But then Amelia whispered words that gave the iron purpose. If magic had been cast here, the nail's point would show the direction it came from.

The thread trembled; Cormac tried to hold his hand especially still, but this was the trouble with physicality: the more you thought about holding still, being quiet, breathing slow, the harder controlling yourself got. Movement amplified.

Vibrations traveled down the thread, shuddered through the nail—which swung to point straight down.

Interesting, Amelia declared. *I said it felt like a hole. But this is some kind of vortex. There's a pull here.*

Is there still a danger? he thought to her.

I'm not sure.

He suddenly wanted to get the hell out of here.

What's next? Cormac prompted.

We need to have a very *good look around*, said Amelia. *Not just here. The whole area. To see if this is happening anywhere else. And to see why anyone would want to target* this *cabin over anywhere else.*

"Could Weber have done it to himself?"

I wouldn't have thought so—this isn't the cabin of someone magically inclined. But. . .we can't discount the possibility.

"You found something?" Domingo sounded hopeful.

Cormac shook his head. "Not sure. Need to look around some more, I think."

"Will this happen again or is it a one-time thing? How worried do I need to be?"

I don't know, Amelia admitted.

Maybe this was just about Art Weber. Maybe he'd just been in the wrong place at the wrong time. Maybe this was a one-and-done. Cormac's silence was answer enough—he was worried.

"I'll call you the minute I have something," he said.

They stepped back outside, and the sun seemed bright, and the air clean. The death and uncertainty, that creeping primal fear, was closed up in the cabin. Cormac suppressed a shudder.

There isn't much that frightens you like this, Amelia said.

Frightened might have been a strong word for it. But she was right—he didn't like it. Usually when he felt something off, he could tell what it was. He could at least make a guess and start hunting. He'd faced down werewolves, vampires, demons, ghosts— This was like water coming through the roof and he couldn't find the leak.

We'll find it. Her optimism could be annoying sometimes. She didn't have physical skin to feel the gooseflesh, or hair on the back of her neck.

As he and Domingo walked back to her truck, another truck pulled in behind them, a basic Chevy pickup ten or so years old. Maybe another Park Service official, Cormac thought, until Domingo groaned with annoyance.

"God, not again," she muttered.

A man in his forties climbed out of the truck and marched to intercept Domingo, fists clenched and eyes glaring. He was a white guy with thinning hair, wearing a rumpled button-up shirt, khakis, and hiking boots. An outdoors type. He gave Cormac a brief once-over and frowned. All his attention was on Domingo.

"Annie. What's going on? They tell me the area's still restricted."

Domingo reclaimed a professional demeanor, standing tall and relaxed, speaking evenly. "Mr. Peterson, hello. We can't open that area until we get the okay, and we haven't gotten it yet."

"Then it's true, that you won't let the police close the investigation?"

"It's not up to me one way or another."

"You just don't want me here anymore. You don't want me to continue my work, to finish my book—"

Domingo waited with apparent patience, as if she'd heard all this before. Finally, Peterson's rant landed on Cormac.

He pointed. "—And who is this? I suppose you're going to tell me he's part of the investigation? More like some buddy you brought in to gawk—"

The ranger's job might not allow her to step on this guy, but Cormac didn't have to take this. He stepped forward, stuck his hand out, and grinned aggressively. "Hey, name's Cormac, and you are. . .Peterson? Just Peterson?"

The man blinked, nonplussed, and reflexively took Cormac's hand. His grip was hesitant and he let go quickly.

"Elton. Elton Peterson."

"Elton, yeah, good meeting you." Cormac could be as backwoods amiable as Andy Griffith when he needed to be. Best part, it threw people off when they noticed his eyes weren't smiling. "As a matter of fact, Ms. Domingo here did ask me to come in and help with the investigation. You seem to think you know this area pretty well—you notice anything off around here over the last couple of weeks? Anything suspicious?"

The guy took a minute to stare, probably wondering if Cormac was for real. Cormac just smiled back at him with the patience of a rock.

Peterson shook his head quickly and looked away. Gritting his teeth, like he was trying to keep from shouting. "No, I didn't notice anything. I thought it was just an accident, the police said it was an accident, and it's very sad but I need to get back to my research—"

"You said you're writing a book?" Cormac prodded.

"I'm a historian. I'm writing about the Donner Party."

"Huh," Cormac said. "Seems like there can't be that much more to tell about the Donner Party. Folks have been writing books about it for a hundred and fifty years."

"Everyone thinks that. There's *always* more to say. And I've found something. I'm telling you, I know more about what happened than anyone, just wait—" He clamped his mouth shut, glared. Tried again. "And what exactly is your expertise?"

"Oh, nothing special, I'm just having a general look around."

Domingo stood back to watch this exchange, considering Cormac with particular interest.

Peterson simmered. "Oh yeah?" the historian shot back. "And what do *you* think happened here?"

Cormac shrugged offhand. "I'm not at liberty to say until the authorities close the investigation."

Peterson glared one last, fuming look before storming off. Out of the corner of his eye, Cormac saw Domingo hiding a smile.

"You didn't close that gate behind us on the way up, did you?" he said, his voice turned flat again.

She sighed. "No, I didn't. He must have passed by and seen it open. Like a big welcome mat. Arty was able to get him banned from the park entirely for awhile. He was hiking all over the backwoods without a permit, disrupting wildlife surveys. Whew, you should have seen the guy blow his gasket then. But Peterson took it to court, got the ban rescinded, and now here he is."

"Who all has a key for that gate at the end of the road? Does Peterson?"

"No, but that hasn't stopped him from parking and hiking up. The sheriff's office has one, most of the emergency services have a master key, the rangers, the handful of people who own cabins up here."

"So it's not hard to get past that gate."

"No. It's mostly there to discourage tourists, not to really close off the area."

Good to know. "What's Peterson's real story?"

"Just what he says. He thinks he's going to tell the real story of the Donner Party, like everyone else."

"And what's the real story, that they ate each other or they didn't?"

"It's what happens when you put a few dozen people in a pressure cooker. You know something'll pop, but nobody really agrees on how."

He looked around at the trees, at the bright blue sky beyond them. Chickadees were calling in the branches. "Yeah, sounds about right," he said. "And Peterson thinks he has a new 'how,' does he?"

"He won't tell anyone what it is. Doesn't want anyone stealing his idea."

Cormac chuckled. Yeah, the guy seemed like one of those. "Right," he agreed.

"So—you need anything else?" Annie said.

"A place to stay in town. A quiet place."

Truckee had two sides to it. "Old" Truckee was the tourist side of the town, where you couldn't get a hamburger for under $15 or a hotel room for under $200. Exactly the kind of mountain tourist town that made Cormac's skin crawl. Colorado was lousy with them, and he'd spent too much time in places like it as a kid, working instead of playing. Cormac had started going along on trips to help his father when he was a teenager. The façade of it all—the high-end stores in fake-log-cabin buildings, the so-called rustic vacation lodges that had granite counter tops and hot tubs—was symbolic of the prepackaged experiences people came here for. They didn't *really* want to rough it in the wild, just pretend like they could. And they needed people like Cormac's father, like Annie Domingo, to keep them from getting hurt.

Domingo directed him to the other half of town, that had an actual supermarket and looked like any modern main street of any small town. Normal, in other words. The old highway ran through here, from before the interstate went in, and this was where he found the old-style motor lodges and almost-forgotten vacation spots from decades before. Domingo guessed, correctly, that Cormac would be happier on this side of town.

He found a low-key place that had cabins tucked back by a rushing creek. He'd have plenty of space and privacy, and they rented by the week. The sign with "Donner Trail Inn" spelled out in rustic log-shaped letters might have dated from the fifties.

Everything around here seemed to be named "Donner" something. He couldn't tell if it was good branding or a kind of wretched product placement.

He went into the small lobby of the Donner Trail Inn, glanced over the rack of tourist brochures and the faded moss-green carpet, a refugee from another decade. He searched for a bell on the wood-laminate counter, found it, but didn't need to ring it, because a young woman dashed out of the back office at his approach. She had honey-brown hair in a ponytail, a round face, and adjusted her glasses as she looked Cormac over. She was maybe twenty. In college, working for the summer?

"How can I help you?"

"Need a room. One of the cabins if you have one. Farthest from the road."

She smiled happily. "I certainly do. And how long will you be staying with us?"

"Not sure. That a problem?"

Her smile grew sly. "It certainly isn't. My name's Trina, just let me know if there's anything I can do for you."

She tapped the keys of a very ancient computer and made some kind of affirmative noise. Cormac couldn't see the screen to tell what she was nodding at. She kept glancing at him out of the corner of her eye, her lips locked in a smile.

"I just need to get your name and information," she said, sliding a card across the table for him to fill out. Dutifully, he did so. She studied it when he handed it back over.

"So, Mr. Bennett, what brings you to town?"

"Just having a look around."

"Nice. It's a great town. You'll love it here."

"You from around here?"

"My whole life! My grandparents build this place!"

He tried to turn his wince into a smile. "Nice."

"I mean, why would I leave? And you know what? People come to visit here and like it so much they *never leave.* Half the people in town have a story like that! Car broke down, liked it so much they decided to stay. Came for vacation, liked it so much they just stayed. Neat, huh?"

Along with the sign out front, the keys on a plastic key ring—no magnetic key cards here—might have dated from the fifties. Trina put the key on the desk and kept her hand on it. He couldn't just reach out and grab it from her.

She beamed. "So, you know, just watch yourself. You might never leave, too!"

Through Amelia, he felt the sudden urge to make a warding sign against evil.

"We'll see about that," Cormac said, since he wasn't able to manage a polite chuckle.

Trina slid the key across the counter, along with a strip of paper with a wifi code on it, because God forbid anyone have a mountain vacation without internet access.

"Anything else I can help you with? Need a place to eat? Maybe rent a mountain bike or something? Anything?"

Cormac gathered the Donner Trail Inn didn't get a lot of business this time of year. Trina was leaning on the counter now, making it hard to look away from the low-cut scoop of her purple T-shirt. She wore a woven leather necklace and had a tattoo of roses on her left bicep.

Amelia seemed rather nonplussed, expressing roiling discomfort in the back of his mind. *What. . .is she. . .what would you call it?*

She's flirting, he thought back. He pressed his lips into a thin smile, amused and a little annoyed. Trina was cute because she was young and bright eyed, but she wasn't his type.

Do you have a type?

He had to think about that a minute. And realized he wasn't sure he did. He liked what he liked.

"I'll let you know," he said, leaving without a backward glance.

The photocopied map she'd given him highlighted which unit was his. She'd also written her name down and circled the phone number for the front desk. Just in case.

"What do you think so far?" Cormac asked, back in the fresh air and sunlight, crossing the parking lot to the row of little cabins nestled among sparse pines. A raven sailed overhead, and chickadees called from the trees. "Is Donner Pass haunted?"

You mean other than Art Weber's cabin? No sign at all. This place is so bright, it's the opposite of haunted. After another moment of thought she added, *You never hear so many birds around a place that's haunted.*

117

Five

First thing they did—or rather Amelia did—was cast protective magic over the room. Just a basic spell to keep the bad stuff out and make sleeping at night a little easier. In her first life, when Amelia was traveling all over the world, she made a habit of protecting her room wherever she stayed. She'd taken up the habit again, with Cormac. He was skeptical that the magic did much good. It might keep out an angry ghost, but wouldn't stop anyone who decided to drive a truck through the wall. The odds of either thing happening were pretty slim. But the spell didn't hurt anything, so why not? *The one time I don't do this will be the one time something terrible happens.*

They had an argument about whether lighting a sage smudge would violate the motel's no-smoking policy—$250 fine for smoking in the cabin, a plastic sign on the nightstand declared. Cormac thought it probably would, Amelia didn't much care, and when did Cormac worry about following the rules anyway? Answer: since he got off parole after his felony conviction. Given the unknown nature of what they were investigating, Amelia was adamant: they needed the spell, and the spell needed incense. They could add any fines to their list of expenses when they handed Domingo the bill.

You could probably persuade that very helpful young woman at the front desk to dispense with any fines, should the issue arise.

Cormac didn't want to go near that conversation.

So they cast the spell, filled the room with haze from a smoldering bundle of sage, and hoped they wouldn't need it. When Amelia murmured the last syllable of her chant, using his voice, Cormac felt something like a wall going up, a thin sheet of bluish light, invisible to anyone who didn't know what to look for. He did breathe a little better when it was done.

Next, he wanted to have a look around town. He found a sporting goods store where he bought a detailed map of the area, and put a mark at the rough location of Art Weber's cabin. The road it was on barely showed up as a faint dotted line. The woods around here probably had dozens of cabins tucked away on back roads, in addition to the ones prominently overlooking the lake. Still, the area had some remote stretches—part of the Pacific Coast Trail went through here. The Tahoe National Forest reached in all directions.

Amelia circled maybe a dozen or so areas equally spaced around the location of Weber's cabin. She wanted to raise her pendulum and take readings at each spot—a magical survey. An almost scientific approach, taking measurements that would help them discover if whatever supernatural influence they'd located only affected that one spot—if this was an isolated event—or if that magical sink they'd sensed had appeared anywhere else.

They started in the woods around the state park visitor center and worked in a circle, west toward the glacial lake between the town and the mountain pass, east toward the town. It took longer than Cormac expected. Not every spot Amelia wanted to check was on a road or hiking trail. In a couple of spots he had to park at a trailhead then hike a mile or so to some grove of tangled underbrush or granite outcrop.

One of the spots was just a few feet off of a scenic overlook. A couple of other cars were parked there. None of the tourists made his nerves twitch, and they didn't even stare when he left the pavement and went through the underbrush. When Amelia found the place she wanted, it turned out to have a view, looking out over a stretch of forested hills to the east, across the lake, to the town beyond. This was the view the Donner Party might have seen if they'd made it this far and bothered to turn around to look.

Weber's cabin was visible from here only because Cormac knew where to look. Its brown shingled roof made an angular line at odds with the vertical trees around it. From here, it looked harmless. Normal. He didn't sense anything like what he'd felt passing through the doorway.

Ready?

"Yeah."

Amelia slipped into his limbs, taking charge of his nerves. She grounded them both, taking stock of the space around them as he uncoiled the nail pendulum. He expected it to swivel, then point decisively to the cabin. But just like at every other spot they'd tried so far, the nail shivered, then pointed straight down before going slack as if tired. Unlike at the cabin, the nails didn't stay pointed. They jerked in the one direction, then returned to neutral. The farther from the cabin, the less the nail moved. The effect disappeared about five miles away in all directions—at least the directions they could check. He didn't feel the need to climb the ridge that rose up south of the cabin. This much should give them something to work with.

I don't like this, Cormac. It's like some kind of bomb went off and flattened the atmosphere around it.

Back at their room, Amelia worked on the map, adding markings, interpreting what they found. She consulted one of her standard research books, one of the first things she'd asked him to track down when he'd gotten out of prison: a study of ley lines, maps marked with color-coded lines and dots that supposedly represented veins and roads of magic existing deep in the earth all over the world. According to these maps, a couple of lines passed through the area, and she copied their routes over her increasingly crowded markings.

When they sat back to regard the whole picture, they found a swirling mass of magical influences, flows of power saturating the area. Nothing indicated why Weber's cabin should be the focus of whatever it was they'd discovered.

"Could what happened to Weber be connected with the Donner Party in any way?"

No, she said, which surprised him. She rarely made such decisive declarations. Usually it was probably not, or I don't believe so. *Look at the map. I've marked the presumed locations of the campsites where the party made shelter, the spots where the deaths occurred, even the ones along the pass and beyond. None of them correspond in any way to Weber's cabin or the ley lines, or influence reaching beyond it.*

She indicated a trio of squares near the visitor center— the Donner Party's campsites. Another set of squares marked a few miles east—the party had separated before getting trapped for the winter. The Donner family itself was at that eastern location.

Mostly, Cormac was amazed that this much information survived about the Donner Party, to be able to mark the deaths on a map.

They're still making archeological investigations to learn more about what happened. It's an obsession with some people.

"Peterson?"

Indeed.

"What now?"

I need more information, she said, with an intensity that might have been, if he could say it, obsessive.

Time to hit the books.

The local library was rustic, but honestly so, a small brown building tucked into yet another collection of pine trees—and right next to the sheriff's department, Cormac noted. He wasn't doing anything wrong, no reason he ought to draw suspicion. A bunch of kids' drawings decorated the library windows.

The nice cardigan-wearing woman at the counter smiled briefly at him as he entered and turned back to whatever she was doing. The place was soft and insulated. Safe, which should have been comforting.

First, he found the local newspapers going back to Weber's death, and read everything he could. He didn't learn much more than Domingo had told him and what he'd read online. The man didn't have much family, wasn't married, and didn't have kids, which was a small comfort, he supposed. Weber had been a popular guide and ranger. He was an authority on the white-headed woodpecker, a local rarity. People liked him. They'd miss him. And he didn't seem like the kind of guy who'd kill himself. There was no reason someone like him should have died so mysteriously—and no reason that he shouldn't, if he was in the wrong place at the wrong time.

Like a lot of libraries in tourist towns, this one had a section of local books about the area. Places like this always had a couple of local authors who collected folklore and stories of regional interest, publishing them in pamphlets just a couple of steps up from homemade. And yes, he found a few by Elton Peterson, the angry historian. He'd written biographies of several of the main figures from the tragedy; an entire book discussing the children who were part of the expedition— as depressing a subject as Cormac could imagine, so he didn't even crack the cover on that one—and another covering the equipment and survival techniques the members of the party would have used to set up their not-particularly-successful camp. As far as Cormac could tell from skimming the work, Peterson hadn't done much original research—the archeological information in that last book was all done decades ago, and he compiled it from other sources and recycled it into the newer book. He'd talked about a new book in his rant at Domingo. Cormac wondered what could possibly be left to cover.

Amelia took notes. Just in case, she insisted. It was probably most noteworthy that they didn't find anything new and interesting. The Donner story was tragic, but it wasn't supernatural.

Next stop was the local historical society, which could be another font of quirky and often useful information in a town like this. What stories were important to the town itself, maybe overshadowed by the notoriety of the Donners? Then again, it might just be a room with lots of black and white pictures of Fourth of July parades of yesteryear. Amelia didn't want to miss anything, so they looked.

The society had a small cabin at one end of a standard city park, with ball fields and a playground, a few kids playing and people throwing sticks for dogs. It all would have looked innocuous except for a couple of vans and a big SUV parked near the cabin, blocking out half the lot, and a series of traffic cones marking out an area of the grassy lawn nearby. The reason for the presumptuous claim of public space became clear quickly: the nearby cluster of people included a man with a big video camera, another with a mike boom, and a few of the others were wearing historical costumes, cheap nineteenth century pioneer outfits, shirts and trousers, skirts and shawls, floppy hats and sunbonnets.

Somebody was filming something. Cormac wondered if the costumes looked as fake to Amelia as they did to him.

How am I supposed to know if they look real? Those costumes represent an era well before my time, she answered with a huff. *You do realize the nineteenth century was a hundred years long, don't you?* She added, *But yes, they look fake.*

An energetic young man emerged from the back of one of the vans. He had slicked-back dark hair and wore expensive-looking shirt and trousers. Clapping his hands, he started calling out orders. The cameraman and mike operator took positions at one end of the grassy stretch, and the people in costume—actors—straightened skirts and hats and moved toward the other end of the grass, against a backdrop of trees, the one and only place they could be filmed without the modern buildings, roads, wires, and so on, intruding. One of them dropped a half-burned cigarette and stomped it out.

The energetic man must have been the director. Cormac scanned the vans for some kind of production company logo, but they looked like plain white rentals. A few more people were on hand with clipboards, bottles of water, and other odds and ends. Some of the dog walkers wandered over, and one of the women with a clipboard marched over to them. "Move along, folks. We've got people working here, we need you to stay out of the way."

That didn't really help. This was too interesting to just walk away from.

"Okay, people! This is part one of the Fort Bridger scene, everybody know where we're at?"

Amelia observed, *Fort Bridger is a thousand miles away, in Wyoming. What are these people doing?*

Cormac believed they were filming a dramatic reenactment for some kind of documentary.

"All right!" the director checked in with his crew while the actors took up places they'd obviously discussed or rehearsed. "Ready? Action!"

Two of the men in costumes began arguing. "We should continue on the old route! It's the safest way!"

"No!" said the other. "This new shortcut will be faster! It will shorten our journey by three hundred miles!"

"But we know nothing about the route and we have no guide!" They made expansive gestures and over-enunciated in a way that made Cormac wince.

"How hard can it be?" the second man declared. Cormac couldn't tell if this was intended to sound as ironic as it did.

Oh dear Lord, are they reenacting the Donner Party? Amelia seemed horrified by the idea.

One of the actresses hefted a bundle of cloth, bouncing it against her shoulder like she would a baby, but exaggerated. The whole thing was exaggerated. "Darling! I'm afraid!" she declared, clinging to the man arguing for the shortcut.

"Don't be, my dear! I know what I'm doing!" The man turned forward, gazing into some invisible distant horizon. They looked very much like the giant pioneer statue over at the state park. This might have been intentional. "Soon, we'll be in California and all will be well!"

"Great, great!" the director said. "Now, let's do it again. Take two!"

Ignoring the film shoot, which had nothing to do with him, Cormac headed over to the Historical Society building. Turned out, the place was closed—a sign on the door helpfully indicated the society was only open three days a week, and not today.

"Sir! Sir, you can't be there, you're in the shot!" The woman with the clipboard hurried toward Cormac. As far as Cormac could tell, the camera pointed well away from him. He crossed his arms, and she hesitated, not coming any closer. "Uh, hi. Can I ask you to please move along? Just for a little while."

"You guys making some kind of movie?" he asked.

"A TV show, yes."

"About the Donner Party?"

"Y-yes?"

He nodded like she had revealed some deep dark secret. "Just give me one more minute." He went to the sashed window to the left of the door, cupped his face to the glass, and looked in.

"Sir!"

The windows weren't particularly clean; he didn't see much. Mostly framed black and white photos of stern men on horseback and parades.

Satisfied, he crossed to the other end of the lot and his Jeep. The director glanced his way, and Cormac caught his gaze. The director didn't look away right off; instead, he gave the impression of making some calculation.

Well, this should make our investigation more interesting.

Cormac sincerely hoped not.

Back at the Donner Trail Inn, Cormac dropped by the office. Trina again tore out of the back room as soon as she heard the door, and her face lit up when she saw him. Unfortunately. He resisted an urge to walk out and instead asked what he came to ask. She claimed to know everything about the area. Time to test that.

"You hear anything about filming down at the park?" he asked.

Trina's reaction was dramatic, as she slapped the counter and rolled her eyes. "Oh my God *yes*, I heard all about it, they're doing some kind of documentary for one of those history TV shows about the Donner Party, including recreations. Like, with kids sitting around campfires licking bones and that kind of thing, can you believe it? I mean there's always somebody or other coming through and making documentaries, but these are apparently *way* out there. The historical society isn't happy but the producer is paying the town off so what're you gonna do? Some of my friends are furious, they thought there'd be some kind of local casting call for extras or whatever, just people standing around in the background, you know? I have this friend who lives in L.A. and being an extra in crowds is, like, her *job*. She just stands around all day and makes pretty good money. Isn't that cool?"

"But these guys aren't hiring locals," Cormac prompted, hoping to move the conversation along.

"No, from what I hear this company does a lot of these reenactments for cable shows and crime shows and stuff and they have their own actors they bring in. Just think how much goodwill they'd get if they hired like at least *a few* locals—"

"You know how long they're supposed to be filming?"

She shrugged. "A week? Something like that?"

"Thanks. Another question—you know anything about Art Weber?"

"Oh my God, the ranger who died last week? That was so *weird*."

"Did you know him?"

"No, I didn't know him. But my friend Katie used to go out with him—just a few dates, you know? She ended up breaking it off because he was kind of a loner. And then he died. . .all alone. . . ." Her gaze went a little vacant.

"But you don't know of any rumors about him that might give an idea what happened?"

She shook her head. "People liked him. He was always around, helping out and stuff."

"What about Elton Peterson?"

At this, she gave a frustrated huff. "He's just your basic know-it-all. Oh my God, don't tell me you've run into him already."

"He was out at the state park."

"He's *obsessed* with the park. Keeps trying to get people to sign petitions to change the signs—not even the information on the signs, it's just that he wants to be the one to write them. He's not even local. He's originally from *Fresno!*"

"Right. Thanks." He turned to go, but she stopped him.

"Are you really a detective? Like a private detective, like on TV?"

"I'm not sure I'd go that far," he said. He was still trying to figure out what kind of detective he really was.

"So is there really something weird going on with Arty? Like some secret evidence that tells what really happened?"

Cop and detective TV shows tended to portray murder as some kind of baroque puzzle, with obscure pieces that only an intrepid hero could discover, that when assembled pointed to the most unlikely suspect imaginable, who had equally baroque reasons for wanting the victim dead. Murder in the real world hardly ever worked like that. Not even when the supernatural was involved. Sure, sometimes a murderer worked out an elaborate plot to kill someone in secret, without getting caught, usually for the most prosaic reasons—sex or money. But most murders were violent, sudden, messy, unpremeditated. People killed people they knew when they got angry. Nothing mysterious about it, and it was often just a case of tracing back the blood spatters, metaphorical or otherwise, to the person standing at the source of them. Trick to not getting caught was not to be the person standing in the spot the spatters all pointed to. Being a professional mostly meant knowing to not be standing where the evidence led back to. Cormac had only failed at that once; that was all it took.

Here, a magical bomb had gone off. Where did the blast point back to?

"Nothing as fancy as that," Cormac said. "I'm mostly just helping Ms. Domingo clean up the cabin."

Trina was clearly disappointed—this probably wouldn't make nearly as interesting gossip as some other tale about a horrifying secret behind Weber's death.

"Ah. And everything else? You getting around okay? You find the grocery store? Gas station?"

"Everything's fine."

"Okay, just let me know if—"

She might have still been calling after him, but he shut the door as he walked out.

I have an idea.

"Oh?" They were back in their sage-scented room, their maps and books spread around them. Night had fallen. He'd grabbed fast food for dinner, and his stomach wasn't thanking him for it. They had only arrived in Truckee that morning, after driving through the night. Really, they ought to sleep. He wasn't quite vibrating with exhaustion, but he was getting close.

Only speculation, really. Someone—or a group of someones—casting powerful spells and not cleaning up after themselves. Not using circles to ground the magic, but rather letting it simply. . .explode.

He could imagine the gesture, Amelia raising her arms and flicking her fingers out to demonstrate.

I want to set up a kind of. . .alarm. In case it happens again, we'll know and can perhaps track down the culprit.

"Can it wait till morning?"

I think so. But right now I want to look for ghosts.

"I thought you said—"

Indulge me.

The Donner Party camped over the winter of 1846 and '47 in two different locations. The first, the main camp, was near the lake, where the visitor center, monument, campground, and park were located. The bulk of the party stopped here, holing up in three cabins. The other camp was some six miles away, near Alder Creek, off a state highway, commemorated by a national forest turnout and trailhead. The Donner family itself, stymied by broken wagons and injuries, had stopped here and tried to tough out the winter under little more than a tent and tree branches. Most of them hadn't made it.

For decades, ghost hunters assumed the whole valley must be haunted. Over forty people had died in one long, drawn-out, horrifying event. Surely the place was saturated with supernatural energy.

Not necessarily, Amelia murmured.

Recently, ghost hunters had done all the usual, taken EMF readings, searched for EVP—but noise from the freeway complicated both those efforts. They always found the usual: vague feelings, unsubstantiated clues. Psychics had their opinions.

But the ghost of Tamsen Donner was said to walk between the two camps, a trek she'd made in life right before she'd died, and—possibly—been consumed by the main camp's last survivor, Louis Keseberg.

After dark, Cormac pulled into the parking lot, turned off the headlights, and shut off the engine. Once again, he had a feeling of disconnect. This landscape was so tame, so populous, how could he reconcile it with the stories of the Donner Party, the twenty feet of snow and pervasive death? Like the other locations significant to the story, nothing here gave any sign about what had happened. He didn't feel a lurking menace, no sense of dread. No hint of the spirits of those who'd died. No, this was another beautiful mountain meadow with a trickling creek running through, ringed by towering pines, all of it silvered by the light of a half-moon. Only the ubiquitous bronze commemorative slabs told the story of what had gone wrong here.

Time erases, Amelia said.

It did and didn't, Cormac thought. Of course a hundred and fifty years would change the landscape. But echoes remained. They changed the names of the pass and the lake to match the party. Everything around here was Donner. You could not know anything about the story and still have some inkling that something had happened here. Like an old battlefield with a single bronze plaque marking an event that no one but historians knew about.

Penlight in hand, he got out to walk around. This spot, some ways down an easy, well-groomed trail, had two markers: one where common belief said the Donner camp was located, and another some twenty feet away where archeological digs determined the camp probably was. Without a time machine, no one would ever know for sure. Unless Amelia decided to run some kind of séance and try to talk to one of the party.

Even then, any spirit raised might not know. The trees are different. The path of the creek will have changed. Memory is a tricky thing.

He kept the penlight pointed down, studied the grassy meadow as well as he could in the moonlight.

Walk that way a bit, I want to see something.

He got the feeling she wasn't looking for anything in particular—she just wanted to look. He scuffed his boots through the grass, drying out in high summer, panned the light back and forth for anything that might jump out.

Meanwhile, he also listened. Kept his awareness turned out to the stands of pines surrounding the meadow, to the shadows around the parking lot a couple hundred yards away. They'd escaped the truck roar on the freeway, but the night wasn't completely quiet, when he really listened. Trees creaked, a bit of underbrush rustled—one nocturnal creature hunting another.

There, Amelia murmured, and he sensed her frustration at not being able to simply reach out. If she wanted to badly enough, she could try to take control of his body—briefly, at least, before he fought back. At the beginning, he'd fought. The headaches had been mind ripping, and she hadn't succeeded. They cooperated now.

He looked for where she indicated, and finally saw it: the glint of something unnatural mostly buried in the dirt, hidden by grass. Crouching, he picked at it, brought it into the light. It was a small brown button, made of bone or horn, polished.

"This what you wanted?"

Yes. I wonder. . . .

The button was old—but probably not that old. This ground had been scoured over so many times, nothing from that time would have been left. Unless some tiny artifact—like a button—happened to bubble up from the ground and appear just for them.

I want to try something, she said, and pressed forward. She wanted his hands, his muscles, his voice, to work a spell that was too complicated to explain. Frustrated, he nonetheless relented. One of these days, he was going to know her entire catalog of spells, every possible thing she could pull out in a situation like this. He hadn't reached the end of her knowledge yet.

"And you never will," she murmured with his own voice, as he slipped to the back of his own mind.

She struck a match from his pocket, started a tiny fire with a bit of grass—and was careful to clear a space around it and keep it barricaded, in response to his spike of anxiety about accidentally setting the entire forest on fire. Sprinkled some herbal mix into it, releasing a scent of earth and spice. Whispered words like she always did, that he couldn't quite catch and could never quite remember. He was about to ask what this was supposed to do.

Something caught his—her—eye. She didn't notice, she was so intent on reciting the spell and pressing the old lost button between her hands, calling forth whatever thread of power she was searching for. He tried to get her to turn her head, or at least shift her gaze to a sliver of movement, light where there shouldn't be any. He didn't have as much practice catching her attention as she had catching his.

At last she flinched, startled into paying attention to him.

The faintest blur of fog had risen. The night was dry, the sky clear. This might have been the start of morning dew—except it wasn't morning and the gray mist only rose *here*, on this spot, some ten feet away. It had the shape of a woman. Details emerged: she wore a long skirt and a threadbare blanket over her shoulders, and stood with her hands folded before her. She gazed west as if waiting for someone to arrive from over the next hill.

"Tamsen Donner," Amelia breathed.

And the fog slipped away, melting back into the air.

So did Amelia, in that moment. She was so astonished that she slipped out of Cormac's body, back to her usual place lurking around his subconscious. He stretched his fingers and winced, adjusting to the feel of blood and breath again.

They stared at the space where the mist had formed—Cormac resisted calling it a ghost, that explanation seemed too easy—for a long time, waiting for something else to appear, for that unsettled prickling feeling to fade. Finally, Cormac stomped out the wisp of fire.

"Was that your spell?" he asked. "Did you do that?"

I fear it might have been coincidence. Suggestion. I'm not certain she was really a ghost. Merely an echo. Her pain, recorded on the ether. Just one bit of magic calling to another.

"What was your spell supposed to do?"

Recall history, she admitted. *Show a glimpse of what had happened. But when I've used it in the past it's mostly evoked noises and emotions, something linked to the artifact used to recall the image. I really doubt that button was a hundred fifty years old, however much I may wish it.*

"If you want to try again we could always swipe something from the museum at the visitor center."

That won't be necessary. She sounded a little testy. Maybe because she knew he could really do it, and get the artifact back in place when they were done before Annie Domingo found out.

This seemed a somber end to their first day on the job.

Six

The next morning Cormac called the hospital and a couple of local clinics to find out if there'd been any illnesses related to starvation or malnourishment. Since he wasn't asking about specific patients—he didn't bring up Weber's death—he hoped officials could tell him about broad trends. But no, the couple of administrators he managed to get on the line didn't think such a thing was possible. Eating disorders didn't generally come in waves, like he was suggesting. He couldn't get them to understand that he wasn't talking about eating disorders—this was something else. But didn't that generally happen, trying to talk about the supernatural? It didn't fit in the regular categories, so people didn't know what to think. They didn't have a paradigm to follow, and so what he described didn't—couldn't—exist.

I have heard of starvation magic being used in battle, Amelia offered. *A siege tactic, to hasten the suffering within a holding under attack. But spells of that type are usually directed at the food and water supplies— foul the wells, rot the food, the people will starve as a result. That isn't what happened here.*

So much magic worked slantwise—not directly at a thing, but near it. Sympathetic relations. That Weber just *starved,* within reach of food, for no medically obvious reason, was throwing them off.

Their next stop was back to Weber's cabin, to place Amelia's warning system. In the parking lot on the way to the Jeep, Cormac slowed, listened. Trina was standing outside the office, talking loudly on her phone. Her back was to him; he stayed hidden by the wall of the office.

". . .yeah, right. I don't know why he's here, he's asking a lot of questions. . . . Of course I'm keeping an eye on him! Well I don't know. I asked Mag at the diner and she said she talked to Mary over at the park, and Mary says Annie Domingo hired him for *something*. You think it has something to do with Arty? Between this guy asking questions and the Hollywood people it's like someone rigged this whole thing up as a publicity stunt. . .right? And it wouldn't even bother me that much except, you know, what actually *happened*? It's some sick joke, I'm telling you. Do I think this guy has something to do with it? Well, I don't know. . . . Yeah, he's cute—"

Cormac sidled away without a word, however fun it might be to tap her on the shoulder and watch her squirm. The Jeep was waiting at the other end of the parking lot.

Well, you are.

"What?"

Never mind.

The gate at the end of the dirt road to Weber's cabin was already open, so Cormac wasn't entirely surprised when he drove up and found a couple of SUVs and a utility van blocking the drive. At least a dozen people milled in the clearing in front of the cabin. Cormac pulled over and got out for a look around. Then he saw the cameras, the historical costumes, and a woman consulting a clipboard and marshalling forces—the one who'd yelled at him yesterday. The same film crew.

Cormac stood back to watch as some kind of order emerged from the chaos. The director, wearing a different set of slick clothes but with the same polished urgency, shouted, "Places!" and the camera operators took up positions, pointing toward a canvas lean-to set up under a stand of trees, near a weathered cabin wall. Two male actors in homespun trousers, shirts, boots, and large beards, arranged themselves in front of the cameras. One held an axe, and the two were arguing, presumably about the weather since they occasionally looked up at the sky with anguished expressions.

"If we don't cross the pass now, we'll never cross!" one actor solemnly told the other.

"But we can't go on! The storm's too bad. We'll. . .we'll have to wait it out."

"Then we're doomed!"

Both actors again gazed forlornly at the clear blue sky. The axe didn't seem to serve much purpose. Nobody in the Donner Party had axed another member, after all. It mostly seemed to be there to show that yes, these were pioneers. Or something.

"Cut!" the director called out, and the actors sagged. One of them walked over to an assistant who offered him a cigarette.

The caution tape was still up around the cabin. Didn't seem to bother anyone on the crew. A Forest Service pickup truck was parked across the way, hidden by the film crew's vehicles. Annie Domingo leaned on the hood, arms crossed, scowling. She must have been the one to open the gate.

The director spotted him and moved to intercept. However much he wanted to, Cormac couldn't ignore him. The guy was *right there*. He stood with his hand outstretched, and didn't miss a beat when Cormac refused to shake it.

"Hi, I'm Ford Bellamy. And I hear you're Cormac Bennett? Is that right? You have a couple minutes to talk?"

Cormac bristled. Small town—he could make a couple of guesses how Bellamy knew his name. "I'm busy, sorry." He couldn't imagine what Bellamy could have to say to him. Cormac walked around the guy, giving him a wide berth. Bellamy chased after him, still talking, like he was used to chasing after people who didn't want to talk to him.

"Um, so. . .I understand you're a detective investigating the Donner Party tragedy?"

Nothing obligated Cormac to talk to anyone he didn't want to. This basic fact made his life so much easier. People so often relied on the basic politeness of others to get what they wanted, and they always seemed so surprised that Cormac just didn't care.

Bellamy wouldn't take the hint. "Our company produces recreations of historical events, and right now we're making a documentary of the Donner Party. We're interviewing local experts for the show, and we'd love to get your perspective, to maybe talk about some of the more unexplained aspects of the tragedy—"

Cormac stopped, and the guy smiled, victorious. He probably thought everyone wanted to get on film.

Cormac said, "You going to recreate that scene where Betsy Donner fed her children flesh from their own father without telling them what it was?" Amelia had floated that tidbit up from the back of his mind, and he delivered it deadpan.

What did it say about Bellamy that his smile remained fixed? "Inspiring, isn't it, the lengths a mother will go to ensure her children's survival?"

"I'm not a historian, I'm not investigating the Donner Party. You don't want to talk to me." Again, he turned away, and again Bellamy followed. He was reaching out, like he might grab Cormac's arm. The whole time, Domingo was watching from her truck with a kind of wide-eyed appreciation.

"But Mr. Bennett, I think you could really add something to our production. You'll be compensated of course."

He thought about that for half a second and decided he wasn't that hard up. "There's another guy you should talk to—Elton Peterson? I bet he'd love to be on your show."

While Bellamy might have been able to keep his smile in place, he couldn't suppress the eye roll. "That guy would like nothing better than to be our expert commentator. To be *the* expert commentator. But what can I say—he's just not good in front of a camera."

What a punchable smile Bellamy had. Cormac shook his head and tried, again, to walk away.

"But wait! You *are* a detective, right?"

This time, Bellamy actually grabbed his arm. Actually touched him. The only reason Cormac didn't punch him was Amelia anticipating him and whispering, *Calm, calm. . . .*

So, with a great deal of calm—he thought—he stepped away from the other man and out of his grip.

The producer's smile finally fell, as if he realized how close he'd come to injury. He blinked, owl-like, at Cormac, who continued over to Domingo. She seemed to be trying not to chuckle.

"Could have used some help there," he said flatly.

"I wanted to see if you were really going to deck him," she said. "What stopped you?"

"Intervention from the great beyond." Amelia humphed at this. "So how is it everybody around here knows about me?"

"Trina at the inn likes to talk," she said. "And she knows *everyone.*"

"I'm used to being a little more under the radar."

"Too small a town for that, Mr. Bennett. So, have you found anything?"

"I was hoping to do a little work here. Didn't expect all this." He waved at the vans and SUVs. Some of the actors were drinking coffee now, while part of the crew cleared a spot in the underbrush to set up some lights on tripods. In broad daylight. He didn't get it.

"Yeah, I had to let them in. They thought it would be 'atmospheric.'" She shook her head. "They're apparently paying the town a lot of money. But getting in the cabin shouldn't be a problem."

He nodded at the cabin. "What's going to happen to it when this is all over."

"It's Forest Service property, so as soon as I let them sign off on it, we'll clean it out and assign it to the next researcher."

"That's why you're getting pressure to close the investigation?"

"Yeah. But I seem to be the only one who thinks this could happen again, and I can't risk that."

"Even if we do figure out that something weird's going on here, I don't know if I can guarantee it'll never happen again. Not much about this is ever cut and dry."

"I know," she said, sighing.

The longer the cabin stayed empty, the dustier and lonelier it would feel.

The place could use a good cleaning. Magical and otherwise, Amelia observed.

Then why not do it? he thought in response. Clean the place, set an alarm in case that magical vortex struck again. If nothing else, they'd all feel a little better being here.

He went around the whole building, gathering up tape into a huge messy armful, then went back and dumped it in front of the truck, next to Domingo.

"Cleaning house?" she asked.

"Something like that," he said.

All right, we've done this before. Salt, candles, sage.

He could almost picture Amelia rolling up her sleeves and brushing her hands. After gathering materials from her kit in the Jeep, he let her take over, stepping to the back of his own mind. She'd do the work; he'd keep watch. He could still hear and see out of the corners of her vision, sound and movement she wasn't paying attention to while she cast the spell. He became her subconscious, tapping into an awareness she wasn't connected to. If anything happened, he'd shout.

Some of the film crew and actors had stopped to watch him. Bellamy in particular had his hand on his chin, looking thoughtful.

Never mind, we're here to do a job.

A circle of salt poured out of a small tin, candles at the cardinal points, a lit bundle of sage—they were running out of sage—and the words of a spell that Cormac still didn't know by heart since half of it was in Latin and half in what Amelia said was Egyptian. He took her word for it. Three times they circled the house, and back at the north candle she kicked an opening in the salt circle and snuffed the candle with her—with his—hand. And something changed, as if a breath of wind blew out from the house.

Domingo, waiting at the front of the cabin and looked around in wonder. "I felt something. What was that?"

"Check it out," he said. Amelia retreated, and he stepped into his body again. Stretched his fingers, popped a kink out of his neck. Took a comforting breath of clean air to anchor himself. Domingo unlocked the front door and cautiously stepped in. Cormac followed.

The place still smelled musty and sad, but the sense of doom was gone. The place felt abandoned now, not cursed. Domingo sighed as if waking up from a sleep.

"It's gone," she said, amazed. "Whatever you did. . .it's gone."

Not really. The prickling on the back of his neck was still there—they still didn't know what had caused the dank scent of dark magic in the first place. It could still come back. "One more thing I need to do," he said.

He sorted through his pockets—he was going to have to do a major cleaning and overhaul when he got back to the room this afternoon, since he didn't know what he had left in them anymore. But Amelia seemed to know. She knew everything.

Does the plumbing here still work?

Cormac tried the faucet at the kitchen sink, and water ran from the tap.

Even better. Water from the same place will anchor the spell even more firmly.

He held a strip of paper under the stream for a moment, just enough to soak but not so much that it would disintegrate. Following Amelia's instructions, he tied a piece of red string around the paper strip, and tied the other end of the string to a spot in the middle of the room, to a bolt sticking out under the kitchen table. From this spot it was exposed to almost everything going on in the room, yet would be invisible to someone giving the place a cursory look-over.

He must have looked awkward, kneeling under the table, craning up to see, but this was what Amelia wanted so here he was. He closed his eyes, let out a breath—and Amelia was the one who whispered words over the ensemble of materials. Laid out a teaspoonful of incense under the paper, which went up in a flash at the touch of a match and left a spicy scent in the air.

"What is this?" Domingo had been standing watch at the open door, her attention divided between keeping an eye on the film crew outside and watching Cormac. Her nose wrinkled.

"I guess you could think of it as an early warning system," Cormac said.

"So if this is happens again, we'll know?"

It was a little more complicated than that. "Sure," he said.

The strip of paper was dry now, the incense a smudge of ash on the floor, and Amelia retreated. Whatever she needed to do was done, but she had one last instruction for him.

Carefully, he tore the strip in half, left the one piece hanging under the table, and folded the other half and put it in his pocket. If something happened to the first strip, if some kind of magic affected it, the torn piece would be affected as well. They'd know, and maybe be able to get out here to see what it was.

He managed to crawl out from under the table without bumping his head, brushed off his jeans, and considered. He could almost feel the torn piece humming in his pocket, and couldn't decide if he wanted it to go off— smoke or buzz or whatever it was going to do—or wished it wouldn't. He just wanted to *fix* this.

"Now we wait."

Domingo locked the cabin behind them with a sense of finality. "I guess that's it then."

Cormac looked at her. "How so?"

"Part of what's been keeping me from letting them close the case is just how. . .wrong this place felt. That whatever happened to Arty would happen again, as long as that evil was there. Well, now it's gone. I'm going to have to let them open the cabin back up."

"Not sure that's the best idea."

"At some point we have to move on. You fixed the big problem."

"And whatever caused that problem is still out there," he said.

Bellamy was waiting for them outside the cabin.

"Just what exactly are you investigating up here, Mr. Bennett?'

"Oh you know, the usual." Cormac gestured around at the crew setting up for the next bit of filming. "What's this scene supposed to be about?"

"George Donner and James Reed are deciding if they should push on or stay and wait out the storm."

Well, at least the dialog was on the nose. Of course this would be the storm that ended up dropping twenty feet of snow on the area. He looked around at the sun-dappled woods on a bright summer day. "Shouldn't there be some, you know, snow?"

"We'll CGI that in post. You know, I'm still looking for expert witnesses. I think you'd be perfect. We'll give you the script."

Cormac wasn't an expert on anything, and he didn't want to end up on TV. "No," he said over his shoulder, walking with Domingo back to their vehicles. Just in time to get out of the way as another truck barreled up the drive and threw up gravel as it slid to a halt. Elton Peterson just about fell out of the driver's seat. He hadn't appeared to have changed clothes since yesterday, or maybe he just had a lot of the same flannel shirt. The historian glanced at Cormac and Domingo, blinked in what seemed to be surprise, but then stalked toward his original target: Bellamy.

Peterson leaned into his rant, just about spitting at Bellamy while pointing at the cabin.

"You don't have permission to use this spot for your. . .your *theater.*"

"Actually, we do." Bellamy waved a hand and one of his college-age PAs scurried over, holding out a clipboard like an offering. "All the Forest Service and California State Park System permissions are right here. We've paid to be here for a full week, and the filming license is in order. This is all publicly posted at the Forest Service Office."

"You should be talking to *me*. I know this history better than anyone. Nobody from the Donner-Reed Party even stopped at this spot!"

"Sir, I need to ask you to leave," Bellamy said patiently.

"I—I'll give you my new book, the one I'm working on. You'll see, what I've discovered—you should be talking to *me*!"

Bellamy called over to the ranger. "Ms. Domingo? Can we maybe call the sheriff's department to get this guy out of here?"

Peterson managed to look both helpless and full of rage. His eyes bulged, his fists clenched. Cormac straightened, because however laughable the guy looked, he was boiling over. "You have *no* respect for history, for the Donner Party, for. . .for *anything*! People *died*, and this is how you honor them, with this garbage?"

"Yes, actually. We're an educational show. Mostly." Bellamy's smile conveyed an awareness of little ironies.

Peterson did not appear to have a sense of irony whatsoever. He lunged at Bellamy, shouting in fury.

Half of Bellamy's crew lurched to try to grab one or the other of the men; the other half scurried out of the way. Bellamy mostly dodged, so Peterson only clipped his jaw rather than knocking him over. The two switched places in preparation for the next go-around. Cormac chose this moment to act. The actor playing Reed was trying to wade in, but Cormac shoved him aside, grabbed Peterson's shirt, and hauled backward. The man kicked and flailed, but Cormac stayed behind him, out of reach, and nothing connected.

With the instigator out of the mix, everyone else fell back and recovered. Bellamy had a cut lip but was grinning. He probably really did enjoy this.

Cormac dropped Peterson and stepped away, out of reach. The guy'd run out of fight and sat in the dirt, panting.

The cameramen were filming the whole time. Cormac glared at them.

"What are you *doing*?" Peterson yelled at him.

"Saving your ass." The actor with the large beard and axe was standing off to the side, holding it like he might use it.

Bellamy pointed, clearly gleeful. "This is all on film. I'll go straight to the sheriff and have you charged with assault unless you get the hell away from my shoot right now."

Peterson straightened, brushing himself off. Marked Bellamy, Cormac, and Domingo like he was trying to memorize their faces. Then he climbed into his truck, slammed the door hard, and took about three Y-turns to work his way out of the drive and back to the road, while everyone stood watching and he grew increasingly flustered, bent over the steering wheel like he could use it to physically lift the car.

He might be laughable, but this worries me. The stakes here are so low, and yet—

"Thanks for your help," Bellamy said, extending his hand to Cormac, who still refused to shake it. "I owe you one. I'll tell you what—if you don't want to be my expert witness, you want to be an extra? Just a bit part in the background, one of the teamsters in the party maybe."

"No."

He and Domingo walked away, out of earshot. Bellamy went back to the shoot, and the actors went back to worriedly looking up at the treetops as if it were snowing.

"Peterson's really getting to be a problem. I'll talk to the sheriff about him," she said.

"Probably a good idea," Cormac said. "I'll check in with you tomorrow, if that's okay."

"Thank you, Mr. Bennett."

He gave her a lazy salute and headed back to the Jeep.

Peterson was waiting for him at the bottom of the hill. His truck was pulled across the road; Cormac didn't have a choice but to stop.

Elton Peterson stood by his truck, arms crossed. His manner was still hunched over and squirrelly, like he was on the cusp of something earth-shattering that was weighing him down and fraying his nerves. Cormac didn't have time for this. But, as he expected, Peterson got right in front of him and stared him down.

"So. Did Bellamy ask you to be on his show?" Peterson demanded. He was probably trying to be calm.

"You mind pulling the truck over so I can get by?"

"Who are you, that he asks you and not me?"

He doesn't really expect an honest answer to that. . . .

"I don't know," Cormac drawled, looking off into the trees, giving one of his country-boy shrugs. "Don't really understand those Hollywood types."

"No, I mean it," Peterson said, stepped forward. "Who are you?"

If he got any closer, Cormac would be very tempted to deck the guy. Assault charge, that post-conviction ticker in the back of his head reminded him. So he took a breath and just stared. "I'm just looking into some things for Annie Domingo."

"Art Weber? Is that what you're looking into? He was just as bad as all the rest of them, he didn't understand, not really."

"And what is it we're all supposed to be understanding?"

"The possibilities."

Cormac tilted his head, asking silently. What was it the guy had found, or thought he'd found?

Peterson shook his head, as if acknowledging that he'd said too much. "You won't find it. People have been in this valley for a hundred and fifty years looking for something. They haven't found it. None of them." His eyes blazed, and the tiniest smile twitched on his lips. "Stay out of my way, Mr. Bennett. Everyone needs to stay out of my way."

He clambered back in his truck, roared down the road.

What has he done? Cormac—what has that man gone and done?

"I have no idea," he murmured, watching the dust kicked up by Peterson's departing car.

Seven

melia paced back and forth, her skirt swishing through the lush grass of their shared meadow. "I wouldn't have thought the man had a magical bone in his body, much less the knowledge to evoke. . .well, whatever it is that's been evoked."

"The memory of starvation," Cormac murmured.

Frowning, she looked at him. "Well yes. Exactly."

They'd argued, after Peterson drove away. Cormac wanted to go after him right that moment, run him off the road, put his hands around his throat and demand answers. Amelia argued for restraint, and not just because Cormac couldn't afford to get caught assaulting someone. "If he really did do something that resulted in Weber's death—on purpose, even—we hardly want to confront him directly. Neutralize his power first."

Which sounded good, but they didn't know what his power was. The hint of a magical vortex, the open knife, the scrap of bone. Nothing in Amelia's catalog of experience accounted for it. She needed to think. They needed to plan.

And so, however much he hated the idea of doing nothing, he went back to the motel, had dinner, and went to bed early. Sort of went to bed. Rather, he dreamed, and watched Amelia pacing.

In the valley in his mind, the one place he could look at Amelia— or at least an image of her, whatever that meant—he studied the map she'd spread out on a rock. She'd reproduced their map of the area—or drew on his memories to create an image of it, he still wasn't sure of the mechanics and didn't think about it too much. She'd marked it up with circles and diagrams to show what they'd done, what spikes of magic they'd found, and speculated about what might happen next. The Alder Creek campsite, all by itself on the upper right corner, had a star in a different color. They'd encountered something there, but it wasn't connected to the magic centered around Weber's cabin. Probably.

It should be her with the body, dealing with all this. He felt like a poor translator.

"Does it bother you?" he asked.

"Of course it does, if Peterson really is some amateur would-be wizard dealing with powers of which he has no idea and little control—"

"No, I mean. . . this." He gestured around at their meadow, the place in his mind they shared, this strange dream-place existence. The one place they stood face to face.

"Oh. Being effectively if not actually dead? I try not to think of it. I have plenty of other things to think about instead. I'm finally learning Aramaic, after all—when you'll actually open the book. This is certainly better than it was, trapped in a brick wall with no access to the world. You can smell the pines and revel in that sensation, and I can appreciate that feeling, even if I can't smell them myself."

"Can't you?"

She closed her eyes, tipped back her head, took a deep, full breath that she didn't need and wasn't real.

"Almost. . .like I'm right at the edge. . .and then. . .it vanishes." She opened her eyes and frowned. "I sometimes think of the mummies in Egypt. The mummification process was meant to preserve them for the afterlife, so they could continue on as they were, in wealth and luxury. And I think—is this it? Is this some sort of afterlife? If we traveled to Egypt, would I meet the old pharaohs, lounging on their boats on the Nile, ancient spirits living strange little half lives?"

Someone clever would probably offer some kind of sympathy, some kind of comfort. But he didn't know what to say.

"I am grateful for what I have, for what I'm able to do," she said, determined. "We will meet true death someday, you and I. No need to rush into it. In the meantime, we have work to do."

Pure impulse made him reach out and tuck a strand of her hair back behind her ear. This cleared the view of her profile, the slope of pale cheek, the slender shape of her nose. Glinting dark eyes turned on him, startled but unafraid.

The touch was real. The impulse, the gesture, even if the physicality of it was an illusion, nothing more than shared neurons.

"You're smiling," she observed. A question was implicit in the statement. And then he couldn't stop smiling.

"Yeah, I guess I am," he said. He couldn't have said why, but she didn't ask. Why didn't matter. Just that he was smiling, and wasn't that a thing?

Then she smiled too. "There are a number of spells—more active protection than throwing sage and salt around a room. They're rather generic—it would be useful to know exactly what we're up against—but we can perhaps throw them at Peterson and do some good that way."

"A curse?"

"No. . .more like a wall. We just have to contain the man."

"Can't hurt," he agreed.

She pursed her lips, touched her nose, looking especially thoughtful. How many times had she stood like that in life, considering some problem or other? Did she even realize her quirks had followed her into her afterlife? "I don't suppose we can get a lock of hair from him, or a fingernail clipping?"

"What was that about assault charges?"

"Right then. We'll work with what we have."

Part of him never really slept, waiting for. . .something. There was always something. It wasn't paranoia—he'd been a hunter too long not to be aware of what was coming up behind him, and there was usually something coming up behind him. So when a knock came at the door, he merely opened his eyes. Nothing startling about any of it. The sky outside the window was dark. Middle of the night, chilled and quiet as stone.

Cormac reached for a gun at the bedside that wasn't there. Clenched his fist in frustration.

Something's wrong, terribly wrong.

Yes, of course it was. He checked his phone, in case he'd missed a call or message. Nothing. Time was shy of midnight. He'd slept through the evening.

The knock at the door came again, and Trina's voice called, "Mr. Bennett? Cormac, are you in there?"

Wearing nothing but sweatpants at the moment, he wasn't especially interested in opening the door. Let her think he was a sound sleeper.

"Cormac," Trina called again from the other side of the door, her voice fast and anxious. "I know you're here because your Jeep is here and the police are here and really want to talk to you."

He rubbed his face. Then he smelled smoke.

He froze. Nothing seemed to be on fire. This was a flash, like catching a whiff of cigarette smoke. It jolted his nerves.

Oh no.

He'd left his jeans flung across the end of the bed. The front pocket, where he'd left the other half of the magical alarm, was warm. When he reached in, he found only ash.

We need to get to the cabin.

Yeah, but first they had to get past the police outside.

"Just a minute!" he called as he pulled on clothes. He also called Domingo. The phone went straight to voice mail. Cormac paused. He tried again—it was late, she didn't strike him as being much of a night owl. Maybe she'd just shut her phone off. Or maybe something was wrong. "Goddamn it."

Taking a deep breath, he opened the door and found Trina looking back at him, along with a pair of burly men in beige state trooper uniforms.

Cormac didn't want to talk to cops. He didn't want to deal with the police ever again in his whole life, if he could help it. He'd been off parole for a year, he shouldn't have this reflexive knee-jerk. . .annoyance at seeing men in uniform trying to stare him down. But he was still a convicted felon, and he could assume that Trina told them everything she knew about him, that they'd run the Jeep's license plates, and when you had a mystery no suspect looked quite as good as the one who already had a record.

This will be fine. They are not the enemy.

Yes, they are, Cormac muttered back at her. They had their own agenda. They got in the way.

Trina's nose wrinkled. "You haven't been smoking in there, have you?"

Cormac stepped out, leaving the door cracked. "What is it?" he asked evenly. If he tried to sound innocent he'd only sound more guilty.

"Cormac Bennett? That Jeep in the parking lot is yours?" The cop pointed at the only vehicle in the lot with Colorado plates.

"Yeah." He read the names on their badges, Jankowitz, Stanley. He ought to ask for their identification. He didn't really want to stall these guys.

"Ford Bellamy. You know him?" The shorter one was doing all the talking. He was a white guy, stocky, with a buzz cut. The taller one was blond and glared at Cormac like he expected him to bolt, and yes, his right hand was at the holster on his belt.

Cormac let out a breath. He'd expected them to mention Annie Domingo.

"Yeah, just met him yesterday. He tried to rope me into his film thing, but I said no."

"Too busy? And what're you doing in the area? A long way from home, aren't you?"

"Not that long. I'm just looking into a few things for Annie Domingo over at the state park." There, that got him a uniform on his side. The taller of the two cops still looked like he was waiting for Cormac to do something threatening. Trina stood to the side, looking back and forth with round eyes.

"When was the last time you saw Bellamy?"

"This afternoon at the park's research cabin. Why, what's happened?"

"He's missing," Officer Stanley said.

"Oh yeah?" Cormac tried to sound startled. But he wasn't surprised. They needed to get out of here, now. . . .

"Yeah. We're checking in with all the people who saw him last."

"You talked to Elton Peterson yet? The two of them argued this afternoon. Domingo was there, she'll tell you."

The two officers glanced at each other. "We haven't been able to reach Annie yet. We're still looking for Peterson."

Shit, Cormac thought, and felt Amelia's urgency as a jolt in his hindbrain.

"You seen any of them since this afternoon?" Stanley pressed.

"'Fraid I haven't."

"Found your record," he said next, as if this was a surprise. "Seems like you've been around a lot of missing people in your time."

Cormac almost chuckled, because that was such a roundabout way of putting it. "Yeah, I can see how you'd think that. How about if I hear anything about Bellamy I'll let you all know?" He needed to circumvent this conversation entirely. He needed to get back to the cabin.

Stanley drew a business card out of his trouser pocket and handed it over. Standard contact info. "I'd appreciate it if you'd do that."

The two went back to their patrol car; from inside, a radio scratched out indecipherable news.

"What's going on?" Trina asked, still gaping.

"We need to get ahold of Annie Domingo. She's not answering her phone."

"I'll try calling. I know her neighbor, I'll call her too, have her knock on the door of her house—"

"No," Cormac said, holding out a hand. "No one goes into her house. No one gets close. Just keep calling, maybe she'll answer."

"Okay. Okay, yeah. I'm sure everything's okay—"

"And Elton Peterson. You have any idea where he is?"

"He lives south of here, out on the highway. I don't have his number, I mean who'd *want* his number—"

"You think you can find out where he is right now?"

She nodded quickly. "Yeah, yeah, I think I can do that."

"Good. You find out, and call me. Don't talk to him, nobody goes near him. Call me, got it? Here's my number—"

"I already have it. It's on your registration card."

He smiled back. "You think that's my real number, you got something to learn about paranoia."

Her eyes widened. Then she grinned. "Yes, sir."

The missing director wasn't his problem. Let the cops deal with that.

Except he disappears, and the warning alarm at the cabin goes off?

Amelia didn't believe in coincidences. Worry about the cabin first, then Bellamy. The cabin was the center of it all.

"So tell me this," he said out loud, as they roared up the service road toward Weber's cabin. The alarm had been triggered; the slip of paper in his pocket had burned to ash. Whatever had gotten to Weber had returned. "Bellamy and maybe Domingo are both missing. Peterson's pissed off at both of them, which means he's also pissed off at me. So why are we okay?"

I told you we'd need that protection magic someday.

He gripped the steering wheel, wrestling the Jeep around curves, and was still half a mile from the cabin when he put on the brakes and skidded to a stop. In the headlight beams the dirt road ahead showed ruts where the tires of a vehicle had kicked up trenches of gravel as it lost control and skidded. The tracks disappeared into the trees.

"You don't think. . . ." Cormac murmured.

Be careful, Amelia murmured. His first impulse was to snap that he didn't need reminding. On consideration, he appreciated the reminder. He needed an extra set of eyes. A sixth sense. Clairvoyance. The ability to channel the dead. Omnipotence.

I am a mere magician, she said.

Cormac walked a little ways from the truck, keeping his gaze soft enough to catch unexpected movement in his peripheral vision, but focused enough to notice details that didn't fit. Anything out of place, from a recently fallen tree to a newly dug ditch. If he knew what he was looking for, he wouldn't need to search.

A soft breeze rocked the pines above him. Living wood creaked, a perfectly natural if ominous sound. An owl grumbled a little ways off. The world around him appeared perfectly ordinary, except for the place where a car had obviously skidded off the road, suddenly and violently.

He left the road and followed the tracks through the pathless forest.

He didn't have to go far. The ground dipped, sloping into a shallow gulch, and a black SUV sat innocuously shored up against a big pine. It hadn't been moving fast enough down the track to do more than crunch the bumper when it hit the tree.

This was Ford Bellamy's car.

This is not good.

Maybe the driver had lost control, managed to brake hard enough to keep the crash from being a total disaster. And then what, walked away? Then where was Bellamy? Why hadn't the cops found this? Cormac approached, still looking around for. . .whatever.

He reached the driver's side door and looked in through the tinted window. Someone was sitting inside; Cormac could only see the driver's shape. He pulled a pair of gloves out of his jacket pocket, slipped them on. Old habit, but even now he wasn't willing to leave behind any confusing prints that would have to be explained. He let out a breath, hoping the door would be unlocked.

More than that, it was open a crack. As if the driver had moved the handle but hadn't had the strength to push the door any further. Cormac opened it. The man's hand flopped down. A sour smell came out—a sickroom reek, as when someone had been ill for a long time.

The driver, Ford Bellamy, was dead. Clearly dead, his eyes open and clouded, his cheeks sunken, his body slumped in a limp, familiar manner. Nothing looked quite like a dead body. His stylish, expensive clothes hung off him as if they were too large, and seemed to drape around a too-thin frame. The bones of his hands stood out, skeletal, the flesh shrunken away.

He looked like he had starved to death.

He can't have; he's only been missing a day. Half of a day. A body like this—he would have had to be starving for weeks. Months, even.

"Your spell," he said. "The one that lets you talk to the dead—"

I fear there isn't enough body left to hold a soul. Besides—do you think he understood what was happening to him?

Cormac guessed he didn't, that the man had been overcome with— whatever it was that overcame him. Probably in the middle of driving back down the mountain. When he tried to open the door, to get out, to escape—he'd been too weak to do even that much. He must have been terrified, though the desiccated features didn't reveal any dying expression.

A phone rested in a drink holder between the front seats. Cormac checked it—the battery was dead. Like something had sucked away all the energy in the car, not just Bellamy's life. He put the phone back, just like he'd found it. He did some more searching—and found a keychain-sized Leatherman dropped on the floorboard at Bellamy's feet. Knife blade open, ready to use and then abandoned, just like at Weber's cabin.

On the dash, tucked right up against the glass, a piece of bone. A bit of rib, the length of his thumb.

The cabin—we must get there immediately.

"No. We need to get the hell out of here. Get back home," Cormac said. His first job, always, was keeping themselves safe. He was ready to hit the freeway and never come back.

We can't do that.

Whatever this was. . .it wasn't going to stop. Was Domingo already dead too? Cormac tried to call her again—and couldn't get signal.

We help her by stopping this at the source—the cabin. You aren't one to run. I know you.

When you have the skills, when you have the tools—you need to use them. His father had taught him that. Should have applied to carpentry, not. . .whatever this was. And his father had died young. "I usually know what I'm up against when I stay to fight." Whatever this was. . .could they even fight back?

Sacrifices, Amelia murmured finally, from the back of Cormac's mind. Thinking out loud, as out loud as she could. *He's making sacrifices.*

"What kind of sacrifices? I don't get it."

A sacrifice presumes that the deaths will end when the perpetrator attains whatever goal is aspired to. But then what is the goal? To feed whatever got fed a hundred and fifty years ago when the Donner Party was stranded here? But what did that accomplish? All those people died, and for what?

"Fame," Cormac murmured. "A hundred and fifty years later, we're still talking about them."

He felt Amelia give a frustrated huff, and could picture her brushing the fabric of her skirt in irritation. The wrinkle to her brow, the lines around her mouth. *There are easier ways to achieve fame, even as a killer. Jack the Ripper didn't go through this much trouble.*

"Maybe this isn't about fame as a killer."

That leaves us back where we started. These deaths are sacrifices. They're fueling something. But what?

"Do we go back down the mountain to tell someone about Bellamy, or check out the cabin?"

Cabin. While the scent is fresh.

So be it then. Report the body later.

Sometimes Cormac really hated magic.

Me as well, Amelia said, which surprised him, and she explained. *It never occurred to me to use magic to hurt anyone. I only observed so many inexplicable details in the world, and I wanted to know more. I wanted knowledge. And yes, power. But I hoarded my power like treasure. I didn't have a purpose for it. Not like this. Any purpose that could be derived from this must be terrible. We are moving toward a very dark place, Cormac.*

Wasn't the first time. They were better equipped than most to go there. "So let's do it," he muttered.

What made it hard, they weren't looking for an assailant, an artifact, a *thing*. A target he could hunt and kill. Instead, they were looking for a curse, a black hole, a free-floating area of ill intent. Invisible, deadly, that also seemed to have intent and a vast capacity for evil. This force wanted to kill painfully. Vampirically, almost. Not consuming blood or energy or spirit, but the basic physicality necessary for life. It was vicious in a way that most people wouldn't think of. Not even someone like Cormac. There were faster, nastier ways of killing.

If only they could set out a net to catch the thing, like a bird.

The gate at the bottom of the drive was closed. Holding his penlight in his teeth, Cormac picked the lock quick enough. Slower than he wanted, though. He forced himself to keep calm, keep breathing steady. He might not have had his guns, but this was a hunt just the same. Like his usual prey from the old days, the vampires and werewolves and so on, this target was hunting him, too. He just had to get there first. Easy.

Finally, the gate swung open. He returned to the Jeep and raced up the hill to Weber's cabin. A half-moon didn't do anything to make the forest any clearer. Looking up through the treetops, stars blazed.

He reached the clearing, which this time of night was stark and full of shadows. The cabin lurked, the pair of windows somehow darker than everything around them, something out of a goddamn horror movie. Striding toward the front door, Cormac reached into his pocket for one of the charms Amelia had him put there, a glass Turkish eye the size of a quarter. Not that it would help, but it was something to do.

At the steps up to the porch, he stopped.

What is it?

He simply nodded at the piece of rib bone sitting there. He'd have to walk right past it to get inside.

Two things, she demanded. *A protective circle, and alarms. It's coming, we'll know when it gets here.*

He got to work, quick and calm.

Pouring from a bag of salt, he made a circle some twelve feet in diameter. At the four cardinal points Amelia set a new alarm spell, string and paper resting on the ground. He kept the torn pieces in his hand. If any magic passed this way, they'd know. In the center she had him build a fire, but not light it. He set out a bundle of sage, a candle, a knife. He and Amelia weren't quite sure what they were up against. Something that killed with malice. But they would be ready.

"Now what?"

Patience, Amelia said. *We just have to be patient.*

He sat on the ground in the center of the circle, to keep watch on the trap they'd set. The summer night was crisp. No breeze touched the air.

He scratched his jaw, which was going past feeling like sandpaper into actual beard territory. Waited. This was so like a hunt it was almost comforting. Up at dawn, waiting for a bull elk to walk into his sights. Time seemed to freeze in those moments. He closed his eyes, just for a moment.

Cormac, light the fire. Light it, now!

He smelled burning and tried to swat it away, as if it was part of a dream, as if he was still asleep. He didn't think he'd been asleep for that long, but a chill had settled over the forest. He shivered.

Cormac!

The scraps of paper from the magical trigger had turned to ash. They'd been on the ground in front of him; a wisp of smoke still lingered. He was supposed to be watching them. He looked around—which trigger had been sprung? Which direction was the danger coming from?

All of them at once. All four scraps had burned simultaneously. The danger was here, and everywhere. He felt strangely leaden.

This is it! Cormac, it's here! The curse is here!

The circle of protection hadn't worked because it was already here; they'd locked it in with them. He couldn't stand up. He knew that he ought to. He was sure he needed to stand, right now.

Cormac!

He remained rooted to the ground, nerveless. "I can't move," he murmured, staring at his legs like they belonged to someone else. Fear blasted through him—Amelia's fear, a panic rooted in the back of his mind. He'd never felt fear like this from her. Something was very wrong.

When was the last time you ate?

Dinner, a fast-food burger before going back to the motel. His stomach cramped, far beyond hungry. He was starving.

Don't you have a. . .a. . .what is it, a power bar in your shirt pocket? Some jerky? You always carry around a bit of jerky. Eat it. Just a bite.

"I can't." He winced, knowing he should be angry, unable to find the energy for it. Well, at least he was right—whatever had gotten Weber and Bellamy was right here. Maybe it'd been here the whole time. They'd finally managed to draw its attention.

Cormac, did you hear that?

He listened. Held his breath to hear better, and there it was. Not a voice, this was only a suggestion. A thought on the air, directed at him. He'd probably heard it before, but not with his conscious mind. Now, he listened hard and heard the words.

What's it saying? What's it telling you?

"It's telling me to eat."

But it wants you to starve—

"No. This is about torture. It wants me to eat."

He picked up the pocketknife, the ritual blade she'd had him set by the unlit fire. Yes, for this, the curse let him have free rein. No trouble at all moving for this.

He stabbed the knife into the ground next to him. His hand was shaking. He was gritting his teeth hard, and forced himself to unclench his jaw.

Cormac. She was worried, with a sharp edge to her presence. *Please, Cormac. What is this?*

He looked at the knife. He looked at his thigh, the thick, fleshy stretch of muscle laid out under the fabric of his jeans, just below the skin. Fresh, bloody meat.

Understanding dawned on them both.

All Cormac had to do was cut into himself. Then he could eat.

Eight

melia could do nothing.

The cruelty of the spell was breathtaking. No, upon consideration, much crueler tortures were possible—she could even think of some herself involving children, involving long roads of pain that only ended in death. Involving the kind of hopelessness that did not end in death at all.

This spell had an end to it, a decisive end that she preferred not to think of. The cruelty of this spell was obsessive—taking the fascinating horrors of the Donner story and turning them upon the victim. Amelia had no body. She was unaffected by the curse that had trapped Cormac, pinning him to the ground and sapping from him his will.

She had to do *something*, but she didn't know what. She wanted to reach out, grab Cormac's collar, shake him until his teeth rattled. She couldn't. She couldn't even scream in his ear, because he was drifting away. They were locked together in the same damned brain, and she could feel him losing focus as his energy faded. As he starved, the hunger of weeks compressed into moments. The pain gnawed at him; she watched from a small distance, as if behind glass.

If he died, she would lose her anchor to the world. She would be helpless, and the last part of her still living would dissipate.

This was magic. She *knew* magic, knew a thousand spells and the arcane lore that crafted them. She could solve this, counter it in a way

161

that Weber and Bellamy couldn't have hoped to. God, they must have been terrified, having no way to understand what was happening, thinking the curse of this place must truly be striking them down—

She pulled her thoughts back to the problem at hand. This was not natural, clearly. It was magic. So, what was the magic driving this? What was the power that had invaded their circle and struck Cormac down with so little warning?

A trap. It had waited for a target, then sprang to catch it, without mercy. If this had been old—some spell or curse from the previous century, some leftover magic, there would have been some warning. Some randomness. This was new, and malicious. And very likely the kind of trap that the more one struggled against it, the tighter it held.

They needed some kind of protection, and they needed to draw the perpetrator—the maker of this trap—into the open. Confront the person, turn the spell back somehow. She had charms—she was constantly filling Cormac's pockets with charms and odds and ends, anything that might be useful, a magician's toolkit. If she could remember what he had there, cast her own magic, hope it was strong enough—

And keep Cormac alive. This was all on her now.

This was what Weber and Bellamy had both faced. Lying paralyzed, one option open before them as they watched the skin draw back from their bones and felt their stomachs contract, the hunger of weeks collapsing into hours. All they had to do was eat the one unthinkable meal. Bellamy had dropped his knife rather than give in. Weber, the same. Neither one of them could do it. So, did that make them courageous, or cowardly?

"I could do it." He wasn't weak. He could do whatever he needed to survive. No one would blame him.

You will not, Amelia declared.

"I wouldn't even die. Just a little piece. I could survive. Tell me why I shouldn't."

It's not civilized. Her English accent was so prim, so offended, he had to chuckle. Right, then. He couldn't do it because the prim English lady said not to.

You are very difficult.

His hands looked different. Thinner, more gaunt. The bones seemed more defined. He touched his face—did his cheekbones seem more pronounced? His life was draining away physically as weight vanished from him in defiance of all the laws of physics.

No you will not. You will not starve, I forbid it.

"I'm trying not to," he murmured.

He was starving; she wasn't. Would her spirit survive without a body, the way it had back in prison for a hundred years? Would she be able to find another body out here? Or would Donner Pass really be haunted now?

We must fight. It's simple, really.

"Amelia. . . ."

Annie Domingo. Was she going through this now, right this minute? Had Peterson got her, too? Maybe there was still time. . . .

That's right. We must fight so we can save Annie. There's a spell. You hardly have to move, even.

"Or I could cut. Just a little. Then this all goes away." A piece off the tip of his finger. He wouldn't even miss it, and there'd be enough meat in that one bite, a bit of fat and enough blood to suck on to satisfy the monster—

Cormac! She had to shout at him.

He shook his head to clear his mind. He wasn't thinking straight, he knew he wasn't. He should throw the knife away, like Weber and Bellamy had. Or finally use it to cut, maybe a strip off the curved muscle of his forearm. . . .

No. Those two men had been stronger, to refuse that voice.

I daren't ask you for a drop of blood, you're liable to slice a whole limb off, the state you're in.

"Blood sacrifice. That's what you said, what all this is—someone needs sacrifices, that's why Weber died, why Bellamy died—"

Yes. And if there is a sacrifice, there is someone performing the sacrifice. Someone who wants something.

"I've never been this weak." He was lightheaded. His energy had fled, and his body was throbbing. It wasn't pain so much as. . .need.

I know you haven't. But so much of your strength is in your mind, my dear, we simply have to use it. Ignore the rest. Can you do that?

It was like he had Mary Poppins in his head urging him on. How could he say no? "Yes."

I'll help. Let me in, let me have your body so I can—

"No—you take over, you'll be stuck too. We've done this enough, you can tell me what to do. But you need to stay safe."

As long as you're like this I am not safe.

"Amelia. Please. You don't want to feel what I'm feeling. Just tell me what to do."

How was it he imagined her taking a deep breath? Brushing her hands and rolling back her shoulders like she was about to push a boulder up a hill? She had no body. But she was as real and solid as if she stood next to him. He could almost feel her holding his hands, gazing into his eyes.

Show me what's in your pockets.

The action seemed to take a very long time, far longer than it would have under normal circumstances. Every inch of movement seemed to require a renewed force of will. Move hand to jacket pocket. Put hand in pocket. Rest. Grab items, which amounted to simply closing his hand and keeping hold of what he could. Drop hand to his side, letting items spill. Repeat until he had everything out. Then on to the next pocket. No wonder the other victims hadn't called for help.

Amelia was thinking faster than he was—her mind wasn't clouded. She surveyed the pockets' contents as he laid them out, recognizing them even in the near dark. His phone—drained and dead, of course. A bent nail. Matches. A couple of chunks of quartz. Black string, red string. A pillbox filled with dried clover. Paperclips. Feathers.

Black string, she said. *Wrap it around your right forefinger. I'll say the spell.*

He focused on her words, but they were in another language, Latin maybe, so instead he let the sound of her voice flow through him and concentrated on the string, clasping it with his thumb and clumsily twisting his hand until the string looped around a couple of times. He didn't have the energy for more, but when he finished, so did the words, and he could feel power rise up, a magical energy that hadn't existed before, created by her words and securing him like a brace.

He took a deep breath—he was *able* to take a deep breath. He didn't feel particularly stronger, but life had stopped draining from him. The spell was an anchor. Whatever happened next, his life would hold here for a little while. She'd bought some time.

Next, we draw out the killer.

This would be a summoning, she explained. Not traditional demonic summoning like in the stories. Rather, this would be like a fire alarm, a strobe light—a disruption, to force the target to look over. Shake the spiderweb to see what came out of hiding.

Cormac didn't much like that metaphor. He was already caught— what was he supposed to do, when the spider approached?

Smash it, Amelia declared.

"I hope this works," he murmured.

So do I.

She didn't sound as sure as he would have liked.

Next, they'd be writing in the dirt, symbols and signs, messages sent to the ether. She wanted to use a stick to write; he didn't have the strength or attention to look for one. Wasn't sure he'd be able to hold onto it. He could use his finger just as well. Put whatever strength he had left into the spell.

I wish you'd let me do this.

"No. I need you in reserve."

If you're trying to spare me pain—

That was it exactly. No reason both of them had to suffer.

Cormac—

"Show me what to write."

He closed his eyes to better focus on her presence, her disembodied voice calling to him. He didn't sink all the way into their meadow, the space of their shared consciousness. But he could see what she wanted him to see, the patterns she needed written. Methodically, he scratched them into the dirt beside him. First left, then right. Then another, and another. She spoke a simple phrase with Cormac's voice:

"Acclare! Acclare te ipsum!"

Silence returned. The nighttime forest was more still and ominous than a graveyard. Easy to remember, how many people had died just a few miles from here, and how horribly.

"What now?" he said.

A beam of light panned through the trees. A flashlight, accompanied by soft footsteps on the earth. The sudden motion was shocking, a jolt to his system that was almost painful. His heart raced, and it didn't have the energy to work so hard. He looked, winced, figured out that someone was approaching, searching for the exact spot where he sat. Part of him grew hopeful, ready to call out for rescue. But he knew—this wasn't rescue. This was a man come to see how his sacrifice was progressing. Maybe even alerted because things weren't going the way they should. Someone had gummed up the works.

The light came to rest on him. Cormac squinted into the beam, only able to see a silhouette approach, a ghostly shape moving toward him. He felt worse than helpless, on the ground, looking up, barely able to move and no weapon to hand but a stupid knife.

Finally, as he came around to face Cormac the man lowered the flashlight, revealing himself: Elton Peterson.

"You're dying, aren't you?" Peterson asked, oddly toneless.

"Starving. Just like they were. You can't stop it. Now you know how it feels. Now you understand them."

One thing at a time. This wasn't over yet. Cormac said, "You hated Weber because he blocked your access to the park. Tried to keep you away from the Donner sites. Because you're a nuisance. Bellamy— wouldn't acknowledge your expertise." And he hated Cormac just for hanging around. "What do you want, Peterson? What're you doing all this for?"

The corona from the flashlight shone up, painting skull-like shadows on his face, like he was starving, too. "The usual reason. I want to live forever."

Cormac chuckled. "Need a vampire for that. I know a couple who'd oblige. Or maybe not. They'd have to put up with your bullshit for eternity."

Peterson sneered. "A vampire? Only awake at night, drinking other people's blood? That's not living. I said I want to *live*."

"And you had a plan." Statement, not a question.

"Yes. I will make myself a god."

Well, Cormac hadn't expected that. "I don't get it," he said, unable to hide his confusion. He hadn't meant to say it out loud, but he was losing hold of himself.

"What happened here a hundred and fifty years ago was a stupid tragedy, the end of a long string of stupid mistakes—and yet everyone knows the name Donner. Everyone knows what happened here. And why? The fear. The *power* of it. Starvation is horrible because it's slow, because you see it coming. And yet people die of starvation *every single day*. A whole country starves and a bunch of celebrities sing a song about it! *That's* power! That power will make me a god. But it's more than that, more than just going hungry—there's what people will do to avoid it when they have to. A boat is lost at sea—did they do it? A plane crashes in the Andes and we all want to know—did they do it?"

Cormac coughed at the pain welling in his gut. "You want to be the god of cannibalism?"

"Of hunger," he said, his eyes gleaming. "Of starvation. The thing that has the power to make people do the unthinkable."

Ask him a question, if you will.

"What question?" he murmured, and Peterson looked at him strangely.

Ask him if the power he seeks to wield was already here, at Donner Pass, or if he had to raise it from scratch?

Cormac tried to think of a simpler way to ask this, and couldn't, so just repeated it. "The power—was it already here at Donner Pass, or did you have to raise it from scratch?"

Peterson looked away. Chuckled, a bit madly. "That was the funny thing. I thought. . .all that pain, all that hunger—the place was famous for it. Here, here is where I would stake my claim, I would draw that power, that despair all to myself—"

"But?"

"There wasn't any. There's just. . .the bronze plaques and the tourist shops and the badly named restaurants. The tragedy didn't leave a mark. Not a supernatural one."

Ah, Roland did his work well. He'd be so pleased!

"So I had to do it myself. Make my own mark." He grinned. "Shouldn't be long now. You're almost there. Thank you."

"Yeah, fuck you too."

There is one more symbol to etch, Cormac. The summoning isn't finished. There's more to this than Peterson.

She showed him the sign, a medieval hermetic symbol for strength, for truth. Carefully, line by line, he drew it in the earth at his feet.

"What are you doing?" Peterson asked.

Cormac ignored him. A vertical line, a widdershins curve—

"Stop that." The man stepped forward like he might actually try to stop Cormac. Wouldn't take much; he could probably just push him over. But Elton Peterson held back, acting like someone who'd lit a fuse and wasn't sure what the explosion was going to look like.

Two more marks, dashes over the first line. Amelia murmured

arcane words, and much like with other battles they'd fought, he felt their spirits twist together and become something stronger than the sum of their parts. Her knowledge and age, his physical being anchoring them to the world—it shocked him every time. The first time they'd come together like this, back in prison, he'd almost flinched away, afraid of losing himself—and afraid of what he might accomplish. But he hadn't. He'd reached out to Amelia, she'd grabbed hold, and they'd become powerful. Like they did now. A summoning went out, a flare without light. And then it was gone, finished.

Again, a pause, stillness.

Peterson gripped the flashlight hard and looked up and around like he expected to be attacked by a swarm of wasps. "You can't stop this," he declared in a tight voice. "You're already dead! There's nothing you can do to stop it, the power of your death is already mine—"

"Wait for it. . . ." Cormac murmured. He didn't know what was going to happen but he expected it to be good. By some definition of good.

Right. . .about. . .now, I think.

There was a soft groan, then a rushing sound, a growing breeze blowing through the pines, which creaked at the pressure, the sound increasing until the breeze turned into a gale, tightly focused, whirling in a space with Cormac at its center. He ducked his head, and Peterson put up his arms to protect himself. The flashlight fell out of his hand and broke when it hit the ground. Somehow, though, the spot of forest remained lit by an indistinct glow.

Cormac knew this sound, these smells. The fierce, unnatural wind that suddenly whipped by, bending trees at dangerous angles, snapping branches. Dust rising up in a whirlwind, obscuring sight. The smell of something unnatural burning to death. This was a doorway from somewhere else opening up before them. Any moment, they would see what demon came through to their world.

Times like this, he missed his guns, even as he knew that none of them would help here. Instead, he wished for holy water and wooden stakes, silver bullets and crosses of gold. Anything.

Faith, Amelia whispered. *Have faith.*

Faith in what?

Faith that whatever is about to appear isn't here for us.

A ritual sacrifice had three components: the person making the sacrifice, the thing being sacrificed—and the god or being the sacrifice was offered to. One figure in this tableau was still missing. Peterson had forgotten something important—he thought he was making sacrifices to himself. But power like that attracted attention.

Cormac missed the moment when the thing took form. The wind and swirling dust became a shadow, and the shadow gained mass. A huge animal came through the trees, stepping toward them. A medieval war horse, pitch black and massive, with steps that shook the ground. Its eyes, peering out from behind a thick fall of mane, were glints of obsidian, and it studied them with disturbing intelligence. Measuring them.

The rider was cloaked, billows of thick fabric falling around his saddle and legs, draped over his shoulders, as if he had come from a very cold place. Leather gauntlets on his hands, a close-fitting bronze helmet settled over his head. A bearded chin was all that was visible of his face, apart from another set of black, glinting eyes. In one hand he held the horse's reins; in the other, a sword, but where the cross guard should have been was a set of antique scales. He could hold the sword vertical and measure the world in those bronze bowls.

Amelia quoted: *And lo a black horse; and he that sat on him had a pair of balances in his hand. And I heard a voice in the midst of the four beasts say, A measure of wheat for a penny, and three measures of barley for a penny; and see thou hurt not the oil and the wine.*

"That's the Book of Revelation," Cormac said softly. And this was the Third Horseman. Famine. What did it mean, that Famine should come to this place? "You have some kind of spell that'll protect against this?"

If she had been standing beside him, she would have shaken her head slowly.

Peterson stood aghast, his eyes wide, arms spread. He seemed frozen, in shock. Then, incredibly, he laughed. The look of joy spreading over him seemed hideous.

"I've done your work! Haven't I done it well?" he demanded of the figure.

Cormac somehow found the strength to prop himself up. Not quite standing, but enough to lean toward Peterson and point at him in accusation. "You wanted to be a god. You came up with some fucked-up ritual to do it, but you needed dead bodies. *Starved* bodies. What the hell kind of god did you think that would make you?"

"Famine," Peterson said simply. Cormac was taken aback. "Famine, here, just like this, yes!" He was still smiling, with such a look of triumph.

"No," a voice said. A deep, resonate voice, much like the clomp of a giant hoof on soft forest ground. At that, *everything* went still. The wind vanished, trees stilled. Cormac held his breath. He could feel Amelia with him, close as she'd ever been, with a mental gesture that was much like gripping his hand.

Peterson, gormless as he was, had the nerve to chuckle, confused, and ask, "What?"

Famine tapped his mount with his heel, and the horse stepped forward, closer to Peterson. It was such a human gesture, such a normal set of movements, Cormac was startled. That the Four Horsemen of Biblical legend might actually exist didn't shock him—he'd seen some unbelievable shit in his time. What shocked him is that they—or at least this one—should be so human-like. With weight, with physicality. The fabric of the cloak rustled as the Horseman moved.

Peterson's ecstasy seemed to be fading. The back of the horse was taller than he was, and the rider loomed over him. He maybe didn't quite realize the powers he'd been messing with until just this second. Like the Donner Party, when the snow began falling.

"I. . .I thought it was just a myth. A story. I mean, it's the *Bible*, no one takes it *literally*. . .do they? I was going to turn myself into the story—"

Peterson grappled with his pockets a moment, turning out some familiar items—matches, string, a piece of slate. Charms and scraps of spells. A couple of pieces of rib bone. Famine ignored them all.

"You think this suffering belongs to you," the rider said in that rumbling voice, like a trumpet sounding from far away. "It doesn't."

The historian stammered, "I. . .I only wanted. . . ."

The Third Horseman grabbed Peterson by the throat. The man didn't have a chance to cry out before he began to shrink, to desiccate. Skin turning bloodless, cheeks growing hollow, skeletal. Peterson clawed at Famine's arms with increasingly bony fingers, but had no effect on his captor. His movements slowed, slackened, stilled. His shirt billowed over a gut that had gone concave. The fabric of his clothing disintegrated, fell away until the man was naked. The same curse, the same progression—starving, happening here in seconds. The pain must have been dire. He was gulping for air like a fish.

When Famine let go, the historian was a skeleton with a covering of skin, his hair dried up and falling away in clumps. He might have been dead for years and mummified.

But he still moved. Ghastly, yellowed eyes still blinked. The laddered rib cage drew in air. A leg twitched. A shaking arm reached. Somehow, Peterson was still alive, imploring his god and idol.

Peterson had tried to make himself something from a powerful legend, but he hadn't believed enough to recognize: The job was already taken.

Offhand, Cormac wondered what the Fourth Horseman, Death, could do just by holding someone by the throat.

The black horse snorted, stamping a front leg a couple of times— right on top of Peterson's body. That ended him, collapsing the rib cage, smashing the brittle skull. He lay still, a pile of bones and dried-up skin. He was done.

Cormac wasn't sure if Famine had seen him. He wanted to run—he really ought to get the hell out of here. But he also didn't want to draw attention to himself. He waited. . .waited. . . .

The rider shifted the reins; the black horse turned, pivoting on hind legs. The pair paused a moment, appearing to study this stretch of forest. Cormac couldn't be sure; he couldn't see the rider's eyes. The horse wuffed a breath as if he'd smelled something he didn't like.

Barely breathing, Cormac remained still, thinking over and over, he had nothing to do with this. He meant nothing to the Third Horseman. They could go their separate ways, no harm. Maybe it wasn't magic, some kind of spell to turn away the evil eye. But maybe the hope would be enough.

Amelia added to the hope. *Please, look away.*

And then, they did. The horseman gave another nudge with his heel, and the horse moved off at a jog, weaving through the trees and vanishing in what might have been fog, or light, or a crack in the air, or nothing at all.

Cormac heaved out the breath he'd been holding. It echoed among the trees, dead quiet in the still air. His next inhalation smelled of pine, thick with vegetation and life. It was a good smell.

Peterson's body lay crumpled, not ten yards away. Cormac looked away.

I think the sun is rising.

Looking up, squinting past the canopy of trees, he tried to see what she was seeing, and sure enough, the sky was the muffled gray of predawn. He hadn't been paying any attention. But this—this was hope. In the growing light he held up a hand, turned it this way and that to study it. It wasn't gaunt. It didn't hurt. He tested more movement, pushing himself to his knees, pausing to take stock. Then, he stood, without dizziness, without trembling.

How do you feel? Amelia waited tensely for the answer.

"I feel. . .tired. But normal tired." Not dying tired. He knew the difference now.

His stomach rumbled. He was still hungry. But not starving. That could wait, though. "We've got to find Annie," he murmured.

But first, they scattered the remains of their spell, all trace of magic at the cabin. At Amelia's direction he went around the clearing, taking down all the bits and pieces of her spells, kicking dirt over the symbols etched into the dirt, burning the last bits of string and sage, then stomping out the ashes. He left Peterson's body where it was—let that be someone else's problem.

No one else would starve on Donner Pass. At least not like this.

He charged his phone and made calls as they roared down the mountain in the Jeep. Domingo's phone still wasn't picking up. But Trina's was.

"Trina. You get ahold of Domingo?"

The girl sounded exhausted. "Yeah, yeah. I'm sorry, I tried to call but you weren't picking up your phone."

"Never mind, is she okay?"

"She's okay. I mean, she was in bad shape when we got here, but she's okay now."

"I told you not to go near her."

"But we had to, she was sick."

Trina. Fluffy, happy, gossipy, heroic Trina. God. "You with her now? Tell me where you are."

She gave him the address. He raced on.

Trina was making soup in the cozy, trim kitchen of Annie Domingo's own Forest Service cabin, down near the visitor center. "My grandma's soup," she said, smiling. "Good for anything."

The plain chicken broth was the perfect food for people who'd been starving.

Domingo had been struck after Cormac. She collapsed, and Trina and her neighbor found her curled up on the floor, groaning. And then. . .it had gone away. Cormac found a piece of rib bone on her front porch and smashed it under his heel.

Now, the ranger sat at her small kitchen table, wrapped in a blanket, regarding Cormac with confusion. Her cheeks were gaunt, her skin ashen, but growing more flush and lively by the moment. "I don't understand."

Neither did Cormac, really. He could explain what he'd seen, explain to her what she'd experienced. But that didn't mean the explanation made any sense. Not to someone in a uniform who had to write a report about it.

"If you're looking for a culprit, it was Peterson. If you're looking for a cause of death—call it poisoning. Whatever it is, it won't happen again."

"You sure?"

"I'm not real sure about anything these days. But yeah, I think it's done."

"Wow," Trina said from the sink, pausing in the middle of washing dishes. "That's *wild.*"

Domingo smiled weakly. "Trina hon, you probably shouldn't go telling this story around to everybody."

She huffed. "Yeah, I know. Who'd believe it?"

Domingo scrubbed her hands over her face and sighed. "I don't know whether to be relieved or disgusted. Peterson? Nebbish annoying Peterson? For God's sake, why? Why would he want to kill anyone?"

"He wanted this," Cormac said, gesturing around the cabin, and by extension to the land outside, the visitor center, all the bronze plaques and pine forests, the creeks and mountains around them. "He was obsessed. He wanted to be a part of it. Take some of the glory for himself."

The ranger stared. "There's nothing glorious about the Donner Party. What they went through—it was five months of hell."

"But can you name a more famous set of settlers?" She pressed her lips together; she couldn't. Very few people who knew about the Donner Party could name any of the other tens of thousands of people who'd made that journey west. However horrible their ordeal, it and the sensational reporting of it after had made them famous. "He thought their fame made them great. And he wanted it." He'd made a mistake so many made: no one could understand this thing as well as he did, therefore it ought to be his.

Trina shook her head. "I knew something was off with that guy. He's from *Fresno*."

Domingo sighed. "Thank you, I suppose. The police will probably want to talk to you again—"

"I'd rather not."

"But I'll need to tell them—"

"Call it an anonymous tip. Someone found their bodies and left voice mail."

After a moment, she nodded. "I may need to call in a favor or two, but I'll leave you out of it."

"Thanks."

She went to a kitchen drawer, opened it, drew out a fat envelope, which she set on the table in front of him. It was full of cash, just like he asked. "I think I totaled up your expenses all right. Let me know if it's short."

"And the cabin?" Trina said. "Don't worry about it. Free of charge. Just for, you know."

He almost pushed the envelope back. He liked Domingo. What had happened here? That needed to be taken down. This wasn't a job, this was a crusade for the public good.

Is that a little pride I sense, hm?

The altruistic thing would be to refuse payment and drive off into the sunset. But he took the money because the gas he'd burned to get here was more than he could afford. Besides, he deserved a little compensation for that nightmare. For facing Famine itself and living to tell about it. But he at least counted out what he would have spent on the cabin and gave it back to her.

"Thanks," he said. Annie and Trina shared a wry smile.

"Anything else?" she asked.

He could ask her out to dinner. He could maybe stick around a couple more days. He could do a lot of things, he supposed. But he wanted to get back home.

"I'm happy I could help, Ms. Domingo," he said, and offered his hand for shaking.

"I'll call you if we get any other weird trouble around here, yeah?"

"You've got my number," he said.

Amelia had one last task she wanted to perform before they took to the interstate to head out of the valley, so Cormac went to the supermarket up the road and bought a bouquet of flowers. Plenty of daisies this time of year, and Amelia liked daisies. Next, they drove out to the Alder Creek site, where the Donner family had camped. Camped, starved, and mostly died. Half the kids had survived. None of the adults did.

At Amelia's direction, he stepped a few feet off the trail and found a likely spot, near a living pine and hidden in the grasses where a conscientious ranger wouldn't be likely to see it right away. There, he laid the thin bouquet on the ground, and thought about Tamsen Donner.

Not just her, Amelia thought. *All the mothers, really. If I was in the habit of praying, I would pray for them, trying to keep all those children alive through the nightmare. It's the women of the camp I mourn.*

They couldn't change anything. The prayers, the flowers—they were never for those who'd died. They were for the living, who wanted to help but couldn't, not a hundred and fifty years later. So you lay down flowers and try not to think of what you'd have done if it had been you in that camp.

He stood for a moment enjoying the clean air, the pure morning sun blazing down. Soaking in some of that elusive peace. If he felt a hand in his, giving a comforting touch of pressure, surely it was his imagination.

I think it's far past time we leave this place and go home.

Cormac knew she was right.

Epilogue

Kitty and Ben stared at Cormac across the table, and the longer they did the weirder this got. Obviously he hadn't explained things very well, but he wasn't sure what else he could say to make his trip out to Truckee sound more reasonable. They'd wanted to know what happened. Maybe he shouldn't have told them.

Finally, baby Jon fidgeted in Kitty's arms, and that distracted them from their astonishment. He still wasn't used to seeing the couple with a baby, but that was another issue. Babies were something that happened to other people, not anyone he knew.

"Famine? The Third Horseman of the Apocalypse Famine?" Ben said.

Cormac shrugged. "Don't know that I'd swear to it in court. But it was pretty convincing."

"I shouldn't be surprised," Kitty said. "Why am I even surprised? The shit we've seen? Sorry, pardon my language, don't learn that word." She kissed the baby's fuzzy head, and he yawned.

Ben was Cormac's cousin and sometime lawyer. Kitty, he'd planned on killing the first time they met. Now, in one of the stranger mysteries in Cormac's life, they were friends. The couple were both werewolves. Cormac had introduced them to each other, and. . .well. That had turned out all right, in the end.

Today, they occupied a corner booth at Wild Things, Kitty and

Ben's new café slash coffee shop venture. More upscale than these places usually were, the café gave the impression of being part of the atrium of a modest country house, refined yet homey. Well lit and furnished, it had a good selection of art on the walls, books in scuffed bookshelves, and inviting sofas, chairs, and tables distributed throughout, with enough space in between that people weren't likely to jostle each other moving around. Werewolves were territorial and sensitive to that sort of thing.

Cormac still kept a silver-laced penknife in his pocket, just in case.

"But it's okay?" Ben asked. "It's. . .not going to follow you or try to take revenge."

"No, I think it got whatever revenge it needed when it killed Peterson."

And good riddance. Let that be a warning if we ever tend toward hubris, hm?

"So why do you still look worried?"

Cormac gave a quick, wry smile which vanished almost instantly, and looked away. "I'm always worried."

Kitty got that look, then. The focused one that meant she was studying him, getting ready to ask a question he wouldn't be able to dodge. But Jon fidgeted again, emitting a spectacular amount of drool, and she grabbed a napkin to stop the flow.

They are a bit like alien creatures, aren't they?

Cormac had never held a baby in his life until this one came along. Kitty had insisted. "You're his godfather. Just hold him once, so you can say you did. Maybe Amelia wants to hold him, ask her." And, surprisingly, Amelia—whom Kitty had gleefully dubbed the fairy godmother—did. *Just to see what it's like,* she'd said. The baby had been surprisingly solid in his arms, a firm weight pressing against him. Cormac had held his breath, hoping the baby didn't wake up, that he didn't drop him, and that Jon would grow up to be nothing like himself. Cormac as godfather was a terrible mistake. At the same time, he knew, in some fundamental and horrible way, that he would do anything in his power to protect this small life. They were a pack, Kitty liked to say. So, he now had a godson to go along with his cousin and whatever the hell Kitty was. And Amelia, whatever *she* was. It was illogical. It was family. Strange and comforting, all at once.

"So what's different this time?" she asked. "Something's different. If this wasn't bothering you, you wouldn't have told us about it."

He almost hadn't. He didn't want them to worry, not about him. They had more important things to worry about. Like that kid. "I don't know. We thought we'd seen it all. I've never felt like I crossed a line I couldn't handle before. Then this happens." Maybe he was just getting old.

"You're not thinking of quitting, are you?" Kitty asked.

He hadn't meant to hesitate, but he took an extra breath. And another. The couple exchanged one of those couple-glances, worried and full of questions as well as secret, silent plotting. Like they were thinking, No, you say something. . . .

We aren't quitting, Amelia said. Then added, more softly. *Are we?*

"Amelia says no," Cormac says. "And no, we aren't."

"Well, good," Kitty said, decisive. "Because the both of you have a really unique set of skills."

Yes. Exactly. And we must use those skills. You understand, don't you?

He could almost imagine Amelia sitting next to him, explaining. Persuading. He chuckled.

"Now what?" Ben said. "This isn't funny, this is some kind of Biblical shit—"

"Language," Kitty said.

"Kitty, hon, he's six months old—"

"And I swear if 'shit' ends up being his first word—"

Jon grinned and burbled something that was, fortunately, incomprehensible.

"Maybe that's it," Cormac said. "There's some crazy stuff out there and we have these skills. . . . I just never had, I guess you'd call it purpose before. Not like this."

"Well," Kitty said. "Purpose seems to suit you."

"I was worried," Ben confessed. "When you put the guns away, if you'd find something else. And here you are."

Cormac smirked and looked away. This was getting too serious for him. "We'll see."

In a meadow in his mind, Amelia smiled.

3.

"I always thought the Four Horseman were just a metaphor. A symbol," the man said.

"For what?" his partner answered.

"I don't know." He sounded frustrated.

"Not that it matters, you can't really trust any of the symbology from Revelation given the cultural context has shifted so radically—"

Ooh, I think I like her.

They didn't *sound* like bad guys. The magician had an academic streak—most magicians did.

"Well," Cormac said. "I think it really was Famine and it turns out the Four Horsemen don't like competition."

In a tone of vague longing, the woman said, "Can you imagine what the others must be like? What they would all be like together?"

"Don't really want to." Cormac never, ever wanted to find out, because he was pretty sure seeing all four of them together would mean very bad things were happening. Honestly, he'd rather avoid situations where he was meeting *any* Horsemen of the Apocalypse.

"Are you Christian, Mr. Bennett?" the man asked.

"No? But I gotta be honest, at this point I believe just about everything. I've met the Monkey King."

"You...you what?"

Cormac pointed. "That one isn't in your reports, is it?"

"What's he like?" the woman asked wonderingly.

"Kind of a pain in the ass, to be honest."

"Well, of course—"

The man butted in. "Your next case was in South Dakota, in the Badlands area."

"Let me guess, another park service incident report?" Cormac muttered. An awkward silence followed, which gave him his answer, and maybe another one besides. He leaned forward. "Wait—are you guys Feds? You're government agents, aren't you? What is it, that new outfit—the Paranatural Security Administration?"

"Agent Stein said he'd figure it out," the woman muttered.

Pieces fell into place, even as a few more gaps opened up, but overall this made him more annoyed than worried. He'd dealt with Federal agents before and could do this dance. Cormac chuckled. "I have a pretty good lawyer who'd be really excited about a civil rights violation like this."

The man put his hand on his forehead and sighed. "We can make a good argument for probable cause."

"*What* probably cause?"

"You," he answered. "Federal park land is our jurisdiction, no question there. You go into these situations, things happen that no one can explain, and the only common factor is *you*."

He wasn't wrong, was the bitch of it.

The woman explained, "We merely took precautions before bringing you in for questioning. Even a little warning would have given you time to prepare."

"You really are that scared of me?"

How many people have you killed, anyway? Amelia said this gently, with sympathy. But in the end, the list was long, and he had, once upon a time, been a killer.

"Death follows you, Bennett," the man said. And it was true.

"Is this an interrogation or a trial?" Cormac said. "Am I defending myself from something?"

They didn't answer, and he started to worry again. Amelia, we need to figure out how to get the hell out of this.

I'm working on an idea. I would really like to see you right now but I know that isn't possible. Just...keep them talking is all we can to do for the moment.

"Right," he said, sighing. "Here's what happened in the Badlands."

BADLANDS WITCH

One

Something's not right, Amelia murmured in the back of Cormac's mind. Cormac scanned the depressing parking lot outside his apartment building, half-full of beater cars. Orange streetlights bathed the washed-out concrete walls. The roar of cars on the nearby highway beat at the air. His shoulders ached. They'd spent the afternoon putting up magical protections around a dog park on the other side of the city, which seemed weird to him but he didn't question anyone willing to write a check. Amelia knew the spells, but Cormac did the work, seeing as how she didn't have a body. That meant he'd been the one with his arms raised, waving sage and candles while walking around a couple of acres of territory. He was tired.

Amelia could only see what he saw, but she'd honed some magical instinct in him. When she said something wasn't right, Cormac listened. Which meant he didn't walk straight into the ambush at the base of the stairs.

Movement flickered, a shadow breaking away from the concrete and launching straight at him. He knew right off what it was. Nothing moved that fast, nothing was so at home in darkness. This was how vampires got the reputation of vanishing like smoke. You'd look and the vampire simply wouldn't be there anymore. Cormac dived for shelter, hitting the asphalt and rolling under the nearest car, a sedan with busted fenders, while reaching inside his jacket for a stake. To think, some people made fun of him for carrying stakes everywhere.

A thump pounded the top of the car as he rolled out the other side, and the vampire came pouncing down on top of him. Cormac braced the point of the stake upward. The guy kicked it out of his hand, midair, then kneed him in the gut. Move like that shouldn't have been possible, but then neither should vampires. Ignoring the pain, the air knocked out of his lungs, the shock in his back, Cormac writhed and kicked up, catching the guy in the nuts. That still worked on vampires at least.

The thing about fighting vampires, your defenses had to be solid. Not a crack. That was the only way you'd get a chance to strike back. They moved so fast, their reflexes were so sharp, they'd be on you and breaking your neck or ripping out your throat before you knew they were there. You couldn't let them get close, bringing their power and experience to bear. Couldn't let them catch your gaze, stare in your eyes, and immobilize you.

This one must have followed Cormac home. That was his mistake, thinking no vampire would ever be caught dead—undead— in this low-rent neighborhood off the Boulder turnpike. So he came home to the run-down two-story apartment block and relaxed before getting to his own front door.

Cormac recognized the guy. Sharp nose, long face, a flop of hair. The permanently offended snarl of a self-important minion. About ten years ago in Chicago, he took on a gang of vampires running a protection racket on a human neighborhood. He wouldn't dignify the group with the label Family, though they were sure trying to act like one. They hadn't been old enough, rich enough, or smart enough to avoid trouble. Cormac took out the leader of the bunch, a guy calling himself Lord Edgar, and half his followers. The rest had scattered, gone to ground.

Turned out, at least one of them had just been biding his time.

Cormac managed to shove himself out from under the guy, looked wildly around for the stake, raced for it—the vampire grabbed his ankle and he fell. Cormac immediately kicked, smashing the guy's nose. Didn't kill him. Not much would.

Nothing in Amelia's magical arsenal could help them unless he could get away, get a little space and time for her to work a spell. But that was just it, vampires never gave you that time. She stayed quiet and let Cormac's body and fighting instincts try to save them.

He ran. Didn't think he could get to his front door and the safety of the threshold before the vampire caught up to him. He needed a weapon. The apartment building had exterior stairs leading up to the second floor. Cormac dodged behind the steel frame of the staircase and spotted the door to the janitor's closet.

"You'll pay for what you did!" the minion yelled, from the other side of the stairs.

"That was a long time ago," he shot back, which was a stupid thing to say to a vampire, which was only part of why Cormac worried that he was getting soft.

He had one more stake tucked in his inside jacket pocket. Pulled it out, held it outstretched while the vampire ran at him. Alas, the vampire wasn't stupid enough to just run right up it. He grabbed Cormac's wrist and squeezed, causing him to drop the stake. He could have broken Cormac in half right there; instead, he paused, savoring the moment, leering with bared fangs and bringing himself closer, closer. . .

Cormac's other hand was on the utility closet's handle. He yanked open the door, fell in, knocking the vampire off balance and shutting the door behind him. As he hoped, a stack of mops and brooms lay piled up in the corner. He grabbed a broom with a wooden handle, set it under a foot and snapped it in half.

When the vampire opened the door, Cormac rammed the broken handle into his chest, right through his heart. The guy screamed, expression twisting with anguish.

The vampire couldn't have been that old, a couple of decades at most. The body blackened, but it didn't shrivel to a husk and turn to ash the way the old ones did, the rot of the grave if they had been allowed to rot in a grave. Becoming a vampire only delayed the inevitable. Vampires like this, throwing themselves on stakes for a Master who had been destroyed years before—what a waste. But nobody held a grudge like a vampire. They had the time to burn. Cormac let go of the stake, and the rotted body dropped at his feet.

Well, that was bracing.

Because the vampire didn't turn to dust and blow away, conveniently disposing of itself, Cormac now had a body to deal with.

"I do not need this shit," he muttered. Irate, he kicked it. The leathery skin made a disconcerting squishing sound.

It's better than letting him kill you, Amelia stated, sounding nonplussed. *But yes, it is a bother.*

He dragged the body someplace where it would be exposed to sunlight before anyone found it. The apartment building's dumpster had too much foot traffic, but behind the building lay a gravely stretch, a foot or two wide, between the building and a boundary fence. A couple of scraggily dead shrubs poked up through the rocks. No one went there, and it faced east. As soon as the rays hit it, it would burn to ash, then poof, gone. Hell, this was such a clear case of self-defense maybe he should call the police. Except no, not with a manslaughter conviction on his record. Besides, come dawn, there wouldn't even be a body. Nothing to report.

Finally he got safely into his apartment and took a very long, hot shower to get the stink of dead vampire off him.

Explain it again, Amelia said when he finally got out of the shower. She'd at least given him some peace until he got clean. *You went after an entire vampire Family by yourself?*

"Wasn't much of a Family. Most of them weren't any older than that guy."

You could have been killed.

"Turned out okay."

There are times when I am grateful I didn't know you earlier in your life. You seemed to have engaged in quite a lot of reckless behavior.

He barked a laugh. "If you only knew the half of it."

She could know, if she wanted. But she was English, overly polite, and didn't pry too much into the mind where she lived. That would be like rifling through the linen closet in the house where one was a guest, she insisted. Even though they were more like roommates.

Except with her, the door was always, always open. When he toweled off, she was there. When he slipped on sweatpants, so did she. Whatever he touched, she felt. They didn't talk about it. Ignored it as much as they could. He avoided mirrors. When he needed to jack off, she pretended to leave the room, as if she could ever leave the room. And once in a while, he found himself in front of the mirror and hoping she *was* looking.

She wasn't real. It wasn't real.

Two

Cormac slept and dreamed in their valley.

His father had taken him camping here, a high valley in the Colorado Rockies where a snowmelt creek cut down through a meadow bowl, bounded by a pine forest. The sky above was searing blue, smudged with white clouds. No air smelled cleaner than this. No place felt safer. He and Amelia had built this shared space—part guided meditation, part visualization exercise— where they could talk. She'd had a body, once. Here, she did again, resembling the single old sepia-toned photo he'd seen of her, with her serious demeanor, her hair in a prim bun, her clothing precise, long Edwardian skirt and high-necked blouse. He liked being able to see her, to talk to her.

He lay back in the grass, hands laced under his head, eyes closed. Sleep within sleep. He thought he heard chickadees in the pines up the hill.

She sat nearby, leaning against an outcrop of rounded granite. Her hand tapped nervously against her knee in what seemed to be an unconscious gesture. A disembodied spirit shouldn't *have* nervous ticks. If she existed only as consciousness, could she be unconscious of anything? This was why Cormac avoided the philosophy of it all.

"What?" he asked brusquely.

"Would you like to apprise me of any other outstanding grudges we might encounter?"

"Not particularly," he said. "I didn't even remember that guy until he was hissing spit in my face."

"You destroyed a gang of vampires. How can you forget something like that?"

She wasn't going to like the answer, so he waited, but she remained expectantly silent. "Because I used to do a lot of that sort of thing," he said finally, and she blew out a frustrated breath. "They usually don't come back for revenge."

"*Usually.* How are you meant to protect yourself from random vampires seeking vengeance?"

Do a better job of keeping stakes and holy water in his pockets. Live in a never-ending state of vigilance. "I figure one of these guys'll get me, sooner or later." These battles just delayed the inevitable.

"If you die, I die."

"You already died."

"You know what I mean."

"We've talked about this."

"Yes, I know. I just felt so. . .*helpless.*"

He hesitated. The chickadees had stopped calling. "I'm sorry you felt helpless."

Her lips pursed in a tight smile, but her gaze remained troubled. "I died once, you'd think I'd be less frightened of it happening again. But I'm not."

He straightened, sitting up with his arms around his knees. She rarely got this worked up. "I suppose I could get one of these guys to make me a vampire. . ."

"You're joking." She looked sharply at him. "You *are* joking?"

"Yeah."

"Because I don't think you becoming a vampire would stop anyone with a grudge from trying to kill you."

"No, probably not."

"Besides, I'm not sure I'd survive the transformation. I have no interest in attempting the experiment."

"So you like being here?" He looked up, around. Quirked a smile.

"I suppose I do."

"Could be worse, I guess."

"Cormac, what did you ever do before you had me looking out for you?"

"Got myself sent to prison is what I did."

"Ah, yes, see. That's just the sort of thing I'd like to avoid."

"Yes, ma'am."

"Spiritually cleansing dog parks. Let's keep to that." She settled back against her boulder and closed her eyes.

Chuckling, he lay back in the grass and let a real sleep overtake him.

A few mornings later, their email delivered a more interesting proposal than magically protecting dog parks.

An archeologist at a dig in South Dakota had found an unusual artifact, a clay pot in a style and with markings that didn't match any other pottery styles of the time and region. The archeologist, Professor Aubrey Walker, claimed to have some magical sensitivity, and believed that the artifact represented something otherworldly. Would Cormac please come and examine it, to see if he could tell if it was magical, or merely odd?

"'Otherworldly.' That could mean anything," Cormac murmured.

I'm not sure we have the expertise to evaluate such an item.

"We can be up front about that. Walker has to be willing to pay travel expenses and a consulting fee, even if the answer is we don't have a clue."

We can't guarantee an absence of magic. We can only state definitively if we do find something. It seems unsatisfying.

Amelia insisted on doing initial research to determine if they were even qualified to take on the job. Cormac did a web search on Walker and her credentials, and the trail of online breadcrumbs led to the home university of the archeology team and information about the dig, which was investigating hunting and camping sites of Plains Archaic cultures from about fifteen hundred years ago. So, there really was a dig, and their correspondent really was a scientist there. A scientist who wanted a magical consult.

Amelia was intrigued. *An artifact such as intact pottery seems very incongruous with other information about the culture. You'd expect to find bones and fire pits, maybe a few tools, nothing more.*

"Maybe that's why she thinks it's magical."

If something magical, some sort of spellcraft, has survived from that era—that would be phenomenal.

So she was all for taking the job. Cormac replied to the email, laying out his requirements, a hefty fee, and the fact he couldn't make any guarantees. A response came back almost immediately: that was fine, Walker had nowhere else to turn, and even a small amount of information would be better than nothing.

"Here's the thing," Cormac said to Amelia. "University archeology departments don't usually have a lot of funding to spare for paranormal investigators and that's a pretty big number we gave her."

I doubt she even reported it to her department. She might be planning to pay out of her own pocket, to keep this out of the books.

That made sense. He checked the email again—it wasn't a university address. So, keeping it really off the books. A serious archeologist wouldn't exactly want to advertise that she was consulting with a paranormal investigator. It also made him nervous.

We will be careful, Amelia assured him.

They were always careful. At least, they always tried to be careful. But you couldn't plan for all the things that might get you. The one that got you would be the one you didn't expect.

So, we go with caution.

Always, always.

Three

Getting to South Dakota took half a day of driving across an unending sweep of classic Great Plains rangeland, miles of rolling prairie and cattle country, driving on a grid of state highways set at right angles to each other, on and on, punctuated every now and then by some microscopic town that had looked exactly the same for the last fifty years. Cormac preferred the mountains, someplace to put your back against to see what was coming. Out here, there was no place to hide.

Amelia was riveted. *This sky, look at it! This wonderful huge sky! I can almost see it curving around and under us to the other side. It's like being under a bowl.* Three hours into the trip, she still hadn't gotten tired of it.

Walker had asked to meet them at a turnout on a county road near Badlands National Park. She had to give him GPS coordinates. Cormac wasn't sure he'd still have a phone connection by the time they got there—in another two and a half hours of driving.

I never got to this region in my travels. I had meant to. I was so looking forward to seeing the great herds of bison.

"They'd mostly been killed off by your time," Cormac said. Amelia had been so fascinated by stories of the American West, but by the early 1900's that world had vanished.

Do you think we'll see any bison?

"I don't know."

And Deadwood—do you know we'll only be a couple of hours away from Deadwood? After we've consulted with Professor Walker, perhaps we can visit?

"What's in Deadwood?" Cormac asked tiredly.

Calamity Jane's grave. And Wild Bill Hickok's. It's where he was shot. There's a museum there I'd like to see.

"Why?" he said curtly.

Well. Just to see it.

"We won't have time—"

This meeting will surely not take very long, and since we're already in the area—

"Can we talk about it later?"

She fell silent, finally, thankfully. He didn't want to see Deadwood, he didn't want to do anything but the job. The bison around here were probably all kept on farms. There wasn't any point to it.

Cranky and sweaty after a day on the road was probably not the best way to meet a client, but he didn't think the job would take more than an hour. Amelia would take a look at the artifact, decide it was nothing special, and they could turn around and go home.

No, she muttered. *You will not. We'll find a room, rest for the night, and explore tomorrow.*

He'd see how they felt at the end of the day.

A room and a hot shower.

"We'll talk about it later."

Somehow, she managed to pout without having a tangible face to pout with. He felt her testing. She could take over his body—if he let her. A good guest, she usually asked first. She hadn't tried to take over since they'd first met, back in prison. He didn't know if she ever thought about it. Or rather, he didn't know how much she thought about it.

He squeezed the steering wheel. He was in control, he was driving. But Amelia had probably learned enough about driving by watching him to do it herself. . .

The turnout Aubrey Walker had directed him to was just west of the national park boundary, on a dirt road. She had explained in an email, "The actual dig site is restricted, and I have to be careful. If word gets out that I contacted you, I could get in trouble."

I'm not sure if what she's doing is entirely legal, Amelia observed. He was pretty sure this particular chunk of land was part of the Pine Ridge Reservation, so yeah, they were probably breaking some rules.

"As long as nobody steals anything or breaks anything, we'll be fine." He hoped. If things got weird he could always walk away.

The dirt road cut across a sagebrush plain, straight as a line. To the west, the Black Hills rose up like a crumbling wall, dark with the smudged color of forests. To the east, the badlands, desolate gullies and washes, pinnacles of eroded stone. Hard to believe anybody could live out here.

Up ahead, right where Walker had asked him to meet her, a Honda CR-V with mud-spattered Illinois plates was parked in a rutted turnout. A woman waited there, leaning against the driver's side door. She was white, average height and build, had on khaki cargo pants, a shapeless sweatshirt, and dusty work boots. A plain baseball cap mashed down a mess of black hair pulled back in a bun. She looked like someone who'd been working on an archeological dig.

Cormac parked the Jeep alongside her. "Professor Walker?" he asked, stepping out, shutting the door behind him.

She brightened, smiling broadly. "You must be Cormac Bennett. Call me Aubrey. Thank you so much for coming." She clicked open the back hatch of the SUV with her key fob. "You ready to take a look?"

Amelia definitely was. *All this anticipation.* He could almost picture Amelia straining forward to get a first look at the artifact.

He explained again, "You understand I may not be able to tell you much. It may be dormant or have some kind of protection on it."

"Yes, I understand. I'll be grateful for anything you can tell me." Once the door was open, she stepped aside, gesturing. "Here it is."

A beat-up cardboard box sat alone in the back. Inside was the artifact, a piece of dusty pottery, no packing material around it. All by itself, it seemed to lurk. The pot had a round body, a flat base, and a long, narrow neck with a small, spout-like opening. Maybe eight inches high, six wide. The reddish color made it look like a lot of Native American pottery from the Southwest, but the markings on it seemed more like Norse runes. The shape wasn't like any tradition he—or Amelia rather—knew about.

"What makes you think it's magical?" he asked. "Anything weird been happening around it? Anything that started when it was first excavated, or when people touched it?"

"Mostly it's just the way it looks, the way it doesn't fit with anything else from the time or region. Like it came from another dimension or something, you know? It just makes me nervous." As if to emphasize this, she shivered and seemed to draw away from it.

That hardly seemed likely, but given some of the shit he'd seen in his time, he wouldn't discount it. He nudged Amelia. Sense anything?

There's definitely something. I can't make it out in detail, though. Magical, yes, but I don't know what it's supposed to do. We could try some scrying spells, try to work out what it's for.

He squinted at it from a couple of different angles. Leaned in to try to get a look down the neck, but he couldn't see inside. The opening wasn't wide enough. He'd need a penlight to look down in there.

"Well, what do you think?" the woman asked eagerly.

"Not sure," Cormac said. "I need to spend a little more time with it."

Let's see if there's anything inscribed on the bottom.

Cormac picked up the pot, turned it over.

And blacked out.

He woke up flat on his back with a raging, hangover-like headache that throbbed from the top of his skull and reached down to his gut. He rolled to his side but didn't vomit. Felt like he wanted to, though. Resting a moment, he caught his breath, steadied himself. The headache dimmed a little. He squinted against westering sunlight—shadows stretched long over the sagebrush.

Amelia?

She didn't answer. "Amelia?"

Nothing. Really nothing. He prodded that place in the back of his mind that he thought of as hers, where he usually felt her. It was open, blank, empty.

Amelia was gone.

Four

The ground under Cormac seemed to tilt. How could his brain feel physically empty, an open warehouse echoing with the absence? He squeezed his hands over his ears, as if he had to hold his skull together. Grit his teeth. Swallowed back an incipient scream.

She'd just been knocked unconscious, like him. But nothing like this had happened before. She was nothing but consciousness, she couldn't be *un*conscious. That would mean she was— He waited. The sun inched lower, toward dusk. Amelia was still gone. He kept thinking, What do I do? Amelia, what's happening? The answering silence hurt his skull.

His Jeep was still parked here. Walker's SUV was gone. In a panic he patted himself down, found his phone and wallet in his pockets where he left them. So he hadn't been robbed. Just left for dead. This was a trap, a trick, and he'd walked right into it.

But what was it? What had *happened*?

Amelia was gone. Just gone.

He was free.

No more voice talking at him, no more presence looking over his shoulder. For the first time in years, his mind was clear, light. Alone.

He didn't know what to do.

Just move. One step at a time. Something would come to him. Leaning against the Jeep's rear bumper, he stood, swayed a bit. The ground still felt like it was trembling. Like an earthquake, but he was the only one moving. He waited until he felt steady, and eventually he could stand. He drew a deep breath into exhausted lungs.

He still wanted to scream.

The plain around him was empty. No cars traveled the straight road, not so much as a cloud of dust rose up. A wind blew, whispering through the brush. His face felt raw—sunburned. Walker had fled hours ago, leaving him lying in the dirt. Had she thought he was dead? Had she really tried to kill him?

What had *happened*?

Since he barely knew what Amelia was to start with, he couldn't guess what had happened to her. Just that she was gone. Dead? For real this time.

Aubrey Walker knew what had happened.

Cormac took a long draw from the water bottle jammed in by the Jeep's gear shift. It was hot, metallic, and made him feel a little better. But that gaping silence still bore down on him.

What do I do?

No one answered. He couldn't seem to think on his own.

He tore out of the gravel pull-out and drove.

He ended up in Rapid City before he decided he couldn't just drive around looking for that pale SUV, pulling into parking lots, studying every car, every license plate. Driving at random was stupid and he'd never get anywhere this way. But it meant he didn't have to think. He didn't want to think, because that meant turning to his own mind and acknowledging the silence.

"Fuck it," he finally muttered, pulling into a McDonald's parking lot and shutting off the engine. He could figure this out. He used to hunt people down for a living. He could find Aubrey Walker, and she would tell him what she'd done. Maybe Amelia was only asleep, maybe—

Find Walker. Then worry.

Using his phone he started hunting with a little more focus. The phone number Walker had given him turned out to be disconnected. He re-did some of the digging he and Amelia had done before, through her university and the sponsors of the dig she was working on. Her department's website showed a picture of her, smiling, along with a group of grubby graduate students wearing hats and scarves against a bright sun, in the middle of a series of precise, squared-off pits. She looked so harmless, there.

He could call her department. Except it was after dark now, after business hours. He could spend all night driving around and it wouldn't help. Morning, he would have to wait until morning to make calls, but that was too long. He needed to find her *now*.

The water bottle was empty; he hadn't eaten all day. He stalked into the restaurant and got a burger, devoured it without thought. Drank something.

If Amelia could still speak to him, she would tell him to sleep. They had been arguing about whether to get a hotel room.

Cormac drove some more because he couldn't think of what else to do. Finally, he found a dark corner of a box store parking lot. Tried to think, but his brain wasn't working any better that it had been earlier. Sleep, Amelia would tell him. He could almost hear her.

He tipped back the seat and closed his eyes.

No sight, no sound, so sensation at all. Not even an echo, because echo implied space, and this. . .was confinement without space. She had no breath or heartbeat with which to monitor the passing of time.

This, this was death. Cormac was dead, she hadn't noticed, and she was. . .trapped? But where? In his body. . .no, *that* she would have felt.

Her consciousness would not have stayed in dead flesh. This. . .she had been here before, she *knew* this state. This nothingness, a consciousness with no anchor, residing in some solid prison. Trapped.

She screamed, or tried to, or would have if she still had a mouth. Cormac's mouth. Where was Cormac? What had happened?

While her mind, her self, whatever this was, screamed, she could do nothing else and so waited for a small space in the panic she could wedge herself into and take stock. She could not scream forever, though she wanted to.

In this state, Cormac would take a deep breath and settle himself. She had no lungs, she had no breath. Panic returned, until she imagined lungs, imagined breath. Imagined stillness. Her mind paused. A firefly in a canyon, blinking where no one could see her.

She had no way to judge where she was, what she was. She could do nothing.

But no, her mind was hers. She could think, and if she could think, she had some small hope. Memory returned, slowly. They had met Aubrey Walker on a deserted road, and she showed them an artifact from an archeological dig. But no, there was no possible way that artifact had come from a Plains Archaic camp, not a thousand years ago, not yesterday. Which meant it was something else.

A trap. It had been a trap.

Amelia hadn't been looking at the woman when Cormac reached out to pick up the piece of pottery. He'd dutifully focused on the target, so Amelia could study it. What would they have seen, if they had looked at the woman? The eagerness of a hunter closing in on her quarry? The bait had been so carefully laid and they had fallen for it. Amelia might have been furious, if she had blood and nerves for it. But she didn't.

What had the trap done to Cormac? He might be dead. He certainly was not here. She was. . .she did not know, and without Cormac had no way to tell.

She tried futilely to scream, and what was left of her mind folded in on itself.

Five

The exact dig location and its headquarters were confidential, to protect artifacts from black market dealers, which was apparently a real thing. So while Cormac could find out a bunch of information about Walker, the internet couldn't give him a clue about where she was right now. He still had a few tricks, though. He picked up a pay-as-you-go phone from a local drug store and prepared to talk fast when he got the archeology department secretary on the line in the morning.

"Hi, yeah," he said, putting on a clueless tone. "I'm here in Rapid City, I've got a delivery of bottled water for the dig out at Badlands but they didn't give me real good directions for getting to the site, I wondered if you could help me out?"

"Oh, of course," she said, and gave him precise directions.

People were so trusting. Yeah, he knew all about that, didn't he? He thanked the secretary profusely and set out.

The dig's headquarters was at the end of a pair of rutted tracks pretending to be a road. The only prominent structures were a single-wide mobile home that had seen better days and a couple of campers. Just two other cars were in the open space that served as a parking lot. Neither one was the tan CR-V.

He was still sitting in the Jeep, coming up with a good cover story for knocking on the trailer's door and explaining himself to whoever was inside, and for why he needed to find Walker, when the woman herself appeared. She looked just like she did in her university photo, with the dark hair, floppy hat and ratty clothes. Olive-colored pants and a loose white T-shirt today.

She saw the Jeep and her gaze narrowed. Yeah, she was surprised see him, he bet. He got out of the Jeep, expecting her to make a run for it, to break down into some kind of panic when he approached. But she didn't. She approached him.

"Can I help you?" she asked. "We don't get too many visitors out here." The suspicion in her tone was plain—visitors weren't supposed to just show up here.

"I want to know what you did to me yesterday."

She tilted her head. Now she looked confused. "I'm sorry?"

"Yesterday, you wanted me to look at a clay pot, and then you. . .you did something."

"I've never seen you before in my life."

He believed her. She spoke with such plain, stark truth, he couldn't help but believe her.

"You left me for dead," he said, trying again.

"I was here all day, until nightfall. Really, I don't know what you're talking about." She had begun inching back toward the trailer.

He clenched his fists against his head. What was going on here? "Do you drive a tan SUV?"

"You see a tan SUV here? Mine's the blue Subaru." She pointed.

"Well goddamn it," he muttered. Walker—no, not Walker, someone pretending to be Walker. They'd needed credibility. Credentials. Someone Cormac would believe and agree to meet without question. So they'd borrowed her identity. *Really* borrowed it, using magic. He'd never even questioned.

"Do I need to call the cops? Because I will." She'd taken out her phone and held her thumb poised over the phone's screen.

"You actually get a signal out here?" he asked.

She frowned and put the phone away. "Who are you?"

"I'm a fucking idiot is who I am. I don't suppose you have a twin sister?" He needed to think. Someone pretending to be Walker would still have some kind of connection to her. He could pick up that thread and follow it.

"No, why?" she said.

What were the odds she'd actually believe him? "I think there's someone out there pretending to be you."

Her confusion deepened. "Why would they do that? *How* would they do that?"

He shaded his eyes and looked around the lot, and the dusty trailer and camper. One bare-bones light post had a floodlight, just enough to cover the parking area. And a surveillance camera. "Where do you save your security footage? Mind if I take a look?"

"Do you really think someone is out there pretending to be me?"

"Yeah. And I need to find them." He sighed. "My name's Cormac Bennett, I got mugged on the side of the road and I'm just trying to figure out who did it." No reason she should believe him. But she nodded.

"I'm Aubrey," she said.

"Yeah, I know."

"Okay. Just a minute." She went to the Subaru, popped open the back hatch and rummaged around for a set of clipboards. He waited as patiently as he could. He really wanted to get on this woman's good side.

With less hesitation than he expected, Aubrey invited him into the trailer. A fan sitting to the side and going full blast didn't do much to move the air, which was hot, heavy, dusty. One half of the space was an office, a couple of card tables pretending to be desks, folding chairs, computers, and piles of paper. All of it looked temporary. The other half—that seemed to be where the real action was. Cormac stepped over to look. Cramped metal shelving held tubs, trays, and *stuff*. More tubs and trays sat on a table, where a couple of people worked with lamps, magnifiers, brushes, and tiny picks on pottery shards. Dozens of shards, stone tools, arrowheads, other bits and pieces, detritus. It all looked like junk but the pair of what must have been students or interns or something, as young they seemed, worked with a focus that suggested it was treasure.

Amelia would love this. Cormac shunted that thought aside. Best he not think about Amelia until he had a real plan of action. A target.

The people working here, grad students or archeologists or whatever, looked up at him, glanced over at Aubrey skeptically. "Everything okay, professor?" one of them asked.

"I think so," she called back.

Aubrey was waking up one of the computers. "The security footage all comes through here. If we have someone sneaking around who shouldn't be here, I'd really like to know about it."

He pulled over a folding chair and sat next to her.

"When do you think this person was here?" Aubrey asked and brought up a list of video files.

The person impersonating Walker had contacted him a week ago, and he'd agreed to the job a couple of days after that. "About four days ago," he said. "Let's start there."

She clicked open the file and fast-forwarded through the footage. Time zipped by on the screen, the sun rising, shadows in the parking lot shifting with the hours. Cars drove in, parked. People got out, gathered. The dig's day seemed to begin at dawn with a group of people meeting by the front door, then they scattered to cars and drove, presumably to the actual dig site.

"You'd recognize a car that wasn't supposed to be here?" he asked.

"Oh yeah," she said. "We're a pretty tight group. You just about have to be, working on a project like this all summer."

She'd called him out straight off, so yeah, that made sense.

Nothing from the first day's videos caught their attention. The second day—same cars, same people. Then—

"Wait," Aubrey murmured and paused the playback. She rewound, played again.

In the middle of the day, when only her Subaru and another SUV were parked there, a tan CR-V pulled into the edge of the surveillance range. A woman got out, glanced around, and marched with purpose to Aubrey's Subaru. Her features were obscured; she wore a coat and wide-brimmed hat even in the summer heat. But she was tall, svelte, and moved with confidence. Quickly, methodically, she popped the lock—she must have had some kind of tool to help her—and opened the driver's side door.

The woman reached in and slipped something into an envelope she'd had in the pocket of her coat. She didn't waste any time looking around, just closed the car door and walked away. The whole thing took no more than ten or twenty seconds. If no one had had a reason to review the footage, she might never have been discovered.

"What's she doing?" Aubrey asked, leaning in, fascinated.

"She's taking a hair off the headrest," Cormac said. And with that hair. . .it would be a powerful, complex spell, using a hair to form the basis of a disguise. But it would also be a really good disguise when it was done.

Aubrey sat back in her chair, nonplussed. "A hair? That's it? Why?" It wasn't like she'd sabotaged the car or tried to steal artifacts. It must have seemed so harmless.

"She's a witch," Cormac said simply.

"Huh. Like, for real? Like eye of newt and magic wands and the rest?"

"Yeah, afraid so."

He expected her to laugh, to express disbelief. A witch, for real? But she merely looked thoughtful. "And why me?"

"Credibility. She came after me. You just happened to be someone around here I'd listen to, so she used you. Sorry you got wrapped up in it."

In the video, the woman looked around briefly before climbing back into her car. Cormac leaned in suddenly. He recognized her.

"Can we freeze that, blow it up?" he asked, and Aubrey slid the computer mouse to him. He backed up the footage, zoomed in. She had on sunglasses. Her dark hair was in a braid. The features were fuzzy in the low-res footage, but there was something about the tilt of her head, the way she moved, and the bright red lipstick she wore. "I'll be damned."

Amelia wanted to know how many people from his past might be holding grudges. He wasn't expecting this one.

"You know her?" Aubrey asked. "Who is she?"

Maybe Cormac was wrong. This was a mistake. Maybe. "Don't worry about it."

"Is. . .is this going to be a problem?"

For him or for her? Best she not get involved. "You see her around here again, call me." He wrote his number on a notepad tucked under one of the stacks of paper.

She never stopped with the skeptical sidewise glances, but she pinned the number to a nearby corkboard, next to diagrams of excavations and photos of broken pottery in dirt.

She walked him back to the Jeep, maybe to make sure he really left. She also studied him in a way that seemed academic. What sort of sense would an archeologist make of his T-shirt and jacket, brown mustache, sunglasses, and constant frown?

"What exactly is it you do, Mr. Bennett?"

"Travel. Look out for things." He'd never been able to explain what he did, not since his days of hunting vampires and werewolves and everything in between. He'd gotten in the habit of delivering the vague and ready answer.

"Ah," she said. Then put a thoughtful hand on her chin. "Would. . .you like to go get a cup of coffee or something? We don't really have much here, but there's a good diner back on the highway to Rapid City. I'd like to hear more about witches." Her interest might have been merely academic.

The archeologist was cute, under the dust. Round face, bright eyes. She probably had some great stories. Maybe some other time. . . He shook his head. "I don't really have time right now. Maybe later."

She smiled wryly. "Good luck. If you find anything out about this impersonator, let me know."

"Sure." He walked out, ready to follow the next lead.

Driving away he thought: Amelia would have told him he should have gone for the coffee.

Clearly, he'd left too many threads hanging after that job in Chicago.

Lord Edgar hadn't been the Master of Chicago. Chicago technically didn't have a Master, as far as Cormac knew, though how the vampires themselves decided these things seemed arcane to him. But Lord Edgar aspired. What he wasn't was discreet, and while running a protection racket to make money he'd been leaving bodies. Vampires usually policed their own, but Chicago didn't have enough of a presence to manage it. That was exactly where folks like Cormac came in. Cormac had been hired to finish him by a local cop who knew and believed. He'd taken up a collection to pay Cormac.

Isabel Durant had been the primary human servant of Lord Edgar. She called herself a courtesan, but really, she was a human servant, which meant fetching and carrying in daylight hours and serving as a food source. Vampires didn't really need or want sex. For them, physical desire was tied up with drinking blood. So she could claim to be his beloved mistress and sex object all she wanted, and that might be what she got out of the relationship. But really, a human servant had more in common with livestock.

Ten years ago, she'd been stunning. Model-beautiful, aristocratic features, impeccable taste, and a stately manner. A trophy a would-be Master vampire would keep hanging on his arm, another pretty thing to go with all his other pretty things. She had seemed to enjoy being kept. Maybe Edgar had even promised to turn her, after a suitable apprenticeship. Well, so much for that.

Once he got rid of Edgar, Cormac had left her alone. She hadn't been a threat. That'd teach him.

Isabel Durant, from what Cormac knew of her, wasn't a witch. So what was she doing taking hairs from other people's cars? She'd either learned some witchcraft in the last ten years, or she'd hired someone. But why? If she'd wanted to leave him for dead she could have just shot him. She'd knocked him out, hadn't robbed him, but Amelia was gone. No way Durant could know about Amelia to target her. Something wasn't fitting together.

If Durant had been learning magic or had hired a magician, he ought to be able to track that. However, this was Amelia's area of expertise. She was much better at it than he was. He had learned from her by watching, but not enough for this.

Some quick searching revealed that Durant had no internet footprint to speak of. She might have been savvy at keeping her information offline, or she might have been one of those fringe freaks so suspicious of technology they never left an imprint. Not surprising, hanging out with vampires. So how did he find her?

He went back to Rapid City, forced himself to eat another burger, downed a large coffee, and sat in his Jeep to make another call.

"Manitou Wishing Well, may I help you?" A kindly voice answered, which meant this was Judi. Her partner, Frida, was more brusque. They owned a souvenir shop in Manitou Springs that served as cover for more occult dealings. Judi also ran a ghost tour in the historical town. First time he'd met them, they spotted Amelia right off—Cormac had two auras, Frida insisted—and hadn't batted an eye. He wondered what Frida would see in his aura now.

"Judi? This is Cormac Bennett. I could use some help."

"Cormac, how nice to hear from you!" A muffled shifting sounded, as if she tilted away the phone and said over her shoulder, "It's that tough fellow who knows Amelia Parker."

"What's he want?" Frida muttered back.

Judi came back on the line. "If I can help, I'll certainly try."

"You ever hear of someone named Isabelle Durant?"

"No, should I have?"

"Just thought I'd try. I think she's either working some bad magic herself or hiring someone to do it for her. I spotted her in the Rapid City, South Dakota area. You know any witches out here who might be casting spells to impersonate someone using their hair?"

After a pause, Judi answered, her voice gone from cheerful to somber. "That's some very unpleasant magic."

"Yeah, it is. I've got a whole lot of unpleasant going on up here."

"I see."

"I know it's a long shot but I thought you might know someone or have heard something, given your contacts." Judi played the part of an unassuming dabbler, but she had serious chops. "I was hoping you could maybe ask around."

He heard whispering—the two women in a hushed conference. He waited patiently.

Judi returned and asked, "Are you still there?" He murmured that he was. "Rapid City is it?" Yes. . . "You'll want to talk Gregory at Tea on the Range, in Deadwood." Tea on the Range? In Deadwood? Seriously? "I'm not saying he has anything to do with whatever trouble you're mixed up in, he's much too sensible for that. But if there's something fishy going on, he might have caught the scent."

He wasn't quite able to keep the skepticism out of his tone. "Okay. I appreciate the tip."

"I promise you, you won't regret meeting him," she said cheerfully.

"So do you guys have an organization of unassuming shop owners who are also magicians, or what?"

Judi deftly ignored him. "And how is Lady Amelia?"

Cormac hesitated, frowning. He wished he knew. "That's part of my problem right now. I'm not really sure."

"Oh, dear." He could sense her worry. But then, he suspected Judi liked Amelia better than him.

"If. . .if you hear anything from her, can you let me know?" That was a long shot. He wasn't even sure how that would work. But he would try anything at this point. He'd even ask for help.

"We certainly will. Good hunting."

"Thanks," he said, clicking off before she made him explain any more of what was happening, or worse, deliver any soothing platitudes.

Could Amelia be out there. . .somewhere? If so, would she be able to contact him? *How*? This was her area of expertise. He was at a loss.

Six

A great deal of magic was imagination. Visualization. Picturing what one wished to accomplish. Ritual helped focus that intention; ingredients and symbols with inherent properties could be manipulated. But before any ritual could be enacted, one must know what one wanted to accomplish, specifically and with confidence.

Amelia still had that tool, at least. But so much of her thoughts were currently occupied in just keeping herself whole. She had gotten out of the practice of doing this.

Back at the Colorado Territorial Correctional Facility, when her physical body had been hanged for murder, she had transferred her mind, her consciousness, into the very foundation of the place and had stayed there for almost a century. She had learned to travel through brick and stone, to possess in a minimal way some of the people there. With practice, she could see and hear and feel, at least enough to plan. Finally, she had met Cormac, and he had let her in. He understood something of what she was, and they had been able to work together. When he left the prison, he took her with him.

Now, though, she didn't even have those rudimentary abilities. She could sense no foundation, no pathways through stone or wood that could help her. There was no one here at all. Then, she had been disembodied. Here, she was entirely trapped.

Her mind would split apart if she kept screaming. So she stopped.

First, she must find some way, however small and slim, to reach the outside world. Second, she must discover what had happened to Cormac, learn if he was still alive and what had uprooted her.

He could not be dead. She refused to believe it.

More than a hundred years ago she had known she was dealing with dark, powerful, unpredictable magic. Had it been even more powerful than she thought? Had she somehow removed her own soul from the possibility of death? No, that wasn't it. She still had form, boundaries. She was restricted in some physical, concrete way. Trapped. Her soul hadn't been set loose—it had been *put* somewhere.

The clay pot. This had happened when Cormac picked up the artifact. Oh. . .this made sense. This was the anchor holding her in place. With this image firmly in mind she was able to collect herself and identify the boundaries trapping her, like some genie in a bottle. Her mind was contained, which meant she could use her thoughts for other things.

The woman, the archeologist, Aubrey Walker. She had not seemed magical to Amelia. She wore no charms or talismans and had seemed exactly as she appeared. But she had done this. She must have lured them out, set a trap—and captured Amelia.

But how could the woman have known about Amelia? Nothing about this made sense.

Unlike her time in the prison, she could not reach out to try to touch some nearby mind. To communicate, however little she was able. There was no one here, and the walls of this prison were secure.

Damn. Damn damn damn.

Impossible to tell how much time passed, without the body to mark heartbeats and breath, or eyes to watch sunlight come and go. She could count seconds ticking by, if she wanted to do nothing else. Amelia had spent years counting the seconds, in prison.

She had survived prison once and would do so again.

As it happened, she had not been abandoned here. She had been made captive. It stood to reason that a captor existed, and Amelia had only to wait for her captor to make itself known. And it came as lightning. A bolt of pain, scattering the self she had worked so hard to keep whole. The strike came once, a streak and flash launching through her prison. The second time it came, she was ready for it and was able to watch. The third time, she stood fast against it.

This was magic, it had to be magic. All that was left of Amelia was her magic, the soul of her that made magic possible. This was not physical torture; this was designed to tear at her soul. By the same token, one could not bind a soul as one could bind a body. She could resist in ways a tortured body could not. Magic was thought, was visualization, so she made herself a wall, a shield between herself and the torture. A prison within the prison, in a sense, but this one she controlled. The soul-blast came again, and Amelia was insulated. It did not touch her. Then it struck again, even more fiercely. Her shield held. Three more times, faster and harder, as if whoever cast the bolts was growing frustrated. As if they tried to shake Amelia out of her defenses.

Then the attacks paused. Amelia counted this as a victory and waited for the next assault. Her captor was active and meant to punish her. She would be ready.

The next attack came as heat, a slow simmering, as if she sat in a cook pot waiting for the water to boil. Clumsy and inelegant. The same defenses she had used before held.

Then came nightmares, but they were mere illusion, black swarms of demons, showers of knives, as insubstantial as she herself was. Amelia was able to step aside, detach herself from the onslaught directed at her, and observe.

Then came the voice. *You can't resist you can't stop me how are you doing this how are you surviving. . .*

So this was what it was like, having a voice in the back of one's mind, nagging.

Her captor expected some reaction that Amelia was not delivering. This gave her satisfaction. But she knew nothing of her captor's purpose, why the torture was happening at all. Her attacker expected her to be helpless, to have no experience of magic, of the occult practices that were required to stage such immaterial tortures.

If only Amelia could reach out, find some way to discover what was outside her prison. Think, she had to think. But she felt like she was a small fox hiding in an even smaller cave while the hounds bayed outside. If she moved, she was finished.

No, she was bigger than this, better. Whoever her torturer was, was clumsy, unskilled, using brute force instead of precision. Amelia represented a hundred years of magical experience. This was a duel, and she had the advantage, because her attacker didn't know she had initiated a battle. That the lioness was unchained. Amelia rolled up metaphorical sleeves and got to work.

She imagined sending a message. She imagined all the ways she might scry, looking for such a message from the beyond, and then thought of the process in reverse, sending instead of receiving. Trying to control which way the runes turned up or how the tea leaves scattered at the bottom of the cup. If she could not reach any nearby minds, could she reach out to magic itself? Magic trapped her here; she was half magic herself. Surely she could use that. She must.

Trying anything was better than trying nothing. She would start with a simple S.O.S. A cry, I am here, I am still here. She did not know if Cormac was still alive to hear it. But they had other friends, other magicians who might be receptive to her call. If they heard her, they might be able to help.

For now, she only wanted to be heard. S.O.S., S.O.S., S.O.S.

Cormac expected, maybe he hoped for, a classic Hollywood image of an Old West town with dusty storefronts and maybe a tumbleweed or two rolling down the street. But he drove around the curve and into the steep, wooded gulch where the town lay, and his heart sank. Casinos, everywhere. Too many shiny new buildings, tour buses with tinted windows, dozens of weekend motorcyclists. Another mountain town turned into a tourist gambling center, just like Black Hawk back home. Place like this wouldn't have enough magical savvy to fill a shoe. What was Judi thinking, sending him here?

A billboard hung on a corner of a building: *Witness the Thrill of a Main Street Shootout! Realistic! Fun! Family Approved!* Live shows three times a day recreating the murder of Wild Bill Hickok. Well, there was that, he supposed.

The address Judi gave him was at the end of the old main street, several blocks away from where the bulk of the casinos and T-shirt shops and crowds gathered. He parked, which was a challenge in itself in a town like this. He tried not to get annoyed. Trouble was, he'd started annoyed and was edging into rage.

Even though he knew exactly where it was, he walked past the place three times before realizing he'd arrived. The storefront was unassuming, weathered brown, with a closed door and dusty windows. A small sign hung above the front door, words painted in a touristy old-timey font: Tea on the Range.

The tourists walking up and down the sidewalk didn't seem to notice it. No one went inside. Frowning, Cormac pulled open the door and entered.

The floorboards were worn from decades of feet passing over them. The ceiling was high, and had what must have been the original pressed-tin decoration. The sunlight coming in through the windows filtered hazily through dust that might have been hanging in the air for years.

To his right, what must have once been a bar now served as a counter. An old mirror, worn and pitted, hung behind it, surrounded by shelves, which didn't hold bottles of booze but rows of labeled tea tins, along with mismatched cups and saucers and mugs. A display case of pastries sat nearby. A half a dozen bistro tables and chairs spread out in the front half of the shop. The place was empty of customers.

The back half of the store looked more like what he expected, what the back half of the Manitou Wishing Well looked like: shelves of books, handmade soaps and herbal sachets, crystals and tarot cards, all of it innocuous enough you could take it as seriously or not as you chose. Cormac looked around for the signs that he ought to take this place seriously: charms hanging above the doorway, spells worked into the signage. The pressed-tin ceiling was mostly made up of a flower motif that repeated, nothing mystical to speak of, but here and there a newer piece had been placed over the old, symbols that didn't go with the other decoration.

The whole place smelled of herbs and age.

If at any point, some classic Old West town had had a shop like this, this is what it would have looked like. Then again, maybe there had been shops like this, full of books and herbs and esoterica, the equivalent of a New Age apothecary and fortune-telling emporium but with a historical patina. Maybe they hid in plain sight, that unassuming tea parlor or what not. Amelia had traveled the world, looking for magic, and had found it. Maybe it showed up in places just like this.

Amelia would love this.

A young-looking man stood at the counter, reading a book lying flat on the counter. He had brown skin, short-cropped curly hair, and wore a long-sleeved, button-up shirt, a vest, wire-rimmed glasses. As old-fashioned as the rest of the place. He had a leather cord wrapped twice around his right wrist, which might have been jewelry except it didn't much go with the rest of his outfit. Might have been a spell.

Cormac didn't waste time and went up to the counter, putting his hand on the varnished wood. The guy looked up. His smile was perfunctory, the bland face of a customer service professional.

"What can I get for you?" A chalkboard on an easel listed a menu: tea in three sizes, prices for the pastries.

Cormac said, "Judi Scanlon said I should look you up. Might be able to help me with a problem."

The young man regarded him a moment. Sizing him up, and Cormac put up with it. Considered what he'd do if the guy denied knowing Judi, played dumb about the whole magic thing. But eventually he turned up half a grin. "She did, did she? I didn't think you looked much like a tea drinker."

Amelia was. He drank it for her, when they couldn't get coffee. "Don't seem to be too many tea drinkers around here." Through the windows, people passed by and never even looked at the shop.

"Folks have to really want to find the place." Which meant maybe Cormac was supposed to be here. That seemed to be enough for the guy. He closed the book and slipped it under the counter. Cormac caught just enough of a look to see that it was bound in stained leather, no title, no other markings. "And you are?"

"Cormac," he said. "You must be Gregory?"

"And Judi thinks I can help you."

"You can call her and get her to vouch for me."

"That's all right. You don't go around dropping a name like that for the fun of it." Cormac realized he really had no idea what Judi's reputation was outside of the nice old lady who gave ghost tours in Manitou Springs. He wondered if he wanted to find out. Gregory continued. "What's the problem?"

"You know her?" He unfolded the sheet of paper with Isabelle Durant's blurry, security camera picture and lay it on the counter. The man studied it, and his gaze narrowed in what might have been recognition. Cormac waited to see if he would deny it or dodge the question.

He lifted his gaze. "Why are you looking for her?"

Cormac's lip curled. "I just have a couple of questions I need to ask her."

Gregory's lip curled as well, a mirroring half smile, just as cynical. "That right?"

"She's probably laying low at the moment. She's been working some powerful magic over the last couple of days. Or she might have hired someone to work the magic for her. Judi says you might have a sense of who around here might be capable of that." *Or that it might have been you...*

"Let me ask you a question. If you know enough to know about that kind of magic, and Judi Scanlon trusts you enough to send you to me, why can't you find this person yourself?"

"That's just it, normally I would. And now I can't. That's what I need to ask her about."

The implications sank in—that Durant had done something to Cormac's magical abilities. It wasn't a lie, per se. Gregory raised a brow and blew out a breath.

"Why don't you step back to my office?" He went to the front door and turned over a painted wood sign from "open" to "closed." In the back of the shop, Gregory gestured Cormac to a chair at a small, linen-covered table. "Yes, I've seen her. I don't know her name but she's been in a couple of times, picking up odds and ends. It's not my place to ask my customers what they do with what I sell them."

"I've heard the same argument at gun shops," Cormac said.

"Yeah. Well." From a nearby shelf he retrieved a silk bag and drew out a deck of cards, which he began deftly shuffling.

"Tarot?" Cormac asked, smirking. "You think this will track her down, give me an address for her?"

"This isn't about her. I want to know what *you're* about."

Cormac leaned back and crossed his arms. He didn't much feel like being tested. On the other hand, he was kind of curious what the guy would come up with. This was just parlor tricks, though Amelia would say that in the right hands tarot could be more. And he wished he could stop thinking about Amelia. "If I pass your test, you'll help?"

"What's your connection to this woman?"

"Old grudge," he said.

"Mutual?"

"Honestly, until today I'd completely forgotten about her."

Gregory glanced at him. "Scorned lover? You dump her at the altar or something?"

"No. Never date anyone crazier than yourself, I've been told."

Gregory chuckled. It struck Cormac that he couldn't really tell how old the man was, a weathered thirty or a youthful fifty. He seemed young but his manner was confident.

He finished shuffling, squared the deck in the middle of the table. Cut it into two piles and turned over a single card from the cut. The image showed a woman with long black hair in an Old West get-up: pleated skirt, boots, a tailored jacket, wide-brimmed hat. She held a rifle. The pen-and-ink drawing was based on an old publicity photo of Annie Oakley.

"Queen of Swords," he said. He turned the deck over and fanned it out so Cormac could see the image in context.

The whole deck was Old West themed. Not Rider-Waite or one of the traditional decks Amelia was familiar with but something you'd expect to find in a tourist shop in Deadwood, and not in the hands of a serious magician. Six-shooters and rifles, horses and stagecoaches, cow skulls and lightning strikes over rocky mesas. The suits were rifles, arrows, gold pan and sheriff's star. The Major Arcana were famous figures and tropes of the genre. Tombstones and card tables, nooses and cactus. It was cheesy, and it made Cormac nervous.

Gregory turned the cards face down and shuffled the deck again. Spread the whole deck out in a fan, face down. The art on the backs showed a pen-and-ink drawing of intertwined tumbleweeds. "Now you pick."

Cormac didn't think. Reached out and put his hand on the first card he came to. Pulled it out and flipped it over.

The Queen of Swords.

That was just a little too pat. For all he knew Gregory was working with Durant. He met Gregory's gaze across the table. The man swept up the deck, shuffled, fanned the cards again. "Choose."

Cormac did. The Queen of Swords. Annie Oakley, who'd been alive at the same time as Amelia Parker, who had the same thick black hair cascading over her shoulders.

Gregory's eyes widened. "I'm not stacking the deck."

Cormac knew he wasn't. "Try it again."

He did so three more times, shuffling and cutting the deck differently each time, drawing from the bottom, the middle, laying a spread face down and turning up one. The Queen of Swords. The Queen of Swords. The Queen of Swords.

"This is a message," Gregory said finally, squaring the deck and leaning back from it.

"Yeah," Cormac said, uncertain what to do with the wash of relief. It made him almost light-headed. This was a message. This was Amelia.

"You know what it means," Gregory said, a statement. "Who is she?"

"What would you say? If this was a reading and not. . .something else, what would you tell me?"

He hesitated. "She's important to you. She's powerful. It's not the woman in the picture you showed me."

Cormac smiled and glanced away.

Gregory pushed away from the table. "I'm going to make myself some tea, you want anything?"

"Just water," he said. Cormac flipped the cards over, spread them out, studied the images. Found the Queen of Swords and pulled it front and center. The odds of a flipped coin coming up heads or tails was fifty percent, every time. The odds of drawing one card out of seventy-odd was the same, every time. But the odds of drawing that same card a half a dozen times in a row? This wasn't about odds. It was, as Gregory had said, a message. A voice reaching out, but unable to speak.

Cormac found the ace of the suit. Ace of Swords. A Winchester rifle, resting in a rack above a fireplace containing a blazing fire, in what looked to be a cozy cabin. He put this and the Queen next to each other. Not a message but intention.

Gregory returned with a tray holding a glass of water, and a small steaming teapot with accompanying china cup, saucer, and sugar bowl.

"Going to read tea leaves next?" Cormac asked.

"No, I'm not sure I can take any more messages." He looked at the cards Cormac had matched together. "Not the King?"

He shook his head. He didn't know what he was doing.

Gregory sat and told him the story: Durant came in looking for some arcane ingredients. Way beyond the quartz crystals and sage smudges he sold to low-key kitchen witches. She was looking for powdered puffer fish, poison arrow frog, that kind of thing, which he didn't have. Or at least wasn't willing to sell to someone off the street. She'd bought some plain green tea and a couple of chunks of hematite, and left.

"I need to find her," Cormac said decisively.

"She paid cash. Sorry I can't help track her down via her credit card. You're. . .not going to hurt her, are you?"

Why not? She left him laid out on a road in the middle of nowhere. She had done something to him and Amelia was gone. Yes, he was going to try very much to hurt her. "I just need to talk to her." He wasn't sure Gregory believed him.

"If she's staying in the area she might come back. I can give you a call if she does."

Cormac didn't want to wait. He thought for a minute, tried to imagine what Amelia would suggest. He'd learned a lot from her. Not enough, not for this. But maybe he didn't need to go looking for her. Maybe he could draw her out. Set a lure. Not even a summoning spell. Just. . .a sign in the window. A text message, hinting that he knew what she'd done. That someone was watching her.

"I can't wait. I need a signal," Cormac said. "Nothing big, not too powerful. Just. . .an urge to look inside." He flicked a hand, an acknowledgement of how much of this relied on chance.

"That kind of thing is real risky in retail," Gregory said. "You cast 'come buy me' over your shop and before you know it you're out of stock and everything is back-ordered and you have to close up. I cast things like safety and comfort so people feel at home here, wards so the drunk yahoos stay out, and the spending takes care of itself. This. . ."

"Not a big spell. Just a suggestion. Just for one person." He tapped Durant's picture. "A message that there's something here she wants."

"Why are you assuming I know how to do that sort of thing?"

"Judi Scanlon wouldn't have sent me to you if you didn't."

He offered a wry smile. "All right."

"All right you can do it, or you will?"

"I have an idea."

"I can pay—"

"I want the whole story. I want to know who the Queen of Swords is."

The whole story. . .he'd never get that. This story had no boundaries, and Cormac didn't know the end. "If this works, you will. Need anything from me?"

"Oh, the usual. A hair."

Of course he did. If he was going to be handling this shit in Deadwood at least he could get into actual straightforward gunfight. Nothing in this magic business was ever straightforward. "You got a plan for that hair?"

"It's a test, mostly. To see if you trust me."

Cormac felt blind. He'd spent most of his life without Amelia looking over his shoulder, why did he feel so lost without her now? He ought to leave here, get away, go back to the life he would have had without her—

Without her, he'd still be in prison, he was pretty sure.

Amelia had become the voice of his conscience, the voice of reason. Even now he was waiting for her to tell him yes or no. He didn't think he'd become so dependent. He reached above his ear, yanked on a brown strand. Barely long enough to matter.

Gregory produced a glass vial as long as his finger and held it out. Cormac dropped the hair in, Gregory corked it, wrote something on it in Sharpie. The vial disappeared into his pocket and the shopkeeper seemed far too pleased with himself.

What was Cormac getting himself in to?

"Give me until tomorrow. I'll need tonight to pull this together."

Now. He wanted to confront her *now*. "Durant might have protections—"

"We'll see."

"What exactly are you going to do? If you don't mind me asking."

From a different pocket, Gregory drew out a different small vial. This one contained a long, coiled black hair. "Pulled it from the sleeve of her shirt while she was looking the other way. I had a feeling."

"Shit," Cormac muttered, and Gregory chuckled. A powerful magician could do so much with just a strand of hair, as he'd already seen. If you had the hair of another magician their protections against your magic might not work. There were dark and powerful spells you could use to control someone, with just a bit of hair or a nail clipping. The cost to one's own soul for such magic was generally pretty high and not worth it. Except that Durant had happily used such magic to impersonate Aubrey Walker. Turnabout was fair play.

Isabelle Durant had been a servant to vampires. She didn't seem to hold her own soul in much regard. He wasn't too sure about Gregory.

"I'll text you tomorrow when I start things rolling," Gregory said. "I'll text again when she arrives. You'll want to be close when she does. This will likely only work once."

Handing over his phone number seemed even more momentous than giving the man a hair. Well, why not? This whole thing was already too personal.

"Till tomorrow then," Cormac said, and walked out.

Somehow, he had to sleep, but he didn't want to close his eyes. He should probably find a room, but he didn't want four walls around him. He wanted to be able to run, if he needed to. Run from what, and to where, he didn't know. His own mind wasn't secure, and he couldn't do anything about it.

He had stopped being able to make decisions without that feminine voice adding her opinion. He had thought he resented that voice.

Finally, he broke down and found a run-down motor lodge outside of Deadwood. The walls were thin and didn't block the sound of motorcycles roaring down the highway. Sturgis was an hour away, and it didn't seem to matter that the rally wasn't for another month, the hills still filled up with the machines.

He found some take-out Mexican, took a long, hot shower. He'd started smelling rank. Watched TV for the rest of the night, old movies on HBO that left no impression on him. He should sleep. But he didn't want to sleep. Usually, at night, she talked to him.

The only place he felt truly safe was in the mountains, so in his mind he came here, built up this memory of a valley ringed by a pine forest, a rocky creek tumbling down the middle, thick grasses where elk sometimes grazed. He could sit at the edge of the meadow and be calm. Back in prison, the memory had become the chink in his armor. This was how Amelia had reached him. He'd tried to keep her out, but when dark magic, a demon feeding on pain and blood, invaded the prison itself, they had to work together to defeat it. Since then, this valley in his mind became theirs. She would stand right there, by those rocks, her hands folded in front of her. . .

Without her, it no longer felt safe.

He could not see the sky overhead. It ought to be searing blue, he ought to feel the sun on his face. Before, he could always hear the rushing, trickling water in the creek, smell the pines. Feel the grass under his hands. Now, the vision became dreamlike, and not in a good way. Some form of vertigo overcame him, as he squinted out to a scene that wasn't any clearer than a faded picture. He could not feel the ground under him.

Several times that night he started awake and didn't know where he was. Yesterday. It had just been yesterday that he lost her.

In the morning, he found breakfast at a coffee shop. Around the same time, Gregory sent him a text message: *trigger pulled*.

Seven

Cormac parked the Jeep in an alley the next street over from the tea shop, out of sight. Waiting gave him time to think. His mind felt empty and hollow, with nothing rattling around but his own neuroses. The trick to getting along was never giving himself time to look at his own head. He didn't much like it in there.

Maybe he should read one of the books lying discarded on the passenger seat. They were Amelia's: a history of Jerusalem in the twentieth century. *The Serpent and the Rainbow* by Wade Davis. A Georgette Heyer novel. They read together. She used his eyes. Now, his eyes were his own again.

He waited.

He didn't know if Gregory could do what he said he could or if he played the odds and hoped for the best. He had seemed confident. Cormac wasn't sure, but what did he have to lose? Magic was influence, not science, Amelia always said.

His phone dinged. Text message: *now.* Which meant Isabelle Durant had walked through the door.

Cormac took a deep breath, got out of the Jeep. Closed the door, locked it. Patted his pockets for the charms Amelia always made him carry, protections against curses, magic, evil eyes, whatnot. Could never protect against everything, though, could you? He checked for a gun in a belt holster that wasn't there, years after he had stopped carrying. Never mind. He'd strangle Isabelle Durant with his bare hands if he had to.

Calmly, he walked around the block and up to the door of Tea on the Range. Couldn't see much through the front windows, past the reflection of sky and street. He opened the door, strolled in, like he was just another customer on any average day.

She was there at the counter, in tight designer jeans, tall boots, and a silk blouse, hair bound up with a jeweled clip, her face perfectly made up. This was just how she'd looked when she was with Lord Edgar. A brown packet of herbs or tea sat in front of her, while Gregory typed something into a tablet. They both looked up at his entrance; Gregory backed away a step.

Durant's eyes widened, and her hand went to her chest.

Cormac moved toward her, away from the glare of the front windows. Just in case she hadn't gotten a good look at him.

"You," she whispered in a choked voice.

He grinned. "That's right."

"No. . ."

"Yup." He advanced, intending to close on her.

"You're supposed to be dead!" she yelled, very much like she had seen a ghost. "I took your mind, why aren't you dead!"

He hesitated. "What do you mean, you took my mind?"

She laughed, a mad giggle. "Death is too good for you, so I took your mind!"

"You. . ." He had to stop and think. This. . .this suddenly all made sense. "You took it and did what?"

"I took your mind!" She backed away, looking around wildly as if for a weapon or an exit. Out of the corner of his eye Cormac saw Gregory, hands under the counter. Did the guy have a weapon for this sort of thing?

"What did you do with it?" Cormac demanded, the words raw.

"I put you on my shelf, so you would be mine forever, mine to have and torture. It worked, the spell worked, I trapped you, how are you here!" She grew shrill.

Almost, Cormac laughed. The pieces fell into place. She had a spell to take a mind, to trap it. . .and she had taken Amelia. Her spell took the wrong mind.

He pressed toward her. "Here's what you're going to do. You're going to bring me that clay pot, and you're going to put back what you took. Got it?"

"No, no. . ."

She hefted a chair from one of the bistro tables and swung it at him. He ducked, put up an arm to block and grabbed one of the legs. Yanked it out of her hands and closed on her. Durant didn't try to struggle with him, just let go and ran for the front door. Disentangling himself from the chair took a moment; he shoved it out of the way, sent it clattering on the hardwood floor, and ran after her.

Outside, he looked; she pounded down the block to the right. He followed. She was in a panic; he would catch her.

She turned a corner. He grabbed the wall to haul himself around after her—

She was gone. Here, the street led to an intersection, another pair of streets, and she hadn't had enough time to turn again. She hadn't needed to. While she probably didn't have a spell to make her vanish outright, plenty of spells could cause someone to look away, so they couldn't quite see her, or make her blend in, a kind of camouflage.

"Fuck," he muttered. He could keep running after her but would only look like an idiot.

Back at Tea on the Range, Gregory was still behind the counter where Cormac left him. The guy held his hands steepled under his chin. "And who is the Queen of Swords?" he asked again.

The question felt personal. "You got anything stronger than tea?"

Gregory drew out a half-full bottle of some obscure, probably local, craft whiskey, which he set on the counter with a *thunk*. "Now, who is the Queen of Swords, and what did Isabelle Durant do to her?"

Cormac wasn't going to be able to handle this on his own. He'd already decided that. He might as well tell it all. "Amelia Parker. She needed a body and I loaned her mine. Durant thought she was trapping my mind and leaving my body to die. But she got Amelia instead."

If Gregory didn't understand it he at least didn't scoff. "Lucky for you, I guess. That's some very unpleasant magic she's dealing with."

Cormac snorted a laugh. "Amelia would be better at sorting this out than I am." It should have been him. . .except he had no experience being a mind trapped in stone. She did. And she was trying to reach out. . . "I need to get her back."

"The pot. . .the reliquary, let's call it. You need to find it. So you need to find where Durant is hiding."

"Yeah."

If Durant were smart, she'd leave town. Flee. Cormac would have a tough time finding her then. But maybe Durant wasn't all that smart. She wanted Cormac, not Amelia. She'd be back. She'd find another way to take revenge on him. So yeah, she'd probably stick around.

Gregory continued, "I've still got her hair, I could try some scrying—"

"You have a map?" Cormac asked. He was a hunter, he'd been a hunter long before he'd known anything about magic. "Let's start with a map first."

At the age of twenty Amelia Parker left her well-born family's comfortable estate in Kent forever. She wanted to learn magic. All of it.

She hadn't started particularly well.

A woman could travel alone, even at the turn of the last century, but she had to be prepared, to plan ahead. To walk with a certain swagger that no one could question. Having a lot of money to smooth the way didn't hurt. Additionally, as young as she'd been she had had to remain on guard—primarily against a certain type of older gentleman, entrenched in colonial bureaucracy, who simply had to be *helpful*.

She didn't want help. She wanted power. So she buttoned herself up tight, put her hat firmly upon her head and kept her parasol close at hand, and set out, determined.

And still, despite it all, she would find herself on foreign shores, in an exotic market, staring around her with wonder and thinking this was it, this was all she wanted. To be part of the world.

At a market in Marrakech, only a few months into her journey, she grew drunk on the smells of spices and herbs, held back from pawing at baskets of dates and figs. Meat sizzled over braziers, and voices cried out, hawking their wares. This was just like she'd read about, exactly how she'd imagined traveling would be. The whole world was a market, but now that she was in the middle of it she didn't know what to try first. She bought a packet of figs and another of almonds, and tried to simply take it all in.

She mostly spoke French to get by, learned some basic Arabic. She searched for magic.

When she found a series of medieval alchemical symbols carved into the wood frame of an awning outside one shop, she stopped and stared. So far she had seen Turkish eyes and blessings in Arabic, some Sanskrit and even a bit of Hebrew. Common prayers and blessings, no more remarkable than a cross in a Christian country. But she had not expected to see such an arcane set of writing here, like this. To the casual gaze the symbols did not stand out among the other whorls and arabesques of the decoration on the shop's lintel. But to Amelia's eye they blazed, incongruous. This was not mere decoration. It was intentional, from another time and place and with its own meaning. It was a warding, for protection.

This was magic in the wild, and the thrill of finding it rooted her to her spot.

"Miss? Miss?"

She started back to herself, gripping her parasol. She really needed to be more careful. The person who had spoken to her was a woman, shorter than Amelia, round of face and stout of body, long black hair with a few gray streaks touching it. She wore a printed blouse, full skirt and vest in wild colors, and seemed like exactly the sort of woman who would inhabit a stall decorated with an alchemical ward.

"Are you all right, miss?" the woman asked in lilting English, and Amelia was a bit annoyed that she was so easily identified.

"Do you know what that means?" Amelia asked, pointing at the markings on the lintel.

The woman's lips curled in a half smile. "I hope so, I put it there."

"I beg your pardon, but I had not expected to find such symbols outside of a book, ever. I'm quite astonished."

"I see that."

Amelia blushed, looked away. She wasn't acting like a worldly woman of knowledge and consequence at all. She ought to be more circumspect. She had no idea what to say next. Only that she wanted to know everything this woman knew. But the shopkeeper wouldn't just *tell* her, would she?

"My name is Amelia Parker," she said, and held out her gloved hand. "You have a very nice shop here."

"And you are interested in alchemy," the woman said.

"I'm interested in everything," she confessed, a bit breathlessly.

"Here, come in off the street. You draw a lot of attention." The woman touched her arm and gestured into the warm, hazy interior of the shop. "My name is Mariam."

Amelia ought to have been careful, ought not to have trusted strangers. But she eagerly followed the woman in, and within moments was seated on cushions, at a low table, with a cup of sweet mint tea before her. Amelia drank, half expecting hallucinations, some magical concoction that would send her mind to another plane of existence—or knock her out entirely while the Mariam robbed her. She hardly cared, this was an adventure. But the tea was only tea, brightly flavored, a bit on the cool side.

Mariam offered Amelia a job. At first, Amelia balked. She was a lady, an English lady, she did not work in market stalls in North Africa.

But she quelled the old, stodgy sensibilities. That was her family talking.

This was, she realized, a test. And so, for the next six months, she worked in Mariam's tea and herb shop alongside her two young daughters, sweeping the floor, dusting tins and jars, cups and pots. Things got very dusty. Every now and then, Mariam asked her to translate a letter or part of a book. Amelia learned not to beg to be taught alchemy and magic. She learned to be grateful for whatever Mariam decided to teach her, which was, in the end, what Mariam decided she most needed to learn. A thing that could not be found in any book.

How to be still. How to breathe. How to be inside one's own mind.

Imagine an apple. Don't just think of an apple. Picture all aspects of it, the smooth texture of its skin, the weight of it in your palm. What color is it? Red, of course, yes? But no, it's more than red. Once you can feel the apple in your hand, really look at it. It isn't just red, as in a child's drawing. It has shades, freckles, streaks. A bit of gold on the underside, a bit of brown around the stem. To imagine the apple one must be able to picture it in hand, turn it this way and that, feel it, hold it to one's nose and smell the fruity sweetness of it. Or for a challenge, imagine it rotting. You hold the apple, and as you watch the flesh grows softer, spots appear, turn brown, weep fluids, until the whole of it is a sickly mash dripping through your fingers.

Until one can imagine all of this, can one really work magic? Can you cast a spell, unless you can imagine exactly what you want the spell to do? When you cast a protective spell around your room, are you simply saying the words, or are you building a wall, a shield, a barrier that ill intent cannot cross? Can you *see* it?

Magic is in the mind. So the mind must be sharp and specific. You must be able to create what you need with thought, when no other materials are at hand, when stress and violence assail you from without. When you have no other weapon but your mind, will it be sharp enough?

The work was exhausting and thrilling.

"Where did you learn all this?" Amelia asked Mariam one day, as they sorted a new delivery of teas into the right jars and tins. Amelia had shuffled off some of her staid English clothing, trading the high-buttoned blouse and long skirt for a tunic and loose trousers, a linen coat over all. She still kept her hair up and under a scarf, as if she was hiding. As a white woman, she still looked out of place here.

Mariam smiled slyly and looked out to the market, which was busy in the hour before dusk, merchants closing up booths and workers hustling back and forth on errands. "I have very wise ancestors."

That could have meant anything. The answer was a deflection. "Then why would you pass such knowledge on to me? I'm an outsider. You owe me nothing."

"Good of you to notice," Mariam said. "But you've learned to sweep the floors well." Amelia blushed, ducked her gaze. More kindly, her mentor said, "Some little instinct tells me the world might have need of such wisdom, passed along through you. The world is changing from what it was." This sounded like a mission, a directive: use what you have learned. Make the world better. The words felt like a burden.

"I can never thank you enough."

"No, my dear, you can't, but we all walk through life with debts. It comes out even in the end!"

At the end of six months, Mariam announced she was closing the shop. Her mother, who lived in a village several hours away, was ill and needed care. If she wanted, Amelia could continue running the shop. Instead, she decided it was time to travel on. She still had so much to see and continents to cross. Mariam agreed that her path lay away from here.

When she left, Amelia embraced Mariam and her daughters and promised to return to visit someday. She never did. She had not returned to visit any of the friends she had made on her journeys. When she emerged back into the world, she learned of computers and the internet and spent some time searching for the people and places where she had been. There was some small chance that Mariam's daughters, or perhaps their children, yet lived. But the market in Marrakech was long gone and Amelia could not find them.

That Amelia survived all that she had, she owed to Mariam and her teaching.

Amelia knew how to build walls with her mind, to imagine the color of the stone, the texture of them, the strength of their foundations. She also knew how to break them down. Particularly the walls people built up in their minds to keep their inner selves hidden, their emotions in check, to function in the world. Or not, sometimes. She had driven people mad, beating down their walls.

With Cormac, she finally had to simply ask him to let her in. And where was he, was he all right. . .

Had he just walked away?

When a presence tried to break down the wall she'd built to hold herself together, Amelia held fast. She had a century's worth of experience doing this. She wouldn't bend. The presence, however, was filled with rage, and this gave it power.

Who are you who are you what are you who are you tell me tell me.

Well. Something had happened, clearly.

You are not him tell me who are you who are you who are you.

Amelia couldn't be expected to carry on a conversation with someone who had so little control. So she didn't. She merely listened and tried to learn.

It was supposed to be him in here, why isn't it.

Ah, the situation started to become clear. Amelia was the victim of an entrapment spell, a powerful and dangerous piece of magic derived from voudon traditions that sought to control a person's spirit. Rather than focusing on control of the body, her assailant wanted to possess the mind.

The strike had been directed at Cormac. This was someone from Cormac's past, then, seeking revenge? They hadn't known that two souls resided in Cormac's body. The irony was rather delicious, that rather than trap the oh-so-physical bounty hunter, this assailant had caught perhaps the one magician in all the world who was well equipped to deal with such captivity.

Amelia very nearly relished the coming battle.

Who are you who are you who are you.

Amelia reached out, ever so slightly. Like plucking the branch a spider's web was anchored to, to see what reaction she got from the spider. Donned a bit of a careless tone.

"Got yourself in a bit of a fix, have you?"

Screaming answered her. The shocked reaction of someone who had not expected her prisoner to have a voice. This was someone who had a plan, and the plan was not going well.

"Ah yes. Would you like to talk about it?"

More screaming. So no.

To work magic one needed a sharp mind. One also needed a physical connection to the world. Amelia no longer had this. But she had a voice screaming at her. Wasn't much of a wedge, but it would have to serve.

Eight

Gregory pulled out a basic road map of the area and spread it on the counter. A pair of women came in, and he had to leave off to help them. They smelled about ten different teas each before picking one, and seemed delighted by everything about the experience, from the old-timey shop to the cute little teapots. Gregory charmed them. Cormac waited patiently and resisted an urge to break something.

"If they were able to come in here, they needed something, even if it was to smell ten different teas and walk out with a smile," Gregory explained.

Durant was close enough that she could be affected by Gregory's summoning spell and arrive in no more than an hour or so. The kind of magic she was working, she'd need to be isolated. Away from town, away from people. She was crazy enough to be neck-deep in weird, but not so crazy that she wouldn't try to hide it. She was used to a certain standard of living, a high level of personal decorum, so she wouldn't be camping in wilderness. That narrowed things down. Isolated vacation rentals, resorts. Cormac pulled up a map on his phone so he could look at satellite imagery. Separated town from wilderness, searched for dirt roads and isolated buildings, all within an hour or so. National forest surrounded Deadwood. East was open prairie and Badlands National Park. Southeast was the Pine Ridge Reservation. Durant would draw attention at any of those places, a random white woman off by herself working dangerous magic.

That still left a lot of ground to cover, but not an infinite amount. Cormac knew what her car looked like, what she looked like. She would be on the defensive after their encounter. That was fine. He found a pencil and started circling spots on Gregory's map. Old-fashioned footwork might just do the trick, no magic needed. That was the trouble with magic. Once you had it, you stopped using other tools.

"There," Cormac said, tapping the page. "I bet she's in one of those spots. I can probably check most of them before dark."

Gregory studied the map as if checking his work, then rocked back, nodded sagely. "I guess you don't need me."

"Wouldn't say that. I don't drink tea, but Amelia does."

"Well then. Let me know when I can brew a pot for her."

Cormac slipped on his sunglasses, took the map, and walked out.

He thought of renting a different car so that Isabelle Durant wouldn't see the Jeep coming and know it was him. Then he thought, fuck it. He knew his Jeep, relied on it, and this hunt was going to take him on some pretty sketchy roads. Let her see him coming.

The Black Hills were familiar territory, reminding him of the Rockies. Curving mountain roads cut through vast pine forests, tourist spots mixed with out-of-the-way farms, weathered ancient houses and more modern but no less weathered mobile homes. Cormac looked for public parks and abandoned lots, three or four turns off the main highway but not so out of the way that a parked car would draw attention. Every tan SUV he saw, he looked at twice.

Then he turned east, through Rapid City and to the prairie beyond. County roads stretched for miles. Along these he found a patchwork of farms and homesteads. He looked for the kinds of charms and runes and talismans a desperate magician might put up to keep someone like him out.

At one point he found himself on a rise, a hill that overlooked miles of sweeping prairie and winding gulches. He got out his binoculars and searched, as if he could spot a flare of magic boiling up like a wildfire. He could not.

He got out a thread and nail, Amelia's magical pendulum that would point directly to powerful magic. Dozens of times, he'd held the thread, let the nail dangle and point, and Amelia had interpreted its movements. Now. . .the nail just hung there. He couldn't tell anything.

Coming on sunset, he still hadn't found signs of Durant and her car, but he still had a few more roads to drive down. Patience, always patience. He'd hunted tougher prey than this in his time.

Twenty miles north of Rapid City, flashing red and blue lights lit up his rearview mirror. They seemed particularly glaring in the half-light of dusk. And yes, they were targeting him, because no one else was driving on this stretch of road. He did not have time for this. . . He hadn't been doing anything wrong, he was sure of it. He usually even kept to the speed limit, just so he'd never have to talk to cops again. That might have been his biggest goal in life, never talk to cops again as long as he lived. He considered punching the gas, running, but only for half a second. He was on a long, straight country road with no turns ahead and a line of sight that went for miles. No place to hide. Running would just hand them an excuse. Dutifully, lawfully, he pulled over, turned off the engine, kept his hands on the steering wheel. The window was already rolled down.

Two officers stepped out of the patrol car. Both male, white, on the young side. If they'd run his plates they'd already know about his record. At least they didn't have their weapons drawn. Then again, Cormac was white, too, even if he was a felon.

The taller one had light hair, a bit of paunch. His buddy had dark hair and a sour expression. Cormac didn't even try to smile. He waited for them to ask for his license and registration before moving to get them.

"Sir, please step out of the car," the tall cop said.

His breath caught, and his hands tightened on the wheel. Cormac wasn't prone to panic. He was used to being in control. This, the instant racing heart and sweat on his palms—this was trauma. Everything he'd been through, and what got him were a couple of regular cops standing outside his car.

Taking several slow breaths, he steadied himself. Kept his hands in view and moved slowly.

"Is something wrong?" he asked stupidly. Of course something was wrong.

"I just need you to step out of the car please, sir." The voice was calm, professional. Arguing would do no good here. Cormac opened the door, climbed out. Steady. . .

"ID please?"

Slowly, always slowly, Cormac reached into his back pocket for his wallet and handed over his driver's license. The taller cop perused it, handed it back. The second cop walked around the Jeep, studying the tires and wheel wells. Cormac tried not to watch him.

"Can you tell me where you were between three and six this afternoon?"

"Driving. Seeing the sights," he said.

"Can anyone confirm that?"

They were trying to establish an alibi. What was going on? "I think I stopped for fast food in Rapid City. You can ask them."

"But no confirmation for the rest of the time?"

Calmly, carefully, he asked, "What's the matter, officer? What's happened?"

"We'd like you to come to the station with us, to answer some more questions, if you don't mind."

Not enough calm in the world for this. "Am I under arrest?"

The cop regarded him a moment. He exchanged a glance with his partner, now standing near the Jeep's left front wheel. The second cop shook his head ever so slightly.

"No, sir," the taller cop said. Frewer, the name badge on his uniform read. "We just need you to answer some questions for us. You can follow us to the station in your Jeep."

"Saves you having to tow it later, I guess," Cormac said with a sour grin. Frewer matched it.

They were looking for something. Cop two, checking out the car—maybe a hit and run? No, they'd get his contact info and let him go for that. This was something else. Something worse. They drove off, and he followed in the Jeep just like they asked, nice and steady, with exactly enough space between them.

On the way, he called Ben, his cousin and sometime lawyer. Ben picked up on the first ring.

"Cormac. What's wrong?"

Yeah, he guessed maybe he should call on birthdays or holidays or some time when he wasn't in trouble. "I've just been pulled over by cops and I'm on the way to the police station in Rapid City, South Dakota."

In the pause that followed, Cormac listened for background noise, but couldn't make out anything that would tell him where Ben was, and what Cormac was interrupting.

"Okay," Ben finally said. "How bad is it?"

"Don't know yet. They say they want to ask questions, which probably means something's happened."

"And you're the guy standing in the wrong place with a criminal record."

"That's what I figure. Just thought I should give you a heads-up."

"Thanks," he said wryly, almost but not quite chuckling. They'd had plenty of conversations like this before. Well, not just like this. More often than not, Cormac actually *had* done something that the police would be interested in. "And why are you in Rapid City, South Dakota?"

"It was supposed to be a job. Things aren't going well." Cormac blew out a sigh.

"Okay, if you want me to worry, I'm worried."

"Let me see what these guys want. I'll call you back and try to explain."

"What's Amelia say?" Ben asked.

He definitely didn't want to talk about her just now. "Look, I can't really talk. I just wanted to let you know where I am."

"Do I need to drive out there?"

"No. Well, not yet."

"Cormac. . ."

"Fine. It'll be fine." He clicked off before Ben could be any more admonishing.

At the station, Officer Frewer placed him in his very own conference room and offered a cup of coffee, which Cormac accepted. Was desperate to accept. He didn't feel sharp, wanting only to wrap his hands over his head and shut out the world. Amelia, what would she say, where was she, what was happening to her. . .

He waited another twenty minutes before the door opened and a woman in a pantsuit entered, a couple of manila folders in hand. A detective with a case, looked like. This definitely didn't look good. Cormac straightened and was determined to be as polite and straightforward as he possibly could. He needed to get out of here.

"Mr. Bennett?" the woman said in a business-like manner. She was average height and build, maybe forty. Her brown hair was pulled back in a bun, and she wore dark-rimmed glasses. "I'm Detective Nielson. I need to ask you a few questions."

"Yeah, so I was told. What's happened?"

Frowning, she looked him over. Sat across from him and set down the folders. "Where were you between three and six today?"

"I told Officer Frewer, I was driving. I don't have any corroborating witnesses."

"You sound like you've been questioned about this sort of thing before."

She might have been making a joke. Then again, maybe not. He couldn't win.

Opening one of the folders, she studied a page there. It was a show; she wouldn't have come in without her questions already lined up. "You did time for manslaughter in Colorado?"

"I did," he said, looking off to a corner of the room, wondering what he'd have to say to make this finish sooner. "Time off for good behavior even."

"Hmm," she murmured. "What brings you to Rapid City?"

"Work," he said truthfully.

"What kind of work?"

"I'm a freelance investigator." Also not a lie.

"Investigating what?"

He winced. Yeah, that was going to be the hard part to explain. "Usually stuff that no one else wants to investigate. Haunted houses, old cursed burial grounds." He shrugged, as if it didn't mean anything.

The way she stared, he couldn't tell if she was a believer or a skeptic. "There a lot of that going around? Cursed burial grounds?"

"Google Cheesman Park in Denver. You'd be surprised."

"Aubrey Walker hired you?" Nielson asked.

That made Cormac sit up a little straighter, and the skin on the back of his neck crawled. "That's. . .a little complicated. Someone pretending to be Aubrey Walker hired me. Used Professor Walker's credentials to get me to take a job. There was a mix-up." How much of this was he going to have to explain? Because he wasn't sure he could, not in a way that would make sense to a hard-assed police detective.

"But you met with Professor Walker yesterday?"

"I did, yes. She helped me figure out that someone was pretending to be her. A woman named Isabelle Durant. We tracked her down on the security cameras over at the dig headquarters."

Nielson betrayed nothing, not so much as a flicker of understanding. "Have you seen Professor Walker since your meeting yesterday?"

"No, I've been trying to track down this Durant person, find out what she really wants." Cormac was just about done being polite. "Detective Nielson, what happened?"

She pressed her lips together and drew a couple of eight-by-ten photos from the second folder. Crime scene photos showing Aubrey Walker's dead body. She looked like she was on a gravel road, sprawled at awkward angles, legs bent, arms flung out, head to the side, eyes staring. Blood covered half her face, pouring from a combination of abrasions and a gash across her forehead. Her shirt was spattered with blood, her hair disheveled. Like she'd been hit by a car or something.

He closed his eyes. This wasn't fair. This was wrong, and he couldn't do a damn thing about it. He hadn't done the deed but he was pretty sure Aubrey was dead because of him.

"Aubrey Walker was alive the last time you saw her?" Nielson asked. "You're sure?"

"What happened?" Cormac asked again, his voice rough. "She was hit by a car, wasn't she?"

Nielson nodded. "Probably at high speed. She probably went over the top. Death would have been almost instantaneous."

"People always say that like it's a good thing."

"Some of us don't like to think about innocent people suffering. I very much want to know who did this."

He flipped through the pictures, not spending much time on them. Aubrey had suffered, even if only for a few seconds. Nielson had to know that. One of the pictures set the scene, a country road, probably near the dig headquarters. Durant had known where the dig headquarters were. So did Cormac.

"Your patrol officers searched the outside of my car," he said. "They didn't find anything."

"You could have washed it."

"Go out and take a look at it yourself, I haven't washed it in months."

"I already did, Mr. Bennett. And you're right. You really should give that thing a wash."

That was why they let him drive here himself. He ran a hand through his hair, wondered what else Nielson was looking for. She was looking for a confession. For a missing piece that would give Cormac a reason to kill the archeologist.

Cormac couldn't get arrested. He couldn't go back to prison. He wouldn't. He had to get out of this room, he had to—

"Mr. Bennett? Tell me about your contact with Aubrey Walker. From the beginning."

"I'm not sure I can explain it. It's. . .strange."

"Even more reason for you to explain it."

"You ever met a werewolf or a vampire, Detective? Or a witch?"

"Like. . .on that crazy radio show?"

The Midnight Hour. Kitty's show. Cormac knew the talk-radio advice show well and had accidentally appeared on it a couple of times. "Yeah," he said, chuckling. "Exactly like that."

"There's some weird stuff in the world, is that what you're saying?"

"That's exactly what I'm saying."

He told the story as simply as he could, leaving Amelia out of it because that really would complicate things. He produced the printout of Durant's picture from his pocket and smoothed it flat. Nielson studied it.

Cormac tapped the photo. "I think I'm being framed. Durant's first hit against me failed. So now she's trying something a little more dramatic."

"And where is Isabelle Durant now?"

"I'd sure like to know."

The photos of Aubrey's body remained on the table. Cormac couldn't not look at them. This woman was dead because of him. He'd come into her life and this was what happened.

Finally, Nielson collected the photos and other papers and slipped them back in their folder. "Mr. Bennett, I'd like you to give me a full accounting of your whereabouts, where you've been and anyone else you've talked to, since you arrived in the area."

Which included hours and hours of sitting in the Jeep with no one to verify. "Am I being charged with anything?"

"Not yet. Finish that accounting and you can go."

"Can I talk to my lawyer first? I have him on speed dial."

She frowned; he was making her job difficult. "How about this. Just don't leave town. You think you can do that?"

"You know I didn't do it. But it would sure look good on paper to charge me with it. Durant's counting on that."

Scowling, Nielson drew a card out of her pocket and slid it across the table. "You think of anything you forgot to tell me, or if you get a lead you think I'd like to know about, you call me."

"I can go?"

"For now."

She was going to have a patrol car on him until he left the state, he was pretty sure. But at least she let him go.

Outside, away from prying ears, he called Ben back.

"They let me go," he said in greeting.

"Are you going to tell me the whole story now?" Ben demanded.

Cormac started to. He intended to. But Ben would have too many questions. "It's complicated," he said, and Ben's sigh of frustration on the other end of the line was obvious. "I've been told not to leave town."

"That's just in case they need to talk to you again. It doesn't mean anything." He didn't sound convinced.

"There's a body, Ben. Someone I had contact with a couple days ago. I didn't do it." What did it mean, that he had to say that out loud, even to Ben? "They don't have any physical evidence. But my record's raising eyebrows."

"What's the detective's name? I'll see if I can hit up my contacts, call Detective Hardin here, find out if we can pull any strings."

"Put in a good word for me?"

"Something like that. Meanwhile don't do anything that'll get you in trouble. In any *more* trouble."

He chuckled. "Thanks for the vote of confidence."

"Call me if you need me out there. I'll drop everything."

A baby started crying in the background, which meant Ben was home, and Kitty and their son Jon were there, a nice domestic scene, and that was where Ben ought to be putting his attention. He shouldn't be worrying about Cormac.

"You don't need to do that," Cormac said. "It'll be fine."

The baby cried harder. Cormac couldn't imagine what must have been going on there. He still wasn't used to the way babies could just *wail*.

"Cormac—I gotta go. *Call me.*" It was a command.

"Yeah." The line clicked off.

Amelia skirted around her captor's mind. This was not an orderly collection of thoughts. Cormac was perhaps not entirely stable, but he had structure, order. A predictable set of strategies by which he interacted with the world. He could converse.

This mind had none of that. It was all panic, all hate. But she learned what she could, watching at a distance.

This was a woman, not young but not old. Privileged, she was used to living in comfort. Used to doing what she needed to keep herself safe, usually under the protection of others. But she had nothing now. She felt herself wronged. The details of it weren't clear. But knowing Cormac, Amelia could make a guess.

This woman, her nemesis, would destroy herself to take revenge on him.

Now, how could Amelia use that? Goad her into some kind of rash action? She almost relished the challenge. The woman kept the clay pot, Amelia's prison, close. Her wild mind was never far away. Amelia could brush it. Breathe the equivalent of a soft sigh upon it. Her captor would feel it as a nagging instinct. That voice that tells you there's something under the bed. Something hiding in the closet. It could just be a branch, knocking against the window. Or is it something else? Something dangerous? Her stomach would clench, her heart would race.

Amelia and Cormac had their place, their meadow, beautiful and calm, where she had first been able to speak with him. Approach him. Befriend him. This mind had no calm space, no safe refuge where Amelia might have a sensible conversation with her. How did this mind see itself? There had to be some kind of self-awareness, even if it had no visual component. Amelia needed to understand her, but however much she probed, she couldn't find a center.

I am your friend, Amelia prompted, not hoping to be believed. She did not need to be believed. She merely needed a space where this mind might listen to her, if only for a moment.

Who are you? Show me. Take a breath. Picture yourself in the place you feel safe. What is under your feet, what is over your head? When you put out your hands, what do they touch? Build me this picture. Show me where you go when you need peace.

The reply came, *There is no peace.*

In spite of herself the woman showed her an image of which she was mostly unaware, rising out of her hindbrain. They were in a stone room with no adornment. A cobbled floor, narrow windows close to the ceiling, the dank smell of a cave. Amelia would have called it a dungeon, but it was a modern American's imagined version of a dungeon, too wide and clean for its truly medieval predecessor. Amelia was not there, could not picture herself there, but she saw her captor.

She was a girl dressed in a froth of lace. Like the room, an adolescent conception of a historic romantic aesthetic. She was slim, long brown hair brushed to a soft sheen. Her hands were folded before her, and her head was bowed, contrite. She did not move, she did not speak. She might have been a statue.

"This is how you see yourself?" Amelia asked.

This is how I am for him. It was a thought, not vocalized. As if she had no voice, not even in her own mind.

"But how do you see yourself?"

I don't.

Amelia sensed the captor had the experience and bitterness that only came with age. Something had happened to her, and her sense of self had not grown past this place, the prison. This was where the woman's rage came from. She did not see herself without her master. She was doing what she believed her master wanted of her.

Oh Cormac, you would be able to tell me where this comes from, how it happens that someone so buries themselves within another. I do not understand. Amelia ought to try to help her. To free her. But she couldn't afford to. She had to look after herself.

"What will you do, after you have taken your revenge."

It doesn't matter.

"Do you think. . .you might ever break free of this place?"

It's too late. I killed her.

"Who—"

I have killed. I will kill again, to do what I must. The figure in the stone room never moved.

Amelia was missing information.

She had to get out of here.

Nine

Cormac got back to the motel for another hot shower and another sleepless night.

In the morning, he went back to looking for Durant's car. Checked the rearview mirror frequently—and yes, as soon as he left town he had a tail, an unmarked car. Two men sat in front, one of them talking on a phone most of the time. Cormac stayed five under the speed limit just to annoy them.

He had a couple of spots left on his map and took his time with them. Some of it was rangeland, some of it out-of-the-way forgotten places with trailers and junked cars around. Cormac searched for the tan SUV. The cops kept their distance—letting Cormac do their work for them.

On a forested road in the choppy foothills, he found Durant's car, seemingly abandoned. Parking some ways behind it, he got out, approached cautiously. It had been recently washed, so any evidence of the hit and run was erased. A forensics team might be able to get something. The inside was empty. Even the usual detritus that collected inside most cars—coffee cups and food wrappers—had been cleared out.

Another dead end. Well. Nothing to do but turn around and find the next road. He walked away without touching anything and called Nielson.

"You can tell the officers you've got following me that I found Durant's car," he said. "It's been washed and looks abandoned. No idea where she could have gone."

"Damn," Nielson muttered. "I suppose you expect that calling me gives you points in your favor?"

"Naw, the fact you've got me doing your leg work is all the points I need. I'll talk to you later, I'm sure—"

"Mr. Bennett."

He hesitated. He could pretend he hadn't heard and just hang up. But he answered. "Yeah?"

"If you find her, call me. Don't confront her."

"I'll talk to you later, Detective," he said and hung up.

He'd talk to her after he confronted Durant on his own terms, to get Amelia back.

Amelia could not save her captor. She should not need to. She wanted her body back. To do this she had to get the woman, the cage where she was keeping Amelia's consciousness, and Cormac all in the same place. And she had to do it with no body of her own and no voice. By mere mental persuasion. She had to lay out a path and hope this woman followed it.

And then hope Cormac anticipated her. How well did the man know her, really?

Her captor had to sleep. No matter who she was, how mad she was, she had panicked herself to exhaustion and had to rest. This made her vulnerable, and Amelia came to her in dreams.

Tauntingly, Amelia's mind whispered to hers, "You want him, not me. So how are you going to get him? Draw him out. Try your spell again—"

Too hard, too hard.

"Ah yes, a very dangerous, difficult spell. Where did you learn it? Very few who know such spells would dare to teach it."

Paid. I paid.

Which meant somewhere in the world was a dangerous, unscrupulous magician selling their knowledge, unmindful of the risk. A problem for another time. "You might think of trying. You've come too far to give up, don't you think? You would need to make a new vessel from scratch, enchant it, arrange another meeting it, get him to pick it up, except that he'll be ready this time, cautious. On the other hand. . ."

What?

"You wouldn't need to work the spell from scratch, perhaps. Perhaps. . ."

What? What?

"Oh that would never work," Amelia thought slyly, prodding, withdrawing, pulling her captor closer.

What?!

"You could simply swap us out. Send me out and take him. It wouldn't even be hard. I could show you."

Her captor's mind settled into something like planning. Strategizing.

"Lure him," Amelia urged, gently as she could, trying to mask her own urgency. They both wanted the same thing, didn't they? They both wanted her out of here. And to find Cormac, though Amelia didn't know where he was, what he was doing. Her captor didn't offer any argument so this must have been possible. Cormac was still out there. He *must* still be out there. He wouldn't just *leave* Amelia here.

Would he?

"Set a trap."

How?

"Send a message." Amelia knew exactly what would get his attention, what would bring him into the open without raising her captor's suspicions. "Tell him. . ."

Cormac had to eat, but he wasn't happy about it. He was living on fast food because it was convenient. He ate better, with Amelia around. With Ben and Kitty looking after him. With friends. He wasn't used to thinking of himself as a man who had friends. Especially not when all his meals for the last few days had been eaten in parking lots, in the front seat of his Jeep. Better off by himself, then no one got hurt, no one got killed because they just happened to be standing in the way—

His phone rang. Caller ID said Gregory from the tea shop. He shoved the burger wrapper aside and answered. "Yeah?"

"Hi, Cormac? Can you get over here?" His voice was on edge. The man always had an edge to him, watchful, as if always solving puzzles. This was different—anxious.

"What's wrong?"

"I got a message."

And wasn't this interesting? "I'll be there in half an hour."

Back in Deadwood he parked a couple of blocks down from the main street. The shop's sign was turned to "closed," but the door was unlocked so Cormac went in. Gregory was sitting at the table in back, the Deadwood Tarot squared neatly on the table, a small piece of paper resting on the felt in front of him, along with a steaming cup of tea. He glanced up at Cormac's approach and frowned.

"What happened?" Cormac asked, pulling out the seat across from the magician.

"Isabelle Durant came in. Threatened to burn the place down if I called the cops on her. I told her that'd be a little extreme, when all she did the last time she was here was throw a chair. But I take it something's happened since then."

"You could say that."

Gregory waited for Cormac to explain, but he declined to. The man glared. "I'm going to have a word with Judi Scanlon about bringing you and this mess down on me."

"Aren't you the least bit curious about what all's going on?" Folks who worked in the shadows like this loved a good mystery. Or even a bad one. "What did Durant do?"

"Said to give you this. What did you do to her to piss her off so bad? She wants to kill you." He slid the folded paper across to Cormac.

"Yeah, I know. I—" He wasn't sure how to put it. She had been a servant to vampires, guilt by association. But Gregory might not see it that way. "She lost her job because of me."

"That must have been some job."

"Yeah." He read the message, written in sloppy cursive.

I can tell you how your father died. Be here, in the street, at midnight.

Why was it always midnight? These jokers never had any imagination. The rest of it confused him for a moment. He knew exactly how his father died—he'd been there, he'd witnessed it when the werewolf they'd been hunting mauled him to death. Cormac had killed the monster; it had been his first kill. He'd been sixteen.

But Durant. . .Durant didn't know how Cormac's father died. It would seem like a good mystery, wouldn't it? Something sure to draw him out, if she believed that Cormac didn't know and that he would want to.

Amelia. Amelia had given Durant that clue as a lure. It would fire up Durant, but Cormac would know it was fake. Amelia had somehow got a hook into Durant, and she had a plan. He crumpled the page in his hand and chuckled. For the first time since losing her, he felt back in control.

"What's it mean?" Gregory asked.

"You read it?"

"Yeah. I mean, clearly she's trying to set a trap for you. Do you really need to know how your father died that badly? Maybe you should just let it go."

"Oh, it's a trap all right, but not for me." Cormac turned the deck over, intending to fan them out to find the card he wanted. But it turned out she was sitting right on top. The Queen of Swords. He tapped his finger on it. "She set the trap. I just have to spring it."

Gregory stared at him, nonplussed, and Cormac relished his confusion. "Can I watch?" he asked finally.

"Yeah. I might need your help." He went outside to make his next call, to Detective Nielson.

"Mr. Bennett?" she answered.

"Do you trust me, Detective?"

A pause, then, "I can't say that I do."

"I can give you Durant. But you have to promise to wait until I give the signal. I have some business with her first."

"You can give her to me now, or I'll charge you with obstructing justice," she said evenly.

Yeah, he should have expected that. "She has something of mine."

"We can get it from her once we know where to serve the search warrant."

"It's not. . .it's not really a *thing*, it's. . .it's not really tangible. It's weird, it's crazy, I can't explain it. But I just need a little time before you swoop in. Can you give that to me?"

"If what you say about her is true, Isabelle Durant is a very dangerous woman. And you're just going to, what—ask her nicely?"

Not *nicely*. More nicely than he wanted, for sure. "We'll see if that works."

"If you're having one over on me, there'll be consequences. I know that means something to you."

"Yes ma'am, it does. You know where Tea on the Range is, in the old part of Deadwood?"

She groaned. "For the love of God please don't tell me you're arranging a standoff on the streets of Deadwood."

"Durant will be there out front." He made a guess. Took a risk. "Ten minutes after midnight." He had no doubt Nielson and her people would be there long before. He just had to hope that gave him enough time with Durant.

"Well, what have I got to lose, right?"

"You? Nothing. Thanks, Detective." He hung up.

Gregory was waiting just inside the door, leaning close enough to the glass that Cormac was sure he'd been eavesdropping. His gaze had narrowed and turned appraising. "Are you sure you're the one setting the trap?"

"I'm the one who knows where all the pieces are. Now, we just have to wait until midnight. I'll be back around ten till." He started walk away, when Gregory put up a hand to stop him. He held two cards. The Queen of Swords, and the Ace.

"Take them. For luck."

More than luck, they might have been a lifeline. Magic was all about symbols and thought. Cormac might need a focus, and that card, the woman with the black hair and determined expression, weapon of choice in her hand, might do it.

His familiar valley was dark, overcast, only the milky light of the moon bleeding through. He could sense trees, imagine wind rustling the leaves. But the image, the scene that was so familiar and so comforting to him, was indistinct. He was losing it. He called out; the sound should have echoed. But his voice fell flat, as if the space had become small. Dead.

He was a better person with Amelia. His mind was a better place. This would work.

The night was warm, dry and sharp, smelling of smoke. Maybe campfires somewhere, or maybe a wildfire was burning up in the hills. It felt dangerous. Or maybe he was projecting.

A couple of old-fashioned streetlamps lit up the corners, that was it. The casinos further up the street were still jumping, but this part of town rolled up the sidewalks after dark. They had the block to themselves.

Gregory spent the last hour before Durant's arrival walking three circles around his shop and marking all the doors and windows with runes.

"It's me she's after," Cormac said. He was trying for reassuring but it came out sarcastic.

"Can't be too careful," Gregory replied.

He wasn't wrong. The pockets of Cormac's jeans were filled with talismans and charms, so it wasn't like he was one to talk. But they hadn't done much to protect him the last time Durant confronted him.

"I still don't know who this is a trap for," Gregory said, coming up alongside Cormac where he stood on the sidewalk outside the shop. The night had turned cold; the magician rubbed his hands together. "Do you trust this Queen of Swords?"

Amelia could be ruthless. She gathered power to her. She had driven men mad, she had made them kill themselves. She had a hundred years of history he knew very little about. But they were partners. A team. She'd said so herself.

He chuckled. "We'll find out, I guess."

Shortly before midnight a figure emerged from darkness. Like a vampire, it seemed to move in the shadows, hiding until it came into the circle of a light, then it marched toward them, up the middle of the street. Isabelle Durant, looking elegant in silk slacks and a tailored suit jacket. Her hair was loose but still perfectly styled, her makeup expensive. She looked so out of place here. Cormac might have taken everything from her when he killed her Master, but she didn't have to look like it.

She held something cradled in her arms, covered with a woven, patterned scarf.

A mad glaze in her eyes, she caught sight of Cormac and gave him a weirdly flirting smile, looking him up and down like he was on a shelf at a store. She believed she had the power here.

"You came," she said, haughty and condescending. "I wasn't sure a man like you could be lured by such an emotional appeal."

That she could be so wrong and so right at the same time. A harder man would not have been swayed by emotion and would have walked away from Amelia. Cormac was going soft, and maybe he didn't mind so much after all.

When he didn't answer, her smile turned brittle. "Well, aren't you going to ask how your father died? Aren't you going to ask how I know such a thing?"

Cormac said, "My father died when a werewolf ripped his throat out. I watched it happen. I'm not here for that. I want what you're carrying there."

Her expression crashed into hard, stony hate. She'd been tricked; that had to sting. But she still had what he wanted. Question was, what was she going to do about it.

With a flourish, she removed the scarf, revealing the clay pot. He studied it as best he could at this distance and was pretty sure it was the same pot. Same shape, color, and markings.

He started toward her, one slow step at a time.

"Back," she ordered. "Stay back."

He held up his hands. No trouble, no trouble at all. "A lot of people looking for you, Durant."

Ignoring him, she set down the pot and drew something out of the handbag hanging off her forearm. The bag was stuffed full of who knew what. Cormac's heart started pounding hard; he had to work to calm himself, to not march straight over and put his hands around her throat.

The pot drew his attention. He held his breath, listening—would he even know if Amelia was there? Could she reach him?

Durant had taken out a piece of chalk and drew a circle on the asphalt, maybe four feet in diameter. Biting her lip with concentration, she worked quickly, marking symbols around the circle. Messed up a couple of times and had to awkwardly rub out the mark and try again. This wasn't second nature to her. She was acting like she was following someone else's instructions. That arcane circle—that looked like Amelia's work. Durant only thought she was working her own spell. Cormac had never had a harder time waiting for a trap to spring.

He tilted his head at Gregory. "What's that look like to you?" he asked softly.

"That's out of my league," he answered. "That lady's going to blow something up if she isn't careful. Magically speaking, I mean."

Nielson and her crew were probably here already, lurking. They were well hidden. Would they give Cormac the time he needed? And how much time was that. . .

"Durant!" He walked into the street. "Why come after me now? Why come after me at all?"

She wouldn't look at him. "A good plan takes time to pull together. Darius wanted to just kill you and be done with it. I told him he'd never succeed. And he didn't. My plan was better. It might have taken time to learn what I needed, but I can be patient. My Lord Edgar would be proud, don't you think?"

Darius? Was that the vampire who'd come after him last week? And what would she say if he told her that he hadn't thought about her, Edgar, or any of his vampires in years?

The chalk crumbled out of her fingers, all used up. She stood. Her hands were shaking. "She's important to you, isn't she?" she said, taunting, glancing at the clay pot. "You'd do anything to save her."

"Just about."

"Well. Come on. Pick it up." Backing away, she nodded at the pot, which was sitting in the middle of the circle she had drawn. Both it and Cormac would be contained within its boundaries, if he stepped up to it.

Slowly, he approached. A sign, if Amelia could just give him a sign . . . No, he'd had plenty of signs. "How do I know this isn't just going to knock me out again, or worse?"

"What you think doesn't matter. If you want to save her, you'll do it."

"I'm not convinced you know what you're doing."

"Quit stalling," Durant said. "Pick up the jar."

"Just like that?"

"Yes."

This was Amelia's spell. Cormac was sure of it. Which raised a new question: how much did he trust Amelia? How much would she love to have his body without him to argue with over it? Maybe she didn't need him. What would this spell do, really? Did he trust her? They had walked out of prison together. She had called them partners.

He flexed his hands. Tried to settle his mind. Be calm. Imagine the valley. Build up that space. That safety.

Durant pulled something else out of her bag. A 9mm handgun, pointed at him. "Pick it up!" she screamed.

In the end, he had only to ask himself one question. Which of them was stronger, Isabelle Durant or Amelia Parker? No question there, no question at all. He knelt by the jar and filled his mind with the thought: *Amelia, I'm here.*

He wrapped both hands around the pot.

Now. Now now now.

Imagine a rope and throw it to him. *Cormac, grab hold. Grab hold, now!*

They were now two minds with no body, and they needed an anchor.

He responded to her voice instantly.

Now imagine an anchor, holding them fast. *Hold on to me, hold on.*

I've got you, he said, and she could very nearly feel his arms around her. She almost laughed.

Where are we, where, where. . .

They stood in a valley, high in the Rockies. A pine forest bounded the grassy bowl through which a stream rushed and sang. Above them, blue sky. Home.

He stood before her, gripping her arms. His eyes were closed. She clung to him.

"Cormac," she murmured.

His eyes opened. They darted, taking her in, all of her, and his hand cupped her cheek. "Amelia," he breathed out.

She fell into his arms, laughing, and he held her tight. This was not real, this was only thought, but she *felt* him, a powerful embrace, full of desperation.

"What the hell happened?" he whispered to her ear.

"A bloody mess is what," she answered, holding him. She didn't want him to let go. May he never let go. . . "Where are we? Cormac, where are we?" She forced herself to pull away, but he kept his hands on her arms. An anchor.

"You don't know?"

"There was a chance it could go wrong. Horribly, awfully wrong. I tried to anchor us to your body, but if I missed, if I got it wrong—" They might have ended up back in the jar. She tried to reassure herself that at least they would be together—

But Cormac donned a slow, sly smile. A hunter's smile. "I think it's time we have a word with Isabelle Durant."

And he opened his eyes.

No more than a couple of seconds had passed. Durant was still standing here, backlit by washed-out streetlights, pointing the gun without conviction, waiting. She might have been holding her breath. Gregory waited in front of the shop, hands clenched into fists. The burnt smell of tension in the street was the same. Everyone waited to see what the trap had caught.

Cormac rubbed his fingers along the surface of the jar, its rough clay, the symbols in raised paint. It was inert now.

Amelia? he queried the back of his mind.

I'm here. Oh, I am here!

His mind felt right for the first time in days. He chuckled softly. Do you have anything you'd like to say to her?

Did she ever. He let her slip into control of his body, to use his voice. This was what Durant expected after all. Cormac's body but not Cormac. Let her think she won, just for a second.

"Hello, Isabelle." She caused Cormac's body to stand, the clay pot resting in her hands.

Durant's eyes lit up. She gasped a laugh. "It worked? It worked!"

Amelia, through Cormac, said, "Look at you. In so far over your head you don't even know you're drowning."

Durant put her hand to her mouth, grinning. "He's there, he's trapped in the jar now, just like you said—"

"Oh, my child." Amelia shook Cormac's head. "You've no idea what just happened, do you?"

Durant's smile fell. "What. . .what happened?"

"Exactly what I wanted."

"Who are you?" Durant's voice pushed to the edge of a scream.

Amelia retreated, leaving Cormac back in charge of his body and his voice. The timber of his speech changed, from Amelia's clipped aristocratic accent to his flat midwestern. "Durant? You lose."

He let the pot fall. It tumbled, and Cormac's—and Amelia's—heart lifted at the sight of it, all that trouble, the terrible trap. It smashed against the asphalt. Clay shattered. A thousand pieces, a cloud of shards and powder expanding. The cracking song of it rang out.

Durant screamed. It might as well have been a baby's skull that shattered, so much anguish filled the sound. Cormac lifted his hands, brushed his fingers in a show of dismissal. He smiled, victorious.

"Put the gun down! Put down the weapon! Hands up!" Urgent, professional voices called out. From side streets Detective Nielson and what must have been every uniformed officer in the county closed in. "Put it down!"

She'd waited. Thank God and all magic she had waited.

Cormac stood very still, his hands raised and harmless. Durant looked around with the panic of a trapped animal. Then her gaze rested on Cormac, and some decision settled over her expression.

"No!" Nielson ordered. "Drop it, drop it now!"

He knew it would happen just as her finger tightened. Time slowed, and a strange confidence settled over him. Whatever was going to happen would happen, he could only do so much to stop it. But that little, he would do. He breathed out, watched her hand, saw the twitch. And he dropped, dodged, rolled to the side in a way that he hoped she would not anticipate.

The gun fired, the air exploded with the crack.

The bullet hit. Knocked back, he fell prone.

Cops shouted. Everyone shouted. Somebody wanted an ambulance. Cormac lay still. He couldn't tell what got hit. He blinked up at sky.

Cormac? Cormac!

He passed out.

The scene was vague. Rushing water chimed nearby; birds sang. The air smelled of springtime, lilacs and warmth. He was in a boat, a small craft drifting lazily. He was unstable, but if he lay still, the soft movement lulled him, and he let himself drift. He wore a suit, something out of a Victorian movie, tailored and perfect, with a neat cravat. His mustache was trimmed. He was the dashing hero of a romantic novel. He lay with his head in someone's lap. Gentle hands stroked his forehead. A woman, wearing diaphanous silk that frothed around her in a gown that was complicated and angelic. Her dark hair lay around her shoulders in waves. If he reached up, he could wrap a lock of it around his finger, and it would feel like satin. The woman, Amelia, pressed her hand to his face and gazed on him with such care and longing. He wanted to pull her down with him and hold her close, but it was all so impossible, and a thick haze blurred everything, and he couldn't move, and the boat drifted on and on. Nothing here was right and yet he didn't want to leave, this was too perfect—

"I will be here when you wake up, my heart," the woman breathed, and she faded, until all was white silk and rocking waves and she was gone and there were other voices—

"Mr. Bennett? Cormac? Can you hear me? Open your eyes if you can hear me."

Opening his eyes was a chore, but he did it, blinking into too much light, so that he winced and turned away. He was cold, his mouth tasted like metal, and the air smelled like a hospital.

"What. . .what happened. . ."

"Mr. Bennett, do you remember being shot?"

Oh yeah. He remembered that.

"Bullet hit your left shoulder. You've just come out of surgery. Everything's fine, but you'll be out of it for a while. Just rest, all right?"

"Amelia. . ."

"Amelia? Is that someone we should call?" The nurse seemed concerned that she might have missed something.

I am here.

He chuckled. "No. . .she's already here."

"Oh yeah," the nurse chuckled. "You're on the good drugs, aren't you?"

Satisfied, he dropped back into the haze.

Ben came in not long after he'd been wheeled into a private room. His cousin, pushing forty like Cormac was, rough brown hair, shadows at his eyes clearly indicating he'd missed sleep. Cormac tried to figure out if he'd had enough time to drive here from Colorado and who might have called him to tell what happened, but that was all just a bit too complicated right now. Ben looked him over, in the bed and hospital gown, IV bag dripping into him, monitors clicking away. He sat heavily in a chair and folded his hands in front of his face.

"You didn't have to come here," Cormac said. His voice sounded kind of vague. A lot more than saline was dripping out of that bag, he suspected. He knew he ought to be in pain but he didn't much care at the moment.

"Jesus." Ben looked away, chuckling through his scowl. "You almost got Kitty and the Junior League, too. I talked her into staying home. But you should call her."

Maybe he could just lie here a moment, not thinking of anything.

You owe Kitty a call.

Yeah. Okay. Later.

"Still—"

"Yes, Cormac, I had to come here. Practically our whole lives I've been waiting to get a call from the cops telling me you're. . .that something had happened. Now here we are. It really did."

"Yeah, I guess so."

"You ever going to tell me what happened?"

"Maybe. . .maybe later."

"And how is Amelia?" Ben and Kitty knew about Amelia and that whole history. They practically treated her like one of the family, which was weird if he thought about it too much. Then again, they were werewolves. They knew weird.

How are you, Amelia?

Tell him I am doing quite well now that the trouble is past, thank you, and it's very kind of him to visit.

"She's fine."

Cormac. . .

"She says it's very kind of you to visit." Cormac shifted, trying to sit, then gave up. The needle in his arm was starting to itch. So was his shoulder, which was swathed in bandages. "Maybe it's just as well you're here. The cops are probably wanting to talk to me."

"Yeah, I already met your Detective Nielson. Sensible woman, there."

He chuckled. "She tell you what they're charging Durant with?"

"A handful of breaking and entering and theft charges for her shenanigans at the dig site. Attempted murder for shooting you, and murder one for Professor Walker."

"Not vehicular homicide?"

"They started with that. Then Durant explained in great detail how she planned it out, and why. So, it's murder one now. I expect she may not be competent to stand trial. That's where I'd go if I were her lawyer. But I'm not, thank God."

"It's my fault Aubrey is dead."

Ben didn't answer right away. He couldn't deny it—if Cormac had never come here, the archeologist would still be alive. Finally, his cousin sighed. "I don't think you need to carry that one around with you. You nailed Durant, and that matters."

Woman nailed herself. If only she had just let it all go. Her Master, the man she was avenging? He hadn't given a shit about her.

"When can I go home?" Cormac asked. Not that he could drive. Not that he actually felt like getting out of bed at the moment.

"They'll spring you tomorrow if you promise not to be an ass about it and then see an orthopedist the minute you get home," Ben said.

That sounded bad. "Yeah, I think I can do that."

A knock came at the door. The way both he and Ben flinched, it was like they had people with guns coming after them on a regular basis. The door opened, but instead of a nurse, Gregory from the tea shop leaned in. "They said you were awake. Up for a visit?"

"Yeah," Cormac murmured.

He looked like he hadn't gotten any sleep, ashen around the eyes, moving carefully. But his clothes were neat and polished as ever. "I am glad to see you in one piece."

"Mostly," Cormac said. "This is Ben, my cousin. Ben, Gregory."

They shook hands, exchanged pleasantries.

Who is this? Cormac had to quickly explain who Gregory was, the tea shop, all of it. As he expected, he sensed some faint jealousy from her—Tea on the Range was exactly the kind of place she loved. Then she said, *We owe him a great deal, then.*

Yeah. "Thanks," he told Gregory, on her behalf. "We couldn't have got through this without you."

"We. You mean the Queen of Swords?"

"Amelia. Yeah. She's happy to meet you."

Gregory pressed his lips together, appearing thoughtful.

"Takes some getting used to," Ben observed.

"Well, it's worth it for the stories." He drew a small, silk-wrapped bundle from his pocket. "I decided this wants to live with you. You seem to have a connection to it."

Cormac rested the bundle on his lap, unwrapped it. The Deadwood Tarot deck. He flipped the first few cards up, the cow skulls and lightning strikes, barbed wire and six-shooters. Amelia let out a mental sigh of pure admiration.

"Thanks. Amelia loves it."

"Good," Gregory said.

I cannot wait to explore this. But what did he mean, the Queen of Swords?

It was a message, he told her. The card kept coming up. "Ben, my jacket. There should have been a couple of cards in the pocket."

Cormac's belongings had all been shoved in a plastic bag when he'd landed in the emergency room. The jacket was ruined—big hole in the shoulder, covered in blood. But they'd cleared out the pockets before throwing it out. Ben dug through the bag, now sitting at his feet, and found the two cards. Cormac reunited them with the rest of the deck, setting them face up where Amelia could see.

Annie Oakley. I sent an S.O.S. out to the universe. . .and this is what turned up? I am astonished.

So were we.

I saw her once, when I was a girl. Buffalo Bill's Wild West show came to London. I saw it. I saw her. I thought she was so beautiful.

I think she looks a little like you.

The Queen and the Ace. Is that what we are?

Maybe.

The valley was home again. Amelia was back home.

They both sat in the grass on a lazy summer day, taking in the warmth and not worrying too much about anything.

Amelia looked at him. "Do you have any more old enemies with deadly grudges you'd like to tell me about?"

"Honestly, I wasn't expecting this one."

"You must never again mock me for spending so much time on magical protections."

"Never again," he agreed. But it had been the gunshot that almost killed them this time, and what did she propose to do about that?

She grew pensive, uncertain. He thought he knew what was troubling her. Hell, they shared a brain, how could he not know everything about her? Maybe those hidden parts, what they couldn't know about each other—that was what kept this interesting.

"What is it?" he prompted.

"Did you know? Could you guess what had happened, that she aimed for you and struck me instead, with that trap?"

"I knew it must have been something like that. She was shocked to see me walking around. She thought she'd left me for dead."

"Yes, I think I know when that happened. We had. . .some sort of connection. Nothing like what you and I have, but she could sense me. I could push her."

"I noticed."

All in a rush she said, "You could have left me. You could have walked away. Your mind, your body could have been your own again. I know I have been a burden to you, and you were free at last—"

He got up from his spot and settled on the ground next to her. Right next to her. He moved with the intention of getting her to stop talking.

"But you didn't walk away. . ." she continued. "You came back for me."

He took her hand, which was just a little chilled, and maybe even trembling. He touched her chin. Leaned in, waiting for her to pull away. Expecting her to. But she didn't, so he kissed her. Realized he'd been wanting to do that a very long time, just to see if he could.

She put her arms around him and kissed him back. The touch was a spark that shocked them both. They lay back together, cradled on the grass. Clinging to him, she pressed her head to his shoulder. Here, he wasn't injured.

"I can feel you," she whispered. "I don't have a body, I am not real, how can we feel this?"

He rested his chin on her head. She tucked so neatly in his arms. "I don't know."

"Sensation is a response to stimuli detected by the brain. We can't simply be telling our brains that we feel this—"

He could smell her hair, a scent like wheat in sunshine. It shouldn't have been possible, but there it was. "I don't know anything at all."

"You came back for me," she said again.

"You could have kicked me out of my own body, but you didn't."

"I would never."

He held her close. "Neither would I."

The valley wasn't real. It wasn't. But maybe it meant something that they imagined it together. The sunlight was warm, and Amelia felt solid enough in his arms. He wouldn't ask questions.

Suddenly, she sat up on an elbow and looked down at him. "Might we go see the bison in Custer State Park on our way home? And Mt. Rushmore, we must see Mt. Rushmore."

He hadn't thought that far ahead yet. They'd probably need to get a ride home with Ben, which meant coming back for the Jeep, or towing it, or something. He didn't want to think about it. He just wanted to be. "Didn't we see bison when we went to Yellowstone a year or so back?"

"No, because we were there at night and too busy battling the hosts of Hell."

He chuckled. Everything she'd seen and done, as powerful as she was, and all she wanted to do now was go look at buffalo. He couldn't argue with that. "Fine. Okay, we'll go see the bison."

4.

Cormac let Amelia drift into his vision, so she could judge the scene for herself. The woman—he still hadn't gotten their names, this would seem just that little more manageable if he knew their names—hadn't moved after resealing the circle. She stood just outside the light, an ominous shadow. She did not seem to be working any magic currently. No candles burned, no scents of herbs or incense drifted. She might have been wearing charms or talismans—they were both likely wearing some kind of talismans of protection, given how dangerous they apparently thought he was.

The woman had cast a circle that held not just demons, but anyone rooted in magic. Whatever bound him and Amelia had enough magic to count. She was powerful, not to be underestimated. The man probably had a weapon, anything from a Taser to a gun, and it didn't matter how magical you were, a bullet went through you just the same. His shoulder twinged at the memory.

First thing wasn't actually getting past the salt circle. First thing was figuring out how to get past the agents. *Then* he could figure out the circle.

"Does it worry you?" the man asked.

Cormac tilted his head. "Does what worry me?"

"That there are these random, powerful magicians out there? Like Elton Peterson, like Isabel Durant. That there's all this power that most people aren't even aware of, and wouldn't understand even if they knew about it."

"You mean like computers? Electricity? The stock market?" Cormac chuckled. "Magic's just another tool."

"That's a simplification," the woman said.

"Clearly you're worried about it. You bring the others in for questioning, too?"

"They keep dying," the man said. "In proximity to *you*."

"It isn't a competition," Cormac said. "It's not like magicians are out there battling each other to see who can be top magician. Are they?"

Again, that brittle silence, as they didn't answer. Had he gotten neck deep into something without even noticing? Vampires spoke of a thing—a process, a tradition—called the Long Game. And for them, that really was long. Thousands of years, in at least a couple of cases. It was about gathering power. About bringing other vampires under one's influence, control, and spreading that control out. Eventually, they believed, all their power would be gathered under just one of them, who would then control...everything.

Kitty had cut the whole thing off at the knees by destroying the man who had been about to win it. And yes, Cormac had been there for that, too. From that perspective, he did start to look a little suspicious.

He didn't want all that power. He was just trying to make his way in the world without screwing up too badly. As for Amelia... He wasn't quite sure what she wanted. To survive, of course. That had been her driving motivation for over a century. A vampire-like length of a life.

All I ever wanted to do was learn, she said.

He could imagine a cabal of magicians, vying for power in a cutthroat competition with huge stakes... And these agents were worried that he was part of it. A tool, a string they could tug on to find something bigger. If these guys were watching him, had been tracking his career so carefully—who else was doing so?

A problem for another time.

"Look, I'm not *always* going up against weirdly powerful rogue magicians."

"Then what does a normal case look like for you?"

He hesitated before answering. "Normal's not really a good word for what we do."

"Okay, what does a *regular* case look like for you?"

He had done everything from cleansing Ouija boards to convincing old men that their elderly cats were not, in fact, demonically possessed. He staked out haunted houses and made protective wards for friends. Kitty had suggested he start selling herbal concoctions and charms on Etsy but he wasn't ready for that.

But if we had that herb garden I want... Later, he told her.

The case that came to mind just then hadn't been ordinary, and hadn't even really been magical.

"Well, one of the things I do is check out if haunted houses really are haunted."

FATAL STORM

One

The problem wasn't how often Cormac ended up in proximity to brutally murdered bodies. The problem was how often everyone else assumed he was the one responsible.

The guests who'd gathered at Wright House, a Victorian-era lodge in the mountains outside of Buena Vista, Colorado, were crammed in the kitchen, staring at the body of Monty Connor, which was lying face down on a steel prep table. Blood had dripped off the table and gathered in a wide, sticky pool on the floor. The blood was cool now, which meant the man had been dead for hours. That much blood, he'd probably been stabbed. They wouldn't know for sure without turning him over.

Beck Anderson, the house's owner, was a steel-haired woman in her sixties. She had been a friend of Cormac's father back in the day. Normally active and bustling, she was now frozen, with her arms around Frannie Ng, who had her face pressed to Beck's shoulder. Frannie, the young woman who was cooking for the guests, discovered the body when she came into the kitchen that morning to start coffee. Her scream had awakened the rest of the house and brought them stumbling in to see what was wrong: Cormac and Beck; Vane, just Vane, a professional psychic hired to assess whether the house was haunted; Lora Mirelli, the online personality Vane had brought to document his assessment; Monty Connor's wife June, hand over her mouth, pressed to the door frame after trying to stumble out the doorway and missing. And Glyn Farrow, another friend of Beck's, who was here because Cormac hadn't quite figured out why. He was near forty, British, neat in slacks and a pressed shirt—the only one of them not in pajamas and robes.

They were pressed to the edges of the room, in a half circle around the body. Cormac looked at each of them, noting whose eyes were wide and shocked and whose were more studious, curious. He and Glyn had somehow ended up on either end of the row, closest to the body. Both of them ready to step forward to touch it, to learn more about what had happened.

Amelia? Cormac asked the question at the back of his mind, to the not-quite-a-ghost who lived there. His constant companion, his trusted conscience. She was being unusually quiet.

I'm horrified. I... don't know what to think.

She retreated, full of anxiety that found its way into Cormac's nerves. He wanted to get out of here, to punch something.

"What do we do?" Beck asked in a thin, reedy voice. "What are we supposed to do?"

"Call the police, one should think," Glyn said.

"There's three feet of snow outside," Cormac said. "Police aren't coming." He glanced out the window over the kitchen sink. The blizzard that had made his drive up here last night harrowing was still on, thick snow pattering against the glass in the muted morning light. Nobody was going anywhere.

Likewise, no one could have arrived here in the middle of the night. Whoever killed Monty Connor was standing in this room.

"I'll call. I can at least call," Beck said, but didn't move. As if time had stuck, none of them moved.

"How did this happen?" Lora murmured. She was one of those twenty-somethings who'd managed to build a career off of Instagram and YouTube videos on paranormal topics. In flannel pajamas and an oversize sweater, she looked very different than her public persona, which involved lots of eye makeup, miniskirts, and black tights with spiderweb patterns.

"I'm guessing stab wound through the front of the ribs," Glyn said. "With that amount of blood, it had to be an artery pouring right out. We'll have to look to be sure, of course."

There was a big carving knife missing from the knife block on the back counter. The gap among the other polished brown handles was a glaring void.

"So where's the knife?" Cormac said, circling the table, careful to keep his socked feet out of the blood. He knelt, looking under the table, along the edges of the nearby cabinets. No knife. Monty's face was tilted to the right. He was a big man in his sixties, a musician and performer, an old-school cowboy poet in a snap-front plaid shirt, with a fringe of white hair brushing his neck, just like Buffalo Bill. His eyes were half open. He must have bled out in seconds.

"He could be lying on top of it," Glyn said. He glanced over at the knife block—he'd noticed it, too. "I rather think at this point the weapon itself is less important than the person who wielded it. As Mr. Bennett observed, there's enough snow outside that no one could have come up the mountain during the night."

"What are you saying?" Vane said, which was almost laughable for a psychic. Like Lora, his public persona—all black, showy jewelry and lots of glaring—was gone. He wore a gray T-shirt and sweatpants, and without eyeliner his face seemed plain and tired.

"It had to have been one of us," Cormac answered.

"Indeed," Glyn said, studying him with a calculating furrow to his brow. "Tell us, Mr. Bennett. What did you spend time in prison for?"

They all turned their gazes from the body to Cormac. The mysterious man who'd come in from the snow, who didn't say much, who didn't smile, who couldn't talk about his job. And who it turned out was a convicted felon.

He met Glyn's gaze and chuckled. "You know the answer to that or you wouldn't have asked."

Another long pause drew out, and Lora finally burst, "So what was it? What did you do?"

It had been self-defense. He had been protecting his friends. "Manslaughter," Cormac said. "At least, that's what they tell me."

They all looked again at the body and the awful pool of blood.

Yeah, today was going to go *just great*.

Two

Cormac should have turned around and gone home when he had the chance.

He'd arrived last night, later than he'd intended, because the snow had been falling hard, reducing visibility to nothing and making the roads an ice rink. The headlights turned the snow into a shifting wall, so he dimmed them. He had to carefully steer the Jeep around switchbacks growing dangerously slippery.

"This is a bad idea," he muttered.

This is a paying job, Amelia noted.

"There'll be other jobs. We're going to be snowed in up here for days."

Ask for hazard pay. It will be lovely. I've never seen snow like this, it's marvelous.

"Yeah, wait 'til there's three feet of it and you can't open the doors."

Donner Pass, she murmured, recalling memories of an earlier case. They had explored the area around Truckee, California in high summer, wondering what the area must have looked like with the twenty feet of snow that had piled up on the ill-fated members of the Donner Party. Yeah, it might have looked a little like this. They must have felt something like this sense of foreboding, suspecting that they should have turned back only when it was far too late.

Even with chains on, the tires spun briefly on the next incline, and he grumbled.

Finally, the road leveled out, the pine forest thinned, and their destination appeared: Wright House. The ornate hulk of a Victorian lodge occupied what in summer would be a wide meadow, hemmed in by a forest which loomed in the fading light. Now, snow blanketed the area, erasing details. The house itself was an artifact from the gold rush days, restored and turned into a vacation lodge. Three stories tall, it was full of gables and bay windows, scalloped trim, and painted shutters. A long porch with carved rails stretched across the front. Warm light glowed from several windows, and smoke rose up from one of a pair of chimneys. The whole scene was obscured by a lacework veil of immense snowflakes. Well, at least it would be warm and dry inside, though heat in these old houses could be tricky. He hoped for the best.

A collection of other cars already occupied the circular drive curving up to the front porch. Mostly SUVs and other four-wheel-drive vehicles but also, incongruously, a tiny Miata convertible. With a foot of new snow mounded on top of it, it looked like some kind of cute pastry next to the others. Clearly it had arrived early.

"We're definitely getting snowed in," he said, parking his Jeep at the end of the row, front end out. Forecast said this was going to keep up all night. He pulled his duffle bag out of the back, wincing as his shoulder twinged. The gunshot wound from last summer—acquired in Deadwood, South Dakota, of all places—might have healed, but it was feeling the cold now and stiffening up. He switched the bag to the other hand and bent his head against the weather.

A warm fire, a nice drink… really, Cormac, you need to be more positive.

Maybe if it was just him in the house, and not him and a bunch of strangers. Maybe if this wasn't a job. He paused on the steps leading to the front door. Snow instantly collected on his hair, the shoulders of his leather jacket, and his bag.

"There's still a chance to get back down the mountain before the snow socks us in."

We're here now. Might as well see what's this is all about, yes?

He thumped up the remaining steps to the shelter of the porch, brushed the snow off, and knocked on the door. A murmur of voices within was audible. He watched the shadow of a figure appear beyond the frosted-glass decoration in the door. At last, the door opened, revealing an older woman smiling up at him.

"Cormac! Well, just look at you!"

"Mrs. Anderson," he said politely, out of twenty-five-year-old habit.

"Oh, don't Mrs. Anderson me, not when you're all grown up now. Call me Beck. Come in, come in!"

"Yes, ma'am," he said wryly as he followed her into the foyer.

"Thank you so much for coming out in this weather. Snow like this isn't really surprising this time of year, but it's still a hassle. Here, let's get your coat off, just set your bag down for now. We were sitting down to dinner, you're just in time."

The jacket went on a hook on an already-filled coat tree. The decor here was warm, invitingly vintage, giving the place an authentic rather than ostentatious atmosphere. Dark wood paneling on the walls contrasted with the brass light fixtures. A couple of fancy side tables and an upholstered wingback chair stood watch, and he could imagine a gentleman in a bowler hat sitting there, reading a morning paper, a hundred years ago. In his jeans and plain T-shirt, Cormac felt out of place.

A gentleman doesn't wear a hat indoors, Amelia observed. Well, good thing Cormac didn't have a hat. He shook snow out of his hair.

A couple of paintings of western landscapes hung on the walls, and a copy of a Remington sculpture, the one of the horse and rider navigating a steep downward slope, had pride of place on one of the tables. A Persian rug softened the wood floor. He was almost afraid to step on it.

"This is nice," he said, for lack of anything more creative.

"It's been a bear getting the place ready for paying guests." She scowled, but her eyes gleamed with pride. "We're almost there, I think. This weekend's the dry run."

"What exactly do you want me to be looking for?"

Her voice dropped, a soft conference between the two of them. "Keep an eye on my psychic. If he says the place is haunted—well, you're my quality control. I'm hoping you can let me know if he's the real deal or blowing smoke."

Wright House was supposed to be haunted. A lurid tale of tragic murder and violence, the way these things usually were. Two brothers, an argument, a shootout... and now a ghost. Cormac and Amelia had examined a lot of haunted—and so-called haunted—houses. Investigating a medium on the sly? That was new, and now that he was here, Cormac discovered he was looking forward to the challenge. It felt a little like a hunt.

"This is just the kind of thing I would have called your father about, back in the day. When I heard you'd followed in his footsteps—"

"Not quite. Maybe followed him on the next wheel track over."

"Good enough for me." She took hold of his elbow companionably. "Let's go meet everyone."

She guided him through an inviting parlor with that blazing fire in the fireplace Amelia had been so looking forward to, through an archway to a formal dining room. With a long, polished table and a crystal chandelier over it, it looked like something out of a British period TV series. Beck had really gone all out putting the house together. China place settings, high-backed mahogany chairs, a long sideboard with graceful, curving legs, and another Persian rug, all plush and glowing in warm light.

The five people sitting around the table turned to stare at him, which made his shoulders bunch up.

"Here he is, he made it after all. This is Cormac Bennett, friend of the family."

Be polite, Amelia murmured, and Cormac managed a stiff, fleeting smile.

He spotted the hired psychic right off: Vane was a young punk to Cormac's eyes, with spiky black hair, a slick goatee, a lot of jewelry, and a disdainful way of looking down his nose. Seated next to him, Lora Mirelli was just as image conscious, ostentatiously goth, with the tips of her brown hair dyed in fiery shades of orange. She sneered a bit at Cormac, who must have looked ancient and old-fashioned to her, with his mustache and western slouch.

On the other side of the table sat Monty and June Connor, in matching pearl-snap western shirts, blue jeans, and cowboy boots. They smiled broadly in the way of people used to being on stage. They were singers and storytellers, kitschy cowboy poets Beck was planning to bring in as entertainment. They were probably going to sing at some point this weekend, and Cormac thought that asking for hazard pay wasn't such a bad idea after all.

Lastly, Beck introduced Glyn Farrow, seated at the end of the table. He gave Cormac a slight nod.

Monty Connor greeted him in a booming down-home voice. "Quite a storm, must have been a heck of a drive!"

Cormac agreed. "I wouldn't have made it if I didn't have the Jeep. Whoever's got that Miata is lucky they got here early."

"That would be me." Glyn raised a glass, a tumbler with some amber liquid in it. "Seemed such a good idea to have a neat little convertible for a mountain drive. Ah well." His accent was cultured, precise.

I wonder what part of England he's from? You'll be sure to ask, won't you?

Before he could do so, a young Asian woman bustled in from the next room—the kitchen, by the glimpse of tile and stainless steel appliances visible through the swinging door. She was dressed in a practical T-shirt and jeans with a smudged apron over them, and her silky black hair was tied up in a sloppy bun.

"And that's Frannie, she's a friend helping out for the weekend," Beck said.

Frannie donned a big smile. "Hi, nice to meet you. Food'll be out in a sec; how is everyone doing for drinks? What can I get you, Cormac?"

"Club soda, thanks."

It didn't seem possible but her smile brightened even more, and she ducked back into the kitchen.

"What is it you do, son?" Monty asked Cormac, who smiled a little at the *son*. He pegged Monty as a certain kind of guy from a certain familiar demographic. One of his father's several careers had been leading backcountry hunting parties. His clients were usually rich and full of themselves, wanting to play tough guy without the work necessary to back up the appearance. When teenage Cormac started going along on the trips to help, guys like this would ruffle his hair and call him *son*. What kept him from getting too mad about it was knowing they'd die out there without his father holding their hands, figuratively speaking.

"Oh, this and that," Cormac said, letting his own drawl thicken. "Dad was a hunting guide. Family business."

Douglas Bennett had also been a bounty hunter specializing in supernatural creatures. Vampires, werewolves, and the like. *That* was the business Cormac had mostly kept up. His shooting days were behind him. He hoped.

"Well, how about that! Tell me, what's the biggest moose you ever shot? You ever go for bear?"

Cormac suppressed a grumble, and Amelia murmured, *Patience.* He'd been here five minutes and he was already exhausted. "I never kept track," he said. Now, if he'd asked how many vampires he'd staked...

Beck took a seat between Monty and Glyn, leaving Cormac at the opposite end of the table. Frannie swept in a moment later, somehow balancing three big platters in her arms. Glyn immediately rose to help her deposit them on the table. It turned out to be a great spread of southwest cooking: enchiladas, beans and rice, homemade tortillas, and all the fixings. Suddenly, Cormac was starving. Maybe this wouldn't be so bad after all.

"I was expecting you'd make chow mein or something like that," Monty said, chuckling.

"Monty, hush," June said, then pressed her lips together in an apology.

Frannie's smile dropped for a second and she glared.

Vane's lip curled. "Is this chicken? I'm sorry, I thought I made clear that I'm vegan—"

Frannie held up a hand, stopping him mid-sentence. Turning on a heel, she retreated back to the kitchen and returned a moment later with an additional steaming-hot plate.

"Squash and quinoa-stuffed peppers. *Organic.*" She set the plate before him with a flourish.

"Oh, uh. Thanks. It's because I have a deeper connection with the spiritual world if I don't rely on death to sustain me."

"You're welcome," she said pointedly, and took the last empty seat at the table.

Monty turned to Beck. "You let the help sit at the table with everyone else?"

"Oh my God, are you serious?" Lora exclaimed.

Beck said evenly, "As I've already told you, Frannie isn't 'the help,' she's a friend who agreed to come in for the weekend and help me take care of things."

"Maybe you'd prefer it if she were in a uniform," Glyn said. "Go for the full *Downton Abbey* experience, hmm?"

"Don't get pissy with me," Monty glared back.

Beck was determinedly scooping food on her plate and passing dishes around. "I think we should all enjoy our dinner and think good thoughts for the séance later. Right, Vane?"

Vane shrugged. "We'll be channeling a murder victim, but sure. Good thoughts."

"I hear you put on a pretty good show," Monty said.

Cormac wished the guy would be quiet. Shovel some food into his mouth. Not that that would necessarily stop him talking.

"You can watch the videos on YouTube," Vane said.

The man huffed. "An internet show is one thing, real life is something else."

"He's got a million subscribers," Lora said. "How many do you have?"

"We don't have a YouTube channel," June said a bit stiffly. "Monty doesn't think it's worthwhile. We've had... discussions about it."

Lora opened her mouth as if she might argue, then thought better of it. "I see."

"We do just fine without the internet," Monty said. "Keeps us honest." June's hand clenched on her fork.

"This is great, Frannie," Cormac said, indicating his plate full of enchilada. Frannie smiled gratefully across the table.

June jumped in. "Glyn, I understand you're a writer?"

"Cat's out of the bag," he said.

"Have you been published?" Vane asked, like he was expecting to catch him out in some deception.

"A bit." He studied the pattern in the fork's handle.

"Glyn writes bestselling mysteries," Beck said. "Ten novels so far, is it?"

"Twelve." He smiled wryly.

"They're really good, you should try them," Beck continued. "They're about a detective who used to be in the army before joining the police in London. I feel like I'm actually there when I read them."

"The invitation to come visit me in Brighton still stands," Glyn told her.

"Oh, that would be nice. Once I get this place going, we'll talk."

"Are you going to write about the murder of Tobias?" Lora asked.

Glyn said, "It's my understanding the trial concluded Tobias Wright's brother Jacob killed him in self-defense. That there was an actual shootout. So perhaps technically not a murder."

Cormac could almost sense Amelia leaning forward, intent on the conversation. A little bit frustrated that she couldn't jump in herself, without his help.

"Whatever you call it, it's a violent death," Lora explained. "They were both in love with the same woman, and Tobias threatened Jacob if Clarice wouldn't marry him."

Beck shook her head. "The story Jim's family passed down is that

Clarice had agreed to marry Tobias, but then Jacob threatened to cut him off from the inheritance. That was what they had the shootout over."

Vane said, "And these are the questions we hope to find answers to. This is the *perfect* subject for a séance."

I'm looking forward to this séance. We'll see if he has any true abilities beyond showmanship.

All they had to do was get through dinner.

"It's a load of bunk," Monty muttered under his breath, but not really under his breath. Vane glared.

Mr. Connor doesn't seem much interested in making friends.

Cormac was feeling downright sociable in comparison, in fact.

In another valiant effort to haul the conversation to back to something resembling civility, Glyn said, "Jim was related to the Wrights, yes?"

"Their sister Alice was his great-great—I think it's just two greats—grandmother. She'd married and moved away by then so never really got the whole story. But that's Tobias's pocket watch sitting on the mantle. That's stayed with the house this whole time."

They all glanced through the archway to the parlor, where they could make out the mantle over the fireplace, and the antique watch displayed on a polished wooden stand right in the center, pride of place.

"Perfect," Vane murmured.

Frannie served flan for dessert, which inspired a round of very small talk about flans of dinners past, and finally the meal was over and the guests stood to make their way back to the parlor. Out of habit, Cormac started stacking plates and gathering silverware.

Beck moved to intercept him. "Oh Cormac, you don't have to do that—"

"I'm happy to help." Gave him something to do besides sit there not talking.

"Your father did raise you right, didn't he?"

Cormac wasn't so sure about that. His father had receded to memory, and most of those memories involved guns and a command to continue in the family business—hunting.

His first kill was the werewolf who had killed Douglas Bennett.

These days, he wanted to stay out of prison more than he wanted to continue his father's monster-hunting legacy. He had a lingering sense that his father would have been disappointed, so he tried not to think about him at all.

Beck, Frannie, and he cleared the table, carrying plates and empty serving dishes to the kitchen. The rest of the house had preserved the late Victorian aesthetic, but the kitchen was modern, built for commercial use, with a wide three-section sink, stainless-steel appliances, lots of counter space, neat racks and shelves for pots, pans, professional-grade chef knives in a big wooden block, serving trays, dishes, glassware. The floor was classic black and white tile, with matching backsplashes behind the sink and stove.

A window over the sink looked out over the back of the house. The snow was still coming down hard. Large flakes beat against the glass.

"We're going to be snowed in all weekend," he muttered.

"Oh, it'll be cozy!" Beck said, rather desperately.

Cormac had noticed a guitar case leaning on the wall in the parlor. Monty Connor's, presumably. A cozy weekend? Maybe, but definitely a long one.

He said, "Must have taken a lot to get this place up and running."

"I'm mortgaged to the hilt," she said softly, and her smile thinned. "If next summer's tourist season doesn't pan out, I might lose it all." She had presented such a cheerful, confident picture. She couldn't very well confess worries to the people she was trying to win over.

"I thought you inherited the place from your husband?"

"I did. But Jim sold off most of the land and the water rights that went with it—you know how screwed up those old water agreements get. Turns out Jim didn't keep up with his inheritance quite as well as he let on. Had a whole lot of business debt he never told me about. He was trying to do the right thing, pay it all off with what he got from the land. But, well... a house like this gets expensive." She waved a hand dismissively. "Never mind, nothing anybody can do about it now, is there? Let's just go and have a good time. Let me get you a drink." She bustled out.

Back in the dining room, Vane had taken over the table, spreading a black-on-black embroidered cloth over it and drawing a number of arcane items from a travel case.

Let's stay and watch, Amelia suggested eagerly. *If he's going to be setting up wires or sound effects, now is when he'll do it.*

Cormac leaned against the doorway, arms crossed. Vane arranged a couple of silver candlesticks, a trivet shaped like a pentagram—

"Please, I need privacy!" Vane insisted.

He's definitely setting up wires and sound effects.

Cormac could imagine her rubbing her hands together. He slouched away from the wall and continued on to the parlor...

Where Monty was in the big armchair by the fireplace, tuning his guitar. June sat nearby, beaming, looking friendly but coming across just as stiffly as she had through dinner. They made a calculated picture of archetypal folksiness. Cormac almost kept going, to the foyer and straight out of the house, to try to drive out of here despite the accumulating snow. Maybe there were more dishes to wash. Maybe he could go to bed, except there was still the séance to get through.

Sometimes he really hated people.

He settled into one of the wingback chairs as far away from the fireplace as he could get. Lora was on a sofa, checking her phone. Beck stood nearby, hands clasped nervously. Glyn was by one of the windows, tumbler in hand. Cormac couldn't recall him actually taking a drink from it, not even during dinner.

"What should I start with, darlin'?" Monty said to June in an affected drawl as he strummed.

"Oh, let's go with a classic!" She delivered the scripted response, and the random strumming turned into a series of chords—for "Home on the Range."

Cormac slumped back in the chair and sighed.

"Not a fan?" Glyn murmured.

Cormac wasn't a fan of easy sentimentality. "Around the time this was written, the Great Plains bison population was already crashing from overhunting. Buffalo weren't roaming all that much, it turns out." The home the song talked about didn't exist, which might have been part of the point, but that wasn't how guys like this sang it.

"Well, that takes some of the romance out of it. I suppose people still expect the local color."

The song ended, and Monty segued into the next one. "'Oh bury me not on the lone prair-eeee...'"

Cormac wasn't getting paid enough for this.

A thin, wind-borne howling cut through a pause in the song, and the curtains by the nearby window rustled in a draft. The storm was worsening, beating snow against the sides of the house. Couldn't have been more atmospheric if the Connors had planned it.

Lora shook her phone and looked up. "Connection's down. Is anyone else getting a signal?"

Monty stopped mid-line and glared.

Beck said, "It's satellite internet way out here. Connection's dodgy at the best of times, and with this storm, well... nothing I can do about it." Lora heaved a frustrated sigh.

Then the lights flickered.

"And... maybe I'll get some candles out, just in case."

"Perfect weather for a séance, anyway," Glyn said with a grin.

"But if I can't post about it what's the point?" Lora replied.

Monty strummed harder, letting a discordant note twang out before settling back into the classic folk-western three-note rhythm. "This all reminds me of a story you might have heard, about a group of pioneers making the dangerous trek to California, and the storm that trapped in them in a place we now call Donner Pass—"

Oh no, Amelia said. *You were right. We should have turned around and gone home when we had the chance.*

Vane appeared in the doorway to the dining room and clapped once, loudly. June jumped, Beck gasped and dropped the handful of candles she'd brought in from the foyer, and another bad chord strummed out.

Vane had made a quick change of clothes, trading his plain long-sleeved shirt for a leather vest, revealing complex tattoos covering both arms. Amelia spotted a number of arcane symbols, alchemical notations, and figures in a dizzying spiral. Hard to be sure if it actually meant anything.

"If you'll come join me, I believe the spirit plane is calling to us." He glared menacingly from under arched eyebrows, and the rings he wore seemed to make his hands flash.

Well, he certainly had his shtick down.

Three

melia had never seen a setup like it, and Cormac trusted her experience more than his own with this sort of thing.

Along with the trivet, the candlesticks marked out a pentagram. The candles in them, all black, were lit, and the flames were each a different color: blue, red, yellow, green, and white. There had to be some trick to it, chemicals in the wick. The effect was unsettling. Apricot-sized quartz crystals sat at each place around the table. Incense burned in a ceramic bowl—sharp, with a bitter edge, not like what Amelia used, or the usual sage and sandalwood.

Rowan, with a bit of anise. Something else I'm not sure of, but I'd use those in a divination spell at least, I'll give him that.

A small gong marked with Chinese characters sat near the head of the table, where Vane stood, presiding. Lora, camera in hand, moved around the room snapping photos and taking video. She came in close to frame an artistic shot of thick gray smoke rising up from the incense, then moved to the back of the room to encompass the whole setting.

"Well, this is downright Satanic," Monty said, frowning.

"The pentagram is an ancient symbol with many meanings," Vane said. "It represents the four earthly elements, plus the ethereal plane. Now please, sit."

Cormac. Try to sit next to Vane, if you can.

Amelia wanted to be able to tell if Vane was pulling strings under the table, or flexing to activate hidden controls. However, Beck and Lora had already crowded in, while Cormac's tendency to linger in the back of rooms defeated them.

Glyn was also hanging back. He gestured to Cormac. "After you, Mr. Bennett."

"You go on."

They stared at one another, neither willing to have the other at his back.

Oh for God's sake, just go.

Frannie arrived last, and Monty glanced at her with what seemed like surprise, faintly sneering. Like he really couldn't see her as anything other than hired help. The singer started to say something, but June hushed him. For her part, Frannie seemed eager, leaning right up to the table and focusing on Vane. When the medium stepped back to turn off the lights, the room transformed. The cozy home-like setting was remade by the uncertain glow of the spirit world. A couple of the others gasped, and Cormac was annoyed to notice the hairs on the back of his neck standing up.

Lora attached the camera to a tabletop tripod and switched a button—setting to video, it looked like. With everyone in their chairs, an anticipatory silence settled over them. The candle flames wavered in an unfelt draft. Silently, Vane settled in the chair at the head of the table and spread his hands in an inviting gesture.

"My friends. Prepare yourselves. We are about to make a journey. There is the world we know. And then there is the one... beyond!"

There was a thump—just his fist against the table, making the candle flames jump and the gong rattle. Frannie gasped, June let out a small squeal. Monty chuckled, but the sound came out nervously.

"My friends, I need your help," Vane continued. "Whether you believe or don't doesn't matter. I just need you to turn your thoughts... to the mysterious. Remain silent. Remain attentive. But most of all, whatever happens... remain *calm*. I beg you." He met the gazes of each of them around the table, so it seemed as if he asked them personally for their help. Drawing them into the ritual. "If the spirits believe you are afraid..." He shook his head slowly, as if to say he couldn't guess what would happen and wouldn't be responsible for the consequences.

Quite the showman, Amelia said. In the dark, lit from below by the multicolored candles, Vane had a haunted expression, as if had seen terrible things and lived to tell.

What are we looking for? Cormac asked. Amelia's attention had become sharp. His own vision went soft, as she stepped into his body, using his eyes, ears, nose.

I'm not even sure. In the old days it was all wires and toe cracking.

Toe cracking wasn't a thing. It couldn't be.

It worked for the Fox Sisters, apparently. I never saw them perform myself. Though in this modern day he might have recordings, smart speakers using voice-activated cues. I'd wager Lora is helping him.

Vane lifted his hands. "Entities on the ethereal plane, draw nigh. We are here to contact the unfortunate spirit that is said to inhabit this place, Tobias Wright. Tonight, we hope to hear his tragic story from his own spectral self. We will open a doorway to the shadow realm and ask Tobias to... step through."

Cormac could almost believe that someone was breathing over his shoulder. He resisted an urge to look behind him.

Vane produced an object: the pocket watch from the mantle over the fireplace. It was antique, tarnished to a dark shade. Holding it flat in his palm, he showed it around the table so all could see, then placed it on the pentagram in the middle of the table. A focus. A connection with the past. Assuming it had actually belonged to Tobias.

"Now, please take the hands of your neighbors," Vane ordered.

"June, switch places with me," Monty hissed.

"What? Monty, just sit—" But the singer was already fumbling out of his chair and pulling at June's arm.

"I'm not holding hands with a man. No offense." He nodded at Glyn in a way he probably thought was polite.

"And what if I do take offense?" Glyn said, leering a bit with an arch to his eyebrow.

"June!"

"All right, fine!"

A muscle in Vane's jaw twitched.

The couple settled in their new seats, which placed Monty between June and Beck. This was apparently acceptable.

Glyn thickened his precise accent to say, "Really, Mr. Connor. I won't bite. Unless you ask nicely." It was an old joke, but nicely deployed. Monty's eyes widened, as if in horror, and he refused to look at Glyn, who seemed to be enjoying himself.

Glyn now arched that same brow at Cormac, who was seated on his other side. "Will you take offense?"

"I'm tough, I can take it," Cormac said, gripping his offered hand.

In fact, Amelia appeared to be delighted by their neighbor. Frannie took hold of his left hand, and the circle was complete.

"*Friends,*" Vane intoned a bit desperately. "We have a somber task before us! Let the light fill your vision, the air fill your senses. Steady your breathing. Focus on your breath, breath that Tobias Wright no longer has for himself. We must breathe for him if we wish him to speak!"

A reliable meditation technique. In spite of themselves, they all began to match their breaths to the rhythm of Vane's steady speech, until they were all breathing together, and even the flickering of the candle flames seemed to settle into the rhythm.

"The veil is thin... the spirits are close..."

The smell in the room changed, the incense abruptly shifting to a sharper, sweeter odor. Cinnamon maybe?

Oh, very nice. Timed release, so once the rowan burned down the next scent is ready. Excellent timing, good showmanship there.

"Is that pot?" Monty exclaimed. June hushed him.

"No," Vane hissed. "It's my secret blend of divinatory herbs."

"He sells it on his website if you like it," Lora added in a loud whisper.

Vane closed his eyes for a moment and seemed to be gritting his teeth. "Please, I'm begging you to be quiet. The spirits are *very close*. But you have to focus!"

The air grew warm, heady. Frannie's hand in Cormac's was shaking slightly. She was squeezing just a little too tightly, and Cormac couldn't get her to loosen her grip without disrupting the proceedings. Her eyes were half-lidded, her lips parted. Falling easily into the half trance Vane was attempting to induce in them.

In a slow, haunted voice, Vane asked, "Tobias Wright. Are you here with us this evening? Can you give us a sign? Tobias Wright, we have opened the door, and we humbly ask for a small sign of your presence."

"I think I heard something!" June hissed.

There had been no sound apart from the room's ambient noise. The wind gusting against the windows was the same as it had been.

The more of a show Vane put on, the less inclined Cormac was to take him seriously. Still, he hadn't sensed any odd movements. No hiss of speakers, no sign of electronics. He watched Lora; she'd remained sitting still.

If nothing happens, that doesn't particularly mean he isn't *psychic.*

Vane continued, undaunted. He took a deep breath... and suddenly tilted his head. His brow furrowed. "I'm sensing... a spirit presence is here. A soul from another realm has joined us."

The tension around the table ratcheted up a notch. Even Monty held his breath. Somehow, Frannie's grip on Cormac's hand tightened even more.

"It's very strong!" Vane said, his demeanor of control slipping in his excitement. "I am sensing... sensing..." Vane straightened, his shoulders stiffening. "There is a spirit here," he said softly, and now he sounded confused. Wondering. He was off script.

"Is it Tobias?" Beck murmured.

"Shh," Vane said. "There's... someone... Died and not dead? Not the murderer but the murdered..."

"That's not *my* ghost," Beck said, blinking.

"No. It's... a woman, maybe?" Vane said, pleading, "Spirit. Can you give me a sign? Reach out, and I'll listen!"

Cormac sat very still.

Cormac. Is he talking about me? Can he sense me?

He asked Amelia, Are there any ghosts here? Is there anything else?

I can't tell, not without working some sort of scrying spell.

Vane shook his head in evident bafflement. He wasn't the only one. "The signs here are jumbled, confusing. Some spirit has come to communicate with us. I need all of your energies to help illuminate the unreal. Your life energy can give power to this otherworldly voice!"

Should I say something? I don't want to be illuminated. Not here, like this.

Although it might give everyone a big shock if Cormac suddenly started channeling the spirit realm.

"There's definitely a presence here," Vane insisted. "But she's not forthcoming. We must make her feel welcome. This is a safe space. Spirit, we ask nothing of you! But if you feel moved to give us a sign. One small sign."

Oh, he sounds sad...

Cormac shifted a foot and cracked a toe. In the breath-held stillness, the noise sounded a lot louder than he expected, especially given his heavy boots. Frannie nearly jumped out of her chair. Beck gasped. Monty muttered a small curse. Vane smiled, a devilish expression in the candlelight.

Cormac grinned a little. So did Glyn, sitting beside him and casting his gaze downward, under the table.

"Spirit, thank you," Vane murmured. "You honor us. Do you have a message for us? Anything. At all."

The moments dragged on, the wind outside kept blowing. The incense burned out, leaving the air smelling sooty. Candles wavered, and Vane let out a sigh.

"Sometimes, the spirits keep their secrets to themselves." His showman's voice of authority returned. "The veil closes. The other plane is out of reach. At least… until each of us in our turn makes that final, permanent journey to the other side. If we are lucky, our journeys will be less fraught than Tobias's. Now raise your hands—" He raised his, along with Lora's and Beck's. The rest of them followed suit. "—and break the bonds, returning our own selves to—we hope!—the safety of the material plane!"

They dropped hands. It was like a rope had been cut, and a weight settled back into Cormac's arms. The material world. Mundanity. Cormac sighed. There was a bit more business with blowing out candles and ringing the gong to "clear the energies." The lights came on, and everyone blinked at each other like mice dragged out of their dens.

Beck leaned toward Vane. "Does that mean I have two ghosts?" Her eyes lit up, excited.

"I really don't know," Vane said. "That was just… weird. That really didn't go the way I expected."

"It's all a show," Monty said, frowning. "That's what I think."

Lora said to Vane, "You got a sign, and you just let it go. Why didn't you follow up? An unexpected ghost and you didn't follow up?"

Vane tipped up his chin. "I do not command the spirits, I am merely their conduit. Hey, that would make a great clip. Can you film that?"

She held up the camera, found the angle, and Vane repeated the line, standing over the remains of his séance in a lordly manner. "I do not command the spirits…"

Glyn sidled up to Cormac and said softly, "Did you really have to crack your toe at right that moment?"

Cormac looked at him. "Maybe the spirit told me to do it."

I did not. That was all you!

Some of the old spiritualists insisted that they really could communicate with the spirit world, that they really were passing along messages. But the bells and tricks and sleights of hand were the only way they could convince anyone else that what they could do was real. That was the problem—unless you had some kind of second sight of your own, how would you ever know they were telling the truth?

Cormac had second sight of a certain kind, he supposed. He just didn't want to share.

Frannie stood, brushing her hands on her jeans; they might have still been trembling a little. "I don't know about the rest of you, but I could use a cup of coffee. Anyone?"

Vane and Lora yes, June yes but decaf, and Monty asked for whiskey. Frannie seemed happy to have a job to occupy her after the small adventure.

Beck approached Cormac, an eager glint in her eyes. Taking him by the arm, she pulled him to the parlor, out of sight and earshot of the others. "Well? What do you think?"

Cormac wasn't sure how to assess Vane and his skills as a spiritualist. His performance was dramatic, but he didn't seem to be using the classic tricks. No stunts, no funny noises. When he said he sensed the spirit of a woman who was dead but not dead... well, he wasn't wrong.

"He puts on a good show. And..." Cormac had to give him credit. "I think he's onto something. Not sure how good he is really, but he's got sensitivity." Not that he was ready to explain how he knew this. He didn't know any of these people well enough to introduce Amelia to them.

He thought Beck would be happy to get an endorsement, but she tilted her head quizzically. "Then why didn't he sense Tobias?"

"Maybe Tobias wasn't talking tonight."

"But then who's the woman he mentioned? Do I have two ghosts?" Her voice lifted at this, as if two ghosts meant twice the marketing opportunities.

"Couldn't say," Cormac evaded.

"Maybe he'll lead another séance tomorrow. Since it looks like we're all going to be here awhile." She glanced out the window and sighed.

Beck went off to check on her other guests, leaving him with Glyn, who was leaning against the doorway, looking off toward the kitchen. And eavesdropping, apparently.

"You really believe in ghosts?" Glyn asked.

Cormac ducked his gaze. "Maybe not the way you're thinking. Glowing shapes knocking things off bookshelves? No. But... there's something out there."

He expected Glyn to scoff. Make some wry British quip, quote a little Shakespeare, "more things in heaven and earth..." Instead, he got a faraway look in his eyes. "Yes. I suppose that's one way of putting it. Something..."

Cormac wondered what the man had seen that he couldn't explain. But Glyn shook off the expression and glanced at his tumbler, which he'd reclaimed. "Well then, time for a touch-up, I think." He strolled to the sideboard with the decanters. The level of alcohol in the man's glass seemed to have hardly diminished. Glyn wasn't drinking, just holding the glass. A crutch.

Back in the dining room, Vane packed up his paraphernalia while Lora watched the video playback on her camera. Could the video have caught anything? Cormac wouldn't have thought so, but he wouldn't put money against it.

They were arguing. "I don't know what it was," Vane hissed loud enough to carry. "I need to sleep on it. Try again tomorrow. I don't know."

"You *usually* know."

He angrily tugged closed the zipper on his case. "Anything?"

Lora continued glaring at the screen. "No. Just... candles. Not even an orb."

"That's because orbs are bullshit," Vane said.

Cormac was liking him better and better.

The medium glanced up and caught Cormac watching. Cormac waved. "Don't mind me, just heading to the kitchen." He sauntered through to the next door.

"There's something off about that guy..." Vane whispered to Lora.

We really ought to tell him about me, Amelia said. *He knows there's something here, centered on you, but because he isn't expecting it he has no idea what to look for.*

Later, Cormac would think about that later.

Monty stormed out of the kitchen just as Cormac reached the door, intending to go in and ask Frannie if she needed any help carrying out the drinks. They'd have crashed into each other if Cormac hadn't deftly stepped aside. Monty drew up short, startled. Glaring, he seemed to be about to spit some insult. Faced with Cormac's impassive response, he walked on by. The man was rubbing his chin and wincing.

In the kitchen, Frannie was leaning on the sink, gripping the edge, white knuckled. He almost backed right out again, uncertain what he'd walked into. But Frannie quickly straightened and wiped away a stray tear. Cormac put the pieces together.

Don't you dare ignore it. Say something. Amelia's fury boiled. She'd connected the pieces faster than Cormac had.

"Did he do something?" He pointed a thumb over his shoulder, where Monty Connor had fled. "Are you okay?"

"Yeah, yeah, I'm fine." She chuckled nervously. "He's just being old school. Thinking he can cross lines, you know? I decked him."

"Good. But you should tell Beck," Cormac said. "She's not going to want him around if he's being an ass."

"No, it's fine. Beck has enough to worry about." She folded a towel, put it by the sink. Looked around the kitchen again. "But, you know, if you could keep an eye on him for me."

"Sure thing," he said, and held the door open for her as she carried out a tray of steaming mugs.

They gathered in the parlor, sipping their drinks and listening to the wind moan. Monty didn't pick up the guitar again, thank goodness. Vane had replaced the pocket watch on its stand on the mantle, its place of honor. Everyone spread out to their own seats; the parlor was almost not quite big enough for all of them. Small talk went on around Cormac, who tuned it out as he looked out the window over the front drive. The snow was still falling hard and had drifted up to the Jeep's front grill. The little Miata was nearly covered. He'd meant to just stay overnight, leave in the morning. But no one was leaving in the morning, not with this.

We'll make the best of it, then. Amelia may not have had a body, but her sigh was evident.

"How?" Cormac murmured. He wasn't sure he could manage being polite for an entire weekend.

We sleep in, she murmured. *We eat a large breakfast. Sit by the fire and read a book. Surely this house has a library somewhere that we haven't seen yet.*

He sensed longing from her. She could have these experiences through him—indirectly, one step removed. Right now, she was thinking what it would be like to have her own body. To smell the old wood and feel the warmth of a wool blanket draped over her lap. He never knew what to say, to try to comfort her in these moments. Only that she needed comfort, which he wasn't very good at delivering. If she had her own body, he might hold her hand. Or scuff his foot on the rug, like he was doing now.

Vane was glancing at him across the room, surreptitiously studying him. Glyn was openly regarding him, as if he were a puzzle. Would it seem strange if Cormac spent the whole day in his room tomorrow?

You'll have to come out to eat sometime.

And Frannie was a good cook. There was that, at least.

Speaking of, Frannie bowed out first, claiming she had an early start, getting breakfast ready for the guests, and fled to her room on the ground floor, behind the parlor. That started the general retreat. Cormac was second. Soon the lights were out, and they'd all climbed the stairs to their rooms.

Cormac's was on the third floor. It was nice, with more of the cozy, Victorian cottage decor. Paintings of flowers on the walls, lace runners on the dresser and nightstand. Overstuffed chair by the window, brocade curtains. A little chilly maybe, like the house's heating system wasn't quite up to the task. The bed was nice. Brass fittings, what seemed to be a handmade quilt. But too soft. Cormac stretched out on it and felt like he was sinking.

The nightstand included a shelf with a handful of books. Including a few by Glyn Farrow, his name glaring along the spine in bold letters. Curious, Cormac picked one out, titled *Fatal Storm,* and opened to a random page to read.

Bryce Stone raced down the icy slope, hot on the heels of the masked gunman, who hesitated, glancing back, his dark eyes glittering malevolently through the holes of his balaclava as he once again raised his weapon—and fired. Bryce reacted instantly, ducking behind a stand of towering pines, feeling the hum of air as the bullet whipped past him...

"I hate this guy," Cormac muttered. "I can already tell I hate him." *It's certainly... exciting?*

Bryce Stone was apparently a police detective as well as a former military officer, and occasionally worked as a consultant for British intelligence. A wide enough range of skills and experience to ensure that Glyn could write about his adventures across dozens of books and never be bored. They might even have been good reads, but the problem was Cormac heard the words in Glyn's voice. He decided he couldn't stand that voice, and therefore couldn't stand Bryce Stone, who didn't even exist.

He shut the book and put it back on the shelf.

Really, I think he's charming. I'd like to speak with him further. Hear about how Brighton is these days.

"I think he's gay," Cormac stated.

She paused a moment—he could just about see the quizzical tilt to her head. *So? I said I wanted to speak with him, not have relations.*

The bedrooms on this floor shared a bathroom. Cormac went out for one last stop, and as he returned to his room, he heard urgent voices from one floor down. He carefully stepped into the shadowed corner to listen. A man and a woman, speaking in a hushed whisper. Cormac just happened to be in exactly the right spot for the sound to carry up the stairs.

"Monty Connor, you got five hundred acres of prime development land out of that deal." That was Beck, her cheerful hostess personality completely replaced by rough tension.

"Not to mention mineral rights." And that was Monty Connor, sounding smug as ever.

She hesitated. "What do you mean, mineral rights?"

"Turns out there's a neat little copper deposit smack in the middle of the plot. Worth quite a lot, I reckon. Did Jim not tell you about that, either?"

"Then why do you need the house, too?"

"Don't *need* anything, now, do I? But I have to say, it's a nice house. You did a good job making it pretty."

"You can't," Beck breathed. "You wouldn't."

"Already have, darlin.'"

Footsteps stormed off, and a door closed harder than necessary. Monty chuckled softly.

What was that about?

None of their business, was what. Jim had been Beck's husband. Cormac vaguely remembered him from back when he was a kid, when his father knew the family. The house had been in his family, that was how Beck got hold of it. Sounded now like it hadn't been that simple. But how did Monty Connor tic in?

He waited another minute before turning back to his room, and spotted movement at the other end of the hall. Glyn Farrow, standing at his open door. He must have heard the argument, too. Cormac met the man's gaze briefly. Glyn pressed his lips together in what might have been an apologetic smile before retreating into his room, shutting his door.

So much for the restful weekend.

Stripped down to sweats and a T-shirt, he shut off the light and climbed into bed. And lay there with his eyes wide open. Maybe he just wasn't used to being comfortable. He punched the fluffy pillows in a futile attempt to flatten them.

Cormac. For God's sake, rest.

He forced himself to take a couple of deep breaths and closed his eyes. Opened them again on a mountain meadow that existed only in his imagination. His and Amelia's.

Winter never came to the forest of his mind. He hadn't really thought about it before, but this mental construct almost always existed in high summer, with wild flowers blooming and a warm sun pouring over it. There had been storms, fog, uncertainty, but never snow. Cormac had to concede: he liked summer.

He lay back in the grass, hands pillowing his head, watching voluminous white clouds against the pristine blue sky. Here, his shoulder didn't ache at all. He could remember what it felt like to not have a gunshot wound, and so that was how he existed here. He listened to birdsong in the trees. Some unfamiliar calls had crept in—English birds, imagined there by Amelia. Made him smile. And this was an odd, uncomfortable feeling. He had income from interesting work, a warm place to sleep, reasons to smile. He might have been happy. Or at least contented. He hardly knew what to do with the feeling.

Amelia was pacing. She always did this when she had some problem to mull, as if this imagined body's movement was enough to simulate the real thing. They had raised the question of how real this all was—if they imagined touching each other, and they felt the contact, was it real or imagined? And then they shied away from it. It was philosophy, and had no answer.

Real or not, she said that pacing helped her think. "Just because there's a story about a ghost does not mean that there really is a ghost." Hesitating, she looked at him. He was not being helpful. She was about to point out that he was not being helpful.

"But," he prompted.

Her expression pursed thoughtfully. "One must consider what is meant by the phrase 'haunted house' to begin with. There are the stories, cursed spectral forms gliding down the hallways, moaning and banging on doors and all that. Hampton Court Palace is supposed to be littered with ghosts. Catherine Howard's is said to run screaming down the gallery behind the chapel. But with so many tourists tromping through does anyone ever see them? Then there's the haunting of an old church that has seen services within its walls for a thousand years. Where all those prayers have seeped into the stone and given the building some weight. Some aura. Is that a haunting?"

Cormac generally left the existential questions to her. He was the muscle. She sighed, and here, in their minds, that finally had some meaning: her lips parted, her chest fell with the exhaled breath. He liked watching her.

"This house has been so remodeled, so done over, any aura it might have carried from its earlier days is lost, I fear," she said. "Who's to say if any spirits linger?"

"You?" Cormac suggested. "Vane felt you because you were sitting right there. None of his séances are going to work as long as you're there. You drown everything out." Which meant Vane really was psychic. How about that?

"I might almost be insulted by that." She crossed her arms, quirked her lips wryly.

Here, she had a body. Here, he could take her hand. "How about we worry about it in the morning? Maybe we can talk to him and let him know what went wrong."

She settled onto the grass next to him, and he did it, took hold of her hand possessively and pressed it to his chest, just as he might have done if they were in that real too-soft bed together. Finally, she settled next to him, her head on his shoulder, and he could sleep.

The light of dawn woke him just before Frannie's scream did, when she walked into the kitchen and discovered Monty Connor's body.

Four

After the awkward gathering around the body, they fled to the dining room, and Frannie managed to bring out a pot of coffee and some day-old pastries. She didn't want to be in the kitchen alone with the body; Glyn stayed with her.

Cormac stood against the wall in a corner. The others kept their distance, which was normally how he liked it. But they all kept *looking* at him. Murdered body in the house, convicted felon standing right there. He had to figure out how to handle this.

Amelia?

She'd gone quiet. Very quiet, so that not even her presence lingered at the back of his mind, where he could almost always find her. His heart rate spiked, and sweat broke out on the back of his neck. Last summer, she'd been captured by a magician. He'd gone a few days without her constant presence and discovered that he needed her. If she vanished again, if the séance had somehow hurt her... Amelia... Amelia!

I'm here.

He tried not to let his relief show. He wouldn't be able to explain it, so he crossed his arms and kept his expression cold.

This has happened to me before.

It was how she had died, before. She'd been discovered kneeling next to the body of a young woman who'd been viciously murdered by a demon. Amelia had only been trying to learn what happened, but the authorities found her, surrounded by her arcane tools, and jumped to the most sensational conclusion. Amelia had been hanged for it. Her spirit lived on; the trauma remained.

We're going to be fine.

How?

He didn't know.

The cell connection was still down, but the house had a land line. In the foyer, Beck finally got through to the police and was explaining the situation in a jumble. Her half of the conversation was maddening. "What do you mean... well yes, I know there's a blizzard... yes... are you sure? But what are we supposed to do? Okay... okay, fine." By her tone, things were clearly not fine.

The police were not coming, at least not right away. Cormac was partly relieved. He didn't want to talk to the police right now.

Beck came back in, looking despondent. "Snow's supposed to taper off this afternoon, but they're not going to get anyone out here until tomorrow morning."

June let out a sob. There were other general gasps of consternation.

"Am I going to have to cook with that in my kitchen?" Frannie exclaimed.

"*That* is my *husband.*" June glared at her.

"No, of course not," Beck said quickly. "The sheriff says we can move him and clean up. Just... we need to take pictures if we can."

"Right," Glyn said. "Best take care of it, then. Ms. Mirelli, if we could trouble you for the use of your camera? And Mr. Bennett, you and I could do the heavy lifting, as it were."

"You trust me?" Cormac said pointedly. "The convicted murderer?"

"Convicted manslaughterer, you said." The author's smile had acid in it. "I'll keep an eye on you."

Manslaughterer? That's not even a word.

Lora ran back to her room to retrieve her camera. They were all still in their night clothes, flannel pajamas and robes. Except for Glyn, who had somehow managed to dress in trousers and a clean shirt before appearing, even amidst all the excitement.

Cormac excused himself to go get dressed, and half expected Glyn to complain, but he didn't.

We've got to figure out what happened, Cormac.

Yes, before everyone here decided on some story starring himself.

They returned to the kitchen door, now dressed in their usual. Glyn reached for the camera, but Lora pulled it close. "I'll do it myself if that's all right."

"Sure you're up for it?" Glyn asked.

She scowled. "Don't be patronizing."

The body lay right where they left it, of course, still jarring, sprawled on the prep table like an ill-prepared slab of meat. And there was Cormac's appetite gone. Staring with obvious fascination, Lora started taking pictures, moving around the body, finding different angles, looking down, kneeling and looking up.

"Watch the blood," Cormac told her. Gasping, she stepped back from the dark, sticky pool.

"I hope you're not planning on posting any of those on your Insta-whatsit," Glyn said.

"Of course not," she said.

"I'm sure you wouldn't kill someone just to get a flashy online story about it," he added.

"*What?*"

Cormac glared. "You just going to go around accusing everybody?"

IIe shrugged, clearly unapologetic. "Just thinking of possible motives. Before last night, none of us knew Monty except for June and Beck. Why would anyone want to kill him? Turns out I can think of all kinds of reasons."

"So what's yours?" Cormac asked.

Lora looked back and forth between them, waiting. Glyn put his hand thoughtfully on his chin. "Maybe I'm a professional hit man, and Monty got on the wrong side of some bad people."

That's just fanciful, Amelia said with a huff.

Fanciful was all they had right now. "Sounds like one of your books."

"Oh, you've read me? I'm flattered."

Cormac nodded at the body. "We should probably turn him over."

A door in the kitchen led to a detached carriage house turned garage, where Beck told him he could find a tarp—and where they could move the body until the coroner could get here. The path there was sheltered and had only a foot of snow instead of four-foot drifts. The stretch was pristine when Cormac went out into it. No one had come into the house this way. He cleared a path by stomping it flat, and found the tarp in the garage, along with two pairs of gardening gloves, stiff with cold but clean. When Cormac offered Glyn the second pair, the man nodded with approval.

"It's almost as if you've done this sort of thing before," Glyn observed.

"Will you stop."

Monty Connor was a big man and there wasn't a lot of room to maneuver. They laid the tarp on the counter, and only then started to shift him, to roll him onto it. The counter was also covered in blood; the entire front of the man's shirt was soaked and growing sour.

"Oh, my God," Lora murmured, continuing to snap pictures, which was annoying, but better too many than not enough.

Glyn's expression never changed. He seemed unbothered by the gruesome job. Then again, Cormac's expression never changed either. He really had moved blood-soaked bodies before; he was starting to wonder about Glyn.

"Hm, I thought the knife might still be under him, but I'm not seeing anything," Glyn said.

"Then where is it?"

"If it were me, I would have gotten rid of it," Glyn said.

"Dump it in a snowdrift outside, let fresh snow cover it up, and no one would find it till spring," Cormac added.

"Indeed." Glyn nodded appreciatively.

"You guys are freaking me out." Lora took pictures of the bloody table, the ponderous body.

They worked the body onto the tarp. Monty Connor lay splayed out, eyes half-lidded, glassy.

"And... there we are. See that?" With the tip of his gloved finger Glyn drew apart a tear in Monty's shirt, a clean slice an inch or so long right below the man's heart. Underneath the fabric, a similar tear in his undershirt, once white but now a vivid red. And under that, the wound. A gap in the skin, blood clotted around the edges. "A clean stab, a good sharp knife. Went straight in and out, up under the ribs. He'd have tipped right over. Lora, make sure you get some pictures."

"You see this sort of thing a lot?" Cormac couldn't help but ask.

Glyn grinned. "We're just going to keep asking each other that sort of question, aren't we?"

Lora dutifully took photos but her face was looking a little drained and clammy. "It doesn't even seem real," she said. "I got my start in true-crime podcasting. But this is nothing like the pictures. It's so much more... sticky."

Cormac said, "Maybe you should go sit down."

"Yeah. Just... I want to find out how this happened."

"We will," Glyn said, with confidence.

Lora fled to the next room.

"All right," Glyn said. "Count of three, we lower him to the floor?"

Cormac nodded and took up two corners of the tarp. Glyn took the other two, and they lifted. Cormac winced and nearly dropped his side, but managed to pause with most of the body's weight still on the counter.

"Everything all right?"

"Hurt my shoulder last summer. Still isn't quite right." No need to give Glyn even more to think about by telling him it was a gunshot that had hurt him.

"Should I ask someone else?"

317

"No, I'm fine." He just needed reminding that this was going to hurt. Setting his grip more firmly, he nodded.

They got Monty to the floor, opened the door, and managed to maneuver their load through the kitchen, outside and to the garage. The wind had stopped; a few thin flakes were still falling from a uniformly gray sky. Glyn squinted into the storm with something like resignation.

A pickup truck was parked in the garage, and they lifted Monty into its bed, to keep it off the ground and away from vermin. They wrapped him up tight in the tarp, making sure all the corners were tucked in, all parts covered.

"It's cold enough out here to store a body, at least," Glyn said. He stepped back, taking one last look over the wrapped corpse. Folded his hands as if saying a prayer.

As they walked back to the house, Cormac felt the need to say, "I didn't do it."

"Everyone in the house is going to say that," Glyn said. "Someone will be lying."

"What about you?"

"Me?" Glyn glanced at him over his shoulder. Grinned. "Of course I didn't do it. Why would I lie?"

Five

As it happened, Glyn also knew a lot about cleaning up blood. He took point, while gently talking Beck through soaking up the spilled blood, wiping the table and floor down with bleach, while wearing thick rubber dishwashing gloves. Frannie had nervously volunteered to help, but Beck overruled her. She'd been through enough, their host insisted. Cormac held open the garbage bag that the bleached and bloodied rags went into.

"You'll need to get someone in here to do a thorough cleaning, but we'll be able to use the kitchen for now," Glyn assured her.

"Thank God you're here," Beck said. "I don't know what I'd have done without you."

"Mr. Bennett would have been a help, I think." Glyn arched a brow at him.

Cormac tried to ignore the guy. *Amelia?* he prompted. She was still being very quiet, retreating to as small a space in his mind as she ever had. He worried, and he couldn't close his eyes and try to see her in their shared meadow. Not when he needed to keep track of what was happening here.

Frannie set up a more substantial buffet of breakfast items in the dining room, but no one was much hungry. Even the coffee smelled uninteresting.

Tea, Amelia murmured. *Tea makes everything better.*

So he drank a cup of tea for her, letting its warmth settle him.

Vane, his coffee cup abandoned on an end table, started pacing, gesturing broadly. "So, are we all just going to sit here staring at each other until the snow stops and the cops come?"

"I don't think I want to let any of you out of my sight," Beck said. "So yes, I think we should all just sit here."

"None of us knew the guy, why would anyone want to kill him?" Lora said. She'd settled in an armchair, hugging herself. Vane came over and rested a hand on her shoulder.

"He wasn't very likeable," Frannie said quietly. Lora looked sharply at her, and Glyn raised a questioning brow. Cormac expected June to shoot back with a grief-stricken and defensive reply, but she didn't, continuing to knead a handkerchief.

"What is it they do on TV?" Frannie said. "Do we know what time it happened? Then we find out where everyone was then."

"Maybe it was the ghost," Lora said. "That unknown spirit in the séance."

They're seriously accusing me? I can't go through this again.

Glyn chuckled. "That would make a good story for your podcast, wouldn't it? Frannie has the right idea, though. The lights went out about 11:30. The blood was already cool when Frannie went into the kitchen, when was it, around 7? So let's say Monty was dead by 4."

"You ask us where we were between 11:30 and 4, we're just going to say 'asleep,'" Vane said.

"Well, you see, I have to confess I have a terrible habit of eavesdropping. Can't seem to keep my nose out of it. I'd apologize, but it's often so useful."

Cormac tried to remember when he'd gone out to the bathroom and seen Glyn standing on the other end of the hall, after the argument between Beck and Monty. About midnight?

What if Monty hadn't gone back to his room after? And what if Glyn hadn't, either? He tried to remember how many doors he had heard closing. Was it just the one?

"So you were awake and out of your room after midnight, is what you're saying?" Cormac countered.

"Touché, sir. But then so was nearly everyone else. Mr. Vane left his room as well, if I'm not mistaken."

"Just Vane," he said testily. "And yes, I left my room. Just getting my toothbrush from the bathroom. Is that allowed?"

"Pardon me for being indelicate," Glyn said, "But you weren't near the bathroom. You went to Ms. Mirelli's room, yes?"

Beck huffed. "If you'd wanted to stay together I could have given you one of the queen-size rooms—"

"We're not—" Lora started, then looked away. Because Vane's gaze was downcast, and they clearly were. "We're not public about it," she finally said.

"We'd lose credibility," Vane said. "People wouldn't take the cross-promotion between our brands seriously if they knew we were together." He gave Lora a wan smile, which she returned. Clearly, there were feelings.

It's... adorable.

"Or you're just waiting for the right moment to monetize the romance?" Glyn said. Both of them sat up in outrage, but Glyn waved them back before they could say anything. "At any rate, it seems that a number of us were up and about in the night. Beck and Monty argued at the top of the stairs at about midnight... June, when did Monty return to your room, and when did he leave again?"

"I... I don't know. He said he was going to get a nightcap, and I went to bed. I'm a sound sleeper, I wouldn't have heard him come back in. That scream woke me up, and... and that's when I realized he'd never come to bed last night." She let out a dramatic, cut-off sob and kneaded the handkerchief even more forcefully.

Cormac turned to Frannie. "Your room's right next to the kitchen. You must have heard something."

Unless she's the murderer. A little revenge for Monty's earlier transgression?

Was Cormac the only one who knew about that? Frannie was the last person here he'd peg as being capable of murder.

"I didn't." She sounded defensive. "I wear earplugs, because of the way the wind hits that side of the house. It's loud. So I wouldn't have heard anything."

Convenient. Everyone in the room was thinking it.

Amelia had a spell. At least, she had once used a spell that could raise the dead. Not really raise the dead—recall their soul for a moment, to ask them questions. The knife had gone through Monty's chest—he must have seen who his killer was.

That spell is so very difficult, Amelia said, as soon as Cormac thought of it. *I've only ever attempted it immediately after death, and even then… it's uncertain any answers would be forthcoming. Monty's been dead for hours.*

It might be worth trying, to get some kind of answer.

She hesitated. *We would have to explain the ritual to the others. Keep them out of the way while I draw the appropriate symbols. I'm not sure they would let us.*

Even if it meant catching a murderer?

It would only increase their suspicion of you.

Glyn was still on his tear. "Mrs. Connor, I know this is difficult, but I wondered if you could go through your husband's things? Just to see if it will give us some idea that might indicate why this happened."

"I don't know, I can't think of anything at all—"

"It can't hurt to take a look."

"All right… just give me a minute to straighten up." June rushed up the stairs. Glyn exchanged a look with Beck, and the pair followed.

Cormac desperately wanted to chase after them. Dig through Monty's things himself, like he was some kind of TV detective. Maybe the room wasn't the only place to look. He set down the mug of tea and paced to the foyer, to the coat tree in the corner, mounded with all their coats and wraps.

He didn't have to work to figure out which coat was Monty's: the big, tan cowboy duster that looked like no drop of mud had ever come near it. Carefully moving aside the coats piled around it, Cormac felt along the side pockets for... he wasn't sure what. A figurative smoking gun. Maybe Monty was blackmailing someone. Maybe he stole something. Maybe he pissed off one too many folk singers.

In the inside pocket of the coat, he felt the hard edge of an envelope, stuffed with folded paper. Crinkling, as he put pressure on it. It would just take a second for him to look at it—

Voices traveled down the stairs. Beck, June, and Glyn. Cormac drew away from the coat tree and waited by the banister. They hesitated on the landing when they saw Cormac standing there.

"Find anything good?" he asked.

"The Connors pack a lot of luggage for a weekend," Glyn said.

June shrugged. "Monty liked his shirts folded just so. Takes up space. I... don't even know what I'm going to do with all his things now."

"You don't need to worry about it, hon," Beck assured her. "Take all the time you need."

June Connor still seemed stunned. She shook her head vaguely, as if the reality of the situation was just now settling on her. "If he had enemies, I'm sure I don't know. If he was keeping things from me— how would I ever know?"

"Why don't you come sit by the fire and rest for now," Glyn said kindly, guiding her into the parlor and steering her toward one of the sofas and not the big chair where Monty had been sitting the night before. His guitar was still propped against the wall.

Beck lingered near Cormac, crossing her arms and sighing. "It's the saddest thing," she said. "All the bags unpacked, his clothes everywhere, and she couldn't seem to bring herself to touch any of it."

"You want to explain what the argument with Monty was about?" he asked.

Her eyes widened. "I didn't kill him, I would never—"

"I'm just trying to understand."

"Monty and Jim did a handshake deal on that big parcel of land, working off hundred-year-old deeds. Then Monty does a mineral survey and bingo, there's a deposit. And I don't get anything. Now, if he bought the land knowing about the mineral rights and didn't disclose them, I could sue. I told him I would... and then he claimed the parcel he bought includes the land the house is on. He'd countersue, get the house, and I'd be skunked."

"So you have a motive," Cormac said wryly.

"With Monty dead, the pressure's off. Oh Cormac, what am I going to do?"

Did she actually do it? Cormac didn't feel like asking that bluntly. "Nothing, for now. Just maybe don't say any of this to Glyn."

"Oh, he already knows. That guy doesn't miss anything."

"Why'd you invite him, anyway?"

"Because he doesn't miss anything." She quirked a smile.

From the parlor, raised voices carried in a sudden argument. Beck went to intervene, and Cormac glanced back at the coat tree. He'd have to go digging for those papers later.

"I don't care about the optics," Vane said. He faced off with Lora in the middle of the room.

"No, I forbid it!" June countered. "Monty was right, you're Satanic!"

"*Seriously?*" Lora exclaimed at her, then turned back to Vane. "Look, trying to summon spirits that have been dead for a hundred years is one thing, but I don't think it'll play very well trying to exploit a death that isn't even a day old—"

"I don't want to exploit anything, I just want to learn what really happened."

Beck put her hands on her hips. "What are you yelling about in here?"

Flustered, June said, "Beck, you can't let them do this, it's... *bohemian.*"

"Bohemian? What are you talking about?"

Cormac looked to Glyn for an explanation.

Wearing a wry, unperturbed smile, Glyn said, "Mr. Vane is going to perform another séance. To try to speak to the spirit of Monty Connor."

Six

Some many years previous...

To meet the most interesting people, one had only to alter one's setting. This wasn't the primary reason Lady Amelia Parker decided to travel the Nile by river boat, but it was certainly a benefit.

Most of the passengers were British or European, though an American couple and a gentleman from India were also present. All were wealthy enough to travel, of course, but some definitely appeared to be rather better off. The number of trunks each traveler brought seemed to be an accurate indication of status. The fine Englishwoman traveling with her son might as well have brought an entire estate with her. The son, set to managing the luggage—or rather managing the valet who had been brought along to manage the luggage—seemed to be eternally grumbling about the situation, but continued to accede to the woman's wishes in everything. By contrast, a young, simply dressed French couple seemed to have but one case between them, and gave the impression that they had scrimped and saved to be able to make the journey. The experience was all, and not the accoutrements. Amelia understood.

As a young woman traveling alone, Amelia attracted attention among the passengers. She did not reveal her own rank as minor aristocracy, to avoid tedious conversations. Nevertheless, she became the subject of much curiosity. From the women, she received interest and varying degrees of shock. One girl of about twelve decided to follow her everywhere and ask questions until her mother demanded her daughter to keep away from that woman. From the men—deep protective impulses. Was there anything they could do for her? She need only ask. They would *leap* to her aid, instantly, with great enthusiasm. Oppressive chivalry.

She managed to have normal conversations with a dapper gentleman from Belgium who was willing to speak with her about archeology and hieroglyphics, and not suggest that she must be in desperate need of assistance. She made sure to sit at his table for supper.

She had her own agenda. She spoke to the dining room attendants, the housekeeping staff, and the crew of the *Nile Dream*. What was it like growing up in Egypt? What stories did their grandparents tell? What meaning did the ancient monuments have for them in their modern lives? They seemed confused at her interest at first, but were kind.

Amelia was not here for Egyptian linen and photographs with the pyramids, camel rides and quaint marketplaces. She was here for Egyptian magic. Ancient lore. The secrets of the pharaohs and their high priests. The river cruise was meant for tourists, but it was also the best way for her to reach the temple complex at Luxor. What would she find there? She wasn't entirely sure but she planned to enjoy the quest.

Meanwhile, she had to deal with days of travel and a series of dull suppers during which she gave the blandest answers possible to the most obvious questions, spoke of other travels only in passing, and was polite rather than interested.

Then one morning, a body was discovered in the forward parlor. The fine Englishwoman's put-upon son was found sitting in a chair with a shot from a small-caliber pistol through his chest. Most of the passengers went into a series of small panics. The doctor on staff determined that the shot could not have been self-inflicted because of various details—no powder burns, wrong angle. The captain confined all to their quarters, and Amelia tried not to be annoyed that her trip to Luxor might be delayed. After all, a man had died and the mother was inconsolable.

Amelia gave an accounting of her whereabouts but seemed to have no suspicions directed toward her. The Belgian gentleman was on hand for all the interrogations. He was calm but asked such pointed questions.

As far as the conventional investigation went, Amelia could do little to help. But she acquired the blood-spattered handkerchief that had been in the victim's pocket—his belongings had been put in a box on the doctor's desk and left unsupervised—and knew several good scrying spells. What information the mundane world could not disclose, perhaps the spirit realm would reveal. Closed in her cabin, she lit candles and made the appropriate circles and marks on the floor with chalk. Each symbol represented one of the people involved in the case. The Belgian gentleman, the wealthy Englishwoman, the valet, the American couple from Boston who had been next door, the French couple who had been on the deck below, and so on. She made sure the air was still and summoned whatever trace of spirit remained on the handkerchief to give a sign. Waited to discern some meaning in the patterns of smoke rising from the tin of burning incense.

The ancient Egyptians believed they held the secrets of the afterlife. That by certain processes they could send their elite to life everlasting in the next world. Amelia was drawn to these secrets, to the vast mystery of Shakespeare's Undiscovered Country. What if one could return? Or at least send a message. If the victim could tell who had killed him...

Nothing. The smoke did not lean purposefully toward any of the markings, thereby indicating a connection, some mortal thread of doom. She had asked a question of this solid piece of matter; it was not required to give her an answer.

While the handkerchief revealed no otherworldly information, it did have a monogram, initials embroidered in one corner. *Not* the victim's or his mother's. Rather, Amelia believed this handkerchief belonged to the woman from Boston.

This seemed important and she wondered why no one had had searched the victim's pockets before this. Carefully and secretly, she returned the handkerchief, hoping that no one saw her and would try to implicate her in the crime.

The handkerchief was discovered and several alibis fell apart as the truth came out. In fact, the victim and the woman from Boston had arranged their itineraries to put them both on this cruise, and they planned to depart together before its end, from one of the other ports. They had carefully pretended that they did not know each other for days now, all the while waiting for the chance to escape together, after a long and secret affair. The woman had ruthlessly hidden her grief at her lover's death for days. Now, both the woman and her husband fell weeping, for entirely different reasons.

The victim's mother discovered his intention to abandon her. The person among them who had drawn the least suspicion because she had seemed like the last person to commit a murder was the one who had pulled the trigger of the gun provided her by her valet, who was also her lover. The son had told his mother that he would fire the man and have her committed to an institution for madness. So she took action. Both of them, the most dignified, respectable passengers on the ship, were led away by the authorities at the next port.

There was a lesson here.

The remaining days on the cruise felt muted and somber. The boat might not have been literally haunted, but the shadow of what had happened lingered. The stewards could not quite get all the blood up off the spot of the carpet where the man had died. They all avoided walking there, if they could.

Amelia reached Luxor at last. From a street vendor, she purchased some amulets shaped like little shabtis, figurines made of blue glaze, which if not authentic were at least charming. She wandered the ruins as long as she could. She could have spent weeks there, copying inscriptions and studying the inscrutable faces of dead pharaohs. She only had two days and tried to make the most of them.

The Belgian gentleman found her standing still, looking up at a wall full of writing, rows of hieroglyphs and images of kings etched into the stone. If she had a hundred years she would not understand it all. Certainly, the meaning of individual images could be deciphered. But the thoughts that went into composing the entire piece? The purpose felt by those who made this, imperfectly interpreted all these millennia later? One could never reach back like that.

"Mademoiselle, you seem pensive," he observed. He somehow managed to keep his pale suit crisp and clean, even in the dust and heat. "I hope the unfortunate events on this journey have not made you disinclined to travel?"

"Oh no, not at all. I just..." She sighed, because she didn't know what to say. Wasn't sure she could even explain. She would sound maudlin. "I just wonder what they were thinking, is all. Why... people do what they do."

"It is a mystery greater than the secrets of the ancients," he agreed. They stood together and studied the record of the ages.

Seven

Beck and Frannie voted in favor of the new séance. Glyn expressed no opinion but regarded the situation with the air of a man watching the creek rise.

Amelia was disturbed. *We can't let him carry on with this, not without telling him why the last one went wrong.*

Cormac didn't trust any of these people enough to tell them about Amelia.

We need to tell him because if he knows, he can work around it, and might actually be able to contact Monty Connor's spirit.

Amelia believed in Vane, anyway. Maybe the guy could do it. Maybe it wouldn't hurt to try. And maybe a séance would keep everyone distracted enough for a little while to not keep pacing around the house like caged raccoons.

At some point, everyone managed to dress for the day, but they watched each other travel up and down the stairs with suspicion, as if no one wanted to let anyone else out of their sight. The others gave Cormac a wide berth, which he normally wouldn't notice, much less mind. But it was annoying, how easily they all assumed he'd done the deed.

We really do seem to encounter more than our fair share of murdered bodies.

Cormac didn't like thinking about it. He'd taken the number of dead bodies in his life for granted until recently. Might be nice, being the kind of person murders didn't happen around.

"Don't you have to do a séance at night?" Frannie asked.

"That's mostly for atmosphere." Vane had retrieved his bag and was setting up in the dining room. The sense of mystery and showmanship he'd evoked the night before was gone. Now, he was practical and workmanlike, setting up the cloth and candles—plain white tapers this time, a dozen of them across the table. "Darkness helps—can you close the curtains, shut out the light as much as possible?" Frannie got to work doing so, both in the dining room and the parlor.

Cormac approached, trying to be casual and nonthreatening. He wasn't very good at it. "I need to talk to you."

Vane actually flinched back. "What? Why... what do you want?" He glanced at the doorway, prepared to bolt.

Like he was holding him up at a liquor store or something. "You think I have a garrote in my pocket? That I did in Connor and you're next? Look, I know what happened during the séance yesterday. I know about the spirit you sensed."

Vane grabbed his arm and drew him into the kitchen. "*What?*" he asked when the door was closed. "That was real? I wasn't imagining it?"

Cormac wasn't quite sure how to explain it. He could never make their situation sound reasonable.

"Well?" Vane urged.

"She's a spirit... she was hanged a little over a hundred years ago and now she lives in my head... sort of." Vane stared blankly. Yeah, this wasn't in any of the books. "Maybe I'd better let Amelia explain."

"Amelia?"

Cormac took a breath and stepped to the back of his own mind, letting Amelia slip forward, to occupy nerves and flesh. This had gotten easier over time, but it didn't make the sensation of being simultaneously awake and sedated any stranger. Especially when she started speaking. His voice, her words.

"Yes, hello. Here we are then. My name is Amelia Parker, and over a hundred years ago I was wrongfully executed for a murder I did not commit. Not a murderer, but murdered, as you said last night. Delightfully accurate, I must say. I have been Mr. Bennett's companion for a number of years now, since his time in the same prison where I... well, now, that's quite a long story and not relevant. You called for a spirit to make its presence known, and you sensed me. I thought you should know before you attempt another séance and confront the same obstacle. Now, do you have any questions?"

The man stared. His mouth worked, as if he meant to say something, but the words didn't come. Cormac—Amelia—waited expectantly.

"This... isn't a trick?" Vane asked weakly.

"I can understand why you might think so, which is why we don't advertise our... situation."

"How... is it outright possession, or some kind of spirit transference?" His brow furrowed. Cormac could almost see the neurons firing behind his eyes, trying to work it out.

Amelia felt a thrill at meeting someone she could talk shop with. "Spirit transference of a kind, yes. Beyond that I'm unwilling to divulge details. Trade secret and all, you know how magicians are. I wasn't ready to die yet. So... I didn't."

Vane finally seemed to collect himself, straightening with a little shiver. "Thank you for revealing yourself. I'm honored. So... Cormac didn't do it, is what you're saying? Or is this one of those situations where you don't remember what he does and he doesn't remember—"

"I'm right here, I remember everything, and no I didn't," Cormac said, and Vane once again flinched back, because it might have been the same voice but it was clear that Cormac had regained control.

"That is so weird," Vane murmured.

"That's kind of hilarious, coming from you."

"So, you can channel her, just like that?"

"She needed a body, I needed to get out of jail. We came to an arrangement."

You make it sound so mercenary.

Well, what else were they but mercenaries? She chuckled.

Suddenly, Vane reached out to touch his arm and it was Cormac's turn to flinch. "Can you help? I can sense spirits sometimes, and I can usually fudge the difference. But this... solving a murder. Anything you can do." His shrug conveyed helplessness.

"Amelia's a magician. She isn't psychic—"

I'll do whatever I can.

"But she'll try," Cormac said, hedging. Vane's expression brightened; he seemed so relieved. "You'll need a focus. Something that belonged to Monty. His guitar, maybe."

"Of course. Perfect." He raced out of the kitchen.

Cormac's shoulders sagged. "I thought this weekend was supposed to be a vacation," he muttered.

Let's just concentrate on keeping you out of prison, shall we?

He left the kitchen, to see Vane striding into the dining room with Monty's guitar, and June rushing after him.

"No! I won't allow it! You put that down!" she said.

"I need something important that belonged to him, this is the best we've got."

"This is a travesty—"

Lora stepped next to her and gently turned her aside while Vane arranged the guitar in the center of the table. "Mrs. Connor, please. Vane's going to do this with or without your cooperation. Wouldn't you rather be here and know what's happening than sit it out and wonder? We need you for this. If Monty wants to speak to anyone, he'll speak to you."

"Oh, I don't know about that." June seemed torn, glaring with contempt at the new séance Vane was arranging, and looking at the others, pleading. "Beck?"

"I think he should try, hon. It can't hurt, can it?"

"Not entirely sure that's true," Glyn murmured.

It would hurt whoever was the murderer, assuming the séance revealed anything.

"Glyn," June said. "Is there anything else we ought to be doing?"

"Search all the rooms. See who argues against it the most. I still want to know where that knife went."

Cormac didn't repeat what he suspected: that the knife was outside, under a snowdrift, and wouldn't reemerge until spring.

"I'm ready," Vane said. "And I could really use all your help. I'm assuming we all want to know what happened."

"All of us except the murderer," Cormac said. Once again, they glanced suspiciously at him—but he wasn't arguing against the séance. A point in his favor?

They gathered around the table.

The room was surprisingly dark with the curtains drawn. This time, the plain candles glowed with normal yellow flames. The blond wood of the guitar, resting in the middle of the table, gleamed buttery in the light.

Lora started setting up her video camera, but Vane put a hand on her arm. "Not now."

She put the camera away. Just a séance, then. No show this time.

As they sat around the table, they were aware of the gap. The empty chair where Monty had sat the night before. Glyn got up to pull the chair away, but Vane said, "No, leave it. It's an invitation."

The gap remained. No moaning wind outside this time, at least. The stillness was almost worse. The candle flames barely flickered. Vane lit incense, and the air's smell turned spicy.

"Friends, I have called you here to find answers. To seek what contact we may find beyond the veil." His voice was somber and imploring. No banging fists, no ringing gongs. "Together, I believe we can call the spirits to us—and learn the truth of what happened here. Settle yourselves, please. Put away your grief and fear, and come with me on the journey ahead. Now, join hands."

June and Beck had to reach across the gap where Monty had been. They did so nervously, as if the space was actually—or might soon be— occupied. Frannie was on Cormac's right again, and this time seemed reluctant to hold his hand, drawing away even as she reached out. On his other side, Glyn held on like he expected Cormac to try to flee.

Steady there. Focus on the task at hand.

Breathe. Open his mind. Let Amelia step forward.

Vane had placed Cormac across from him, so the two could look directly at one another. Their gazes met, and Cormac—Amelia— nodded.

Now you see me, Vane, don't you? Now, step past me. I'm just another soul sitting at the table. You are searching for someone else.

Vane flashed a thin, satisfied smile. Whatever she had done to put herself outside his awareness must have worked. Maybe it was like filtering white noise from a recording.

"If any spirits, any visitors from alternate planes linger here, we greet you and call on you to join us."

A spike of worry came from Amelia: with such a broad invitation, one never knew what might decide to show up. The sense of anticipation grew heavy. Frannie's hand was trembling.

"The veil has grown thin," Vane murmured. "I feel a presence drawing close. Spirit... we greet you. If you are willing to speak to us, make a sign."

One of the candles winked out.

June bit off a scream; Frannie gasped. Glyn leaned in, his gaze narrow and searching. There was no draft, no puff of air. The candle itself hadn't changed. Vane didn't appear to be manipulating anything, but then he wouldn't.

Vane maintained his calm. "We have received a sign. Welcome to our circle, spirit. May you find comfort here. We humbly ask you to share your secrets, in the manner you've chosen to communicate. Did your life end in this house? I beg you, give us a sign."

A second candle went out. With a dozen others still lit, the room's brightness didn't dim, but the shadows seemed to deepen.

Then the air turned cold. Gooseflesh crawled up Cormac's arms, and his breath fogged. Even Amelia's presence shivered. This was the sharp, bone-stabbing chill of a winter night in the mountains. If they'd gone out to the porch last night, this was what they'd have felt.

It felt like death.

"Spirit," Vane murmured. "Were you murdered?"

The flames of every candle wavered, shuddered, and stayed lit. And this was the problem with trying to speak to spirits with signs and symbols: ambiguity.

"What's that supposed to mean?" Beck asked in a strained voice.

Vane met Cormac's gaze across the table and seemed uncertain what to do next.

Cormac—Amelia, rather—said, "You died in winter. You died in cold."

A third candle went out, and the hair on the back of Cormac's neck stood up.

"Am I speaking to Monty Connor?" Vane asked eagerly. Too eagerly, Amelia thought. He would scare off whatever was in the room with them.

The candles didn't waver. No change, no answer.

"Monty would have hated this, he'd never take part in this," June hissed. "It's all bunk."

"Shh!" Lora hissed at her.

Vane was undeterred. "Spirit, we feel your presence. The cold haunts this place, haunts your death. Was your passing from the material plane recent?"

No change.

We're not speaking to Monty.

That seemed clear, and Cormac wondered if June had the right of it: Monty would never have put up with this. He wouldn't do anything Vane asked him to.

"In the past, then." Vane could be forgiven for sounding disappointed. Imagine, solving a murder through a séance? Not tonight, apparently. "Fifty years ago? A hundred years ago?"

Confusion. The candles flickered, but this time the movement seemed in time with the breathing of those seated around the table. The normal wavering of candle flames.

Vane kept trying. "Did you die before your time? Was your death violent? What is your connection to this place?" Wincing, he shook his head. That wasn't a yes-no question.

The cold continued. Next to Cormac, Frannie was shivering.

Murdered, but not...

Amelia, speaking through Cormac, asked, "Are you Tobias Wright?"

All the candles went out. The room went totally dark.

A woman screamed, and there was scrambling as chairs pushed back from the table. Something fell over, maybe one of the candles. Suddenly, with a shushing of fabric, one of the curtains swept open to reveal the blinding glare of snow in daylight. Everybody winced and turned away.

Glyn stood at the window, hand on the curtain. "Well, Beck. I think your house is haunted."

"And we don't have it on video," Lora said despairingly. "How could we not have it on video?"

"Wouldn't matter," Vane said. "People would still say it was a trick."

"What about Monty?" June demanded. "Where's Monty? If you can call up spirits why not Monty?"

"Maybe he didn't have a reason to stick around," Cormac said.

Beck looked at him. "Not even to talk to his own wife?"

It was Tobias Wright's spirit, I know it... but there's something about it I'm missing, another part of the mystery...

Across the table, Vane sat with his hands steepled before his face, his eyes closed. Maybe shivering, just a bit.

"Vane?" Lora prompted.

The psychic sighed. "We could try again, maybe after dark—"

"This is all theater," Glyn said suddenly. "You could summon the ghost of Sherlock Holmes himself and it wouldn't bring us any closer to learning what happened to Monty Connor and which of us is the murderer."

"Maybe the ghost did it." Frannie said. She was hugging herself.

"Ghost wouldn't have needed a knife," Cormac said.

"It's time to get back to good solid detective work," Glyn said. His look hardened, a determined glint lighting his eyes. The manner of someone used to bowling over obstacles when he needed to. He marched to the stairs.

"Wait, does that mean he's going to search all our rooms?" Lora said. She and Vane looked at each other—and raced after him. She called after Glyn, "You can't do that—!"

"I'd better keep an eye on him." Beck went after them. June, eyeing Cormac nervously, followed Beck.

Frannie gave him a wide-eyed, mildly terrified look. "I think I should go help Beck." She fled after the others. Safety in numbers, maybe.

I'm offended that no one wants to be left alone with you.

"I'm not," he murmured. This gave him the chance to go back to the coat tree, to check on those papers in that inside pocket of Monty's coat. Maybe it was nothing, but maybe it would point to why someone would want to kill the man. Pulling back the other coats, he exposed the tan duster.

Someone else had been here since he'd searched. The front lapel was turned back, and the inside pocket was empty. "Well, I guess it was important."

Who else has been by here? Who else had time to search?

Everyone did. Everyone had been going up and down stairs to change clothes, to linger by the door and look out the window at the snowscape. Cormac himself had been back and forth from one room to the other. He hadn't watched the stairs the whole time. Maybe he should have.

What do you think was in that pocket?

Information about his land dispute with Beck? A blackmail letter? Lyrics to a new morose cowboy poem?

"And there he is, the man himself."

A crowd of footsteps rattled down the stairs and stopped on the landing above the foyer. Glyn Farrow stood behind the banister, like an actor in a play. He was holding something, a towel-wrapped bundle.

June came up next to Glyn and leaned on the banister. "What are you doing with that?"

Cormac was still holding Monty's coat. And didn't that just look guilty as hell? He didn't bother explaining himself; this was exactly what it looked like.

"What is it?" he said tiredly to the crowd looking back at him with undeniable shock and horror.

On the other hand, Glyn seemed to be enjoying himself, wearing a small, eager smile. "We found this shoved behind the dresser in your room. Wondered if you could comment on it."

He unfolded the towel to reveal a gleaming chef's knife, the brown handle a match for the set in the kitchen. A red tint of blood still marked the point.

Eight

In the back of his mind, Amelia swore. It startled him.

Cormac grinned, deciding that yes, he definitely should have driven away when he had the chance. "You already know I'm going to say I have no idea how it got there. Somebody planted that."

"I wanted to see your reaction. You don't react to much of anything, do you?"

Cormac spread his arms in a show of agreement. After the shit he'd seen? After helping save the world from a demonic invasion and volcanic destruction? After carrying around the soul of a Victorian wizard in his mind for years? This didn't scare him, and he was annoyed that Glyn somehow thought it should.

The better question in his mind: Why was Glyn trying to frame him? Only one answer: he might have killed Monty himself. But why?

Maybe just to see if he could.

Glyn spoke to the others, "I'll just go put this out in the garage with Mr. Connor, for safekeeping."

June's voice pitched high as she called, "Are we just going to let him stand there like nothing's wrong? He did it!"

"The knife was in his room," Glyn said. "The other doesn't necessarily follow. He's right—someone might have planted it."

"Someone like you?" Cormac said, and Glyn made a little nod as if to say, touché.

"I can't stand this. I can't trust any of you. I'm locking myself in my room until the police get here." June stormed back up the stairs, and a moment later a door slammed.

"Probably for the best," Beck said nervously. "Maybe we should all just stay in our rooms."

And wait like a lamb for the slaughter? No, absolutely not.

Glyn came down the stairs and brushed past Cormac, pointedly meeting his gaze as he passed through the foyer. Cormac followed.

"You watch me, I watch you," Cormac said flatly, to Glyn's look of inquiry.

"Or you murder me when you get me alone in the carriage house?"

Cormac huffed. "How stupid do you think I am?"

Glyn turned his back on Cormac, an obvious snub. He wasn't afraid.

The temperature in the garage was frigid; their breath fogged. Glyn did exactly what he said he was going to do, setting the towel-wrapped knife next to the shrouded body.

They both stood a moment, regarding the bundle. If you didn't know it was a body, you might think it was a tarp, maybe a rolled-up carpet. Since the two of them had put it there, it was easy to see which end had the shape of a head, and which end tapered to feet.

There's another spell I know, Amelia said. *Not to summon the spirit, but a scrying spell.*

They'd never get enough time alone to set it up and go through with it. Not with Glyn watching. He felt a sigh of agreement from her.

Perhaps we could bring him in on it.

Unless he was the murderer. Cormac wasn't turning his back on the man.

If he is the murderer, then the spell should be especially effective with him standing right there.

Tempting.

"Why were you searching Mr. Connor's coat?" Glyn asked as they turned back for the house.

Cormac's first impulse was to blow him off; he didn't need to tell this guy anything. But he said, "There was something in the front pocket. Some papers, I think. I didn't get a chance to look the first time, and when I went back for it…" He shrugged. He should have just looked the first time. Lesson learned.

"Papers revealing motive, you believe?" Glyn said. "Or were you trying to cover your trail?"

"I keep telling you, if I'd done it you never would have found the knife."

They went back to the house. The sun was setting—where had the day gone? From the side of the house he could see the front drive, the cars parked under mounds of snow like igloos, the pine trees beyond weighted down with the stuff. Maybe the authorities would get here by morning, or maybe they'd be stuck for another day, hurling suspicions and accusations. Cormac wasn't sure they'd survive it.

He didn't realize he'd paused, watching the late afternoon sun cut through the forest, until Glyn stopped beside him, looking out at the same scene.

"Can I ask you a question?" Glyn asked.

"Why stop now?"

"Do you believe in Vane's performances? In séances, ghosts, all the rest of it?"

That wasn't a simple yes or no question. It would definitely take too long to explain, standing out here in the cold.

He chuckled a little. "Two of my best friends are werewolves. So yeah, some of it."

"Werewolves? Really? Hm. Then you think Vane really contacted Tobias Wright?"

"Or what was left of him. Ghosts aren't… people. They're reflections. Memories. I'm not sure what they are."

They hadn't worn coats out, and the cold was biting. Cormac was feeling it; Glyn hugged himself. The stars would be glorious on a night like this, the clear sky after a storm.

343

"Then you think it might be possible to contact Mr. Connor, to learn what happened?"

"I think it might be possible to learn what happened." He studied the author, but the man was as unreadable as ever. British reserve, or something else.

Was he worried about Cormac discovering the truth?

"Let's get inside," Glyn said. "My lungs are freezing."

In the kitchen Frannie was putting together trays of food.

"It's just sandwiches," she said. "I didn't feel up to doing much else."

"It looks perfect," Glyn assured her.

"So you two decided not to kill each other?"

Cormac glanced at Glyn, who glanced back wryly. Cormac had a sinking feeling he was going to have to have it out with the guy at some point. He missed his guns less and less as time went on, but he might have wished for a handgun under his pillow tonight.

"Here, let me help you with that," Glyn said, moving to the sink to wash his hands first.

The others, except for June, had gathered in the dining room. Vane and Lora were side by side, hand in hand. Beck stood pensively by the window. No one made a move toward the sandwiches.

Frannie had a separate, smaller tray prepared. "I'll just take this up to June, then."

If anything, they were looking more unhappy and uncomfortable than even this morning. The shock of seeing the body hadn't worn off. Neither had the shock of knowing that one of them had done it. Would the murderer strike again, to cover their tracks?

Or perhaps the ghosts in this place were lonely and wanted someone to sing them morose songs for eternity.

That was a really disconcerting thought.

Frannie returned with the tray, still with all its food. "She said she wasn't hungry."

Are we hungry? Cormac prodded Amelia. She agreed that they weren't. They politely took the offered food, and picked at it. Lora went through a glass of wine and started on another. As appealing as the self-medicated numbness sounded, Cormac needed to stay sharp. No pun intended.

They finally gave up, and Frannie and Beck cleared the table and returned leftovers to the kitchen. When she returned, Beck stood at the dining room table, hands clasped before her.

"I've decided... I think June is right, and everyone should stay in their rooms until Sheriff Andrews and his crew get here in the morning."

Vane leaned forward. "I could try another séance. I'm getting close, I know it—"

Lora put a hand on his arm, and he stilled.

"On the contrary, I think it would be better for us to wait in the parlor, together," Glyn said.

No one sneaking around, no one getting up to anything. Cormac was annoyed to discover that he agreed.

"I can't do it," Frannie said. "I can't sit here staring at each other waiting for something to happen. Beck's right. Good night." She said this in a rush and fled.

"We lock our doors, nothing bad can happen, right?" Beck seemed to be trying to convince herself.

"Locks don't matter in a haunted house," Vane said.

"Great, now I'm not going to sleep at all," Lora muttered. "I really want to go home."

Impossible, of course.

Vane stood, held out his hand, and Lora took it as he helped her to her feet.

"Sleep well," he said wryly to the others. Hand in hand, they went through the parlor and up the stairs.

Glyn watched them go. "I'm trying to decide if one or both of them would be willing to create a ghost, if they couldn't find one for their séance."

"Oh Glyn, really," Beck said. But she glanced after them with her brow furrowed.

Cormac was still betting on the man who just happened to find a knife in Cormac's room. "I'm all right with the two of us sitting in the parlor staring at each other all night."

"Indeed," Glyn said, studying him with a focused gaze that made Cormac nervous.

Beck said, "I'm not going upstairs till you two get to your rooms."

"Don't trust us?" Cormac said with a smirk.

"You two are the ones in this house I *know* are capable of killing someone. The thing is, you two have the least reason to do it."

Whereas Beck might have had the most, and she knew it.

Glyn went to the sideboard and put a finger of liquor in a tumbler. "Well then, a nightcap for me and off to bed. The sooner morning comes the sooner we can put this behind us."

As if Cormac would be able to sleep.

Beck scattered the ashes in the fireplace and turned out lights. The three of them went upstairs. On the third floor, Cormac and Glyn stood at their respective doors, across the hallway from each other. Waiting for the other to enter his room and shut the door first.

"Well then," Glyn said flatly. "Good night."

"Guess so."

Neither of them moved.

For God's sake just get in the room.

He pushed open the door, stepped in with all the leisurely saunter of a western stereotype. Matched Glyn's gaze as the Brit did likewise. Finally, at last, they shut the doors.

On the shelf next to the bed, the name glared out from the row of books. GLYN FARROW.

Why the hell was he letting this guy get under his skin?

Cormac's duffel bag had been moved. Probably the contents rifled through as well. He could see where the dresser had been shifted to hide the knife, by whoever had done it, and to find it again. Who'd had time to sneak the weapon into his room? Everybody.

He sat on the bed and tried to sort out the day's activities. Frannie was the only one who hadn't been upstairs—but no, she'd come up when everyone else did, when Glyn announced he was searching rooms. At some point each of them had come upstairs to change clothes.

Cormac kept coming back to Glyn, who had so grandly appointed himself the amateur detective in charge. As a distraction?

And he keeps coming back to you.

There was a noise at the door. Small, subtle. The slide of metal against metal. The soft thud of a lock turning over.

Someone had the key to the old-fashioned lock in the door.

Cormac jumped off the bed and grabbed the door handle. It wouldn't turn. He shook it, rattling the door on its hinges. The house might have been old, the hardware on the door might have been original, but it was solid. Didn't budge.

He fell to the floor, pressed his face to the gap at the bottom of the door, hoping to see out, any detail. He just saw the shadow of feet walking away. No telling whose.

"Goddammit," he muttered, hitting the floor with his fist. He rolled back and stared up at the ceiling. His pulse raced, and there was nothing he could do about anything.

Breathe, my dear. Just... breathe. I want to see you.

He unclenched his fists and closed his eyes.

Before he opened them again on the mindscape of his ideal mountain valley, he heard pacing. A long skirt swishing against the grass. A frustrated sigh. When he looked, he saw Amelia, her hair pulled away from her face and hanging long down her back. Her blouse was mussed as if she hadn't changed it in a couple of days—and why that detail? Why should her imagined self ever be anything other than perfect? Because their minds were in disarray. His own jeans were faded. His T-shirt itched. He rolled out an imaginary kink in his imaginary shoulders.

She stopped. Snarled a little. "I went to prison for a murder I didn't commit once, I don't intend to do so again."

He was tired. How could he be this tired? He settled on the grass and leaned up against the tree that always seemed to be right there for him to lean up against.

"Aren't you going to say something? Do something? Anything?" Her anger made her flushed. She glowed. She was gorgeous, like an old painting. If he told her that right now, she'd scoff at him. Tell him he was distracted and irrational.

"Yeah. I just need a minute." A minute to not think about it. A minute to just... let whatever he was supposed to be feeling wash over him. If he let himself actually feel it, he might never stop screaming.

The fight went out of her all at once. His exhaustion, spilling on to her. They could never avoid each other's moods, here. She sank to the grass beside him, and her expression turned beseeching.

Suddenly, she seemed young. She was terrified and trying very hard to hide it. "Whatever happens, we're together. You have no idea how much that means to me."

"Yes, I do." He opened his arms and drew her into an embrace. She gave a little sob, quickly cut off, repressed. But he heard it. Kissed the top of her head, because it gave him comfort. Maybe it would comfort her, too. The weight of her—the imagined and no-less-real feeling weight of her—anchored him.

"We'll go mad," she murmured. "We could stay locked here in our minds forever, go mad... and that wouldn't be such a bad thing, would it?"

Right now, it sounded pretty good. The length of her, lying half on top of him, her arms around him. God, he wanted her. He could shift a little, slide his hand down her hip, put his leg between hers—

"We're not going to take this lying down, are we?" she said abruptly. He chuckled. "Oh hell no."

Nine

With a pair of tweezers from his shaving kit and a paperclip from the stash of odds and ends Amelia had him carry around in his pockets, he picked the lock at the bedroom door in less than a minute. Slowly, carefully, he eased it open, muting the sound of creaking hinges as much as he could. He half expected Glyn to be waiting outside, standing guard. But the hall was dark, the other doorways closed.

He gathered a few materials from Amelia's kit: white votive candles, a bit of chalk. More scrying, but not the imprecise business of trying to talk to spirits this time. This involved the material plane entirely. They just needed half an hour without interruption. By this time he knew which stairs creaked, which floorboards would squeal at his weight, and successfully avoided them. Good, old-fashioned sneaking. It was a relief to be *doing* something.

He hesitated on the last flight of stairs. The lights were off, just as Beck had left them. Outside, visible through the window in the front door, faint moonlight turned the snow-covered landscape silver. All was still, perfectly quiet. So why was the hair on the back of his neck standing up?

Stepping softly, he reached the bottom of the stairs, listening hard, muscles tensing. He wanted the lights on. Flush out whatever shadow was waiting for him.

Something struck toward him from a hiding place to the side of the stairs. Cormac ducked back just in time, as Glyn drew back the staff he was holding—broomstick, or walking stick maybe—and thrust again, and again Cormac dodged. This time, he took hold of Glyn's arm. The man easily twisted out of his grip, finessing some martial arts move to slip away.

Cormac's injured shoulder ached—he didn't want to get into a knock-down drag-out with this guy. He'd lose. He pointed and said, "You locked my door—"

Glyn drew back. "I thought you locked my door." Cormac was breathing hard; Glyn wasn't. He lowered his weapon, what turned out to be a carved wood walking stick, and straightened out of his fighting stance. "You were locked in too?"

"Yeah, I picked it open."

"So did I."

"Then who—"

Glyn raised an eyebrow. "Whoever murdered Monty, trying to keep us out of the way."

Enough of this. Time for some answers. Cormac went to the coat tree and grabbed his coat off the top. "Which one is yours?"

Glyn found his coat, a sensible waterproof overcoat, under the layers. "Planning on a walk?"

"Just to the garage. Something I've been wanting to do." You all right with an audience? he asked the back of his mind.

Looking forward to it. He imagined her rubbing her hands together with anticipation.

Glyn followed without a word. He kept the walking stick, Cormac noticed.

They'd tamped down a clear way to the carriage house by now. At night, it had become slick. They crossed it carefully.

The outbuilding was freezing. Thank goodness. Monty's body must have been frozen solid by this time. Cormac worked quickly; moving kept him warm.

He gave Glyn a flashlight to hold until he got the candles lit. He cleared a space on the concrete floor and made a circle of buttery light.

After putting on gloves, he drew out the bundle containing the knife from the back of the truck and unwrapped it.

"What're you doing?" Glyn asked.

"Just watch. And be quiet."

Setting the knife aside, he drew a chalk circle on the floor, with symbols at the cardinal points for insight. For revelation. Amelia told him what to do; usually he'd let her take over but he needed to stay in his body. To stay fast, alert.

He put the candles at the cardinal points, then added more symbols, one for each person in the house, even himself, no exceptions.

"Are you summoning demons—"

Cormac held up a hand, palm out—*stop*. Surprisingly, Glyn shut up, standing back against the wall and watching skeptically.

Cormac tied black twine around the knife's center of balance, leaving it suspended, parallel to the ground. An arrow, with the ability to turn in any direction. Tied off the other end to a broom handle jammed into the truck bed, so his own microscopic movements on the string wouldn't impact the direction. Finally, he burned a pinch of sage to clear the air. The sharp, herbal scent of it changed the space. Took him just a little bit out of reality. The candlelight settled and spread.

Amelia told him what to say, a series of phrases in other languages. Repetition, asking for truth, to banish mystery, to summon insight. The garage was so quiet he could hear the wicks of the candles burning, a spark popping now and then. The fragile stillness stretched out. Glyn was holding his breath.

Monty Connor is not any more cooperative in death than he was in life.

Cormac hummed softy, "'Oh bury me not on the lone prairie, where the coyotes howl and the wind blows free...'"

That is a dreadful song.

The knife... shivered. The string twisted. The point of the blade drifted, drifted... settled. At the glyph Amelia used to represent Glyn Farrow.

Cormac glanced at the man, inquiring.

"What does that mean?" Glyn said softly.

"Each of these symbols stands for someone in the house. That one's yours," Cormac replied.

"But I didn't—"

"That just means you were the last person before me to handle the knife. Let's see if we can find who held it before you."

Repeat the words.

He did, asking for the knife's truth, for the secrets it conveyed. Then, just in case it helped, he murmured the next line of the song. The knife turned, turned again. A shiver, as if a breath of air pushed it. Maybe a draft in the garage was nudging it along.

The next glyph it rested on was June Connor's.

"Whose symbol is that?" Glyn hissed.

"Shh."

He repeated the incantation a third time and added, "'In a narrow grave, just six by three, they buried him there on the lone prairie.'" The knife did not move again.

Cormac sat back on his heels, trying to imagine the picture the scrying had given him. He couldn't quite do it.

"You look positively gobsmacked."

"It's pointing at June Connor," Cormac said.

"Well." Strangely, Glyn didn't seem surprised.

Cormac cut the string and let the knife fall, ringing against the concrete. He wrapped it back in the towel. Another round of burning sage, a few closing words to banish the magic, and he pinched out the candle flames. The flashlight seemed particularly dim after. The knife went back in the truck and he scuffed out the chalk marks with his boot. He felt unsettled, looking over his shoulder. A queasy anxiety wouldn't fade. He wanted to get back in where it was warm. Sit with Amelia in their meadow and figure out what to do next.

"You think she really could have done it?" Cormac asked.

"In hindsight, it might even make the most sense."

"How—"

"Let's get back inside."

The stillness from the garage carried to outside. The wind had stopped. Starlight blazed overhead. A blue, crystalline glow touched the post-blizzard world. Time seemed to slow to an imperceptible pace.

This wasn't just the winter night. Not just the frozen air. Something was... off.

Wait a moment.

Cormac put his hand out to stop Glyn, and they both stared ahead.

A figure stumbled down the steps from the kitchen door as if shoved out. It turned back to the house, shouted—and made no sound at all. A young man, maybe eighteen, with short brown hair and a thin mustache. He wore boots, rough trousers, and a flannel shirt. No coat, no hat, no gloves. Not dressed for the weather, which was already getting to him. He hugged himself, slapped his arms as if trying to beat warmth into them. Looked up at the sky with a wincing expression of consternation. Trudged away from the house a few halting steps, as if he knew he wouldn't get very far—

And then he stumbled down the steps as if he'd been shoved out the kitchen door. Shouted silently. Turned from the house with uncertain steps. Looked at the sky as if he was looking at his doom. It had been a winter night when Tobias Wright died. Maybe as freezing cold as this one. If he'd been kicked out of the house, if he'd been left outside with the temperature dropping like this...

The scene played out a third time.

"Oh, my God," Glyn murmured. It might have been the first thing that had shocked him all weekend.

Tobias Wright wasn't shot. He froze to death. Murdered but not murdered. Oh, that poor young man.

In his—and Amelia's—experience, ghosts weren't spirits so much as they were memories. Imprints. This was the moment that doomed

Tobias. What happened after... his brother might have invented the story about the shootout. He could have shot the body after the fact. In that version, he was defending himself. A player in an Old West tragedy. Not the instigator of an act of terrible cruelty.

Cormac, love. You're freezing. We should go inside.

He hadn't noticed if the chill he felt came from the cold night air, or the terrible scene playing out before him. Didn't really matter.

Just then, the figure's movement changed. Instead of turning away he stopped—and looked at Cormac and Glyn. His exasperated frown deepened into grief. As if he had consciousness and remembered what had happened. As if he sought understanding. Sympathy.

Cormac started to say something—he wasn't sure what. I'm sorry, maybe. Or, How can I help? But in the next breath the figure vanished.

Cormac touched Glyn's shoulder and urged him toward the door. They both skirted the path the ghost had taken. The snow there showed no footprints, no disturbances.

Back in the kitchen, the heated air hit him like a wall, and he shivered. They both did.

"I think I'll go start a fire," Glyn said, propping the stick by the door and nodding toward the parlor.

"I'll be there in a sec." He took off his gloves and went to the sink to wash his hands, which also gave him a moment to think.

"The scrying," he murmured. "You think it worked?"

I do. With the body and murder weapon right there—and that song. I've never seen so much power go into that spell. I think even Glyn's presence helped. He wants so badly to learn what happened.

"But why would she do it?"

I'm not sure any amount of scrying could answer that.

Voices carried from the parlor, just as Cormac stepped into the dining room. He froze and listened.

"What are you burning there, Mrs. Connor?" That was Glyn, asking a smooth, innocuous question, as if he simply happened to be passing through in the middle of the night for no particular reason.

June Connor answered quickly. Rushed, stressed. "Nothing. It's nothing."

Cormac carefully, quietly, edged up to the doorway, to get a look into the room without being seen.

June stood at the fireplace, caught mid-gesture, holding a piece of paper toward the robust fire burning in the fireplace. She held more pages in her other hand. She had apparently been feeding them one by one to the flames.

"That's the document from Monty's coat, isn't it? The one that Mr. Bennett conveniently discovered for you, and you subsequently took."

And just like that, the gaps between a number of puzzle pieces closed, shapes locking into place. Those papers—when the others had come down the stairs and saw him standing there... June had noticed. June had known he'd found something. She'd retrieved the papers later, setting Cormac up for that moment of frustration.

In considering Monty's death and who might have inflicted it, they'd failed to ask the simplest question. Who in the house had the clearest motive to murder Monty? Maybe the person who knew him best.

Moving quickly, Glyn pulled the pages from June's hand. Futilely, with a cut-off sob, she grabbed after him, but he'd paced out of reach. June remained by the fire, hands now covering her face. Glyn tilted them toward the dim firelight to better study them.

"Divorce documents," he said thoughtfully. "And they were not initiated by you. I think I understand, now. Monty wanted a divorce. This might have been a complete surprise to you, but... I think not. Then Monty discovered his plot of land was worth a whole lot of money in mineral rights. He wasn't going to invoke those rights until the divorce was finalized, entirely cutting you off from that wealth. If he died first, however, and if you successfully framed someone else for his murder... you'd inherit everything. How am I doing?"

He remained focused on the documents, no doubt studying every detail, which meant he wasn't watching June. But Cormac saw her lower her hands, an expression of profound loathing twisting her ordinarily gentle features. Her gaze fell on the wrought-iron vintage fireplace tool stand just half a pace away from her. She didn't have to move to reach down and take hold of the poker, weighted with ornate Victorian flourishes. Without a sound, she removed it from the stand. All she'd need to do was swing hard, and she'd smash Glyn's face in. It would only take a second.

In three calm strides Cormac was across the room, at June's side, wrenching the upraised poker out of her hand. She cried out briefly— then folded. Sank to the floor and shook, crying silently.

Glyn blew out a breath. He had seen the blow coming, and he might even have been able to do something about it. But maybe not this cleanly.

"Thank you, Mr. Bennett," he breathed.

"You're welcome. You think she locked the doors, too? Keep us from snooping around?"

"No, I wonder now if that was Beck wanting to be sure we stayed put. She ought to know us better than that, don't you think?" Glyn studied him with more intensity than ever. Even more than when he thought Cormac had murdered Monty. "Mr. Bennett. I might be a little bit in love with you." He did not seem to be joking.

That flush Cormac felt—flattered and pleased about it—came from Amelia. *Cormac. That might be an avenue worth pursuing. I don't have a body but he does—*

No. Just... no. He looked away to hide Amelia's blush.

Glyn flashed a lopsided grin, as if he could guess what Cormac was thinking. But he would never have any idea what Amelia was thinking.

Ten

They waited in the parlor for morning to arrive. June settled in an armchair—the same one Monty had occupied—and stared at the fire. She offered no denials, made no excuses. Cormac and Glyn waited more restlessly. Every now and then Glyn paced to the window, peering out, watching for both the sun and the police, as if they were in a race. Cormac fed more logs to the fire, keeping the flames going. Its light and warmth seemed important.

This was the tableau that greeted the others when they arrived in the parlor, shortly after dawn. Frannie was first, the smell of fresh coffee wafting out from the kitchen with her. Cormac's mouth watered, and his shoulders finally started to unclench. A cup of coffee sounded like salvation right now.

She pulled up short at the doorway to the dining room, with a startled gasp. "Oh! I didn't expect anyone—"

The bleary-eyed expressions looking back at her must have been stark. She seemed to consider the implications, and then froze.

"If it isn't too much trouble, I'll have some of that coffee as soon as it's ready," Glyn said softly.

"I... I'll bring out a tray." She fled back to the kitchen.

The others followed soon enough, and Cormac wondered if anyone had really managed any sleep. Beck gave a startled gasp when she saw them.

"We picked the locks, if you're wondering," Glyn said casually.

"Oh. I mean... what do you mean?" She wasn't selling the pretended ignorance very hard. She crossed her arms. "I just knew you both would wander and get yourselves in trouble. But what—"

"The mystery is solved," Glyn said, just as Vane and Lora came down.

They stared at June. Of them all, Beck regarded her with something like pity.

By the time the morning sun blazed over the treetops, turning the snow-covered world into blinding crystal under a searing blue sky, a big commercial pickup truck with a wide plow blade attached to the front muscled its way up the drive, and a sheriff department SUV crawled along behind it. The cavalry.

Glyn waited to deliver the full explanation, how all the bits and pieces fit together, until the sheriff and his deputy were settled in the parlor with cups of coffee. Cormac was happy to let him do the talking.

June Connor knew Monty had gone as far as drawing up divorce papers. She didn't know he'd brought them with him, and she hadn't known about his argument with Beck until she overheard them in the hallway. Everyone had heard that, apparently. Part of why Monty had accepted Beck's invitation was to use the time here to convince her not to sue him over the mineral rights, which he had, in fact, known about before convincing Jim Anderson to sell. If she agreed, she could keep the house. June realized then that time was against her, and Monty would force their separation sooner rather than later. Their folksy music act had been on the downswing for years. Bookings had just about dried up, and Monty refused to use the internet to revitalize their career. She was tired of the clichés and the down-home shtick, of supporting all his talent by sacrificing her own. He thought he could get someone younger—more attractive, a better draw—to take her place. She had suppressed her fury at this, until she couldn't any longer.

June had confronted Monty in the kitchen, where he'd gone looking for food. He had insomnia. She'd known to find him there.

Glyn said, "My guess is you didn't plan it. But the knife was right there. Just like with the fireplace poker, hm? You confronted him, and he laughed. Brushed you off as if all those years of your partnership meant nothing. Perhaps you only meant to scare him, and then..." He spread his hands, presenting the obvious picture.

"He didn't make a sound," June murmured. "He was so surprised."

The sheriff turned to June. "Ma'am, is this right? Anything else you want to add?"

"I would like to call my lawyer," she said, her voice barely above a whisper. Then, she chuckled harshly. "Monty's lawyer, I mean. Everything I have belonged to him, really, didn't it?"

The strange, grinding tension of the last day and a half lingered, like mist after a rain. More calls were made, the coroner was on the way, and the sheriff took possession of the memory card from Lora's camera. Then they took June away, into the blinding morning sun.

The whole thing was a domestic tragedy that would have seemed ludicrous if they hadn't been in the middle of it.

The cold spell broke that morning, and the snow started melting, sending a rain of drips off the roof. The truck with the plow shoved the bulk of the drifts to the edge of the drive. Cormac went out with a shovel to help clear the cars. Purely a selfish gesture. The sooner the snow was cleared the sooner he could leave. And the coroner's van needed a path to get to the outbuilding. Cormac and Glyn were the only ones who watched them carry out the gurney, the closed body bag secured to it.

"Someone ought to bear witness," Glyn said. "Don't know that it matters. But... here we are."

"Yeah."

The van doors closed, the sound echoing. Some snow fell off the branch of a nearby pine tree.

"I owe you an apology, of course." Glyn glanced at him sidelong. "I really did imagine a scenario where Beck hired an assassin to remove the obstacle to her financial well-being."

"That wasn't a pro hit," Cormac said bluntly, even as he knew the statement didn't paint him in any better light.

"There is that."

"You going to get a new book out of this?"

Glyn smiled. "People *always* ask that."

"Has this happened to you before? Does this happen to you a lot?"

Glyn rubbed his arms in a dramatic show of keeping warm. "It's getting chilly out here. I think I need to pour myself some of that new pot of coffee Frannie put on." He went back up the porch and to the kitchen door.

Cormac blew out a breath that fogged around him.

Beck was the only one who saw him off, standing on the porch amid the sound of dripping snowmelt. Maybe Cormac should have said goodbye to the others. Amelia wouldn't have minded talking more with Vane. But, well... if any of them wanted to talk to him, they could ask Beck to get in touch.

"I don't know if it still matters," Cormac told her. "But the house really is haunted. Focused on that back porch, outside the kitchen door." He and Amelia had considered whether to tell her the true story, that Tobias had been locked out and froze to death, rather than dying in the more thrilling shootout. They decided not to. Let her keep the old family story.

"Well, that's something I suppose," Beck said with a sigh. "I'm sorry this didn't turn out to be much of a relaxing weekend. But... I appreciate you being here." She handed him an envelope with cash. His father's traditional method of getting paid. Cormac accepted with a thin smile and slipped the envelope inside his jacket pocket. "You drive safe now, you hear me?"

"Yes, ma'am."

Beck went back inside, to the warmth and shelter of the house.

Cormac sat in the Jeep for a moment, letting the heat run. Wright House was an impressive mansion, lurking against its mountain backdrop. The windows reflected the blue sky and glared down like eyes. Cormac repressed a shiver. The house seemed to exude a chill. Maybe it would feel different in the summer.

"Any reason to stick around?" he asked his partner.

No. It's well past time for us to be away from all this.

Carefully, avoiding spinning out in the ice and slush, he steered the Jeep out of the drive and on to the road. He didn't breathe easy until the house was out of sight.

We never got our holiday, Amelia thought wistfully. *We didn't even get to sleep in.*

She was right. He was suddenly exhausted. Maybe they did need a vacation.

"We can stop at a hotel on the way home. Someplace with room service."

That isn't at all the least bit haunted.

"Agreed."

5.

"You know, you really do end up around a lot of murdered people," the woman said.

"I had nothing to do with that one. I *solved* that one."

"Is this Vane guy someone we need to talk to?" the man asked the woman.

"Oh no," she said. "I've seen his YouTube channel. But after this... you said he knows about Amelia?"

These two were way too interested in Amelia, and there was way too much they weren't saying. Cormac was torn—he wanted to bust out of here and was ready to brawl to do it. Assuming he managed to get away, he'd be looking over his shoulder forever. For Federal agents, for the next person who was a little too interested in his career. And the next person would be worse—the next person might be whoever these guys were *actually* looking for.

"What're your names?" Cormac asked, wondering if they would really tell him.

The woman shook her head—he could tell by the movement within the shadow. "Names have power."

"Yeah, well, you know ours and that hasn't given you shit." Magically, he couldn't do anything with their names. In the modern era, the use of names was so ubiquitous and the idea of true names had been so diluted that the old folk tales didn't apply. They thought he and Amelia had a lot more power than they did. This made Cormac nervous, because it suggested that something out there had a lot more power than any of them. They were going in circles and he wanted to break out of it. "Look, you know Agent Stein, I know Agent Stein. And Agent Perez. And this one time a couple of goons like you walked into Kitty's studio in the middle of her show...what were their names? Martin? Ivers or something? This isn't my first time dealing with you people. Stein and Perez at least trust me, and I sort of trust them—"

"What does that mean?" the woman asked, sounding offended.

"Agent Perez loaned me her car and then I kind of dumped it. So you, you know, old friends."

"I want to hear *that* story," the man said. "That's not what it sounded like in Perez's report."

"Really? What did she say about me? Then there's the parts that are all over the internet." Yeah, that was his shining YouTube moment, right there.

"None of those sources talk about Amelia Parker," the woman said. "I would like to speak with her."

"No."

He expected them to make threats. They would disappear him in the name of national security for what they thought he knew, for what they thought Amelia was. They would snipe at each other until he either told them, or they let him go, or some other possibility presented itself.

The woman said, "I'm Agent Ilena Dimitrova." She gave the name a lilt, a trill on the "r" that suggested English wasn't her first language even though her accent was plain American. She nodded at the man. "This is Agent Tom Lynch."

Cormac sighed. "Thank you. Nice to meet you, Agents."

"Would you like to see our badges?" Dimitrova asked wryly.

"Naw," Cormac said. "Y'all never hold them up long enough for anyone to read them anyway."

"Younger people have started insisting on taking pictures of the badges when we do hold them up," Lynch said, shrugging.

"That…I'm going to do that next time," Cormac said.

Dimitrova stepped closer to the circle, coming almost close enough to the light for him to see her. She wasn't tall. Her dark hair was braided down her back. She wore gold-framed glasses.

"We have Agent Stein's and Agent Perez's reports on the mermaid, which apparently don't match your experience. I'd like to hear your side, Mr. Bennett."

He sat in the chair, leaned back and sighed, donning a big smile. He just couldn't help it.

It was a good story.

CHARMED WATERS

One

"Explain it to me again," Cormac said with what he thought was profound patience but probably came off sounding harsh.

Kitty didn't seem to notice the harsh, but she was used to him by now. "The story is that a kid fell out of a boat, went under, and everyone was sure she drowned. But an hour later she turned up on shore next to a boat launch, perfectly fine, just soaking wet. She said a mermaid rescued her. So." She glanced back with that wry smile of hers. "We're here to figure out how to get a mermaid to come talk to me."

Dusk gave the water at Horsetooth Reservoir a metallic sheen. Cormac had the feeling of trying to look through a clouded mirror. The surface rippled with its natural movement; nothing unusual appeared. On a weekday evening, not too many people were around, not too many boats were out on the water.

Kneeling at the edge of the water, Kitty helped her own toddler, Jon, pick out stones, which he then hurled, not very far, watching the splashes with fascination. Ben stood back, his arms crossed, wearing a vague satisfied smile. Producing offspring had mellowed his cousin.

The kid had gone from blob-like baby to walking and grabbing and looking and talking in what seemed like the blink of an eye. *That's what children do,* Amelia murmured.

Did you ever want kids? he asked her. Jon wore a T-shirt with a duck on it, kid-sized pants and kid-sized sneakers. A whole world of kid-sized things had invaded Cormac's life.

I didn't really have time to think about it. I might have, someday.

Amelia had been around twenty-five when she was hanged, and her body died, even if her spirit survived. She didn't really get to want anything, after that.

It's all right. I think we make a better auntie.

You mean uncle.

She answered with a noncommittal *Hmm.*

Cormac looked across the water, watchful. Always watchful, around his family. The spring air had a chill to it. Almost too warm for a jacket, but too cool to go without.

"You believe the story?" Cormac asked.

"I'm willing to entertain the idea. This is just such an un-mermaidish place, I don't see a kid making up something like that, not here."

"Enchanted Horsetooth Reservoir," Ben said, chuckling. "Yeah, no."

The reservoir, west of Fort Collins in northern Colorado, was typical for the region, an artificial body designed to provide water for this section of urban corridor. It filled a valley, and hills covered with pine trees and scrub oak rose up almost all the way around it, except for a couple of inlets where boat launches and tiny beaches were located. They had parked in a turnout near one of the dams containing the lake and walked down a short hill to a sandy patch, an easy fishing spot. He'd come here a couple of times to catch smallmouth bass with his dad, when he was a kid.

"Do you know anything about talking to mermaids?" Kitty asked. "Does Amelia?"

"Maybe you just have to ask," Cormac said, half joking. Not that anyone ever recognized when he was joking, his voice always sounded the same.

But Kitty cupped her hands around her mouth and yelled, "Hey! If you can hear me, I'd love to talk! Just for a minute!" In the still evening air, her voice seemed to fade dully. They waited a minute or two; the water's surface still didn't change.

Cormac didn't doubt that mermaids existed—not after everything else he'd seen. But he didn't know anything about them. Not for real. He didn't trust anything from movies or fairy tales—they often got so much wrong.

My knowledge is hypothetical. I never met a mermaid, and I never met anyone who has. They've always been elusive.

"Maybe if I sing a Disney song or two. Can you smell anything?" she asked Ben.

He gave an amused snort. "Just the reservoir. Dead fish and runoff."

Kitty, gazing across the water, narrowed her gaze skeptically. "'I have heard the mermaids singing each to each. I do not think that they will sing to me...'"

"Is that a spell?" Ben asked.

"No, it's T.S. Eliot. I always thought that was such a sad line." She leaned back down to pick up Jon and prop him on her hip. Kid had kept hold of a rock which seemed to occupy his full attention. "Maybe this is a bust."

"You said she rescued a kid?" Cormac asked. "Do mermaids like kids? Maybe you could toss the rugrat in—"

"No," Ben said curtly, at the same time Kitty said, "We are not using my child as bait."

Cormac shrugged. "Just a suggestion."

I have an idea, Amelia said. *A reclusive legendary creature is not likely to respond to a human call. But... there are other legendary creatures here.*

Kitty and Ben were werewolves, and the main reason he didn't trust movies and fairy tales for arcane knowledge. The reality didn't always match up with the myths. The couple had a house in the suburbs, for crying out loud.

"What if one of your wolves called?" Cormac said, and they both looked at him. "You know, one supernatural creature to another. That's Amelia's idea."

"That might actually work," she said, brightening. She started to hand Jon off to his father, but Ben shook his head.

"If you're a wolf you can't talk. I'll do it. You look after him."

"That... makes sense. Thanks." They exchanged one of those couple looks, full of subtext Cormac couldn't interpret.

"You'll owe me one." He kissed her on the forehead.

Ben started off toward a section of scrub, and Cormac was relieved he wasn't going to strip down and shapeshift right here. He'd seen werewolves, including Ben, shift before, and the process was disconcerting.

Magical, even, Amelia observed.

Cormac intercepted him, speaking low. "Sure you'll be okay?"

"Nice of you to ask," Ben said wryly. He glanced back at Kitty, who talked softly to Jon, distracting him. "I think it's worth doing. Just... watch our backs?"

"Yeah," Cormac said. Always.

Ben pulled his T-shirt off over his head as he entered the scrub.

"So what are you going to say?" Cormac asked Kitty. "Assuming there's a mermaid and you can actually talk to her?"

"The first thing I want to know is how she got to Horsetooth Reservoir. After that—you know, the usual. Her whole life story." Kitty grinned.

Five minutes or so later, a big wolf moved along the waterline. Bigger than a wild wolf—Ben's hundred and seventy pounds or so, in fact—and covered in thick fur, dark gray flecked with rust, he trotted on long, rangy legs, ears up and tail out like a rudder. Kitty dropped her shoulders and tilted her head, a wolfish greeting, like a tail and ears dipping with affection. The wolf bumped her hip and rubbed his whole body against her, and she leaned into the touch. The toddler reached to it, and the wolf sniffed back, wuffling its nose all over the kid.

Cormac had gotten used to this, seeing a huge wolf behaving

nothing like its natural counterpart. The rational response, seeing a big predator nose up to a kid like that, would be panic, and to lunge forward to separate them. In the old days, Cormac would have reached for a gun. These days, he didn't even twitch. He would never get used to getting used to this.

In just a couple of strides, Ben as wolf reached the water and stopped with all four legs submerged to the knees. Then, he tipped his nose up and howled.

The thin, haunting note carried, wavering. It rang in Cormac's ears even as it traveled down his spine, raising the hair on his neck. Otherworldly and pure, the call cut across space and froze time.

Oh my goodness, Amelia murmured. They rarely heard this, especially so close.

"A territory call," Kitty said softly. "He's saying I'm here, where are you?"

Ben's wolf howled again, ringing across the water. If anything was out there, they must have heard it. A third howl trailed off, uncertain, and the wolf turned and splashed back to shore, trotting along the edge of the water, glancing out.

"Thanks, hon," Kitty said to the wolf, whose ears were pricked up and out, listening.

A splash broke the water, maybe fifty yards out. It caught all their attentions.

"Fish?" Kitty set Jon down, taking his hand. In any large, stocked body of water like this, you'd see fish jumping, splashing back in.

The splash came again, closer this time. A wide fin, silvery scales. Cormac's heart jumped. Everything they'd both seen, all the supernatural business they'd encountered—he still couldn't believe it.

It's real.

Part of a face emerged. Only her eyes showed, and a trailing length of dark hair, floating in the water.

"Watch him," Kitty said, setting Jon down before she waded into the lake.

Cormac hated when she said that. The kid looked up at him with what could only be described as malevolence, no doubt planning all the ways he could get in trouble. Jon promptly stuck a rock into his mouth.

"Yeah, don't do that." Cormac took the rock away and picked him up before he could start crying. Cormac wiped his now-slimy hand on his jeans and sighed.

Meanwhile, Kitty stood with her hand on Ben's back. "My name's Kitty! We won't hurt you, we just want to talk."

The mermaid moved quickly, sinuously. Diving, a silvery blue tail arched after her. She reappeared closer, her whole head coming up above the surface this time. She extended her arms, keeping her stable in the water. She looked exhausted, her skin pale, shadowed, a frown pulling at her features. She wasn't young—she had crows' feet at her eyes, loose skin at her neck. This was one of the ways the stories lied: they never featured middle-aged mermaids. Merwoman, maybe.

They studied each other across the water: mermaid, wolf, and woman.

"Do you need help?" Kitty asked abruptly.

"Oh yes. Please," the mermaid breathed.

Two

A little ways up the shore they found a stand of boulders jutting into the water. Kitty went out to the edge of this to meet the mermaid. Ben waited on the shore, sitting at attention, ears pricked forward. Cormac deposited the kid next to him, once again overcoming a jolt of panic at the sheer insanity of setting a small child next to a big furry monster. Except the monster was the kid's father. Cormac stopped himself from asking the wolf if this was this okay, mostly because he was afraid he'd understand the answer.

Ben's wolf nudged the toddler, who sat on the gravel and clung to the wolf's leg. It was odd. It was cute.

Cormac needed to know what Kitty and the mermaid were talking about.

The mermaid was holding loosely to a partially submerged rock. She rested at the surface, her body stretched behind her, and Cormac got his first good look at her. Her waist-length hair drifted around her pale shoulders like a shawl. Her head and torso were all human, but the skin of her waist merged into scales. What would have been hips on a human were wide, muscular. Her tail was long, double the length of her torso. A fan-like dorsal fin fluttered in the water; a pair of fins under her spread out, helping her stay afloat. The tail was wide, the membranes tough-looking, iridescent. Her whole tail shimmered between green, blue, and silver. Cormac was entranced.

Kitty, perched at the edge of a boulder, was finishing introductions. "...that's my husband Ben and our kid, Jon. And this... this is Cormac."

The mermaid drew back, sinking under the water a few inches. Cormac stopped, holding his hands up in a calming gesture.

"He's okay," Kitty added. "Most of the time."

"I'm Nia," she said.

"Nia. It's so nice to meet you. I have so many questions. How did you get here? What happened? How can we help you?"

"I want to go home," she said. Her voice was low, musical. A note of whale song turned into speech. "I've looked for a river, but there's only dams—"

"Yeah, this is a reservoir. I'm afraid you're stuck."

She rubbed her face. If there were tears, they'd never see them.

Gently, Kitty prompted, "How did you get here? This isn't exactly mermaid territory."

"I was dumped," she said. She had an accent. Irish, or maybe Scottish, something with a lilt from that part of the world. He wondered where mermaids learned to speak English. "My memory of that time's not good. I was in a tank, in a room full of bad light and bleach. A laboratory?" She tried the word out slowly, like she hadn't ever spoken it before.

Beside him, Kitty flinched, her hands clenching. She had spent her own short but memorable time in a lab. "I'm so sorry," she said, heartfelt.

"The people there... something changed. Some kind of urgency, like the place was shutting down. I wish it was more clear." Nia shook her head, rippling the water around her. "I... convinced a pair of them to help me. But this was as far as they could carry me. I suppose I should be grateful they put me somewhere wet."

"Convinced how?" Cormac asked. And was she "convincing" them now? Vampires could hypnotize people; Amelia knew of spells that could influence the mind. What could mermaids do?

They sing, Amelia said. *Remember the old stories of sirens luring sailors to their deaths.*

Nia wasn't singing now. She looked sad and wilted and deeply out of place in the reservoir's murky water. "I'm afraid they'll come back to look for me. They must be looking for me."

"Where's home?"

"If I can get to the Atlantic, I can get myself home. Is there any way to get there? A river?"

"None that go to the Atlantic. Not from here." Kitty sat back, flustered. "Of course we're in a landlocked state. Because of course we are."

"The only way you could be further from a coast is if you'd ended up in North Dakota," Cormac said.

Nia ducked her face under the water, shivered a little. A mermaid's sigh.

Cormac. We have to help.

Of course they did. "So we drive."

Kitty perked up. "Yeah. Aquariums move dolphins and things all the time, right? How hard can it be?"

"Never ask that," Cormac said.

"I'm assuming you need a tank?" Kitty said. "Can you leave the water at all?"

"I need water. Not much, enough to cover me. But I need it to breathe."

Kitty turned to Cormac. "We're smart people, we can figure this out. Can't we?"

"Can I trust you?" the mermaid asked. Her tone suggested she had trusted before and regretted it.

"I can say yes, but you'd have to trust I'm telling the truth," Kitty said. "I'll just say this: I'm a werewolf, and I've spent time in a cage. I understand. I want to help."

Cormac said, "We get a van, a tank. Then we drive. We can be on the east coast in just a couple days if we don't stop."

Nia's tail turned, the fin splashing in the water. She wiped her face—and yes, there must have been tears there. "I can hardly believe it."

A buzzing noise cut through the air suddenly, and Cormac got to his feet. He knew that sound. In the twilight it took a bit of searching, but he found it: a small drone, about twenty feet up, flying along the shore, then stopping to hover.

"Kitty," he said, tapping her shoulder.

"Shit," she muttered. She reached toward the water. "You should get out of here, we've got spies."

"How will I find you again?" she asked.

"Listen for the howl."

Nia gave a push and slipped under the water. With a couple of flicks of her muscular tail, she was gone.

Cormac looked around and found a couple of good throwing stones. The drone was still hovering. Presumably, it had a camera. He met what he imagined was its beady mechanical gaze, and threw one stone, then another before it could veer off. The first one hit, but only knocked it off balance. It dodged the second stone and then raced inland. He lost sight of it in the fading light.

Kitty had already scooped up Jon. Ben loped beside her, up the hill and back to the car. Cormac looked out over the water for a silvery glint of fin or a splash, but the mermaid was gone. Good. He took a moment to grab Ben's clothes, folded neatly at the edge of the scrub because wasn't that just like him? When he reached the car, he tossed them in the back seat.

Up on the road, an engine rumbled and tires squealed on pavement as a shining black Range Rover came to a sliding stop in the turnout behind their car. It had a lot of fancy antennae on it, and strapped to the roof was an even larger drone than the one that had found them. The driver and passenger immediately got out. The driver was a tall, broad-shouldered man with a thick dark beard and a ball cap, embroidered with the initials FRACH, jammed over his hair. The passenger was a stocky woman with red hair in a ponytail, holding up what looked like a small video camera, filming.

Cormac had to tamp down the thought that it was a weapon and he needed to reach for his own. On second thought... He marched forward. The woman with the camera stumbled back, but not before he could grab the thing away from her.

Fearfully, she pressed herself against the hood of the car. He supposed he ought to feel bad about scaring her.

"Hey, you can't do that, that's assault!" the guy yelled. Cormac ignored him, studying the camera's screen and fiddling with the buttons until he deleted the footage.

"So is this." Cormac gestured with the camera before setting it on the hood.

The wolf stood at the back of the SUV, hackles up, head down, teeth bared. Cormac didn't know if he'd be able to stop Ben if he decided to strike. These two had no idea what they were up against.

Fortunately, Kitty was there. She must have gotten Jon stashed in the car. Now, she came up and put her hand on Ben's back. The hackles flattened—slightly.

"Oh my God, is that a werewolf?" the ponytailed woman said, reaching again for the camera.

Cormac pointed. "Don't."

"You're Kitty Norville!" the driver in the hat exclaimed. "What do you know about the mermaid?"

Ben's wolf growled softly, and Kitty hissed a warning at him, stepping in front of him. "Why should I tell you?"

"The public has a right to know!"

"And what about the right to privacy?"

"There's no privacy in science!"

She gaped. "Is that what you think you're doing here? Science? You maybe have an ethics board to check in with about that?"

Cormac bet the guy was recording audio. The whole setup screamed publicity, that they were playing to an audience somewhere.

These guys had an angle. He walked up to Kitty, said softly, "We need to get out of here. Don't engage."

"Yeah." She patted the wolf's shoulder and started around to the car door.

"Bet you I can catch her before you can," the guy said, his lip curling.

Kitty paused and looked back at him. "But I don't want— That's your plan? Catch her? Then what?"

"Then we'll just have to see, won't we?"

"Kitty, we need to go," Cormac said, and opened the door for her. She urged Ben to hop in first, then followed. Cormac drove, peeling around past Mr. FRACH and the Range Rover. The guy was laughing.

Three

So that made the situation a little more urgent than it had been a few minutes ago.

They headed south, back home. Cormac drove. Kitty got Jon secured in his car seat and calmed down. Once the kid was calm, Ben's wolf stretched out in the back, trying to sleep so he could shift back to human. Kitty was anxious, with one hand on the toddler, her attention divided between Ben in the back and her phone.

"Let's find out who these guys are, shall we?" she muttered in a vaguely predatory tone.

Meanwhile, Amelia was thrilled. *We need a van. We can rent this, yes? And a container for water. Where do we even look for such a thing? And will it even fit in a van? Cormac, I know nothing of these details...*

"Holy cow, that was fast," Kitty said. "Video from that drone is already up on YouTube. The Horsetooth Reservoir Mermaid. Geez. And there it is. Front Range Cryptid Hunters. FRACH."

"That's a stupid acronym," he said.

"I know, right? Oh my God, this YouTube channel is off the rails. They've got twenty low-light videos looking for Bigfoot in Rocky Mountain National Park. And this one—that's not evidence of a Slide-Rock Bolter, you moron, that's tailings from an old mine! How is it I've never heard of these people? You'd think I'd have heard of them."

The staticky, distorted sound of a buzzing drone emerged as she played a video. There were no voices, so maybe the sound wasn't good enough to record what they'd been saying. Small favors. "The light's bad enough they didn't get too many details," Kitty said. "But they got pictures of Nia. And there's you throwing a rock at it. Nice aim, by the way. They've got your face, front and center."

"Shit," he muttered. He'd looked straight at the drone. Whoever this was could probably ID him, dig up his criminal record, his father's connections...

The static dropped out, replaced by traffic background noises and a male voice speaking in an urgent tone, as if he was reporting a news story and not a local oddity. It was the guy who'd confronted them.

"There you have it, definitive proof: the stories are true, there is a mermaid living in Horsetooth Reservoir. And what's more—the creature has been in contact with known celebrity werewolf Kitty Norville. People, this is big. This is a conspiracy. How long has Norville known about this? Why hasn't she come forward with information? *What is she hiding?* We're still tracking the identity of the man with her, but we do know—he's *not* her husband. There's a story here, and she doesn't want us to know! You can bet we're going to be looking into pressing charges for his *unprovoked* attack on our *completely legal* drone activities."

"Oh for crying out loud," Cormac muttered. Did he need to get a lawyer? Ben, who was in fact a lawyer, was still lupine and nonverbal and couldn't chime in.

"Hmm, I smell a libel suit," Kitty murmured. "Go on, keep pushing there, bucko."

The narration continued. "We're increasing our surveillance of the reservoir while we work on the next phase of this investigation. We're going to find this mermaid. If you like what you see, subscribe to our channel and consider backing us on Patreon, so we can continue with our work. I'm Eddie Foster with FRACH, bringing you *the truth.*"

"He called her a creature," Kitty said. "Like she isn't even a person. I don't like him."

"He's not going to let up," Cormac said. "Going to be a lot harder getting Nia out of there with this kind of attention."

"Working on it. I've got some ideas."

That was almost as ominous as learning about the existence of the Front Range Cryptid Hunters in the first place. "What ideas?"

"Still thinking. Gotta talk to the lawyers first."

Kitty's phone beeped, and she studied the screen. Hit a button, and the call cut out. Then it beeped again. She declined that call, too, but the next beep came right after. She hit the mute button and sighed. "I'm going to be getting a lot of calls about this, aren't I?"

"Too many people have your phone number. We talked about this."

"Yes, I know, but it's my job!"

He was off the freeway and nearing Ben and Kitty's house when a groan came from the back of the SUV.

"Hey there," Kitty said soothingly. In the rearview mirror Cormac could see Ben sitting up, rubbing his face. He was naked and looked a mess, like werewolves almost always did after shifting back to human. "Welcome back."

"What happened?" He sounded hung over.

"We're on YouTube!" Kitty said brightly.

"That is never good."

"Your clothes are there."

"Oh, thank God. Did you manage to talk to the mermaid?" Ben asked, pulling on his shirt.

"We did," Kitty said. "We also made some new not-friends. And now we need to figure out how to mount a rescue."

By the time they got back to the house, it was dark and after business hours, but they did what they could. Cormac hated the idea of this Eddie Foster guy going after Nia, but there wasn't a whole lot they could do until morning, except hope FRACH didn't have a way to search underwater in the dark.

That is a large body of water, Amelia reassured him. *And I imagine Nia has a lot of experience hiding.*

Amelia was probably right, but that didn't stop him from feeling like he needed to do something *right now.*

Kitty called her contact at the Center for the Study of Paranatural Biology, the department within the NIH tasked with studying all things supernatural. Kitty tried to keep up a good relationship with them, despite their dodgy past, for just these situations. Cormac didn't catch the whole conversation because Kitty was pacing in and out of the room during the call, displaying increasing levels of frustration.

"But you're saying the Center *did* study mermaids," she said. "Had mermaids in captivity at some point."

The reply carried over the speaker. "Well, yes, but that was under Dr. Flemming's supervision—"

"You know my feelings about Dr. Flemming." She almost growled when she said this.

Flemming had been the director of the Center who had captured Kitty on the night of a full moon and forced her to shapeshift on live TV, early on in her career. Kitty wasn't generally inclined to hold grudges, but this one had stuck. She never let the Center live it down, even though Flemming had been dead for years now.

Kitty pressed on. "Can you just check your records for any listing of a mermaid named Nia, in the northern Colorado area?"

"Does this have something to do with that YouTube video going around?"

"Why, yes," Kitty said bitingly. "Yes, it does."

"She might not have been held at a federal facility, you know. There are private firms who also conduct research into paranatural subjects. Pharmaceutical companies in particular."

Kitty put her hand on her forehead. "Oh my God. That's a can and a half of worms I don't even want to open right now. Just please call me back if you find out anything. Thank you."

Ben stared. "Pharmaceutical? What, like studying vampires for the secret of immortality? I'm not sure that's a crusade you can take on right now."

"Yeah. One crusade at a time. Excuse me, I need to hug my kid."

Cormac pulled up a USGS map of Horsetooth, marking service roads and back ways to the water they could maybe use to avoid being watched. Found a couple of likely spots. He was even getting a crazy idea about how to keep Nia safe during a cross-country road trip.

He called a family friend who ran a junkyard. "Hey, Fred. I need a container of some kind. Maybe seven feet long, three feet deep, that can hold water. It has to fit in a cargo van, and I need it by early afternoon."

"Are we talking... what? Like an aquarium?"

"Not necessarily, it just has to hold water."

"Maybe a bathtub? Like, a big industrial tub."

That might work. "Something like that, yeah."

"Is this about the mermaid in Fort Collins on that YouTube video?"

"I'm starting a mobile dog-washing service," Cormac answered flatly while silently cursing the entire phenomenon of viral videos.

Fred laughed. "Yeah, right."

"Fred. You owe me, don't ask questions."

"Fine. I'll see what I can come up with."

He tried to rent a car online but couldn't find the sort of commercial cargo van he would need for this endeavor and would have to wait until morning. The ticking clock hung over them but there was nothing else they could do right now.

"The plus side is Eddie Foster won't be able to do much until morning, either," Ben said.

"We hope," Kitty muttered. "I suppose we should try to get some sleep. Tomorrow's going to be... something."

Cormac stayed the night in their guest room, and the next morning their kitchen turned into something of a war room. Kitty and Ben traded looking after Jon, making calls, and watching updates on TV. The mermaid hadn't been sighted again, even with news helicopters scoping out the scene. They'd started at first light.

The Front Range Cryptid Hunters video was all over the local news, and even some national outlets had picked up the story. The clip just kept playing, over and over. Nia's silvery form disappearing under the water, Kitty kneeling by the shore, and Cormac looking straight at the drone's camera. Small blessing: the drone had failed to get any footage of Ben's wolf and Jon sitting on the shore nearby. None of the commentary mentioned them.

All the local news channels sent trucks to the reservoir, and what must have been hundreds of gawkers joined them, people lining up along the road and filling the parking turnouts, bringing binoculars and cameras and looking for a glimpse of the mermaid. A festival atmosphere took over, with news reporters delivering breathless accounts and cameras surveying the lines of cars jammed on the roads. Someone had managed to get T-shirts printed overnight—they read "The Horsetooth Mermaid" in big letters with a generic stylized woodcut-style image of a mermaid—and were selling them out of the back of a station wagon.

Whatever chance they had to make a clandestine rescue was obliterated.

A stream of reporters called Kitty, hoping for an interview. She turned them down, even after her nominal boss at the radio station where she based her talk show called, begging her to issue some sort of statement. Kitty told him she needed a plan first.

Cormac was finally able to call about a renting a van. At least that was a little more straightforward. Ben handed over his credit card, which was nice of him.

The rental agent asked, "Shall I add the extra insurance?"

Cormac hesitated a beat, then said, earnestly, "Yes. All the insurance, please."

The main problem was still going to be getting Nia out without drawing attention. Cormac didn't have a solution for that. He asked Amelia, I don't suppose you have some kind of invisibility spell we can cast over the whole reservoir.

The trouble with that is if the whole reservoir turned invisible, someone would notice.

Some kind of spell to avert the gaze? So people don't notice us?

Those sorts of spells work better when people aren't already looking. They're going to be looking very carefully, Cormac.

"I've got it," Kitty said suddenly, grabbing her phone and heading to the other room.

Ben stared after her. "Oh shit."

Cormac knew exactly what he meant. She had that gleam in her eye, the one that usually preceded something dramatic, like unexpected YouTube videos. "Good thing you're around to tell us where the line is between legal and not."

"As if that actually ever stopped anyone from going over it," he said with a huff. "Better if I don't say a word. My professional conscience is clear."

She returned after just a minute, which could have been good or bad. And smiling, which also could have been good or bad. "Well, that's all taken care of."

"What's all taken care of?" Ben asked, a bit desperately.

"You want to avoid attention, you're going to need a distraction," she said. "Well, I'm your distraction. I'm going to run a press conference while you two get Nia away."

Four

I t wasn't a bad plan. Except that it involved putting Kitty in the spotlight, the focus of far too much of the wrong kind of attention.

"I'd be worried except that seems to be her natural state of being," Ben said, when Cormac expressed the fear. "I think it's a good plan."

In fact, just an hour after she'd made a few calls, the news stations started publicizing the presser, and social media blew up with the announcement. She planned to stage the event early that afternoon near the marina at Inlet Bay, on the southwest end of the reservoir. It was something of a bottleneck—one narrow road in and out, on the far side of the reservoir from the town. Cormac picked an escape route at the opposite end, to the north. Satanka Cove—not as crowded, easier to get away from. It had a boat ramp, so they could pull the van right down to the water. Everyone, including Eddie Foster, should be so focused on Kitty, they wouldn't notice Nia making her escape.

"And what are you going to say at this press conference?" Ben asked.

"I'm going to baffle them with bullshit," she said, grinning. "I think I can get you guys about forty minutes before people figure out I'm full of it."

"That going to be enough?" Ben asked Cormac.

"I think it'll be plenty. Just as long as Foster doesn't have a crew watching out for us on the side."

They learned what they could about Foster and FRACH. It seemed to be a newer organization—the earliest video had been posted less than a year ago. Two different teams showed up in the videos, with no more than eight people. Not enough to cover the reservoir—Cormac was hopeful.

They had just a couple of hours to pull it together. Cormac picked up the van, a large commercial model with no side windows and a bare cargo space. Perfect. Next, he headed over to Fred's junkyard east of Greeley, where Fred was waiting with the requested item on a forklift.

"Hey there!" Fred called, after Cormac had backed in the van. Cormac and Ben had gone to high school with Fred's brothers—Fred was a couple of years younger. Cormac's father had bought cars from Fred's father. He hadn't seen him in years, but he recognized him, his heavyset frame and hair in a ponytail. He wore a flannel shirt untucked over faded jeans and biker boots. His smile was jovial. Cormac summoned all the politeness he was capable of and waved a greeting.

Fred had, in fact, brought him a bathtub. Large, plain white, a little beat up. Cormac hoped it was still watertight. Fred had also brought along an armful of rope and tie-downs, and a sheet of Plexiglas.

"It's a lid," he explained. "We can tie it down over the tub. I figure you'd need that to keep the water from splashing out, and to keep the mermaid safe inside."

Cormac took a moment to rein back his temper. "What mermaid?" he asked calmly.

"Cormac. Please. It's not like I'm going to tell anyone."

"Fred, does the phrase 'plausible deniability' mean anything to you?"

"Oh, and I went ahead and caulked up the drain so it wouldn't accidently get unplugged."

That... was actually a good idea. What choice did Cormac have but to say, "Thanks."

"I just know a mermaid doesn't belong in Horsetooth. You're taking her someplace safe, right? Back to the ocean?"

"That's the plan."

He nodded once. "Good."

Amelia's heart melted a bit. Maybe even Cormac's, just a little, if he was honest.

Fred let Cormac fill the tub from his own spigot, after helping him secure it in the back of the van. It took up most of the cargo space, along with a whole web of tie-downs. Weighted down with water, it wasn't going to budge. Cormac was more worried about the van itself tipping. He'd have to drive carefully. Then Fred produced a couple of twenty-gallon coolers, and they filled those, too, to use to refill the tub.

He didn't know if the water needed to be a certain temperature, if the junkyard's well water was going to be safe for a mermaid, what kind of food she needed—surely she'd need to eat before they got to the coast. He packed a cooler and threw in a couple packs of smoked salmon, just in case. Filled up with gas, so they wouldn't need to stop for awhile.

Amelia cast a whole raft of protection spells over the van. General stuff—turn away harm, safety on a journey. Every little bit had to help.

He picked up Ben at a Starbucks where he and Kitty were waiting. Kitty would head out on her own for the press conference.

"I love it," Kitty said, examining the setup. "I gotta go put out the bait. Good luck, you two."

Ben hugged her, long and fiercely. Cormac looked away, and when he turned back, Kitty was driving out of the parking lot.

"Fred really came through for you," Ben said, nodding at the van.

"He was very excited."

"He guessed, didn't he? He going to rat us out?"

"I don't think he will. He really seemed to like the idea of helping rescue a mermaid."

Ben snorted. "Who wouldn't? How often does anyone get a chance to recreate an old Tom Hanks movie? It's great!" Sometimes, Ben got sarcastic enough that he swung back around into sounding sincere.

They weren't going to head to the reservoir until just before Kitty's show. A van sitting next to the water ahead of time would look way too suspicious. They'd drive in quick, get Nia, then drive out. Easy.

He'd just keep telling himself that.

She'd announced a start time at two. Her plan was to start twenty minutes late. More, if she could push it without people getting too restless. Cormac didn't want her by herself, but Ben was on it—he'd called in members of their werewolf pack. They'd keep an eye on the crowd, watch her back, and babysit Jon.

"Nice, having your own gang to call on," Cormac said.

Ben's mouth pursed, like he was going to say something snarky. Then he sighed. "Yeah, it is." He constantly checked his phone for the time, until it was finally time to head over.

This is nerve-wracking. I'm not sure I can stand it.

Amelia didn't even have a body with taut nerves and clenched shoulders. Her nerves were wracked vicariously.

Doesn't matter. I still feel it.

Ben turned the radio to the local public station, which was carrying Kitty's press conference live. Nothing from Kitty yet, just the background hum of the crowd and a reporter repeating a summary they'd probably repeated five or six times already, about the viral video and the possibility of a mermaid in the unlikely setting of northern Colorado.

Afternoon sun was slanting over the water. The cove was startlingly empty—Kitty's announcement had drawn people to the southern end of the reservoir, maybe convincing them the mermaid would be a part of it. Only a few paddleboarders splashed around here, and they seemed more concerned with staying upright than paying attention to the van. Cormac kept his ears open and his eyes on the sky. No drones, yet.

The big question mark in the plan was whether or not Nia would find them in time. They hadn't had a chance to work out a good signal with her. Ben had a recording of a wolf howl—Kitty's, the one she used to introduce her radio show. Maybe it would be enough.

Ben stood at the end of the boat ramp, holding his phone up as the howl played. The recording wasn't quite so piercing and sonorous as the real thing, but the sound still carried. They waited.

And waited.

This whole thing might have been for nothing.

Then, Cormac pointed. A ripple in the water was followed by the arc of a silvery body, the flip of a fin. It happened again, closer to shore. Ben shut off the howl. The paddleboarders didn't see her; they just weren't looking.

The mermaid came to rest in the shallows, leaning on muscular arms, her fins rippling on the surface. There were bare breasts—strategically and artfully hidden under the drape of her hair, as if by magic.

Be polite, Amelia admonished.

Of course.

Since she would recognize Cormac, he approached. "Hi. We've got a van and a tank—sort of. I'm not sure if it'll work, but if you still want to get out of here, we can go."

"Where's Kitty?" she asked anxiously.

"She's the distraction," Ben said. "Hi, I'm Ben, we didn't really get a chance to meet yesterday."

"Oh, I remember you, and your lovely singing voice," she said, and winked. Ben blushed, which was amusing.

Cormac hadn't backed the van all the way down the ramp—its angle was steep enough that water started spilling out of the tub. They'd have to carry her up. Opening the doors so she could see in, he belatedly observed how incredibly dodgy this must look, inviting a near stranger into a windowless van. Trust us, sure.

"It's so dark in there," she said, uncertain. Hugging herself, she rocked back on her tail.

She'd probably been dumped from a setup just like this. Kitty should have been here; Kitty was so much easier to trust than a couple of scruffy-looking men.

Cormac rubbed a hand through his hair and nervously glanced skyward, listening for drones. "Look, you've got no reason to trust us, just because we say so. I get it. But this is Kitty's gig and the thing you gotta understand about her is she just... wants to help. Everyone. And if I let anything bad happen to you she would murder me."

Ben shrugged. "She might not murder you but she'd be very disappointed in you."

"Close enough," Cormac said, and this—that he cared what Kitty thought about him—felt like admitting a dark secret.

In the afternoon light, the mermaid seemed particularly mystical. Rippling water flashed around her like starlight. Her eyes were searching.

"All right," she said finally. "I want to go home."

Cormac checked the time. Quarter after two. Kitty's audience would start getting restless.

"So how do we do this?" Ben said.

They'd have to carry her. "Here," Cormac said, pulling a blanket out of the back of the van. He took one side, Ben took the other, and they lay it out in the water. They were ankle deep in it, their shoes soaked. She regarded the makeshift lift and nodded, satisfied. Maybe this— not directly manhandling her—earned them a little bit more trust. With a thrust of her tail, she hauled herself on the blanket. Gripping each corner, Cormac and Ben lifted. Cormac's shoulder twinged uncomfortably, and he winced.

"You okay?" Ben asked, watching him carefully.

"Yeah, just give me a sec." The gunshot wound in his shoulder was healed enough that he could forget about it sometimes. Then he tried to lift a body and his whole shoulder rebelled. He just had to remember to be ready for it. Ben frowned skeptically at this answer, but Cormac didn't wince again. They moved toward the van.

Her brow furrowed and jaw clenched, she clung to the edges.

She was heavier than Cormac expected. Her tail was long, muscular, and twitching, what seemed to be a reflexive shiver in response to the movement. She was nervous—of course she was, and he wished he knew how to set her at ease. He backed into the van; Ben climbed in next, and they eased their passenger to the tub. What had seemed pretty good for a last-minute plan an hour ago now seemed half-assed and pathetic.

Nia gazed into the water, and to Cormac's relief, she seemed to relax. Pushing down the edge of the blanket, she rolled herself out, for all the world like a fish escaping a net, slipping deftly into the water with barely a splash.

They got the Plexiglas lid strapped into place. It only covered two-thirds of the tub—she could stick her head up anytime she wanted, but it would still keep the water mostly in the tub. She hung her arms over the edge, watching.

"Thank you," she said. "*Mo sheacht mbeannacht ort.*"

Amelia said, *It's Irish. It means, 'My seven blessings upon you.'*

Cormac set his lips in a grim line. She ought to wait to thank them until this was all over. They closed up the van, double-checked everything. He got in the driver's seat, Ben in the passenger seat. Still no drones. They might get out of this without being seen.

The paddleboarders were staring now, pointing. One of them had a phone up, taking pictures. Who the hell brought a cell phone out on the water? These guys, apparently.

They set out, and Nia gave a small gasp as the water sloshed. But everything held together.

The radio was still tuned to the news conference, and Kitty had finally started talking.

"Thank you all for coming and being so patient. These things never quite go the way we plan them, do they?" She sounded bright, cheerful. Drawing them in, being everyone's friend. Cormac didn't know how she did it. "First of all I'd like to confirm that yes, that was me in the viral video that was posted last night. I'll be happy to answer questions about what was happening in that video and my role in it. But I'd like to say a few words first, and if you could please save your questions to the end of my statement, I'd really appreciate it. As you all know, we've been drawn here by evidence of a mermaid living in Horsetooth Reservoir. In case you weren't aware, the first mention of mermaids in the written record can be traced to Ancient Greece—"

And she was off to the races. After five minutes, she had gotten as far as Irish folktales. After ten, she was listing her favorite mermaid movies, and then she launched in on a history of Horsetooth Reservoir. By that time, they were well on their way to I-25.

"God, I love her," Ben said admiringly. "You pick a route?"

They were away from the reservoir in minutes and heading back to the freeway. At I-25, Cormac would have to turn north or south. North to I-80, or south to I-70. Both went all the way to the east coast. "I-80. It's closer and there's less traffic. Unless you think I-70?"

"No, definitely I-80." It was thirty miles or so to Cheyenne and the turn to the eastbound freeway. After that, Cormac could breathe a little easier.

Ben's phone rang just a minute later. He put it on speaker.

"It's me." Kitty. She sounded flustered. Not even a hint of lightness in her voice. "Eddie Foster was here. They bugged out in that tricked-out Range Rover before I finished, I couldn't take a break to call until now. We have to assume he's on your tail."

Five

Kitty ended the call with a heartfelt plea to be careful. It had taken awhile for Cormac not to be offended by such exhortations—of course he was careful, what did she take him for? Because it wasn't really about whether or not she thought they were being careful.

A tricked-out Range Rover could make much better time than an overloaded cargo van. Nothing to do about it at the moment but keep going and cover as much ground as they could. He'd suggest an alternate route, but the problem with the road between Fort Collins and Cheyenne was there were no alternate routes. Nothing else but county roads and open range. They'd make better time on the freeway.

"Shit," Ben murmured, compulsively checking the mirrors and craning around to look out the back. "Do we have a plan B?"

"I'm not going to panic until we spot 'em," Cormac said. The white van stood out, and it would stand out even more after dark. He noted every car around him, every car that passed, wondering if they were tailing him.

Nia sank under the surface of the water and stayed there.

The weight of responsibility for this other being suddenly hit him. He was driving a mermaid across country. He shouldn't be doing this.

You're in it now, Amelia said soothingly.

Got any spells for hot pursuit? Not that he could drive and cast spells at the same time.

Let me think on it.

Ben got out his phone and started typing.

Cormac glanced, trying to see what he was doing. "What's that?"

"You know those hotlines where you can text to report dangerous drivers to highway patrol?" He donned his feral lawyer grin that had somehow grown even scarier since he became a werewolf.

Cormac approved. Now, just twenty-five or so hours of driving to go. Once they took the turn to I-80 east, the trip was practically a straight shot. Nothing to worry about. The exit ramp was wide and gentle; he barely had to slow down.

A car was parked on the verge, a gray SUV with a long CB radio antenna climbing up the back, and a couple of other add-ons beside. Not standard. As the van reached the end of the ramp and merge lane, Cormac watched in the mirror as the SUV pulled onto the road and sped up, following. Wasn't enough traffic around for it to be subtle.

"Ben, look."

Ben cursed low. Turning off on side roads to try to lose them wasn't an option. Their pursuer was faster, more maneuverable. Changing course would only make it easier for them to catch up. And what exactly were they going to do when they caught up? Probably just wait for the van to stop. Everything Foster and his crew were driving got better mileage than the van, which would have to pull over for gas at some point, and they'd be cornered. Then what? That was a question Cormac didn't particularly want the answer to.

"What do we do?" Nia said. This must be maddening for her, not being able to see what was going on. Being helpless to do anything about it even if she could.

"Same thing we've been doing. Don't let on we've spotted them," Cormac said.

"Can you read their plates?" Ben was on his phone again, texting.

"No, they're hanging back."

They called Kitty. Ben put her on speaker. "We've got a car on us, a different one than the Range Rover," he said.

"Not surprised," she said with a sigh. "I'm trying to contact Eddie Foster, to find out what exactly he hopes to accomplish. He's not replying, but he has a live feed going on his YouTube channel right now."

"Wait, I've got to see this." Ben hung up the call and tapped away at his phone.

The video began playing in the middle of a breathless monologue, spoken in Eddie Foster's familiar dramatic voice. "—the Horsetooth Mermaid has been *kidnapped*! I'm very sensitive to charges to libel so I don't want to come out and say that talk-show host Kitty Norville is involved, but I'm currently gathering evidence that Kitty Norville is involved and I promise you I will get to the bottom of why. For now, the biggest question is—where is the mermaid now and why has this happened? I've got chase cars on the freeway, and I'll report back with news. Fans and listeners, I need your help. They're in a white cargo van heading east on I-80, just past Cheyenne. If you see the van, being driven by the man in our original mermaid video, please contact me at the number on the screen. We need your help! FRACH out!"

A lot of background noise marred the recording—a blustery wind and freeway hum. A glance at the screen showed Eddie in the Range Rover, racing on some freeway. Not too close, Cormac hoped.

"Well that's just great." Ben dialed his phone. "Hey hon," he said when Kitty picked up. "Did you catch him siccing his fans on us?"

"Yeah," she said. "Don't worry. Two can play at that game."

"Kitty," Ben said pleadingly. "I think you should try to keep out of trouble, we don't know what this guy is capable of—"

"Ben, my fan base is way bigger than his," she said sweetly. And hung up.

There was a mild splish of water in the tub. "Ach, I'm glad she's on my side," Nia said.

Cormac adjusted his grip on the wheel and glared at the ceiling a moment. The dull black plastic interior was cracking. "This was supposed to be a straight shot. Was there anything we could have done to make this a straight shot?"

"Just drive."

The SUV was still on them. It was clear from the video that Foster intended to get some kind of sensationalized video confrontation he could promote. Cormac didn't know how to shake the tail. Not while keeping them all safe. If it was just him, that would be one thing, but it wasn't. When he asked himself what was the worst that could happen, the answers he came up with were pretty damned bad.

He wasn't used to taking care of other people. Defending, yes. Protecting, definitely. He was fine putting himself between people he cared about and bullets, metaphorical or literal. But this was different.

Let me try something.

He wasn't sure what Amelia could do.

There should be some sage in your coat pocket—

"I can't dig around in my pockets while I'm driving," he said irritably.

"What?" Ben said. Cormac ignored him. He hadn't realized he'd answered her out loud.

Perhaps Ben would be willing to work the spell—

This was too much. Ben didn't have the experience, and relaying her instructions sounded like too much effort. Cormac unbuckled his seat belt. "Here. You drive."

Ben looked back at him, blank-faced. "That sort of thing only works in the movies, you know."

"Just pretend we're still seventeen and unkillable." Cormac thought for a moment, tilting his head. "You being a werewolf means you probably won't die if we get in a big wreck." But Nia might. Easy, then. No crashing.

"Jesus, just stop talking." Ben unbelted and slid over next to the driver's seat.

This really did feel like some of the shit they got up to in high school. He grinned.

Ben gripped the wheel, and Cormac slipped behind him, out of the seat, with his foot still on the gas pedal. Soon, he was crouching between the seats, while Ben settled in. Ben counted down, and Cormac backed out as Ben took over the pedal. The gas was only off for a second or two; the van barely lost speed.

"Hot damn," Ben said, fumbling to get the seat belt buckled. "We are never telling Kitty about this, right?"

Cormac was busy searching his pockets for Amelia's requested materials. Sage. Matches. Blue ink. Paper. She was constantly asking him to fill his pockets with... stuff. He never questioned it, but he was always a little surprised at what he was able to dig out in moments like this.

"Are we all right?" Nia asked. She'd hooked her elbows over the edge of the tub to watch him. Her hair dripped, her pale skin was shining. He was right next to the tub, close enough to catch an enticing, salt-touched scent. She smelled like the sea.

"Not sure," he answered truthfully. "Doing our best here."

She donned a bright smile, crinkling the wrinkles at her eyes, and he hesitated. That smile made him forget what he was doing for a moment.

Cormac, Amelia reminded him.

He might have blushed, and quickly set to work with the sage and candle stub.

"You know magic!" Nia said.

"Sort of," he responded.

The difficulty with casting some sort of diversion spell, to encourage people not to see us, is we're moving at high speed with dozens of other vehicles also moving at high speed. We don't want to be invisible. We need *people to be able to see us.*

Imagine, changing lanes and discovering that spot wasn't empty after all. Cormac wholeheartedly agreed.

Instead, we want to try to appear... different. Just a little. I can't make us look like an entirely different car. But perhaps a different color...

Burning sage tinted the air. Cleansing, protection. A bit of mint, for a new way of looking at the world. Cormac pressed his hand flat to the floor, and let Amelia step into his body, giving her his voice. She breathed out the incantation in a whisper.

Then she stepped back, the candle burned out, and the sage was gone. Only a whiff of it remained. The van felt the same, humming along the freeway. He had no idea if the spell worked. He sat back on his heels and sighed.

"Your aura changed," Nia said. "Just for a moment."

"You can see auras?" he said.

"I can see lots of things. Will you tell me why?"

"Maybe later." He moved back to the passenger seat, and Nia sank under the water.

He studied the mirrors, searching for the gray SUV. "Change lanes. Get some cars in between us and them. Let's see what happens."

"What'd you do?" Ben asked.

"I'm not exactly sure."

"Okay, then what did Amelia do?"

Just wait...

Ben got into the left lane, accelerated around a semi, then moved back.

"Wait, did you see that?" Ben said, glancing at the side mirror.

As they got ahead of the semi, Cormac was able to see more of the freeway behind them. The SUV with the big antenna sped up, zoomed right up behind the semi, jumped lanes—then it fell back. The car almost looked disappointed as it drifted farther behind.

"I swear they were looking right at us and didn't see us," Ben said.

"I think they saw us," Cormac answered. "We just didn't look like they expected us to."

"Then what did we look like?"

He'd love to know. "Just get some distance between us."

"Who is Amelia?" Nia asked.

Ben chuckled a little. "That's a long story."

"We've got time," she said.

They looked at Cormac. Inwardly annoyed, he said to Amelia, I never know what to say. It sounds crazy.

It is crazy. You always seem to do fine. It's not our fault if someone doesn't believe you.

"Amelia's the hundred-plus-year-old magician whose spirit shares my body," Cormac said.

"Really?" Nia said. "She can hear us right now?"

"Every word."

"Then I'm happy to meet her."

"Likewise," Cormac said. Nia had taken the story so matter-of-factly, he was a little bemused.

I love her. Can you imagine all the lore she could tell us? Everything we might learn from her?

They had a lot of hours of driving ahead of them. There'd be time.

Ben's phone rang. He'd left it sitting in a cup holder in the console, and Cormac picked it up. Caller ID said Kitty, of course.

"Yeah?"

"Hey. Where's Ben?" she demanded.

"Driving," Cormac said curtly.

"Wait, did you guys stop? What's happening?"

Cormac exchanged a glance with his cousin, who was gritting his teeth. "I'm not allowed to tell you," he said.

"Oh my God, why do I even ask. I'm still watching Foster's livestream and he just freaked the hell out. One of his chase cars was on your tail and just lost you. They can't figure out what happened. It's not like you guys are inconspicuous. But now he's putting pictures of the van up all over social media."

"We're going to have to change strategies," Ben said.

"Get off the freeway," Cormac said. "Next exit to a state highway. We can change routes then figure it out."

"Don't tell me where you're going," Kitty said. "I'm still trying to call Eddie the Night Stalker but he's only responding to Twitter posts. So we're doing this in public. Performative asshole."

"I'm sure you're holding your own, hon," Ben said.

"I've gotten him to admit he's soliciting corporate sponsorship for this stunt. He did better when he was asking people to feed his Patreon."

Ben leaned in and said, "Talk to Detective Hardin, see if she can help you get a restraining order in place, to keep those clowns away from us. One that'll work in multiple jurisdictions."

She sighed over the line. "This is very complicated."

"Just trying to think of everything."

"Yeah. You guys be careful."

From the back Nia was leaning on the tub, listening, and she called, "Kitty. Thank you."

"Of course." She ended the call.

They exited the freeway and made a couple of turns. Within minutes, they appeared to be in the middle of nowhere, nothing but rangeland marked off with barbed-wire fence in all directions. The road was nearly empty of traffic. Cormac gave Ben a couple of directions to get them back on an eastbound route. They kept up speed. It would be a few hours before they had to think about gas. Finally, he started to relax. Nia submerged again. She must have needed to spend a lot of time underwater, though she seemed able to breathe air well enough. She needed to breathe air to be able to speak, didn't she? He had no idea.

He got out the road atlas he'd shoved in with the rest of the supplies. He always, always kept paper maps in his car, and got teased for it, but if the phones ever went dead—or you ever wanted to avoid having your phone ping your exact location for whoever might be chasing you—you went with paper. The current route was on track, so he looked ahead to the end of the trip. I-80 eventually ran to New York City. To avoid that meant facing a tangle of interstates feeding south, through New Jersey. New Jersey was good, lots of coast line in New Jersey. Maybe too much coastline, because now he had a lot of possible destinations to take Nia to. On one end was Atlantic City and overdeveloped tourist beaches, and on the other the industrial and shipping shoreline of the most populated region of the U.S. This was way outside Cormac's territory and he didn't like it. He just wanted a nice, quiet beach where they could get Nia to the water without drawing attention.

"What're you finding?" Ben asked, glancing briefly at the map.

"I know nothing about New Jersey."

Ben huffed a laugh. "No, I guess not."

"We could try one of the rivers feeding into the bay there, but there'd be a lot of traffic, a lot of chances to get caught. And it's still a long swim to the Atlantic from there."

"I don't mind the swim," Nia said.

"How do you do with shipping traffic, pollution, that sort of thing?"

She hummed a little and said, "The waters run deep, and there are paths you can't see on your maps."

Didn't that sound just a little ominous...

Cormac ran his finger down the coastline, and found a large, incongruous stretch of green jutting into the bay. Gateway National Recreation Area, Sandy Hook Beach. Nothing but wide-open Atlantic Ocean beyond.

"There," he said. "We'll shoot for that spot."

"Nice, having a more specific destination than 'the Atlantic Ocean,'" Ben said.

"I have every faith in you," Nia said.

Now to earn that vote of confidence. Cormac sat back, closed his eyes, and sighed.

"And that's Nebraska," Ben said. One more state down, and too many to go.

Cormac shook himself awake, scrubbing his face. He'd nodded off; the nap made him crankier. According to his phone a couple of hours had passed. Ben seemed calm, which meant nothing was going wrong. Which, perversely, put him more on edge. Things always went wrong. Night was falling; Ben turned on the headlights, and the world seemed to shrink to darkness around them, with just a tunnel of light ahead.

A little while later, the van slowed. Ben had taken his foot off the gas. "You see that?" he asked.

Cormac straightened and studied the road ahead. Distinctive blue and red lights flashed, particularly bright in the twilight. Cop cars. Lots of them, forming a barrier across the highway, maybe half a mile ahead. All their headlights were on, illuminating the spot ahead of them.

This stretch of road had no intersections, no driveways, no place to stop and no way to turn around. Even if they did, the police would have no trouble chasing after them.

"What's going on?" Cormac asked uselessly.

"No idea."

Closer, the scene ahead of them became clear: a dozen cars, everything from highway patrol to unmarked federal sedans, were pulled across both lanes of highway, forming a roadblock.

Six

Several movie-inspired scenarios ran through Cormac's mind. Veering off the road, jouncing over grassland, initiating a massive chase. Doing some kind of squealing one-eighty, burning rubber to race back to some tangled route of escape. Crashing straight through the wall of cars as if the van were a battering ram. Racing the van off a cliff in a misguided blaze of glory.

All those scenarios ended with Nia getting badly injured. Besides, Ben was driving, not him. Ben was a square.

"No," Ben muttered, as if he knew exactly what Cormac was thinking, and that clinched it.

Ben slowed and stopped without any debate. "Keep your hands visible, please," he ordered. His own hands were planted firmly on the steering wheel.

"Yes, counselor," Cormac said, raising his hands. Ben scowled.

A handful of uniformed officers emerged from the roadblock, weapons drawn, and circled the van. The floodlights glared straight at them; Cormac squinted past the bright light, trying to see what was going on.

"You know," Ben said. "All the shit you and I have been through since we were kids and I've never once been arrested?"

"So we're getting arrested?"

"Depends on what excuse they're using to stop us."

So, this was exciting.

You do seem to have these confrontations with law enforcement on a regular basis.

It wasn't like he ever meant to. At least he wouldn't have to call his lawyer this time.

The ones who ended up approaching the van were two agents in suits, each sauntering up to a different window. A pale man in dark blue with a muted tie approached the driver's side. A Latina woman in a gray pantsuit with dark hair pinned up in a bun came to the passenger side. They didn't have weapons drawn. This was only marginally comforting.

"I'm calling it: FBI," Ben said.

"Treasury," Cormac said.

"Ten bucks?"

"You're on."

"Should I be worried?" Nia said, sloshing a bit of water out of her tub as she leaned on the edge.

Ben answered, "We'll let you know in a minute."

"Maybe stay out of sight in the meantime," Cormac added, and she submerged.

Ben waited until the male agent tapped on his window before reaching to roll it down. Cormac did the same on the passenger side. Both agents flashed badges. Cormac had just enough time to read the initials: PSA. Paranatural Security Administration. Oh, this ought to be good.

"Can I see your ID, sir?" the male agent asked Ben. The woman was glancing sidelong, past Cormac, trying to get a look in the back of the van. From the angle, he couldn't tell if she was able to see anything. Nia was being quiet. Not so much as a ripple.

Ben put on what Cormac thought of as his courtroom smile. "Yes, of course. Good evening, Agent... I'm sorry, I wasn't quite able to read your badge there."

"Stein. Agent Stein," the man said patiently. He nodded to his partner. "This is Agent Perez."

"I guess the roadblock means you're stopping everyone? Can I ask why?"

"We have an Amber Alert for a vehicle matching your description. We just need to have a quick look in the back, if you don't mind." That was law-enforcement code for: *Go ahead, try me.*

"The Paranatural Security Administration is following up on Amber Alerts?" Ben asked in mock confusion.

"The back doors. Are they unlocked?" Agent Stein replied evenly.

This whole situation smacked of "kidnapping across state lines," if someone wanted to press the issue. Cormac wondered if they'd been set up. Scratch that, he was pretty sure they'd been set up and he was pretty sure who had done it.

"Cover your ears," Nia murmured from the back.

Cormac froze, not sure he'd heard right. Ben caught his gaze, questioning. Agent Stein also cocked his head, and Perez leaned in.

"Do it!" the mermaid said.

Cover your ears, Amelia said urgently. *Please.*

Cormac put his fingers to his ears and pressed. Ben followed his cue, while the agents looked on, confused. In the enforced silence, he couldn't be sure what exactly was happening. He felt something, a quiet vibration rising up through the seat. The air seemed to move, like a sudden breeze coming in through the window. His breastbone thrummed.

Something was happening, because Agent Stein blinked quickly, and then his eyes glazed over. Agent Perez put her hand against her forehead, as if she was wracked by a sudden headache. She squinted, backing away from the van, and stumbled, only barely keeping herself from falling. A moment later, the cops at the roadblock reacted, leaning on their cars, shaking their heads, their gazes going blank.

Cormac was aware of a sound growing louder, the air growing thick with an otherworldly vibration that made his skin crawl. There seemed to be a melody in it, an enticing rise and fall of notes, a sweet voice... He wanted to hear it, to listen for himself—

Don't do it, Amelia said.

What is this...

Remember Greek mythology.

Sirens, who lured sailors to wreck on rocky shores with their songs. Sirens were said to be a close relative of mermaids. Ben caught his gaze, asking the same question: What is this?

Cormac shook his head and kept his hands firmly on his ears.

Agent Stein's arms fell to his sides. He seemed dazed. They all did; the two agents, all the officers—they stared into space, unblinking, their expressions slack.

The vibrations, the strange thrum in the air, stopped.

Nia leaned as far over the edge of the bathtub as she could and touched Ben's shoulder with a dripping hand. Finally, the two men lowered their hands. The silence felt profound.

"Drive! Go!" she urged.

Ben threw the van into reverse and backed out, swinging around in a turn as soon as he was clear. Cormac checked the scene behind them in the mirror—the cops were starting to wake up, shaking their heads, rubbing their foreheads, still dazed. That wasn't going to last long. Any minute they'd be in their cars, in pursuit. Ben floored it; the van's engine roared. Away from the bright lights, Cormac rubbed the glare out of his eyes.

"Did you do that?" Ben asked Nia.

"I know a few tunes," she said wryly.

They were running out of routes. Backtracking now felt like defeat. Ben turned onto a state highway that traveled roughly toward the interstate. At the moment, losing themselves in traffic still seemed like the best option, if the side roads were being watched. Were the FRACH crew still tracking them? Had Eddie Foster tipped off the authorities? Were they working together, or did the Feds have their own agenda?

He didn't know which one would be worse.

"Thanks," Cormac said to Nia.

"It only worked because the windows were open," she said. "Can't say it'll work again."

"Understood."

"We're not going to get far if we've got the Feds after us," Ben said. "'Nationwide manhunt' is not a phrase I want to deal with, ever."

"We're going to have to stop for gas soon," Cormac said. Making this trek in the middle of the night made it seem that much more daunting. They couldn't see the bad guys coming.

"Yeah," Ben said tiredly. "Call Kitty, will you? Let her know what happened?"

"The Feds are probably tracking our phones."

"Shit," Ben muttered. "Turn them all off, then."

Cormac was constantly checking the mirrors for flashing lights. That he didn't see any didn't make him feel any better, which seemed unfair.

Getting gas involved a whole decision tree of impossible choices. Find a big 24-hour truck stop that would be busy, crowded, easier to hide in—and have lots of security cameras and eyewitnesses. Or find some little farm town gas station which might not be under surveillance, but they'd stick out like a sore thumb. And probably wouldn't be open this late anyway.

In either case, pay with cash. Always pay with cash.

They ended up at a truck stop outside of Grand Island because it was open and because the van's gauge was pointing at empty. They operated on the assumption that they'd be spotted and tracked, and so moved as fast as they could. A pump had never worked as slowly as this one seemed to, but finally the tank filled, and they were away.

Nia surfaced briefly when they stopped, to see what the matter was. Ben did his best to reassure her, and she sank back to the bottom of the tub. Maybe she was managing to get some sleep.

As they pulled back onto the highway, Ben said, "Okay. I've got an idea."

"What?"

"We need another decoy."

Dawn found them near the Des Moines International Airport, smack in the middle of Iowa, on a stretch of road full of industrial buildings and long-term parking lots. They'd found a place to rent a van, but it wasn't open yet, which put them both on the sidewalk in the humid morning, with the sound of jet engines rumbling in the background.

Ben handed the key fob to Cormac. "Just go, I'll be fine. You need to keep moving."

"You sure?"

"I've got a phone and a credit card. It's all good. If we can confuse them a few more hours, well—you're halfway there already."

Splitting up felt wrong. They were both tired and buzzed on coffee. Cormac had managed a couple of hours of sleep. They'd switched drivers when they'd stopped for gas, and then Ben had gotten a couple of hours. They were both okay, but definitely weren't at their sharpest. He just had to be satisfied that Ben could take care of himself. He'd use the credit card to rent the van. That would ping his location to anyone who was tracking transactions and draw their attention. Or so they hoped.

Ben looked in to the back of the van one more time. "Nia. It's been good meeting you. Safe travels."

"I'm grateful for you, Ben."

Cormac drove off, watching in the rearview mirror as Ben made his way to the office to wait. He tried not to think of everything that could go wrong with this.

It'll be fine.

How could she know?

Seven

One problem with leaving Ben behind: Cormac was now the only driver. He was pretty sure he could drive for a dozen more hours, but that meant a lot more coffee in his future.

Soon after dropping Ben off, he had to stop for gas again. Every stop made his anxiety spike. He looked at every single other car in the place, every single driver, every one wandering into and out of the convenience store. They couldn't all be staring at him, but it sure felt like it.

He got himself a large coffee, a pack of energy drinks, some beef jerky, and twenty gallon-sized jugs of water for Nia. The clerk looked at him funny; Cormac glared back.

Water had sloshed out of the tub during the trip, and the extra he'd brought in the coolers went fast. At this point, the floor of the van was permanently wet. What water was left must have been feeling pretty stale. Or maybe tasting stale, or deprived of oxygen, or something. He didn't ask about Nia needing a restroom; frankly, he didn't want to know, so he got the fresh water and didn't ask. She'd found the package of smoked salmon in the cooler and was peeling strips off to eat. For the first time he noticed her fingernails were sharp, more like claws. Perfect for skewering fish and picking at meat. Were mermaids predators? Clearly. Until now, he'd never thought to wonder.

"Need anything else?" he asked.

"If I were going to be here longer than another day, yes. For now I'll manage."

"Shouldn't be longer than another day. I hope."

He really wanted to call Kitty and Ben to find out what was going on from their end. To get any updates on what Foster knew, and if his band of hunters was still after him. They'd gotten lucky, he felt, on their trek across the Great Plains. But now, east of the Mississippi, they were only going to be facing more people, more traffic, more eyes on them. More risk.

I'm still not entirely sure how this tracking phones thing works.

It has to do with the signals and the cell towers.

Let's not risk it, then. It all seems weirdly mystical. Electronic scrying.

He agreed.

Just as he was about to get back into the van, an SUV with a big antenna pulled up the drive. A familiar, gray SUV. It screeched to a stop, literally, tires sliding on the asphalt. The driver, a woman with a round face and her dark hair in long braid, stared at him. And like a moron, Cormac stared right back.

In the passenger seat, a young-looking white guy in glasses held up his phone and presumably started taking video.

"And there it is," he muttered. The other shoe dropping.

"Something wrong?" Nia asked.

"Yeah. We've been spotted." He hopped in the driver's seat.

The problem was, the van was ponderous, with a terrible turn radius and bad visibility. Even pulling straight out of the lane by the pumps required checking all the mirrors and easing around a sedan parked in front of him. The gray SUV was already looping around, clearly intending to cut off his access to the nearest exit. Cormac hauled the steering wheel around, aiming for the secondary exit, but the nimble SUV was already veering to cut him off again. The driver was intent, glaring out with a bright expression of victory, while the passenger talked into his phone. This was probably going up on a livestream.

What the hell did these people want?

A semi-truck, a big red cab hauling an unmarked trailer, pulled into the lane separating the islands of diesel pumps from the passenger cars. The driver's side was facing Cormac; the driver lowered his window. Guy had a beard, sunglasses, and a Turkish eye made of blue glass hanging from his rearview mirror.

He gestured for Cormac to lower his window as well. The SUV had parked on the other side of the lot, engine idling. Just waiting. The van was trapped between the two of them and Cormac was at something of a loss.

He lowered the window.

The trucker called out, "You're Kitty's friend? The one with the mermaid?"

What... was happening? "What about it?" Cormac asked cautiously.

He nodded decisively. "We've got your back. Don't worry, just get out of here."

Cormac could only stare, until Amelia prompted him, *Don't question it. Drive.*

"Thanks," Cormac said finally, giving a brief wave.

"Don't mention it. Good luck out there." The driver grinned at the SUV like he had a plan.

Cormac drove. Swinging back around, away from the SUV and out of the semi's path, he headed back toward the secondary exit. Just as the SUV started to follow, the red semi pulled forward, blocking the way. Then it just sat there.

At the primary drive out, another semi pulled through and stopped. Cormac couldn't see the SUV anymore. Which meant the SUV couldn't see him. He didn't linger to see how this was going to play out, but as he sped out his suddenly clear exit, a third truck came up behind him, turned, and blocked that drive, too. The SUV was stuck at the truck stop until the semis moved.

The van was clear. He raced back onto the road and took the first freeway ramp he came to. Ten minutes later, after pushing the van as fast as it could go, he checked the mirrors. Near as he could tell, they weren't being followed. He blew out a relieved breath, hoping this latest reprieve would last a couple of hours.

"Kitty came through," he said, letting out a nervous laugh. "I hope that FRACH crew got it all on video. She'll love it."

"I told you," Nia said. "I have faith in you."

Seven blessings she'd said, right? Maybe they wouldn't have to use them all up before the trip was done.

The midwest vowel states—Iowa, Illinois, Indiana, Ohio—had a sameness to them that felt oppressive. Giant truck stops, billboards, a flat greenery heavy with a haze of humidity that was utterly alien to him. Not a mountain in sight. Increasing lanes and traffic marked the stretch past Chicago. The traffic turned out to be a boon—it slowed them down, but there were a lot more white cargo vans around. There were toll roads, which he managed to navigate even as he was aware of the security cameras spying on him. In the afternoon heat, he discovered the van's air conditioning was broken, and was a little jealous of Nia soaking in the cool tub.

Amelia, you there? He prodded the back of his mind, and he was tired enough it felt like reaching into a snowdrift for a dropped set of keys. He knew she had to be there, but couldn't seem to find her.

Always, dear.

I really want to see you.

They had a space they shared. A mental construct, a dream—he wasn't sure exactly what it was or what to call it. It used to be his alone, his escape, an image of a high mountain valley that calmed him. But then she came, their partnership started, and it became theirs. They created it, but it also reflected their moods, their inner selves. It was where they had first met when he was in prison, and her spirit had crashed into him, demanding to be heard. Since then it had become their refuge.

But he had to close his eyes to imagine it, to send himself there, which he obviously couldn't do right now.

That would be lovely. I know you're tired.

It was the anxiety as much as anything. He didn't like being hunted.

She said, *I can imagine my hands on your shoulders. It's difficult, on my own. You're the one with the muscles and nerves that work. But if I could, I'd put my hands... there.*

He could almost feel it, her slender hands resting on his shoulders, kneading some of the stress out of them. He sighed, and his muscles shivered.

He asked the eternal question between them: was it real, or were they imagining it? Did their thoughts somehow make it real?

I don't know, she said, and he could have sworn he felt her breath against his cheek. He wanted to close his eyes, fall asleep with her in their meadow... *Cormac. Stay awake,* she commanded sternly. He shook himself and took a long drink of cooling coffee. There'd be time later for philosophical discussions with Amelia about the line between the physical and spiritual planes of existence.

He turned up the radio; he needed some noise.

"Nia?" he asked over his shoulder. The splash of water told him she was at the surface, listening. "Can you talk to me? Help me stay awake." His whole body was vibrating from the hum of the tires. He didn't want to think about the headache starting to pound behind his eyes.

"About what?" she asked in her lilting voice.

Questions. I have questions.

Cormac sighed. "Amelia has questions."

"Oh? Like what?"

The torrent came too fast for Cormac to really convey them, but he tried. Best thing would have been to let Amelia take over his body and have a conversation with Nia herself—but she couldn't drive.

"What's your native language? How did you learn English? When you enspelled those police, did you sing words or is it more about the sound? Do mermaids practice magic? A particular brand of water magic? You would need spells that don't require flames, and would such spells even work out of the water? Could you teach us?"

In the rearview mirror, Cormac saw Nia staring back at him. "That's a lot of questions."

"That's maybe half the questions," Cormac muttered. "Amelia can be a little much."

Really now, Cormac. I'm only curious.

The mermaid wore a wry smile, and craned her neck to look out the windshield. In the back of his mind, Amelia's disappointment was plain. Nia wasn't going to answer her questions.

"Hmm," Nia said, almost a song. "I had no idea how far away from the sea I was. No wonder I've felt so... wrong."

"Wrong how?"

"Weak. Fuzzy in the head. My people's strength comes from the sea."

"The ones who did this to you, you think they knew that? That's why they brought you to the middle of the country?"

"Has to be, I think. Wish I could remember more."

"You think they drugged you?"

She was silent for a moment; he glanced in the mirror, watched her submerge, then come back up, sweeping water back from her hair. "Maybe they did."

"How shitty does someone have to be to drug a mermaid?"

Very, Amelia observed.

"I just want to go home," Nia sighed. "I want to see my children again."

Children. Everybody wanted to talk about their children, so Cormac prompted her. "How many do you have?"

"Two. A son and daughter, all grown up. Nuala and Conn. We... are prone to wander. Long journeys, along the pathways of currents, all over the world. I've been gone long enough they might even have begun to miss me."

Her people, she'd said. A whole merperson society, journeying all over the world. "Are there a lot of you? Are there underwater cities, something like that?"

Atlantis, Amelia murmured. *Can you imagine it?*

He couldn't. It felt like stories to him. If anyone should believe in such stories, he should, but this one was hard to picture.

"It's probably not what you think." She sounded wistful.

"Where—"

"I'm not going to tell you where," she said sternly. "I'm grateful to you for helping me, but I'm not going to reveal secrets."

"Fair," he said, chuckling.

"Now, I have questions about you, Cormac." His name had a lilting cadence in her accent, like it was part of a song. "What's your tale? You're asked to rescue a mermaid and don't bat an eyelash. You've got a wizard living inside you and stay cool as an iceberg. What magic do you have of your own? You must have some."

He'd always thought of himself as the opposite of magic. He hunted magic. Killed it. His father had taught him that it was up to them to protect the world from the supernatural, a duty that had been passed down through his family for more generations than Cormac knew. Cormac had destroyed that legacy in just a few years. Probably just as well his father wasn't alive to see him buddying up to werewolves and vampires, working magic and ferrying mermaids...

"You're not asleep, are you?" Nia asked. A bit of water splashed his arm, where she flicked it from the tub.

"No, just... no one's ever said anything about me being magic. I had to think about it. I used to be a hunter. I hunted werewolves, mostly. But also vampires, skinwalkers, all kinds of monsters."

"I see. But you stopped."

"I met Kitty. Kitty doesn't believe in monsters. There's just people who do good and people who don't."

"And she made you want to do good?"

"Well, a stint in prison might have had something to do with that, too. I don't ever want to go back. Neither does Amelia."

"I understand that very well."

"I bet you do."

"So the magic's rubbed off on you, through the years?"

"Amelia says I'd never have gotten into any of this if I didn't have some of my own to start with."

Indeed, I think in another time and place you could have been a great wizard in your own right.

Well, it's lucky I met you, then. Amelia merely hummed an agreement.

"A wise woman." She cocked her head. "What's that singing?"

"Radio." He bumped up the volume.

"I like those voices."

"It's Simon and Garfunkel, I think."

"Hmm. They're telling a story."

With a splash and ripple, she pulled herself up on the edge of the tub, leaning where the skin of her torso met the scales of her tail, to better hear about the ride on the Greyhound and the New Jersey Turnpike. Her hair dripped water onto the floor of the van. Reaching, she touched Cormac's elbow, where it leaned on the armrest. The damp soaked into his shirt, a chill reached his skin. But somehow, she wasn't cold. Her touch was full of life, conveying affection. It warmed him. He wasn't a hugger; he normally kept his distance. But he shifted his grip on the steering wheel so he could cover her hand with one of his, twining their fingers. There was comfort in the touch. They stayed like that for a mile or so, until the song ended, then she squeezed his hand and pulled away, slipping back into the tub.

At one point he hoped they might reach the coast by nightfall, but he was pretty sure now that wasn't going to happen. The sun was sinking west, and they still had a ways to go.

In Pennsylvania, the landscape grew hilly. Mountainous by eastern standards, but these would never look like more than hills to Cormac, who'd grown up in the Rockies. The trees were different, too. Not pines, but deciduous forests, budding out with new spring growth.

They crossed Pennsylvania. The next state was New Jersey, and he had his route to the coast all mapped out. Mere hours away, now. He left I-80, which felt momentous. It marked entering the last stage of the journey. He stopped again for gas, coffee, the restroom, and fresh water. The hyper-awareness of being in the open woke him up a little. At the same time, getting closer to their destination exhausted him. There wasn't any more tiring phrase than *almost there.*

He weighed the pros and cons of turning on his phone. He worried about Ben, and he needed to get news of what Foster was doing. Kitty would probably appreciate some reassurance that they were alive, random clandestine livestreams notwithstanding. On the other hand, he liked not having the distraction. Putting his head down and just *going.* It was like he was in his own little world, in this van, with a mermaid in the back. It seemed unreal. He could just stay in that world for awhile.

In the end, he needed information.

The second he turned the phone it, it beeped endless notifications at him. He must have had hundreds of messages and voice mails. He didn't want to look at a single one of them, so he just called Kitty.

She didn't wait for him to say hello. "Are you okay? Is Nia okay? Don't tell me where you are, just tell me you're okay."

"We're both okay. Still on track."

"Oh thank God. It's been nuts here. Eddie Foster and I have threatened to sue and countersue each other like ten times and I don't know what even is happening."

"Is Ben okay?" Cormac asked.

"Yeah, yeah. He's on his way home. Looks like the decoy worked for a few hours, but I take it that was enough to get you some distance."

"Seems so. Anything I need to know?"

"I guess you met a couple of agents? Stein and Perez? They called me. They seem nice." Her sarcasm had spikes.

"Well, they didn't shoot, so there's that."

"Foster wants to call you. He says he wants an interview."

Cormac let out an angry huff. "Why? He could have asked for that two days ago and saved us the trouble."

"Yeah, if he just wanted video or some kind of exclusive interview with Nia that would be one thing. But the way he's going after you physically—it's weird."

"I'm not talking to him."

"That's what I told him." The toothy grin in her voice was plain.

"See if you can string him along, keep him distracted. We've just got a few more hours to go."

"Good luck."

In fact, according to the phone, Eddie Foster had called him dozens of times. The guy had gotten his number, which wasn't totally surprising. It did justify Cormac's decision to leave the phone off for most of the trip. Foster left a handful of messages. Cormac only listened to the last one to save time.

"Mr. Bennett. I can save us both a lot of trouble if you'll just talk to me. Neither of us is doing this for fun. We both have our reasons. I'll tell you what I'm willing to do, but not in messages. We need to talk." The line cut off. Foster sounded exhausted, his chipper podcaster voice abandoned. It made him sound rough, threatening.

"He could explain himself to Kitty easier than he can talk to me," Cormac muttered.

Yes, Amelia said. *But Kitty doesn't have custody of Nia. Foster wants Nia.*

The publicity was all a distraction. Cormac had a sudden image of how the confrontation at the gas station could have gone, the pair of Foster's minions successfully cornering the van, then teaming up to pull Cormac out of the driver's seat and steal the van—

It hadn't happened. It wouldn't happen. They were so close to the ocean, now. This was going to be fine.

This time, he left his phone on.

He kept searching for the gray SUV and black Range Rover, but didn't see them. Didn't mean they weren't there, and he was sure Foster had others looking for him. Spotters, fans of the show, whatever. This was confirmed when he noted a car, an older sedan, moving oddly. Speeding up, passing a few cars behind, running parallel with the van for a mile before getting ahead. Falling back and doing it over again, like it was trying to get a good description of the whole vehicle, including the license plates. This hunch was confirmed when Cormac noticed a passenger in the back seat with a phone up, taking pictures.

Then the car changed lanes and pulled up alongside him again, and another passenger pressed a sign to the window, handwritten on paper torn out of a spiral notebook. It read, TAKE THE CALL.

A moment later, Cormac's phone rang, and caller ID listed Eddie Foster.

Answer it, Amelia said. *I'm curious.*

"Shit," he muttered, because he couldn't think of anything better to say, and put the call on speaker. "Yeah."

"Cormac Bennett. Is it you?" It was Eddie Foster.

More often than not, Kitty succeeded when she was just able to talk to people. It had worked on him, at least, when he'd been sent to kill her and he just... listened to her. But she'd been talking to Foster for two days now and he hadn't budged. He was immune to her charm, her own little brand of magic, and that said something about him. Cormac wasn't Kitty. He wasn't good at talking. Cormac wasn't going to try to convince Foster to leave them alone just by talking. So this was about what he could learn from the guy.

"What do you want?" Cormac said in his low drawl.

"I just want to talk. You've kidnapped the Horsetooth Mermaid. We have video evidence, we've tracked you halfway across the country. I want to know why. What are you going to do with her?"

419

Foster's voice was up-tempo, urgent, engaging. Cormac recognized the cadence—a radio voice, a public-speaking voice. Kitty's voice did the same thing when she was on the air during her show. Which meant Foster was live, streaming this online or whatever the hell he did. Foster hadn't warned Cormac that this was going live or being recorded. While he wasn't sure doing that was illegal, it was certainly scummy.

"She has a name," Cormac said, annoyed. "And it isn't 'the Horsetooth Mermaid.' Christ."

"Oh yeah? Then what it is?"

"Not your business," Cormac said, the same time he looked in the mirror and saw Nia shaking her head, then sighing with relief. Yeah, Cormac wasn't going to give this guy anything. "If you wanted to know more you could have played nice from the start and not turned this into a circus."

"People have a right to know the truth!"

"How do they know that's what you're telling?"

"They *trust* me. You—you're a felon. Who should they believe?"

Cormac chuckled. Foster said it like he assumed the label would bother Cormac. That he'd get mad and lose his temper, put on some kind of show for his audience. "Well, I didn't go to prison for lying."

"That's right. Manslaughter, wasn't it?" Foster's tone took on dramatic urgency. "What are you going to do to the mermaid, Mr. Bennett?"

Jesus... "I think it says a lot about you, that you're assuming I'm doing anything but my very best to help her."

There was a click on the line, a shift in the quality of the background noise. "All right, Bennett. I've stopped streaming. It's just the two of us now. No more lies, no more games. I want to make you an offer." His tone was completely different, the dramatic air gone.

A chill shivered across Cormac's skin. This voice was ruthless. Now they were getting somewhere. "Talk."

Foster spoke in a steady, business-like tone. No chance for

misunderstandings. "It's simple. I pay you. I pay you a lot. All you need to do is tell me where you are. Then park the van and walk away. That's it."

Nia ducked under the lid to press herself to the other end of the tub; the shimmery membranes of her tail draped over the front edge. Her expression seemed wary, but not afraid. She was waiting. Surely she trusted him by now. He met her gaze in the mirror, tried to nod, to convey his intentions.

"How much we talking about?" Cormac asked, as if he were serious.

"A million," Foster said.

That's a lot, isn't it? Amelia asked. *Where does someone like him get that kind of money?*

Cormac had some ideas about that. "Now tell me, Mr. Foster— what are *you* going to do with the mermaid?"

"I think my price buys me a little privacy."

Over the years, Cormac had done a lot of unsavory jobs and met a lot of unsavory people. Not much turned his stomach. Eddie Foster was turning his stomach.

"Well? We have a deal?" Foster prompted. Cormac had been quiet for a time. Maybe Foster assumed he was actually thinking it over.

He was not thinking it over. "Naw, we're done here."

He hung up.

With a splashing of water, Nia turned again. "I do not like the sound of him. My scales are twitching."

"I hope you didn't think I would really sell you out."

"Well, no. But I imagine a deal like that is how I ended up needing your help in the first place."

She might have gotten caught in a net—plenty of stories like that in the folklore—or washed up on a beach. It would just take one person carrying her off and finding a buyer. Cormac could probably call a few contacts to find out how to get in on that kind of black market.

A dozen years ago, he might have thought getting in on that kind of black market was a good idea.

The sun was bending west, the shadows growing long, and he wondered if they would ever reach the coast. The sky felt close and small. There were too many people, and he was feeling claustrophobic.

Then he knew he was getting tired because on the last state highway before taking the turn that would eventually get them to Sandy Hook Beach, the gray SUV suddenly appeared behind him. They must have raced to catch up. Cormac's heart fell, because they were so close, and he was out of ideas about how to get away from these guys. The van wasn't going to go any faster. He was running out of escape routes, as the roads funneled him toward New Jersey's northeast corner.

On an open stretch, the gray SUV raced ahead and changed lanes to land in front of the van. A second SUV with one of those oversized antennae took its place, coming up behind the van and matching speed.

The van was sandwiched.

The two pursuing vehicles weren't doing anything overt. This only meant they were tracking him, waiting. He'd have to pull over sometime. He'd have to stop; they were just waiting for their opportunity. Maybe he didn't have to stop—maybe he could find a road or a pier and drive the van straight into the water, and Nia would be home and he... well, he'd figure it out. He'd made worse plans in his time.

Then he saw the third vehicle keeping pace with the SUV behind him. A Range Rover, big and black, with a whole forest of antennae and other equipment, and what looked like a drone the size of a large dog strapped to the roof. Eddie Foster himself.

This was an escort. They already had him nailed; they were just waiting to make a move.

He got his phone, dialed Kitty, put her on speaker.

"Where are you?" she asked, first thing.

"New Jersey somewhere. You have a way to contact Agents Stein and Perez?"

"What's happening?"

"Foster and his crew have three cars flanking us. They haven't done anything yet, but I'm not sure how patient Foster's going to be."

"You trust the Feds more than you trust Foster?"

"Right now? Absolutely yes."

"I'm on it." Her confidence was inspiring. She conveyed not a flicker of doubt.

Nia was gripping the edge of the tub, keeping herself steady in the sloshing water. "I'm glad you tried, however this turns out."

"We're not done yet."

They passed a sign for Sandy Hook Beach. When the exit came up, he veered over and off. He wasn't trying to get away anymore. He just needed to get to the water before they were on top of him. Get Nia to the water, that was all he had to do.

The two cars behind him followed, unbothered by the change in direction. The gray SUV in front had already passed the exit. That didn't stop the driver from slamming on the brakes and swinging over in a one-eighty that left big black skid marks and wisps of smoke from burned rubber. A half a dozen cars behind hit their brakes in turn, swinging this way and that to avoid a collision. Unbothered, the SUV shot back toward the exit.

For a time, he thought he could keep the way ahead of him clear. Win some little scrap of distance and breathing room. But once again, the gray SUV raced ahead, swerved, and jumped right in front of him so he had to slow down

Half the water must have sloshed out of the tub. Cormac glanced in the mirror.

"You okay?"

"You know, I might be a little seasick?"

Nice of her, to try to make a joke. That didn't change how much shit they were in.

His pursuers had him hemmed in again. No question, the drivers of the three vehicles were communicating, coordinating. Cormac was alone and didn't stand a chance.

Any ideas? he asked Amelia.

Caltrops? Explosives?

Wouldn't that be great?

The lead SUV was slowing, slowing. Cormac watched the speedometer creep down to fifty, forty-five, forty, and slower. So this was how they were going to do it. Corral him and force him to a stop.

No. He cranked the wheel over and swerved. Hit the gas, plunged ahead, half on the shoulder, intending to muscle his way around the obstacle. The SUV responded by swinging around to block a lane and a half of the road and stopping dead, lurching on its tires, almost losing stability. Right in front of him.

Cormac slammed on the brakes but there wasn't enough time. The van plowed into the gray SUV with an appalling crunch of metal and shattering plastic, and lurched to its side.

Eight

The following silence was profound.

Cormac's heart was racing, his ears were ringing, and he was unable to make sense of what he was seeing—he'd ended up slumped forward against the seat belt, hanging toward the door, which was on the ground. The windshield was opaque, webbed with cracks. If he breathed on it funny it would shatter.

He didn't feel hurt. He'd just had the breath knocked out of him. Struggling, he tried to unbuckle the seat belt.

"Nia!" he called, craning his neck back to try to see her. The cargo space was a mess, everything inverted and scattered.

She was out of the tub, curled up against the back of the driver's seat in a pool of water that had collected on the side, but was draining quickly. Her tail flopped, dripping water.

"Nia!" he tried again.

"Alive," she said tiredly.

The back doors had popped open, and through them he could see the Range Rover and the second SUV pulling up. Eddie Foster and a couple of his minions rushed out. Foster carried what looked like a handgun at his side. So did his minions, who were spreading out to surround the crash. Their expressions were all hard, professional. Not amateur cryptid hunters and minor internet celebrities, not even a little bit.

Cormac had lost. He'd failed. But they wouldn't get him without a fight.

By some miracle the tub was still secured in place. Nothing else was: water bottles had tipped over, their supplies were scattered and smashed. Nia clung to the back of the seat, gasping a little. Water dripped off her. Scrambling, Cormac pulled himself past her over the side of the tub, to the back. He couldn't tell if he was disoriented from everything being at the wrong angle, or if he was actually dizzy. At last, he got to his feet, hunched down by the open doors.

A tire iron was secured to the side above the wheel well, with a spare tire. He grabbed it, hefting it like a club, and marched out, putting himself between Foster and the van.

"Stop right there," Cormac said. For all the good it did.

Amazingly, Foster stopped. He raised his weapon. The gun didn't look right, and Cormac realized it was a tranquilizer gun of some kind, firing a pneumatic dart.

"You should have taken the money when you had a chance," Foster said, sneering like some movie villain.

"Could have but I'm not an asshole like you," Cormac shot back.

"One last chance. You can walk away from this. Just walk away and you won't get hurt."

"Or?"

"That's a pretty bad crash," he said, nodding past Cormac. "Wouldn't take much to make it look like you died in it."

A flopping, falling noise sounded from the back of the van. Cormac didn't dare take his gaze off Foster, but his heart gave a lurch, thinking of Nia trying to move in the worst possible environment, getting cut up on glass and metal—

"*You.*" Nia had managed to crawl to the van's back, hauling herself with her arms, half-propped up on her tail, which curled behind her. Now, she sat braced on her arms, her hair draped over her chest, and glared out at Eddie Foster. "I remember you," she said steadily, accusingly.

One of the minions aimed; Cormac stood in front of Nia.

"Cover your ears," she murmured, leaning forward.

Foster pointed at her. "Don't sing or I'll shoot him."

"Get back," Cormac said to her. With a muscular lurch, she slipped back, sheltering at the side of the van.

"He was there, where they held me," Nia said. "He worked for them. I remember. I remember now. Two of the doctors helped me escape, but we didn't have time, they brought me to the lake—"

"And they're now being prosecuted for theft of company property," Foster said.

"She's not property!" How hard a concept was this? He needed to call Ben. Kitty. Everybody. "What company is this? Kitty was guessing pharmaceuticals."

"There's a lot to learn from creatures like her," Foster said. "How do they survive in the cold? How do they process oxygen? What will we find when we sequence their genome?"

"And how can you monetize it?"

He opened his arms; he wasn't sorry.

"How many of my people have you killed for your greed?" Nia asked, anguished. "Can you answer that?"

"You know? I don't think I can." Foster said.

Cormac said, "Your show, your whole cryptid hunting shtick. It's cover, isn't it? You've got this whole network of people feeding you information, doing your legwork for you. You put on a show, searching for Bigfoot with night vision headcams and all that. What people don't know is that you *do* find the cryptids you're looking for. But instead of telling anyone about it you disappear them into your private research hell. Jesus."

"It's not like they're people."

Cormac desperately wished for one of his guns. The tire iron would do, though, if he could just get close enough.

"Walk away," Foster said. "Now."

"Not gonna happen." Cormac chuckled a little. Not a bad way to go, really. Protecting—trying to protect, rather—a mermaid. Kind of heroic. It had been a nice drive.

"Cormac, go," Nia said softly. "I don't want you to die for me."

He didn't answer. What could he say? He asked the back of his mind, because Amelia deserved a say in this. *What're you thinking?*

I'm not really sure. I'm just so angry.

You want to walk away?

Oh, no. Not at all.

You got anything we can use here?

Prayer?

"Fine," Foster said, raising his tranquilizer pistol. "We're done here."

A car came screeching up the road, swerving into the midst of the drama. Another followed. Both were driven professionally, stopping to block the other vehicles, facing down Foster and his minions. Both were dark sedans with government plates.

Agents Stein and Perez barreled out of the lead car, weapons drawn. Those guns used bullets.

Cormac dropped the tire iron and put his hands up. And, well, he prayed that this wasn't going to get worse.

Another couple of agents exited the second car, and they all shouted commands—get down, put the guns down—and so on. The occupants of the gray SUV Cormac had crashed into were just now emerging, dazed and bleeding from cuts on their heads.

Cormac waited, wondering how much trouble he was in. Trouble was better than dead.

The chaos resolved somewhat. Foster's minions immediately knelt and put down their tranquilizer guns. Foster stared back at the agents, blinking in confusion. He rested his finger on the trigger, just for a moment, like he was actually thinking about tranking a couple of federal agents. But then he also knelt, glaring hard at Cormac the whole time, as if he had something to do with this.

No one came over to Cormac. The agents noted his presence, but he didn't seem to be their target. He immediately went back to the van to check on Nia.

She was curled up as small as she could get, with her back against the van's ceiling-turned-side. Her tail was pulled in close, the fins clenched and small. She hugged herself and shivered.

"You're bleeding," he said. Blood, thinned by water, traced a trail from a cut on her forehead down her cheek.

She touched her head, looked at the pink on her hand. Such a familiar, human gesture. "What? Oh. What's happening? Are we saved or damned?"

Good question. A few bottles of water remained intact. Cormac gathered them up, because it felt like doing something useful. "Don't know. How long until you dry out?"

"Not long. I need water, it's uncomfortable being out of it." Her body wasn't made to support its own weight like this.

The van was toast. No way they could get it back up and refill the tub.

"Mr. Bennett?" Agent Stein came and stood over him and Nia. She shivered harder, probably more from shock than cold.

"Yeah." He found the blanket they'd used to carry her in and spread it over her.

Stein turned to Nia. "Ma'am?" There was something really odd about the neatly suited agent calling this otherworldly creature "ma'am." Odd and endearing. "Can I ask you to please not do that singing... siren-y thing again? It's disruptive."

"It's supposed to be," she said. "Are you going to give me a reason to?"

The agent seemed daunted at this, regarding her thoughtfully. "Are you all right?" He asked, and a thread seemed to snap, a tension breaking. Cormac started to hope.

"I need to get to water," she said. "I'm not being kidnapped, I asked for help, Cormac is helping me. The one who wanted to kidnap me is that—" Nodding at Foster, she said a watery, guttural word that none of them understood, and yet the meaning was clear.

Cormac said, "We're just trying to get to the coast so she can go home. That's all."

"You should have contacted the agency sooner, we could have helped."

Cormac chuckled a little. "You understand if I don't completely trust the suits and badges. Especially not after what people like you did to Kitty."

Stein frowned. "That was—"

"Before your time, I get it."

"Wait here just a moment."

"We're not going anywhere," Cormac said with a sigh, and slumped back.

Nia took his hand. Just to have something to hold on to, it seemed. "What did they do to Kitty?"

"The first director of the Center for Paranatural Biology locked her up during a full moon and broadcast her shapeshifting on national TV. Ask Kitty, she'll tell you how many hits the video has on YouTube."

"That's awful!"

"You can see why she was so interested in helping you."

"I hope the director was punished."

"Oh yeah, he was." Eventually...

A couple more cars pulled up, including what looked like highway patrol, colored lights flashing. Didn't make Cormac feel much better. But he was *very* happy to see a couple of officers putting cuffs on Foster and company.

Foster, hands cuffed behind him and standing near one of the cop cars, lunged out of the officer's grasp. "I could have made you rich, Bennett! You ruined your chance! I'll remember this, don't think I won't!" He was still shouting when the door slammed shut, and they didn't have to listen anymore.

Stein went back to consult with Perez. The conversation turned urgent, with gestures, and several glances back at the wrecked van.

"I'm sorry," Cormac said. "We almost made it."

"I'm not sorry at all," Nia said, smiling. "Story's not over yet."

They waited, Nia's hand resting on his arm, until both agents came over.

"Everything I've seen in this job and it's still kind of a shock. La Sirena," Perez said. Crouching down to put herself at the mermaid's eye level, she stared; it was a little uncomfortable. "You're not going to do the singing thing, are you?"

"On the other hand," Stein said thoughtfully, "The lab wonks would love it if we got a recording."

Nia looked at Cormac, her gaze pleading. Cormac laid it out. "We need help."

More cars pulled up, filling the opposite shoulder, blocking traffic. The people who stepped out of them looked ordinary, and they had their phones up, presumably taking pictures and video. A handful of cops were put on traffic duty, but the situation was getting increasingly chaotic.

Agent Perez said, "We can take you to a safe place—"

"The coast," Cormac said. "Not that there's anything I can do about it, but she needs to get to the ocean. Ball's in your court."

Nia reached and rested her hand on Perez's arm, met her gaze, and said, "Please."

The crowd was getting bigger, rowdier, and there weren't enough uniforms to keep order. Their window of escape was closing. Stein and Perez glanced at each other. Stein nodded.

Agent Perez pulled her key fob out of her jacket pocket and handed it to Cormac. "We'll clean this up here."

"Thanks," Cormac said with a sigh.

They still had a mess to get through. Perez and Stein made a big show of wrangling the crowd, and uniformed officers managed to get people back in their cars and get traffic moving again. Tow trucks arrived. Cormac gathered up the remaining jugs of water and put them in Perez's sedan, along with a couple of wet towels he'd found. There was nothing much else to salvage.

That left how to get Nia to the car, and Cormac was just about to admit he would need to ask for help when Agent Stein came alongside. "Can I help?"

Yes, Cormac admitted, he could.

The two of them got on either side of Nia and formed a chair between them, while she clung to their shoulders. Even though she'd been out of the water for awhile now, she still felt damp. Her hair pressed wetly to his shirt and Stein's suit. Her scales glittered. All her muscles were clenched, rigid with anxiety. And no wonder.

The cops and bystanders still on the scene fell silent and watched their trek from the van to the car.

"I don't like being seen," Nia said. "We're hardly ever seen."

They managed to get her into the back seat; she tipped herself out of their arms and curled up. Her hair was starting to dry, taking on reddish highlights, with a few streaks of gray around her temples. It would have been beautiful except it meant she was going to be hurting even more soon.

"I'm going to remember this for the rest of my life," Stein murmured.

"Good. You should." Cormac got in the car and drove away.

Nine

Somewhere in the wreck and the aftermath, Cormac had lost his phone. Hadn't even thought about it, and he was weirdly okay with that. It wouldn't distract him. Right now, he just needed to drive.

With another round of splashing, Nia doused herself and sighed with relief.

The sun was behind him, setting. He knew the route he was on; the signs for Sandy Hook Beach came frequently enough he knew he was on the right track. In the mirror he saw Nia folded over her tail, the fins hanging limply. She hadn't spoken in a while.

"Nia?" he called.

"I'm all right," she said, but her voice was weak.

He went faster, checking intersections before running red lights and stop signs when the way was clear. So, really, he shouldn't have been surprised when red and blue lights flashed in his rearview mirror.

The sedan was so much faster and smoother than the van had been, and speeding was an absolute pleasure. This was a car build for chasing down bad guys. And he didn't dare stop. He couldn't see the markings on the patrol car to tell where it was from. County sheriff maybe. Surely they'd run the plates by now and discovered it belonged to a federal agency. That hadn't made them back off.

Didn't matter. They were too close to the goal and Cormac wasn't stopping. He floored it. Entirely predictably, the patrol car's siren howled in response. A mile later, a second cop car joined the pursuit.

They weren't going to make it to Sandy Hook before the cops ran him down.

That was when he spotted another sign: Ideal Beach. With an arrow helpfully pointing the way. They must have had at least one blessing left.

He took the turn and hit the gas. Looking at the map, he'd dismissed this stretch of the shore as being too commercial, but right now it had the significant advantage of being close. They were out of time.

The road narrowed, and there was traffic to dodge. Every time he had to step on the brake made his temper rise, and he was so sure one of these cops was going to jump on a side street to get ahead of him. But the signs gave him hope: Ideal Beach, indeed.

Then the sky opened up. Trees, towns, traffic, streets—all gone. He caught a glimpse of wide gray in the distance.

"I can smell it," Nia said, tipping her head back, closing her eyes. "We're here."

"Almost," Cormac murmured. It could still all go horribly wrong. He hated races. He could be as patient as stone, waiting for something he needed, setting an ambush, springing a trap. But this charging ahead to a finish line he could finally see, still not sure he would get there, was agonizing.

He swerved the car into the first parking lot he came to, a spare bit of pavement with a couple of trash cans in the corner and whole list of rules painted on a big sign. A few other cars were parked here, a few people were wandering farther down the beach. A sandy stretch, broken by scrub, spread fifty yards down to surf. The waves rolling in were low, capped with white. The sky was overcast, turning dark with twilight. Across the water, the lights of skyscrapers, bridges, a whole sprawling city, gleamed. Dusk gave the scene a metallic tone, molten with the last orange blaze of the setting sun.

Cormac kept driving, forcing the car over the concrete parking blocks with a thump and a crunch of shocks. Nia gasped as she bounced in the seat.

"Sorry," he muttered.

He drove out to the sand, hitting rocks, until the tires started spinning and the car bogged down. Sirens echoed and four police cars veered into the lot behind him.

Cormac got out and opened the back door. He regarded Nia, her damp hair and shining tail that made her weigh more than a woman of her size ought to. They were so close, and he was so tired already. His shoulder twinged with anticipatory pain, the old gunshot wound complaining. "I'm not sure I can carry you by myself."

Nia met his gaze. "You can. Slow and steady."

She put her arms around him, and he was again struck by how she could be so chilled by the water that soaked her, and yet her touch was so warm. He got his arms under her, and oh-so-carefully he lifted.

"You! Stop! Turn around, put your hands up!"

The police poured out of the cars and lined up, guns drawn. Wearily, Cormac looked back at them.

"Oh my God, is that—"

He held a mermaid in his arms. The half a dozen cops who gathered to confront him just stared.

"Go," Nia whispered in his ear, and he went. Wanted to go faster, but the sand was slippery, making every step treacherous. Slow and steady, she'd advised, so he stopped trying to run and made sure each step was solid. He locked his arms against her so they wouldn't waver. His shoulder throbbed, and he ignored it. The waves shushed and whispered, a rhythm that drew him on. He expected one of the cops to come tackle him from behind, or just shoot him. But the shouted commands had stopped.

Then, at last, his feet were wet. Then his knees. He shoved his way into the water, even as Nia let go, gave a great muscular kick of her tail, and wrenched out of his arms, splashing into the sea.

He was now waist deep, staring at his own empty arms like he wasn't sure what had happened, because Nia was just gone. Sunk under the surface, just like that.

Then she splashed up and grabbed the front of his shirt, pulling herself close.

"Thank you, Cormac Bennett." She kissed him hard on the mouth.

He had just enough sense to put his arms around her and kiss her back, his lips moving against hers, opening to taste the rich saltiness of her. Then she pulled away, gave him a sly grin, and twisted backward, splashing back into the water. Her tail kicked, and she swam *fast*. Her hair rippled behind her, her scales shimmered silver just under the water. He lost sight of her as she dived into the next wave. Caught what might have been the flicker of a tail in the wave after that. And she was gone.

That is the most wondrous thing that has ever happened to me, Amelia whispered in the back of his mind. Given what had happened to Amelia and how she'd even gotten here, that was saying something. Cormac stumbled back to shallower beach, dropped to his knees, and let the surf shove him where it would.

"Hands up! Hands up right now!" The cops had caught up with him, splashing into the water to get to him.

Cormac didn't even care. Chuckling madly, he put his hands up. He didn't look away from that spot far out in the waves until they dragged him away.

Ten

Cormac was drunk on Nia's kiss. The cops kept asking him questions, and he just grinned stupidly at them like nothing in the world mattered.

They arrested him. Even that seemed like a small thing, after the last couple days. He was soaking wet and crusted in salt water when they stuck him in the back of a patrol car, and him dripping all over the seat seemed hilarious. The cop who drove was a sheriff's deputy, someone-or-other. He kept glancing at Cormac in the rearview mirror, through the Plexiglas barrier.

"Was that really a mermaid?" he asked finally.

"She really was," Cormac answered.

"Wow. But where did she come from?"

Cormac waved his cuffed hands behind him, back toward the ocean. "Out there."

"Just... out there?"

"Yup."

Cataloging his possessions at the jail turned into an ordeal, as Cormac struggled to clean out the pockets of his damp jeans. He kept finding more bits and pieces, all of them wet and sticking together. Candle stubs, a matchbook, some twigs, string, a bent nail—

"I want all of that back when I get out," Cormac said to the officer who dutifully put everything in a plastic bag but was clearly annoyed about it.

"Even the string and twigs?"

"*Especially* the string and twigs."

"Weird," the guy muttered.

"Don't argue with me, I just got kissed by a mermaid," Cormac shot back. Yeah, he was definitely feeling a little drunk.

I like it. Don't fight it.

He chuckled again, and everyone in the place was side-eyeing him.

They stuck him in a holding cell, and he could finally lie down. Two days of exhaustion hit him all at once, and he suddenly couldn't move even he'd wanted to. He'd meant to ask for coffee. Maybe it was just as well he hadn't.

He closed his eyes.

The dream-state valley smelled like a rainstorm had just passed through. Fresh, clean, electric, every blade of grass producing a perfume that smelled like life distilled, infused with fertile soil, and the icy touch of snowmelt. Every pore on his body seemed to take it in, as he stood in the middle of the meadow, surrounded by forest and snowcapped peaks.

As if he had a body here, able to smell and feel. It was just memory, emotion. But it felt real. He and Amelia were constantly discussing the metaphysics of it and never reached a conclusion.

Amelia stood nearby, in her usual pale blouse and full-length dark skirt. Her dark, curling hair was held back from her face by a clip and left to fall loose down her back. She didn't even have a body, and yet here she stood, as she remembered herself in life. When she had first appeared to Cormac, her clothing was more formal, a gown and jacket laced all the way to her neck, gloves on her hands, her hair primly bound in a neat bun. She had grown comfortable with him. First the gloves had gone, then her hair let down. She smiled more.

Closing her eyes, she tipped her face up, took a deep breath, and laughed.

"Amelia," he said.

Smiling, she ran at him and crashed into his embrace. He wrapped his arms around her and held tight. Yes, she was real. Maybe it was all in their heads, they were imagining all of this, but while he was here with her, it was real, and he needed her.

"We did it, we did it!" she said into his shoulder.

"We're back in jail."

"Right now I hardly care. We'll worry about it tomorrow."

He drew back to look at her. He wasn't sure he'd ever seen her this happy, flushed, with the wide smile and shining eyes. She looked younger. He smoothed a thumb across her cheek. This wasn't real, so this should be easier, right? Taking that step. But it was real, and it mattered, and he didn't want to screw this up.

He kissed her. As if he could pass on some of the magic Nia had given him, as if Amelia hadn't been right there, experiencing it with him.

Amelia clung to him and kissed him back, and then they were both in a frenzy of kissing, and she was pulling his T-shirt up and over. His hands were too clumsy to work the delicate buttons of her shirt. He popped the first couple clean off, then decided he didn't care.

Somehow, he ended up lying on the damp grass, and Amelia was on top of him, running her hands down his chest, across his ribs. Her touch on his bare skin was eager, warm. He wanted more. She sat up a moment, struggling to peel off her blouse and the camisole underneath, her weight pressing against his groin, and the pressure lit up his brain and made him even harder than he already was—

He froze, suddenly aware of the uncomfortable pressure in his still-damp jeans, of his physical body in the Monmouth County, New Jersey, sheriff department's holding cell.

Amelia stopped and furrowed her brow. "What's wrong?"

Cormac tipped his head back and chuckled at the unfairness of it all. His hands on her hips, his gaze studied the pale skin of her chest, her breasts, waiting to be stroked and held...

"I'm really turned on," he said.

"Good, that's the idea." She leaned in and kissed his neck, and his body—his physical body—shifted uncomfortably.

"No, I mean I'm *really* turned on. My body. If we keep going I'll have to do something about it and I'd rather not put on a show for the security cameras."

She slid off him, to lie on the grass at his side. He felt a chill when she drew away. He wanted her back. He also wanted privacy. How the hell did his life get so weird?

"Well. That's sobering," she said.

"It's ridiculous," he said, chuckling. "The weirdest shit happens to us."

So they lay shirtless in the grass, enjoying the sun, the spring. She propped herself on an elbow and traced his chin. Stubble had grown in—he hadn't shaved in days. And why should it matter here whether he'd shaved? He had no idea.

She said, "I hope that we can revisit this experiment in the boundaries between the physical and spiritual realms very soon."

"Absolutely," he said, taking her hand, and drawing her in to rest her head on his shoulder.

They let him out the next afternoon. No charges, which seemed a small miracle.

The process of getting his belongings back was just as tedious and absurd as turning them in had been the day before. He made a show of counting, making sure every piece of string and crushed bit of herb was there. He had no idea it if was all there; Amelia was the one who kept inventory and she declined to comment. But he wanted to annoy the officer.

The miracle of his release was explained when he stepped outside and found Ben waiting for him, sitting on a bench by the walkway leading to the parking lot.

"You live," Ben said wryly, standing. "But you look terrible. You'll need to take a shower before we get on an airplane."

Both he and Amelia felt a rush of relief that they wouldn't have to drive the two thousand miles back home.

"How'd you do it?" Cormac asked.

"Which part?"

Cormac realized that yes, there were a lot of questions. How did Ben get here, what happened after they parted ways in Des Moines, and how had he convinced the cops to let him go. He finally settled on the most immediate. "How'd you convince them to let me go?"

"Not sure I can take credit for that one. I did the usual, all ready to ask what they were going to charge you with and getting them to set bail and all that. Turns out Agents Stein and Perez called in ahead of me. Asked the local jurisdiction to just..." He gave a wave of his hand, like a stage magician making something disappear.

"Really," Cormac said flatly.

"I think they're hoping you owe them a favor now."

"I don't think I owe them a favor."

Really, I think you do owe them a favor, for giving you their car if nothing else.

She was probably right, but he wasn't going to admit it. He'd forgotten about their car, left abandoned on the sand of a New Jersey beach. He assumed the agents were smart enough to figure out how to get it back. Hoped they had good insurance.

Ben chuckled. "You might be interested to know that Foster's looking at a couple counts of aggravated assault. He's got some fancy defense lawyers courtesy of his employer, though, so I expect he'll plea down."

"His employer?"

"Eden Medical Advancement. On paper it's a think tank. Off paper? I don't even know where to start."

"Any chance of suing their asses off?"

That toothy grin was pure werewolf. "Kitty's working on that. I've referred her to some people I know. I hope you saved your receipts."

"I wasn't thinking about receipts. Sorry."

"Kidding."

"It'd feel really good to smack him down in court. Nice, not to be a defendant for once."

"It's what I've been telling you all along, you have to work the system when you can." Ben led him to a rental car, a very ordinary sedan this time. "Is Nia okay? Someone posted some video from the beach, but it was from a ways off. Hard to tell what was happening."

"She kissed me," he said, his voice gone a little dreamy. Yeah, he was going to be thinking about that for a long time.

"Well all right then," Ben answered, amused.

"She's home, now. It's good." *Tell him the rest,* Amelia murmured. *He's your cousin, your best friend, tell him the rest.* Cormac set his jaw. He'd nearly died lots of times on lots of jobs. He'd been shot, stalked, threatened. But this... this had shaken him. "It got really bad there, Ben. Foster planned to kill me without a thought. But I just kept thinking how I couldn't save her. She was completely dependent on me. And I couldn't help."

A thoughtful pause followed, and Cormac couldn't read Ben's expression, whether he was confused or upset or just thinking. Finally Ben said, "But you did help. It's a win."

"I was a little surprised at how much it ended up mattering to me. Getting her home."

"Deep down, you're a good guy, Cormac. I don't think you hear that enough."

"Not sure I am. I got a lot of shit to make up for."

"That you're aware of it puts you ahead of the game. Ahead of someone like Foster, for sure. Let's get out of here before someone changes their mind about charging you."

"You're right."

"Hmm?"

"I need a shower."

6.

"Stein can't talk about this without going all misty eyed," Lynch said, sounding disgusted, as if being awed by a mermaid was somehow a weakness. Which suggested he had never seen a mermaid.

"She kissed me, you know," Cormac said, going kind of dreamy.

You will never get over that, will you? But Amelia's voice was kind of dreamy, too. She'd been right there. She understood.

Dimitrova said, "Mr. Bennett, the problem I'm grappling with is that you and Ms. Parker, together, are too powerful to be allowed to operate independently."

He'd been so worried about prison he hadn't considered that others might want to lock him in a cage. His threats about calling his lawyer didn't mean anything if they never let him near a phone.

He had to get out of here.

Amelia murmured, *I have an idea. But...I'm not sure it will work. I need your body, I have a spell that involves walking...it'd be easier for me to just do it rather than explain. But you'll need to keep talking. Can we do that? Can we both use your body at the same time?*

They'd never tried it. Usually, one or the other of them was in control. He'd step to the back of his own mind, a little like trying to fall asleep, and she would take over. Her movements, her mannerism expressed through his physical body. It was weird, disconcerting, and the only reason he didn't panic was because after so many years of this he trusted her.

If I talk, they'll know I'm doing something, and Dimitrova will stop us.

Neither one of them wanted to think about how she would do that.

So he had to talk to distract them. He wasn't a talker—that was Kitty's job. And could they both be present in his body? Nothing for it but to try.

He stood. He thought of...vines, growing along the cracks between bricks of a wall. He thought of dye, swirling through water. Two parts, neither overwhelming the other. Just becoming part of each other.

She imagined a picture for him, of her standing behind him, putting her hand over his. His hand lifted, spread the fingers, turned this way and that—he wasn't doing this. She was. It wasn't so much like being a puppet as it was like dancing. Having a partner. They stepped so you did. He relaxed and let his body move.

They took a step.

She paced. She was smart, she was good—she imitated his saunter instead of her more precise and urgent walking pace. Moving back and forth, she seemed impatient rather than looking like someone who had a plan. Every few steps or so she stopped and scuffed their shoe. It might have been restlessness coming out—tired of sitting, needing to move. Frustration at the bars of the cage, like an animal. Except she scuffed patterns. Runes. Three marks on one side of the circle. Cormac didn't know what they meant, but he let her work without questioning it.

He cleared his throat. His voice was his own. He could talk.

"You ever catch a wolf in a leg trap? You don't really have a choice but to shoot them. You got 'em, but you can't get close enough to let it loose. It might be caught but it'll rip you up as much as it can before the end."

"Are you threatening us?" Lynch sounded amused, like he was daring Cormac to try.

Cormac kept talking, and Amelia kept walking, scuffing patterns on the concrete floor.

"As much as you might want to lock me away or get rid of me, you can't, because people will notice. Kitty and Ben will come after me, and trust me they are *pig-headedly* stubborn about this kind of thing and you don't want to get on their bad side. You can charge me with something—again, good luck with that. You can let me go, but then we're back to Kitty and Ben coming after you to figure out what the hell is going on.

"I'm here like this because you don't trust me. And I get it, I do. I've faced some scary shit and managed to come out the other side in one piece, mostly. You think that makes me powerful, and you want to control that. But honest to god I'm just trying to keep to myself. Now, if you want my help with whatever shit you're dealing with, you could just ask. My rates are pretty reasonable considering I've got over a hundred years of experience."

Now.

He stepped across the line of salt.

Whatever magic had been containing them broke and dissipated like a fog.

Dimitrova raised her hands defensively; she was holding a silver disk, about four inches across with intricate writing etched around the edge. Sanskrit maybe? Lynch aimed a gun at him. Cormac hadn't even see him draw.

He raised his hands and waited.

That was exhausting, Amelia said. He felt her flee to the back of his mind, a small presence there, resting. His body was his own again.

"If you're trying to convince us you're not dangerous you're doing a terrible job," Lynch said.

Cormac bowed his head and chuckled. "Oh, I'm dangerous. I like to leave just how dangerous to the imagination. All I really want is to walk out of here, get back home, and finish taking out my trash. And I think we could all use a cup of coffee right about now."

Dimitrova cupped the talisman, hiding it in her palm, and lowered her hands. Only then did Lynch lower the gun. Cormac sighed. They could disappear him whenever they liked and Kitty and Ben would absolutely tear this shit apart to find out what happened to him. He'd still be gone.

The fact that he was just standing here ought to be enough to convince them he wasn't a bad guy. He was wondering now, though—what bad guys had they faced, to make them so twitchy?

I need to learn some better protection spells.

The two agents exchanged a glance, and Lynch said, "Come with me, please."

He gestured to a door, lost in the darkness against the far wall.

They brought him to a plain conference room, circa sometime in the nineties based on the wear in the carpet and the plastic of the conference table. Cormac had been in a dozen rooms just like it. They could have been anywhere from a university classroom to a police station.

Even the bitter coffee in the plain paper cup didn't give him a clue about where he was. But it was coffee, and the taste brought him back to the world.

The two agents left him there for a good long time to let him think about things, he guessed. He stretched out his legs and closed his eyes—

And was in his valley, in high summer. The searing blue sky overhead calmed him, and the spring-tight tension in his back loosened.

Immediately, Amelia put her arms around him and crushed him in a hug. He held her.

"You okay?" he asked.

"Better now," she mumbled against his shoulder.

Didn't matter if this was real or some shared hallucination. It felt real. That was enough.

A door opened. Cormac opened his eyes to deal with the reality in front of him. The agents entered. Lynch carried a couple of suspicious-looking manila folders. Dimitrova planted herself by the door like a guard. She was holding something in one hand, maybe that same silver disk. Without all the shadows and mysticism, they looked like regular people in regular suits, who would work in any office doing anything from accounting to HR. Nothing about them said, *we cast salt circles and fight demons.*

"Mr. Bennett. You're exactly what you say you are, aren't you?" Lynch said. "An independent operator with some really weird history."

He inherited the history. He wondered if they knew about his father. If they didn't know, he wasn't going to tell them.

"Does that mean I can go?"

"In a moment. First, we'd like to ask you to keep an eye out. If anyone suspicious contacts you, if you come across anything particularly... noteworthy...we hope you'll call us."

"Noteworthy—by whose standards?"

"It's like porn," Lynch said, drawling. "You'll know it when you see it. We can offer a retainer." He set down one of the folders, opening it to show paperwork, what looked like a basic agreement and...a W-9 tax form. Cormac almost laughed.

"Would this officially make me a Federal snitch?"

Lynch rolled his eyes.

Cormac actually thought about it for two seconds. A regular income, that much more money toward getting out of the rat hole apartment...

"No." He didn't run with his uncle's crowd anymore but he wasn't a Fed.

"Mr. Bennett—"

He went on, "Instead of a retainer, how about we keep each other in the loop? A trade. I see something weird, I let you know. You need to ask me something—use the damn phone."

Lynch frowned. "That's unconventional—"

"There's no paper trail," Dimitrova said, smiling. Just a little.

I do like her.

Some other place and time, they could have an actual friendly conversation with her, maybe.

Lynch closed the first folder, and opened the second, revealing yet another dense government form. "Now, if you'll just sign this for us."

"What is it?"

"It's a statement identifying you as a voluntary witness and absolving the Paranatural Security Administration and the United States government of any civil rights violations."

Cormac stared at him. "I want to have my lawyer look at this before I sign it."

"I'm afraid that won't be possible."

"This is bullshit."

"Yeah, it kind of is." Lynch drew a pen from his pocket and set it on the form.

Okay, fine, but Cormac sat there and read every single word on that page while the pair of them waited. But he signed, just so he could get out, aware the whole time that he'd been *handled*.

"I'll show you to the lobby," Dimitrova said, while Lynch gathered the folders, smirking the whole time.

They were in a standard office building, and nothing about it revealed anything supernatural, or even anything suspicious, until they got to the lobby. After a short elevator ride the doors opened to reveal security, metal detectors at the doors, armed guards, the works.

They were in the FBI's Denver field office. God, this made his back itch. Bright morning light streamed through the wall of windows. They'd nabbed him at dusk. They'd been at this all night. Dimitrova didn't seem at all tired, didn't have a hair out of place. Cormac felt like he was made of cotton.

She didn't linger but walked him all the way out the door, to the sidewalk outside, all spartan concrete and scraggily urban trees. The skyscrapers of downtown Denver were visible a few miles away. The fall air held a chill.

"I don't suppose you'll pay for my ride home?"

"I took the liberty of calling a ride for you." She nodded to the street, where a bleary-eyed, sandy-haired man waited next to an SVU. Ben, and how many times had Ben showed up just like this, at some godawful hour of the morning, to pick him up after some harrowing episode? At least he hadn't been actually arrested this time. At least, he didn't think he had.

"Well, thanks," was all Cormac could manage.

"Here's my card." Dimitrova handed him a river stone, gray, smooth, flat.

"What am I supposed to do with this?"

"Ms. Parker will know."

Amelia?

Give me just a moment... And she slipped to the fore, speaking with Cormac's voice for just a moment.

"Delighted, I'm sure." He held Dimitrova's gaze, rubbing a thumb across the stone before tucking it in his pocket.

Dimitrova might have blushed a little.

"And I'm still talking to my lawyer about this."

"As I would expect. Have a good day, Mr. Bennett." She returned to the building, never looking back.

And...now he had to figure out what he was going to tell Ben.

Right. What did they know? First, he'd now encountered a half a dozen agents from an agency that still didn't officially exist, at least not enough to have its own website. Second, they were surveilling Cormac, and probably Ben and Kitty as well. Third, they were looking for something. Someone.

Looked like maybe they had some digging to do.

Cormac and Amelia Will Return

and so will the Paranatural Security Administration

About the Author

Carrie Vaughn's work includes the Philip K. Dick Award winning novel *Bannerless*, the New York Times Bestselling Kitty Norville urban fantasy series, over twenty novels and upwards of 100 short stories, two of which have been finalists for the Hugo Award. Her most recent novel, *Questland*, is about a high-tech LARP that goes horribly wrong and the literature professor who has to save the day. She's a contributor to the Wild Cards series of shared world superhero books edited by George R. R. Martin and a graduate of the Odyssey Fantasy Writing Workshop. An Air Force brat, she survived her nomadic childhood and managed to put down roots in Boulder, Colorado. Visit her at www.carrievaughn.com.

For writing advice and a behind-the-scenes look at Carrie's writing process, subscribe to her Patreon.
https://www.patreon.com/carrievaughn

CPSIA information can be obtained
at www.ICGtesting.com
Printed in the USA
LVHW081932181022
730982LV00002B/441